Selim Özdoğan was born in Germany in 1971 and has been publishing his prose since 1995. He has won numerous prizes and grants and taught creative writing at the University of Michigan.

Ayça Türkoğlu is a writer and literary translator based in North London. Her translation interests include the literature of the Turkish diaspora in Germany and minority literatures in Turkey.

Katy Derbyshire translates contemporary German writers including Olga Grjasnowa, Sharon Dodua Otoo and Heike Geissler. She teaches literary translation and also heads the V&Q Books imprint.

The Blacksmith's Daughter

Selim Özdoğan

*Translated from the German
by Ayça Türkoğlu and Katy Derbyshire*

V&Q Books, Berlin 2021
An imprint of Verlag Voland & Quist GmbH
First published in the German language as Selim Özdoğan, *Die Tochter des Schmieds*.

Translation copyright © Ayça Türkoğlu and Katy Derbyshire
Editing: Florian Duijsens
Copy editing: Angela Hirons
Cover photo © Arun Sharma
Cover design: Pingundpong*Gestaltungsbüro
Typesetting: Fred Uhde
Printing and binding: PBtisk, Příbram, Czech Republic

ISBN: 978-3-86391-294-9

www.vq-books.eu

It is doubtful, of course, that things happened that way, but what we don't know, we don't know.
Mikhail Bulgakov, translated by Pevear & Volokhonsky

Your life has a limit, but knowledge has none. If you use what is limited to pursue what has no limit, you will be in danger.
Zhuang Zhou, translated by Watson, Palmer & Breuilly

I

'Don't make my husband a murderer, I told him. Stop the car, don't make my husband a murderer. Stop the car and let me out, and then piss off as fast as you can.'

Timur exhales and turns his head away so Fatma can't see him tearing up. He's still struggling for breath. He's grateful, so grateful that fate has chosen this woman for him. She must have been written in his book of life on the very day he was born. He doesn't know what's happened to him, where all the time has gone.

Just yesterday he was a little boy in ragged trousers, scrumping pears from the neighbour's garden with his friends. The neighbour had spotted the thieves, and they'd all jumped swiftly over the wall, pockets and shirts full of fruit. All but Timur, who'd been a little too slow, as usual. Though he could run just as fast as the others, he always missed his chance to make a bolt for it. Now he stood there, rooted to the spot, and the neighbour ran past Timur up to the wall and yelled after the escaping boys: 'Come back! Come back, and give Timur a pear, at least. Great friends *you* are…'

Then he turned back to Timur and just said: 'Run.' Timur didn't dare go past the neighbour, so he ran all the way across the garden and jumped over the wall on the other side.

Just yesterday he'd been a little boy, not all that good at school, not all that skilled, not all that popular. Until he began to help his father the blacksmith, helped him blow the heavy bellows and fetch big buckets of water for Necmi to quench the glowing iron. Timur had built up muscles in the workshop, had proved himself hardworking and untiring. He had learned quickly, and he'd enjoyed being with his father all day long. He also enjoyed testing out his new strength. The boy who once avoided fights now let no opportunity pass to show off his superiority.

Timur had a sister, Hülya, and he could well recall the night when she was born, even though he was only five at the time. He remembered the excitement in the house, and above all his father's determined face and his vow to open the girl's feet, no matter what it cost him. *Open*, that was the word he used. Hülya's feet pointed inwards, the big toes touching, and no one who saw them thought she'd grow out of it.

'God means to test us,' Timur's mother, Zeliha, had said in a tear-choked voice, and Necmi had answered: 'If there is a way, I will find it.'

But the doctor had said he could do nothing for the child, Necmi would have to take Hülya to Ankara if he wanted to get help for her. There were specialists there. He had to take her to Ankara and that wouldn't come cheap.

Necmi had money, and although Zeliha was reluctant to make the journey, in the end they boarded the train and went to the big city.

'It's God's will that her feet are closed,' Zeliha had told her husband, but he'd simply ignored her.

In Ankara, the doctor explained the child was too small; they were to come back in two or three years and then he'd operate, but he couldn't promise anything. And it would cost them.

Zeliha gave Necmi a discreet nudge. They were sitting side by side in the surgery, the baby on Zeliha's lap. Stepping on his wife's foot, Necmi stood up and said goodbye, cap in hand.

Outside in the dusty corridor, he said: 'Wife, I can't haggle with a doctor, I'm not a carpet seller, I'm a blacksmith. And he's not a carpet seller either. I don't care how much it'll cost, as long as the girl is cured. I made a vow.'

'We'll end up going hungry just because you've gone and got this idea in your head. If only the Lord had given you a bit of sense to go with your stubbornness,' she added quietly.

They slept in a cheap hotel and returned home the next day with a lorry driver from their small town. Zeliha had arranged it all. It took longer than the train and was uncomfortable too, but it was cheaper.

Her husband could almost be called well-off, but only because she managed to rein in his extravagance and earn a little extra with a few deals here and there. The evening before they left for home, Necmi had taken her to a restaurant and drunk a small bottle of rakı, and they had eaten kebab. As if bread and cheese and tomatoes and onions and a glass of water weren't good enough. No, this man could not handle money; only she knew how to save up and multiply it.

So they squeezed into the driver's cab. Zeliha had the baby on her lap and sat on the far side, breathing in the smoke from the two men's roll-ups, swallowing the dust from the road right alongside them for almost ten hours. During the short stops, she made tea on a gas flame and prepared cold food while Necmi and the driver played backgammon.

Almost three years later, Necmi took the train to the capital city again, but this time Hülya was old enough not to need her mother to come along. When the blacksmith returned after four days, he carried his daughter on his back; her legs were in plaster up to the knees.

Six weeks passed, during which Hülya cried nearly every day because it was so itchy under the plaster. Necmi was standing in front of the only mirror in the house, shaving. Timur stood next to him, but he hardly dared ask him his most pressing question, afraid his father would tell him off.

'Can I come with you?'

'All right,' Necmi said to his surprise, not thinking it over for long, and he stroked his boy's blond hair. 'Run and tell your mother to pack a bit more to eat.'

Timur was waiting impatiently outside the door with the bread and cheese when he heard voices from the kitchen.

'It's absolutely unnecessary for him to go. He's too little, what does he want in Ankara?'

'An adventure,' Necmi said. 'It'll be an adventure for him.'

'It's...'

'Enough. He's coming with us.'

Timur wished he could dash off and tell his friends, but he didn't want to miss the train. The train! He'd never been on a train before.

When a young simit-seller carrying a big tray of sesame rings on his head walked past, Timur piped up.

'Brother,' he said, 'I'm going to Ankara today.'

'To Ankara?'

The boy, who might have been two or three years older than Timur, smiled and said: 'Keep your eyes peeled, they have simit there as big as wagon wheels. The people are rich there, they can afford it.'

Timur was excited to see the big city, the incredible sesame rings, and he was excited to see his sister cured.

He looked out of the window almost all the way, and sometimes he hummed along with the clatter of the train. He didn't want to fall asleep, he was waiting for the moment when the city appeared before them. But the clattering made him tired, that and the endless dry brown of the plains and the hills on the horizon and his father's snoring. Shortly before Ankara, he fell asleep.

Timur didn't wake up until the train pulled into the station with a loud screech of brakes.

'Don't be scared, and watch out for the cars,' the blacksmith told his son as they disembarked.

Timur wasn't scared: he was fascinated by all the people, by the noise, by the big buildings and the cars, which he'd never seen before. When he noticed his sister was afraid, he walked closer alongside his father, who was carrying Hülya on his back. Timur wanted to stroke her, but he couldn't reach any higher than the plaster.

'Why do you keep staring at the simit-sellers?' Necmi asked. And then he laughed and said: 'Did someone tell you they had simit as big as wagon wheels in Ankara?'

'Yes.'

'Ignorant people are always inventing nonsense like that,' his father said, and Timur was proud he was no longer one of the ignorant.

Later, at the doctor's surgery, he did hold Hülya's hand. His sister didn't cry but Timur could see she was stiff with fear.

'Close your eyes,' Timur said, and the doctor added in a warm voice: 'Don't be afraid, it won't hurt.'

Hülya seemed not to hear either of them; she could barely breathe, and when the plaster was sawn open, Timur screamed: 'Dad, Dad, her eyes are slipping!'

But it was too late. From that day on, his sister had a permanent squint.

Sometimes, when the little girls were playing in the street outside the forge, Necmi would go out and call them over. Then he'd take them along to the grocer's, where the girls would scoop up their skirts in front of them to receive a handful of sweets. And Timur's father had enormous hands.

When he began working in the forge, Timur took up this habit from his father. He would often put sweets in Fatma's skirt. He must have been 14 or 15 at the time, and she 10 years younger. He still remembered the girl's smile. Nobody knew anything specific about Fatma's parents; some said they'd been Greeks, some Aramaeans, and others claimed she was the daughter of Circassians. All they could agree upon was that the couple had arrived in the town after the confusion of the First World War. Fatma's father had died before she was born. One day he had complained of back pain, and two weeks later cancer had taken hold of his entire body. Fatma's mother began working as a nanny to a rich family to feed herself and her daughter. When Fatma was six months old, her mother was trampled to death by horses in the marketplace. Everyone told a different story, but all anyone knew for sure was that the horses had bolted, and she had fallen. The family who'd employed her mother had taken Fatma in.

Though she was much older, Timur's sister, Hülya, often played with Fatma, because Fatma never teased her. The other children mocked her squint and her feet, which still turned slightly inwards, making her waddle. But Fatma liked Hülya. Fatma liked almost everyone; she was a happy girl who made friends easily. One moment, Timur had been a teenager, dropping sweets into this little girl's skirts, and now she would soon be a woman.

'Shall we set you up with Fatma?' his mother asked, for the second time. 'You're 25 now, it's time you got married.'

Hülya had been squinting for six years when her father grew sick. He lay in bed for a week and on the morning of the eighth day, he didn't get up again. The first year had been hard for them all, but Zeliha had rented out the forge and managed to make enough money for food and even a little extra. Timur had continued to help in the workshop, and when he turned 17, he took over the forge and earned a livelihood for the family, which his mother managed.

And now he was 25 and he liked his life. He liked working at the forge, sitting at the teahouse and smoking shisha, and every so often he would get drunk. When he did, everything seemed to fall away, he savoured it. He savoured the world, felt nothing but pleasure. It was as if the stars in the night sky rained down on his hair, like sweets dropped into the skirts of a little girl. When he drank, it all became one; beauty and ugliness, heaven and hell, silk and sackcloth, pillows and the hard clay ground. As long as he had this happiness, and his work, nothing could happen to him. And when he needed a change, he would go to the big city and enjoy the sense of adventure he felt since his first visit there. He had no need to get married, but now he was standing drunk in front of his mother on a winter's night, snowflakes melting on the shoulders of his coat, and he said: 'Yes. Go and ask if they'll give her to us.'

And Zeliha said: 'Blessed be the Lord. I'll go straight out in the morning and fix it up.'

'Yes,' he had said, that night, drunk. Yes, as if fate had placed the word in his mouth. It was not the first time his mother had suggested someone, but this time he'd said yes. But was Fatma even old enough? The next morning, he pulled his sister aside.

'You know Fatma, the orphan girl?'

'Yes.'

'Mum wants me to marry her.'

Hülya went to hug her brother, but he held her back. 'Do me a favour, will you? Find an excuse to sleep over at hers. You're friends after all, aren't you? You know each other well enough?'

Hülya looked at him, uncomprehending.

'Have a look to see if she's got breasts. She's still too young to get married, don't you think? What am I supposed to do with a wife without breasts?'

Hülya hesitated, so Timur added: 'Please.' It was a please which sounded more like *go*.

'Okay,' Hülya said. 'I'll try. But believe me, Fatma would make a good wife for you, breasts or no.'

Timur was not convinced, but he couldn't keep it to himself and so he told his friends the news over lunch.

'Mum has gone out today to fix my engagement. Fatma and I are getting married.'

'Fatma, the orphan girl? Get away,' the barber's son said. 'She looks like she's got swamp fever.'

'Swamp fever?'

'Yeah, I don't know, she's so yellow and sickly-looking. Have you seen her recently?'

Timur shook his head. But after a moment's pause, he told his assistant he had something to attend to and would probably be back sometime in the afternoon.

And then, despite the heavy snowfall, he loitered by the big house where Fatma lived until nightfall.

'In spring,' said Zeliha that evening. 'You'll marry in spring. I arranged it all today. She's a hard-working girl and good-natured too, she'll be able to help me out around the house and you'll be less inclined to go wandering about.'

Swamp fever and no breasts. It wasn't quite what Timur had imagined. He found it difficult to say anything, but in the end, he managed: 'It's all happened a bit fast. I hardly had time to think it over.'

'You had 25 years to think it over,' his mother said.

Timur was as strong as a lion, nobody could take him on, he was as strong as a lion and proud – what would he do with a sickly girl? Yesterday, with the stars caught in his hair, he had said yes, but today his feet were back on the ground.

'So?' he asked his sister when she came home the next morning. He had slept poorly and had no appetite.

'So what?'

'So, has she got…?'

'It was too dark in the room.'

'You could have tried feeling for them secretly.'

'Wouldn't have worked.'

'So you couldn't make anything out under her nightdress?'

'No, but she's still very young, they might not be big enough to be obvious yet – that's if she has any…'

That day, Timur again left the forge in the hands of his assistant, who was surprised because Timur never usually stayed away so long.

Once again, the blacksmith went to the house where Fatma lived, and just when he could no longer feel his feet for the cold, she stepped out the door holding a clay jug. He was standing behind a spot where the wall jutted out, and Fatma didn't notice him until she was almost standing in front of him. She knew that this was the man whom she'd been promised to the day before, and she turned around and ran back, only to stop abruptly. It had clearly occurred to her that she couldn't go back into the house without an explanation. She turned around again; she had to visit the neighbour, get some vinegar. She wavered, taking two slow steps forward, hesitantly, her eyes fixed on the ground. Then she took a step back, her cheeks glowing, the snow making an incredible crunch beneath her feet, and stopped. She heard another crunch, then another and another, and as she slowly looked up, she saw the broad back of the blacksmith, walking away.

Timur lit a cigarette and smiled. Maybe she didn't have any breasts, but she was beautiful. She was beautiful, like a piece of the moon. She was beautiful, as if the stars still hung in his hair. Timur didn't go back to the workshop straight away, he went to the shopkeeper, to see the one bed he had for sale. He followed the shopkeeper into the storeroom, squatted down and looked long and carefully at the frame.

'Would you like to buy it?' the shopkeeper asked, scenting a sale. The bed had sat in the shop for six months. Almost everybody in the small town slept on the floor on mattresses or cushions, or on a divan, and even the rich ones didn't seem to want to buy a bed – there was no reason to do so.

Timur didn't respond, so the shopkeeper went on: 'Are you getting married? Are congratulations in order?'

Timur muttered something incomprehensible without looking up from the bed frame.

'We can be a little flexible with the price, of course.'

The blacksmith made no sound and his eyes narrowed a little; he nodded briefly, then stood up and slowly walked around the frame.

Finally, he said to the shopkeeper: 'Yes, I'm getting married. In spring. In spring when everything is green and fragrant. No,

I'm not going to buy the bed, but thank you and have a profit-able day.'

Timur returned to the workshop in good spirits. There was a lot to do, he would have to stay longer if he wanted to make a start on the bed frame. The bedposts were to be exactly like the model at the shopkeeper's; knee-high, round and gleaming. And on top of these, he would lay the slats, just as he had seen. But the headboard would not be made out of straight rods, like a prison cell; they'd be curved, like climbing roses.

He worked in the forge until almost midnight and when he finally lay down on his mattress, he closed his eyes, content. A piece of the moon.

Fatma and Timur slept in a real bed for the first time on their wedding night. Neither of them said a word once they'd entered the room. But later, when Timur was just about to fall asleep, Fatma murmured: 'So this is how kings sleep.'

And Timur was not only proud but also surprised at how ex-actly her words said what he himself was feeling. He felt richer, more powerful, safer; he felt big enough to rule the world.

It was spring and they were newlyweds, Timur had enough work at the forge, they had money, Fatma brought him something to eat every lunchtime, and then they'd sit together for a while and talk and talk until it was time for Fatma to go and for Timur to get back to work. The food was usually still untouched, but Fatma knew that Timur would've eaten it by the evening and that he'd be hungry again by the time he got home; he was a big man who worked hard. It was spring and they had their own room in the house Timur's father had left his mother.

And that was how the problems began. Zeliha saw her son looking after the young woman, this girl, saw him bringing home a little something for her almost every evening: a length of cloth so she could sew some clothes, a simit, a new headscarf, sometimes sweets or a piece of chocolate. Zeliha saw her son wanting to get close to his wife, saw him in love and caring for her.

One evening, it was summer by this point, she drew him aside: 'Your wife, she's lazy, she comes up with excuses not to help around the house. One day she's sprained her ankle and the next she has a stomachache. And when she does do anything, she never tries hard. On our last washing day, she sat down at the trough and didn't change the water once in two hours. She washed our laundry in dirty water.'

'Why didn't you say something?'

'I did. She sighed and said she had changed the water. She heaved a great big sigh. You need to teach her some respect.'

'Mother, you were the one who said she was hard-working and reliable.'

'I must have been wrong. She's lazy and disrespectful.'

That night in bed, Timur told his wife his mother had complained about her. And Fatma said in a quiet voice: 'I'm really doing everything I can. I'm trying my best but your mother... She can be unfair, I think.'

The complaints grew more frequent: Fatma sliced the cheese wrong, she cut the dishcloths in two when she washed up knives. When she went out, she dragged her feet on purpose so she'd get new shoes before the winter, she spread the butter too thickly on the bread, and Timur began to work out what the problem was.

'Listen,' he said to Fatma one evening, 'I think I know what we can do. Next time my mother complains, I'll drag you into our room and then I'll bash the cushions and yell a bit, and you scream with pain, then I'll go out and you stay in here for a while longer.'

Now, every time Zeliha complained to her son about her daughter-in-law, the young couple went to their room and the sound of beatings and screams was heard. The complaints tailed off.

Timur showed off to his friends about the trick, and they laughed together, raised their glasses and drank. And by the time autumn was over, the whole town knew about it.

'We'll have to come up with something new,' said Timur as they lay side by side on the mattress one evening. They had lent out the bedstead; a distant cousin of Timur's was getting married and she wanted to spend her wedding night in a proper bed too. Even the rich envied Timur for this bed, its feet decorated with brass by his own hand.

'We could leave,' Fatma said, 'you could open a workshop, do a bit of trading, I could weave carpets. You've got two horses, we could live somewhere else.'

Yes, he had two horses and a donkey, yes, he had a bit of money, but where were they to go? Leave the town, leave all their relatives and friends, for another small town where they wouldn't know anybody?

'A strange place?' he asked.

'We could move to a village.'

'You have no idea what it's like, life's completely different there. They don't even have toilets, they squat down in the bushes.'

'We could build an outhouse. You could keep the forge and ride into town and back, sell fruit and vegetables at the market on the side. Timur, we could lead our own life.'

'I'll think about it.'

And to help him think better, he took a week off and got on a train to Ankara. He wanted to enjoy life in the big city for a few days, look at cars and rich people's houses, take in the sounds and the scents, the crowds. By day, he sat in teahouses and started conversations with city folk. Some said the war would soon be over, others predicted it would last a long time yet and that the Germans would be at the gates of Istanbul in six months' time, like the Ottomans besieged Vienna back in the day. For Timur, the war was a long way off nonetheless; he listened but changed the subject at the first opportunity and tried to find out who supported Beşiktaş like he did. He was more interested in football than politics.

What interested him most of all were the evenings in the city. Listening to the scantily dressed singers in a bar for a couple of hours, drinking a glass or two, eating a slice of melon, a few chunks of white cheese, and he'd melt into the music after only the third glass. And later he lay alone and relaxed in a cheap hotel room, his worries lifted, his business far away and his mother too. Nobody knew him there, he'd lost himself in the big city, lost himself by losing his greed, ambitions, reservations – all the chains that bound him. He had lost himself only to find himself again, smiling on a hotel bed, his breathing even and calm.

When he got back, he said: 'Winter isn't a good time to move house.'

In the spring, Timur had found a house and taken their possessions there on the backs of the horses and the donkey. He had hired a cart to transport the bed, now returned to them by the cousin, and last of all he had fetched his wife. She'd been on the donkey's back for two hours by the time they got there. The ride on one of the horses took only half that time.

It had been Fatma's idea to move to the village, but she only knew villages from stories people told, and she'd only come across villagers as traders at the market.

Lying in bed on her first day in the new house, Fatma asked: 'Are all the women here related?'

'No, why?'

'They all wear the same clothes.'

Timur laughed: 'That's the way it is here. We're in a village now.'

He laughed but he was worried. He wasn't sure Fatma would get used to it here while he rode into town almost every day to work at the forge. But when he arrived at the village just before sunset a week later, he saw Fatma sitting in the village square, the young women and girls gathered around her, listening.

When Fatma caught sight of him she leapt up, but he gestured to her to stay seated, then he dismounted, led his horse by the reins into the stable and smoked a cigarette on the steps outside the house as he watched the sun go down.

'Fairytales,' was the first thing Fatma said when she came over. 'I was telling them fairytales. They don't know any. Isn't that strange? I always thought fairytales came to the town from the villages… You're back early, I thought you'd be back at the same time as the other days. Dinner's ready.'

Inside, the blacksmith looked at the carpet on the loom, saw that she'd been working, and smiled quietly to himself.

Timur bought green beans from the villagers, bulgur, and in summer and autumn tomatoes, broad beans, melons, grapes, apples and apricots. He loaded up his donkey to sell the produce at the market, and he made a good cut. He bought two cows, a few chickens, and at Fatma's insistence, a small vineyard as well; his workshop was doing well, he was earning more than before.

Towards the end of autumn, he sold the carpets Fatma had woven, and now that the successful summer had put so much money in his pocket, he went to the big city again. Not to Ankara, though – this time he went all the way to Istanbul, because that was where Beşiktaş had their stadium, and the women there were even more beautiful and sang even more sweetly, and the wine flowed down his throat like liquid sunlight.

A week later he was back, having left half of the money in Istanbul.

Fatma got on well with the villagers. They all thought highly of her and valued her, and not because she was the wife of the blacksmith, the wife of the man whose strength was extolled by all, and who was also a good head taller than most of them; the wife of a man with piercing blue eyes, who sat proud and straight-backed on his horse. No, the women of the village liked Fatma because she was still so young, because she could tell stories, because she was always friendly to everyone and didn't think herself better than them simply because she came from the town, or because she had money. They liked her because she was sweet-tempered and always tried to play the peacemaker when arguments arose; they liked that she was soft, but firm.

When Fatma got pregnant in the winter, without having had her period even once, the women of the village shared in her happiness.

The blacksmith had expanded his business, he had made sure word got around the surrounding villages that here was a man who paid farmers a fair price for their wares. One day in spring, when Fatma's belly had grown big and round, Timur took her along with him to a village almost a day's ride away, to give her a change of scene. He still brought her gifts, still fussed over her. Not as much as he had in the early days, but that was the way of everyday life; it did not mean that his feelings had lost any of their intensity. In the village, they had slept at a fat man's house, on a mattress, just as they had recently been doing at home. One of Timur's friends had got married and was borrowing the bedstead. The next morning, Timur spent a good while haggling with a farmer who was determined to squeeze a few more kuruş out of him. It was already lunchtime once the business was finally concluded, and their host did not want to send them on their way unfed. So it wasn't until after midday that the two of them saddled up.

They were still some distance from the village as the sun started to set, but it was dangerous to ride on in the dark; it was so hard to see and they had to be on their guard for highway robbers.

'We'll have to sleep here and ride on in the morning,' Timur said.

'Where are you expecting us to sleep? There's nowhere safe, I won't sleep a wink!'

'I know a place. It's not far.'

At dusk, they reached a graveyard.

'No one else is brave enough to come here after dark,' Timur said. 'Don't be scared, trust me, this is the safest place to spend the night.'

That night, Fatma's sleep was light but peaceful, and from then on, the blacksmith took her with him more often when he had business in villages far away, and she grew accustomed to nights like these. She liked to lie close to her husband in the quiet and the dark, and the ground beneath them seemed to her as soft as down when she lay her head on his shoulder and he stroked her hair and said: 'My girl, my piece of the moon.'

She felt that she had been lucky with this man. It didn't matter to her that he frittered away half the money he earned from the carpets she made, even though they had cost her a whole summer of sitting at the loom. There were things that bothered her, of course. On one occasion, he had lent his horse to the boy he employed to help him in the forge. God knows why he'd done it; the boy was a good worker, but he was a rash young man with a habit of flying into rages. In a fit of recklessness, the boy had ridden the horse at a gallop down the main street. People leapt out of the way in shock, cursing him, and eventually the police caught up with him and took the horse away. The police knew how much the horse was worth to Timur, and he'd been forced to pay a tidy sum to get it back; he had practically bought it a second time over.

On another occasion, Timur had helped out a friend who wanted to buy a field but didn't have enough money. Why was this man buying a field when he didn't have any money? Timur ended up paying for most of it, the field, but it belonged to his friend.

Fatma wasn't worried; he earned well and they always had money, but she understood that he didn't know how to manage it, and she suspected that not all of their days would be like these. But as long as he was by her side, she felt able to face each day with a smile.

On their first night in the graveyard, they lay side by side, eyes open, in silence. Timur thought to himself: *Just two more minutes, just two more minutes to watch the stars and feel my wife in my arms, and then I'll turn over and go to sleep.*

'Gül,' Fatma said softly into the silence.

'Hm?'

'It's going to be a girl, I can feel it. I want to call her Gül, *rose*. I want to have a little girl called Rose.'

The blacksmith placed his hand on her belly.

'Gül,' he said. 'And if it's a boy, we'll call him Emin.'

'It's not going to be a boy.'

Gül was born on a warm September day. When the blacksmith came home at dusk, there was this little creature lying next to his wife in the bed.

'Are her hands and feet normal?' he asked first, and Fatma nodded.

He touched Gül carefully, like the weight of his big hands alone might bruise her. With tears in his eyes, Timur kissed his wife and touched his lips to his daughter's head. Then he went out and sat on the steps outside the house. Something tingled beneath his skin, not like bubbles, more like a warm evening breeze. He felt light, as if the breeze were gently lifting his body, as if he had given over some of his weight to the earth below. He sat on the steps and forgot to smoke.

That autumn, it seemed to him that everything was working out. He bought rich harvests from the farmers and sold them at the market in town; his vineyard bore plenty of grapes; he hired a second assistant to work in the forge; and when it was spring again he bought a summer house with a big apple orchard and a stable on the edge of the town, so that he'd have a shorter journey to work, in summer at least.

Many of the townspeople had summer houses where they would escape the heat, plant a few beds with tomatoes, with cucumbers, peppers, courgettes and corn to eat. They also hoped for a little extra income when their apple trees bore fruit in the autumn. In the summer months, they'd rent out their houses in the town, mostly to rich people from Adana who wanted to escape the heat of the city.

When the heat grew stifling inside the summer house, you could always lie down outside in the shade of a walnut tree. You could listen to the leaves rustling, though it was barely half an hour on foot from the houses in town, lined up side by side with their little backyards with scarcely a tree.

They moved house in early May. Timur had found someone to take the bed and their household goods to the summer house on the back of a small lorry. Once they'd loaded it up, there wasn't even space left in the cab. The driver suggested he take the things to the summer house, find a couple of lads to help him unload, and then come back for Timur and Fatma. Gül was at her grandmother's house already.

'Alright, Timur said, tucking some money in the driver's shirt pocket to pay the lads for unloading. We'll start walking, get a bit of a head start at least.

As man and wife were peacefully making their way along the dusty road, a car approached them from behind and the driver slowed right down. He had soot-black hair, shiny with brilliantine, and bushy eyebrows. Once he'd wound down the window, he asked: 'Where are you heading?'

'Into town,' Timur answered.

'I can give you a lift, get in,' the man said. Fatma had never been in a car in her life. No one in their town owned a car in those days.

She'd been in lorries, in the driver's cab or on the back, but never in a car. She sat down on the back seat and felt briefly trapped as Timur pulled the passenger door shut.

The driver's hands didn't look like he used them to work, but he had a stocky figure that didn't quite match his thin, trimmed moustache.

As they drove up a slight hill the car slowed down, and suddenly it jolted forward and then stopped.

'Damn,' said the driver, then turned to Timur: 'Brother, I can tell you're a strong man. Would you mind getting out and pushing the car up the last bit? It's bound to start again as soon as we're going downhill.'

The blacksmith nodded and smiled, his blue eyes full of zest and pride, and he got out and braced himself against the car. It was easier than he'd thought; he hadn't even broken a sweat by the time they were at the top. The car rolled downhill, the engine started, and the man put his foot down.

He wants to get the engine warmed up, Timur thought first, until he realised the man was simply driving away. His face flushed with heat and he broke into a run, chasing the car. He'd kill that man, he'd kill him. Even if he didn't get his hands on him now, he'd strike him dead if he laid a finger on Fatma.

Timur doesn't notice the car stopping and Fatma getting out; he simply runs without registering anything, and now he sees her standing by the side of the road. But he doesn't slow down, he keeps running until he reaches her. The car is out of sight by now.

'What happened?' Timur asks.

'Don't make my husband a murderer, I told him, don't make my husband a murderer. Stop the car and let me out, and then piss off as fast as you can. He'll find you and kill you, I said, he's a man of honour. I put my arm around his throat from the back seat and I said: Don't make my husband a murderer.'

Timur is grateful. He's grateful and he thinks life will get bigger and bigger and more and more wonderful as long as he has Fatma by his side. Just yesterday he was a little boy, and today he's married to her and thinks they will conquer all dangers together.

Timur bought another cow, he dug the vegetable patches, hammered in the forge, and in the evenings he swept up his daughter in his arms and cuddled her. Fatma made friends with the neighbours, she milked the cows at dawn and then again at dusk when they came back from grazing. When she was alone with Gül, she talked to her daughter, told her what she was doing and who she was thinking of, told her she hadn't had a mother of her own but her adoptive mother had taken good care of her, perhaps because she was the girl she'd always wished for and never had. Fatma hadn't got on well with her three brothers; they'd teased and tormented her, once forcing her to eat a rotten apple, another time hiding her clothes when she was bathing in the river, but all that was long ago. Now she had Timur and she had Gül, and if God willed it, she'd have more children.

Summer passed, and when autumn was almost over they moved back to the village because it had grown too cold in the little summer house without a stove, because there wasn't much left to do once the apples had been harvested, because the neighbours were moving back to town too, back to their homes, now vacated by the people from Adana who would spend a mild winter in the city, probably without a single glimpse of snow. Timur, Fatma and Gül moved back to the village; in the summer houses, there was no one left to talk to, no one left to lend some flour or a barrowful of manure. They moved back to the village without their bed – they had lent it, once again, to someone who had just married – they moved without their bed, but with cows and chickens in tow.

'In a few years' time, everyone in town will know how kings sleep,' Timur said, acting as if he'd find it annoying. In reality, he was proud of the bed, and when it was lent out he'd look forward to being able to wake up in it in the mornings again, without the hard-trodden clay being the first thing he saw and smelt.

Gül had very quickly started talking. But it took her longer than other children to learn to walk. She was almost two and her mother had started to worry, while the blacksmith simply laughed. Gül crawled, but not like the other children; she crawled backwards and was always looking over her shoulder to see what was behind her.

'My crazy rose,' Timur said.

Gül was walking by the time Fatma was pregnant again. One night, Fatma lay once again in Timur's arms at a graveyard and got that same feeling, quite clearly. It was the new moon, and Fatma felt that the spirits of the dead were looking on her kindly, looking on her kindly from surprisingly nearby.

'Timur,' she said, 'would you rather have a son or another daughter?'

'All that matters to me is that its hands and feet are in the right place,' replied the blacksmith, 'that it's healthy and grows up with a mother and a father. That's the most important thing.'

'You're going to have another daughter. Do you know what you'd like to call her?'

'Melike.'

Melike cried through the night, she bawled until her face was purple; sometimes she would nurse greedily, sometimes she wouldn't want anything at all, and sometimes it seemed she would only sleep if all was well. If Fatma was overtired and exhausted and weak, she could be certain Melike would cry all night long. But Fatma never complained.

'What kind of child is this?' Timur asked his wife.

'It's a different child, she's restless and headstrong. You named her Melike, *queen*, and now she behaves like one.'

Timur laughed, took the baby in his arms, gave her a nip on the cheek and said: 'We'll force that out of you yet.'

Fatma smiled. When Timur had fixed the roof, and a raindrop fell from the ceiling into his tea the very next day, he'd hurled his glass at the wall. There was nothing she could do to change it. When Beşiktaş lost, he would be short-tempered for days. When something went wrong at the forge, Timur would hammer away in a frenzy, and afterwards there'd be black bruises underneath his fingernails.

This man would not be forcing anything out of Melike; yes, he loved his daughter, he made time for her, he was besotted with the girl, but he would be as powerless to change his children as Fatma was to change him.

Year after year, they spent the summer at the summer house on the edge of the town and the winter in the village. They made good money and even when they weren't perfectly happy, even when there was lots of work to do, when the winters were hard, when the blacksmith went days at home without speaking a word and Fatma didn't know what was bothering him, when they asked each other in bed at night how they would find the strength to face another day, these were good years. Gül learned to walk, she played in the street with the other children in the village. Melike learned to walk before she could talk, she almost never did what she was told, she protested loudly if she didn't like her food, she yelled if she had the scissors taken away from her. Since developing a big bruise on the back of her head from flinging herself on the floor, whenever she didn't get her way she'd plop down and carefully let herself fall backwards, and only then would she cry and rage and thrash at being told a three-year-old wasn't old enough to milk a cow.

'My little ones are jumpy creatures,' said Timur, 'they might kick out.'

And Melike screamed and shrieked, squeezing the air out of her lungs. She thrashed about and stamped the ground, and Timur was already in a bad mood that evening: two customers who owed him had disappeared without a trace, and Beşiktaş had lost three-nil to Galatasaray, a feeble bunch who hadn't even been on good form. He had fixed the same spot on the stable roof for the third time; the ladder was still propped up against the wall. He grabbed Melike and climbed up to the flat roof with his daughter under his arm. Fatma and Gül stood below, staring up in disbelief.

Arm outstretched, the blacksmith held the still-crying child over the edge of the roof and cried: 'I'm tired of your bawling, I'm tired of it, you hear? Let the devil take you, you can cry in the depths of hell. Now hush, give me some peace or I'll drop you, you hear me?'

Melike fell silent for a moment, but once her father's words had died away she started up again, and in the midst of her cries Gül heard a strange, cutting voice: 'Timur, stop it.'

Gül looked up at her mother and realised that it was she who must have spoken in this quite unfamiliar voice. Fatma's face looked strange too. Melike had stopped crying. For a few seconds, the four of them stood there, unmoving.

'Be thankful for your mother,' Timur said, and climbed back down the ladder with Melike. 'One of these days, I'm going to forget myself', he added.

As soon as he let go of Melike, she carefully lay back on the ground. Fatma seized her by the arm and pulled her into the house. Gül was still standing next to her father, who shook his head, booted the ladder, and went into the stable.

Timur was admired by many in the village; he came from the town, was prosperous, always friendly and generous, and his broad shoulders alone were enough to command respect. But others in the village did not like him – this man who made a profit by selling their harvests at the market, this man who spent the hotter months in his summer house like he was better than them, and who raked in more than enough money come the autumn, when he sold his apple harvest.

One day, the blacksmith received a tip-off from one of the villagers that one of the men who envied him had reported him to the gendarmerie, and they would soon be on their way to search his house. The blacksmith had nothing to hide – he had not grown rich from stealing and flogging stolen goods, he had nothing in his house that he hadn't earned by the sweat of his brow. He had nothing to fear.

As long as he hid his guns. He was a man, the head of a family, of course he had to have a gun. He shot birds with it, rabbits, foxes, making money from their skins, and sometimes in summer he'd shoot moles. If he discovered a molehill in his garden, he would snatch up a spade and shovel away the earth until the underground passage came into view. Then he'd lie down on his stomach some distance away, gun at the ready, and wait. Sooner or later, the mole would emerge to tidy up the hole.

He was a man, and he had two guns which always hung on the wall, loaded. But he didn't have a licence. Timur came home and took the guns down.

'Gül,' he said to his daughter, 'go out and play for a while.'

Gül went out, but once the curtains were drawn, she grew curious. If she stood on tiptoes and tilted her head, she could see exactly what was going on inside. The previous winter, there had been a draught coming from one of the windows and when he repaired it, Timur had noticed a hollow underneath the window ledge. He was a man, yes, he wouldn't entrust his guns to just anyone. He wrenched the board off the window ledge, hid the guns in the space beneath it and hammered the wood back into place.

As the blacksmith was smiling contentedly, Fatima shook her head and pointed to the hooks on the wall. Timur pulled them out with a pair of pliers and they mounted a wall-hanging over the spot, to hide the holes. Three days passed before the gendarmes came. They heard the clatter of hooves just as they were sitting down to eat one evening. Timur opened the door.

'Good evening, gentlemen. I hope it's good news that brings you our way.'

'Good evening,' the gendarmes replied, in chorus, and one continued: 'Can we come in?'

'But of course, do come in.'

Gül was frightened when she saw the strange men, all in uniform, two of them carrying guns. The unarmed one bent down to speak to her.

'Hello, little girl. What's your name, sweetheart? … Don't you have one?'

'Gül.'

'And your little sister, asleep over there, does she have a name?'

'Yes. Melike.'

'Gül and Melike.'

He smiled briefly, then straightened up and turned to Timur: 'You're the blacksmith, Timur.'

'At your service.'

'We've heard you've been keeping guns without a licence.'

'No,' said the blacksmith. 'I don't have guns. You must have heard wrong.'

With a nod, the man directed the others to start the search. They began, unhurried, opening the cupboards, peering under the divan, between the mattresses and pillows and under the rugs next to the loom.

'Can I get you gentlemen anything?' Fatma asked, 'Perhaps you'd like a coffee?'

The unarmed man nodded, and one of the gendarmes followed Fatma into the kitchen while the others carried on searching. The unarmed man sat down next to Gül, Timur took the seat opposite them. He looked completely calm.

'Come here a minute, little one. Come here, Gül,' said the man, once he'd taken off his cap. He pulled Gül into his lap.

'Do you get on well with your sister?'

Gül nodded.

'I bet you're a good big sister, aren't you, you take good care of her?'

Gül nodded again.

'Wonderful, now tell me, how old are you? … Don't you know? You can't be five yet, can you? Or six? Are you at school yet?'

Gül said nothing. She didn't nod, didn't shake her head; she simply stayed silent.

'Come here,' the man said to the gendarme, who was standing about looking hesitant, not knowing where to search next.

'Have a look at this,' he then said to Gül, pointing to the gendarme's gun. 'Look at it, have you ever seen anything like this before?'

He laughed and stroked her cheek.

'There's nothing to be scared of, Gül.'

Gül wasn't scared, she didn't even feel particularly uneasy sitting in this strange man's lap. She simply stayed silent.

'You've seen a gun before, haven't you? Practically every man has a gun. It's quite normal, isn't it? Your dad's got one too, hasn't he?'

Fatma came in with a tray, offering the commander a cup of coffee first, then his two assistants, who accepted their cups but set them down without taking a sip. They wanted to finish searching the last room, the bedroom, where the wrought-iron bedstead had been returned some weeks earlier.

Timur received his cup last. His hands didn't tremble. Even if Gül did say that her father had a gun, it would make no difference, since they'd never find them.

'One of you check the stable,' the commander called to the bedroom before turning back to Gül.

'Your dad's got a gun, hasn't he? And you know exactly where he's hidden it. Be a good girl, Gül, be a good girl and tell me where your dad's hidden the gun. He's got two, hasn't he? You're a big girl now, I'm sure you know where the guns are.'

Thank God we sent her out, thought the blacksmith. Gül said nothing and shrugged.

It was pitch-black outside when the gendarmes abandoned their search, thanked Fatma for the coffee and left.

'Go into the other room and stay there until I call you,' Timur told Gül.

'Can't it wait till tomorrow?' Fatma asked, but Timur just shook his head.

'Go on, Gül.'

'But I already know where they are.'

'Oh really, where?' her father asked, teasing.

Gül ran to the window ledge and placed her little hand roughly over the spot covering the hollow.

Fatma smiled, lifted Gül up in her arms, kissed her on the cheek and said: 'You did very well. It's very important not to tell strangers about what goes on at home. Bravo, I'm proud of you, my darling. You did a great job.'

Timur noticed his hands had started to tremble.

Gül didn't tell anyone at home what went on outside either. That summer, she didn't feel like going out to play with the other children. Even when Fatma told her to look after Melike, who always wanted to go out, Gül would often find an excuse to stay in the summer house or play in the garden by herself, building mud houses in the shade of the apple trees or picking flowers to give to her mother.

'Why don't you play with the other children?' Fatma asked. 'Don't you like them? You always like playing with the children back in the village.'

Gül shrugged and said nothing.

'Melike likes playing with them too. They're nice children, aren't they?'

Fatma had lifted Gül onto her lap. Gül raised her shoulders again, but she leaned her head against her mother's chest.

'Do they tease you? Do they laugh at you?'

Gül nodded.

'And why do they laugh? Because you always get caught when you play red rover?'

Gül shook her head and said: 'Wed wover.'

'You're just as fast as the others, it's alright.'

'Awright,' Gül said, very quietly.

Now Fatma understood.

'They laugh at you because you talk like the people from the village.'

Gül lowered her head.

'But that's not such a bad thing. If you play with them a couple of days, you'll soon sound just like them, you're a quick learner. And they might laugh at you once or twice until then, but they'll soon get bored. There's no need to be ashamed.'

Fatma poked her fingers under Gül's arms and laughed and started to tickle her, first slowly but soon she and her daughter were rolling on the floor. Gül laughed and screeched; she sat on her mother's legs to tickle her feet. Fatma kicked and struggled a little, screaming, and then she let her body go limp and said: 'Now you've tickled me to death.'

She stayed face-down, motionless. Gül went on tickling the soles of her mother's bare feet, but Fatma clenched her teeth and kept perfectly still. When there was no response for a while, Gül stopped, sat up next to Fatma and shook her.

'Mummy?'

Fatma didn't respond.

'Mummy, don't be dead. Mummy?'

Not until Fatma realised Gül was getting scared did she open her eyes with a laugh, hug her daughter and say: 'I'm still here, don't worry. If you go out for a bit today, we can play again to-morrow, awright?'

From then on, they played together every day, and sometimes Fatma played dead. Gül cheated. She went out the front to the children in the street, but she'd soon go into the stable, which had one door onto the road and one to the garden. She was scared of the mice in there, but she simply closed her eyes all but a tiny sliver, held her breath and ran as fast as she could from one door to the other. That was how she spent almost the whole summer before she started school, on her own in the garden.

She liked it at the village school, where all 60 pupils from the first to the fifth year sat in one classroom; she liked it even though the teacher would hit them on the palm with his ruler if they misbehaved. The boys got clips round the head or the ear as well, but the girls didn't need to fear that. Only twice in her first year at school did Gül get hit with the ruler.

Recep, the only blond boy in the village, was in the fourth year and infamous for playing tricks and making trouble. One day he flicked balls of paper across the classroom. When the teacher caught him at it, he smacked him so hard in the face that his cheeks were still red the next morning. But just two days later he started flicking again and hit the teacher on the back of the neck.

Without turning around, the teacher said: 'Recep.'

'It was me,' Gül said; she had no idea why it slipped out. Recep wasn't even her friend. He was the son of a good friend of her mother's, and people thought the reason he was naughty was that he didn't have a father; the man had gone to Istanbul one day and never come back, or so they said.

The teacher turned around and looked at Gül for a few seconds. He knew it hadn't been her, but he called her to the front and made her stretch out her left hand, palm upwards. He had to maintain his authority. Everyone held their breath, and the slapping sound was almost worse for Gül than the pain. As she sat back down, she knew her mother would hear about it. She'd be angry with her for being naughty, she knew she would. Tears pricked her eyes.

'It doesn't hurt any more, does it?' Recep asked after school.

'No,' Gül murmured, looking briefly up into his blue-grey eyes.

'Here.'

Recep took a few apricot stones out of his pocket and pressed them into Gül's hand.

'See you tomorrow,' he added, and then he turned away and left.

At home, Gül smashed the apricot pits open with a stone and ate the nutty innards, not asking Melike if she wanted any.

Gül didn't cry the second time she got hit with the ruler. No one was allowed to be late, not even the girls. And if you came late on Monday mornings, when they were singing the national anthem, you'd get a whack with the ruler. On other days, you had a chance of getting away with it.

When Melike had a bad dream or woke up and couldn't get back to sleep, she'd get into bed with Gül, snuggle up and fall asleep again. At night, half asleep, Gül liked to feel her sister's body curled up next to her.

Sometimes, though, Melike would wake up because she'd wet the bed. She'd soon be four but she still wet the bed regularly. The covers were clammy, the mattress was damp and cold and stank, and Melike would get up and simply lie back down in Gül's warmth.

The night before Gül got her second punishment, Melike woke up from a bad dream and got into Gül's bed. By the morning, however, she was back in her own. And when Gül awoke from the sounds in the kitchen, she thought she had wet her own bed. Her pyjama bottoms were wet, her legs were damp, the cold spot on the mattress was right underneath her.

Gül undressed and thought about where to hide her pyjamas. She wanted to dry them in secret; she was a big girl, she went to school now, she didn't wet the bed any more. At first, she stuffed the trousers under Melike's bedding, and when it was time to go to school, she took them with her to hide them in the stable.

But when she opened the stable door and heard the mice squeaking, sensing rather than seeing their scurrying in the hay, she didn't dare go in, into the dark stable where the cows and horses and the donkey were too. The stable at the summer house had seemed less scary.

Gül stood at the door in her school uniform. She had already smuggled her pyjama trousers out of the house, and she couldn't take them to school. And she couldn't hide them anywhere else, because someone might steal them. It took a long time, a very long time, for Gül to gather up the courage to dash into the stable and hide the trousers in the hay. It took about as long as the national anthem.

A few weeks later, or – more precisely – on the day when their mother told Gül and Melike they would soon be getting a new sibling, Recep was late to school. You could have sung the national anthem 50 times before he arrived. The school day was almost done. It would've been smarter of him not to turn up at all. If you didn't turn up, you wouldn't get caned. The day after, you could always say you'd had to help your parents.

But Recep knocked, opened the door, presented himself to the teacher and simply held his hands out in front of him. And the teacher didn't take much convincing.

Afterwards, Recep squeezed himself onto the bench where Gül was sitting and whispered to her: 'Your dad's got into a row with Tufan, there's going to be a fight in the village square. Your dad's strong, but Tufan has more men.'

Gül was agitated, she felt hot, she felt like she couldn't sit still any longer, but she didn't move. Her father was going to fight someone.

'Why have they fallen out?' she whispered to Recep.

'I don't know. Are you coming with me?'

'Yes,' Gül said. She had never seen adults fight before.

You could've sung the national anthem for a full year before the school day was finally over, that's how slow time seemed to pass. There was whispering and gossiping; the news spread, and when the teacher declared school over for the day, the pupils streamed out of the classroom faster than ever before and ran, breathless, towards the village square. Everyone wanted to grab a good spot.

'Come with me, they'll chase us away from the square,' Recep said.

They climbed up a ladder onto the roof of one of the houses that had a good view of the village square. Two groups of men were standing below them, a stone's throw away. Gül instantly recognised her father in the smaller group. The men were shouting, hurling insults at each other. The blacksmith didn't have the loudest voice, but he towered over the rest of them and stood with his head high, his shoulders slightly back, his chest pushed out: he didn't seem afraid at all.

The men picked up stones off the ground and flung them at their rivals; first someone from Tufan's group would throw one and the others would retreat, then Timur's men would throw and Tufan's friends would put their arms in front of their faces to protect themselves and take a few steps back. One of Timur's mates was hit on the brow, and the left side of his face and his neck were covered with blood, but he shouted the loudest of all. On the other side, even No-Nose Abdul squawked out a few swears. Nearly all the children were afraid of him; his nose had been shot off by his brother when the two of them were young. They'd been playing with their father's gun, thinking it wasn't loaded. Abdul only very rarely left the village, so as not to be at the mercy of strangers' stares. In the village, at least the adults had long grown accustomed to his scarred face, the bridge of his nose ending abruptly just beneath his eyebrows.

'Dishonourable dog!' Abdul shouted, and from behind him Tufan yelled: 'Crook, dirty pig!'

Timur split off from his group and made towards the others. He was lucky, a couple of stones missed him, one clipped his shoulder. When he was standing a good ten strides away from his group, the others stopped throwing stones.

'What's your problem, Tufan, you son of an ox? If you're a man, come over here and fight like one. Don't just throw stones like a woman.'

'In case you didn't already know: in this village, we throw stones to chase off dogs,' Tufan yelled back. 'And what are you but a pesky little dog? What business do you have in our village?'

'A good dog doesn't bite people in his own village,' Timur said. 'Now come and fight like a man.'

Gül would have liked to shout out loud – she would have liked to do something to make them all get along again, but she sat on the roof and held her breath like all the other children who had gathered up there in the meantime, having been chased away from the village square. A few of the children recognised their own fathers among the groups. Recep wished he had a father who could be standing there too, or at least a brother old enough, but he just had four older sisters and a mother. Tufan took a few steps forward, not as energetically as Timur had, then turned around to look at his men. Now there were perhaps 15 strides between Timur and Tufan. The first upright and proud, the other a little shorter, his shoulders sunken.

'You ripped me off,' Tufan said. 'You robbed me blind. I'll tell you again: I want my cut.'

'Cut? We agreed on a price for the beans, you got it. We shook on it, but now you want to go back on your word.'

'You conned me – it was far too little.'

'I gave you a good price. And you agreed to it.'

'You owe me double.'

'Fuck you! Come and fight me.'

Timur took another two steps towards Tufan, who was clearly willing himself to stay standing. And suddenly a stone hit Timur in the middle of his forehead. Nobody saw who'd thrown it, because they had all been mesmerised by the sight of the two rivals. Timur hesitated only briefly, wiped a hand over his brow and then ran at Tufan. But Tufan turned and ran to his men, who were now all flinging stones at Timur to keep him away. Once he'd been hit a few times, the blacksmith stopped and walked back, slowly. When he was far enough away, he turned around again.

'You cowards. Can't even fight like men. If I get hold of any of you, I'll use you to plug the hole you crawled out of.'

He yelled the air out of his lungs, and a single trickle of blood ran between his eyebrows and then down the left side of his nose, disappearing into his thick, blond moustache.

'We're going,' he said.

Tufan had run away, the matter was closed. Gül ran home excitedly and told her mother what she'd seen. Fatma simply nodded; she didn't seem worried.

'Gül, don't mention it to him when he comes home, don't ask him why it happened. Don't ask him. Will you do that, little one?'

It was dark by the time the blacksmith came back. Melike hadn't wanted to go to sleep and was still romping about the room, doing somersaults and trying to climb up onto the window ledge. Once her father had eaten, she plonked herself down in his lap. Gül sat on the floor pretending to do her homework.

'What's that?' asked Melike, poking a finger into the little wound on her father's brow.

'It's where a little girl poked me in the head,' said Timur. 'I was at work and in came a little girl, the same age as you, and she poked her finger into my head and asked if she could be my daughter. And I said I already have two daughters. And maybe soon I'll have a third. And I said my daughters are very kind. But the next time you're naughty, I'll make the little girl my daughter and give you away instead.'

He laughed and kissed Melike, and Gül was sitting close enough to smell his laugh. It smelt hot and sour, it smelt like something forbidden.

At night, Gül heard her parents whispering, but she couldn't understand a word. She would've liked to get up and lie next to Melike, but Melike would wet the bed *and* her from top to bottom. That's what had happened last time. When her mother had found her pyjama bottoms in the stable, she'd confronted Gül.

'Why did you hide your pyjama bottoms?'

Gül had shrugged.

'Did you think you'd wet the bed? It wasn't you, it was Melike again. And even if you do wet the bed, it's not that bad. It can happen to anyone. Just like the business with the teacher when he smacked you. It happens. But it shouldn't happen too often, understand? I want you to be a big girl, one who can take care of her little sister. Now, do you want to help me wash these bottoms of yours, my love?'

Fatma had heated the water and poured it into the big portable copper basin, and while she sat on a low wooden stool washing the pyjamas and the sheets, she let Gül scrub along a little.

Gül lay awake long after her parents' whispering had died away. Her heart still seemed to be beating as fast as it had that afternoon on the roof. It pressed against her chest and wouldn't let her sleep.

One day, Fatma left Gül and Melike with her mother-in-law so she could take care of something in town. While Melike slept, Gül kept jumping off the divan, over and over. She climbed up on one side, walked the entire length of the divan and jumped down at the other end.

'If something gets broken, you're in big trouble,' Zeliha called more than once from the kitchen, where she was rolling stuffed vine leaves with Hülya.

On what must have been her 50th jump from the divan, Gül got cocky, took too much of a run-up and landed in a bowl of minced meat she hadn't noticed was there. She was scared of her grandmother, and didn't want to be in big trouble, so she picked herself up, slipped her shoes on and ran out of the house. There were about as many houses on one street here as in the whole village. Or at least it seemed that way to her. It wasn't five minutes before she lost her way. It was winter, she was freezing cold, and after a quarter of an hour she stopped on a street corner, so scared and cold she couldn't even cry.

A tall man with green eyes and black hair spoke to her: 'Are you lost, little one? I've not seen you around here before.'

Gül nodded.

'Shall I take you home? Come on, first we'll put this jumper on you. That's right… Where do you live then?'

Gül shrugged.

'Whose daughter are you?'

'The blacksmith's daughter.'

'Right, then I'll take you to the blacksmith.'

The young man hoisted Gül onto his shoulders, and Gül enjoyed the perspective from up there; she enjoyed the feeling of being carried for so long and listening to him asking the way of two passers-by. Eventually, the man knocked at a door, lifted Gül down and waited. A woman opened up, and they could see a man and children in the background, eating their dinner.

'A blessed evening and a good meal to you,' the man said, and then he went on: 'Blacksmith, I've brought your daughter back to you.'

'My daughter?' said the man who'd got up and come to the door. 'Don't be silly, that's not my daughter. I've already got four girls, what I want is a son. The merciful Lord hasn't granted me a single son. You get out of here with yet another girl.'

'Oh,' the green-eyed man said.

After the door shut behind them, the man asked Gül: 'What's your father's name, then?'

'Timur.'

'Timur, not Tolga. You're the blacksmith Timur's daughter?'

Gül nodded and said: 'We live in the village.'

'I know,' the man said. 'Don't worry, I'll take you to your father, we'll just have to borrow a horse.'

And so the man, who later turned out to be a sieve maker, took Gül home to her parents in the village and had to stay overnight in the end, because he couldn't ride back in the dark. Gül had thought her mother would tell her off and her father would shout, but neither of them said a thing.

Once the sieve maker had set off for town with her father the next morning, Fatma took Gül aside and gave her a clip round the ear.

'You are never, do you hear, *never* to run away like that again, no matter what happens. And never, never go anywhere with strange men again. They might do bad things to you, very bad things. Promise me you'll never run away again. Promise me!'

Gül got her second clip round the ear then and there, and she saw the tears in her mother's eyes. There was something in Fatma's face that scared her, scared her more than her grandmother's voice.

Fatma pulled Gül into her embrace, stroked her hair and said: 'My dove, never again, promise?'

'I promise.'

It was a hard winter, though they always had enough wood, they had plenty of flour, bulgur and beans, they had thick grape molasses which tugged at the bread when you dunked it in. It was an unusually hard winter, and there were days when the blacksmith did not ride out to work but stayed at home with his pregnant wife instead. It was the first winter that Fatma and Timur had their own bed from the first snow to the last. Relatives and acquaintances married, but there was no chance of transporting the bed through the snow-packed streets.

At school, it was so cold that the firewood ran out. Every day, two children had to bring wood from home, but even then, it was never really warm in the classroom. Fatma spoke to Timur, and one day he rode to the school, taking as much wood as his donkey could carry. Many of the children had fallen ill by then, and the children from the surrounding villages sometimes stayed home because the snow had blocked the roads, and when they'd burned through the blacksmith's wood in no time at all, the teacher shut the school until the snow queen's crown finally shattered; until the snow melted.

Early one morning in the first days of the thaw, Sibel was born. Gül had gone to bed the night before, and when she woke, she had a little sister; a tiny, ruddy little sister, small enough that Gül thought she would probably fit inside her own little belly. Her mother's belly had been so big and her sister was so small. Sibel.

Melike glanced at the new arrival only briefly, apparently uninterested. She was much more interested in breakfast being

43

ready at last and in all the hubbub at the house. People were coming and going, there were well-wishes and little presents, and Timur said again and again: 'Her hands and feet are normal, thanks be to God.'

Good wishes rained down from friends and neighbours: *May she be healthy, may she always have her mother and father, may she be granted a long and happy life.*

By the time Sibel was 40 days old, the snow had melted, the brooks and rivers had burst their banks, the sun was warm – and sometimes Timur sat in front of his house and closed his eyes, rubbed his neck under his coat collar, then held his head still and enjoyed the warmth on his face. And soon the birds were singing, the trees were coming into bud; he had another daughter, named after a fertility goddess. Life was always getting bigger and it had no banks to burst like a river. It simply grew – it grew like his children, and one of these days his life and his heart would grow so big there'd be room inside for everyone, his friends and his foes; there would even be room for Tufan, who'd snitched on him to the gendarmes.

But in the last few days he'd felt a little weak, like he was coming down with the flu. He hadn't had the slightest cold all winter long, so he couldn't understand why he now felt weak and drained, and every morning it got worse, not better. One day his limbs were aching so badly that work was out of the question. Even his clothes made his skin smart, so he left the forge not long after he'd arrived, had a glass of tea at the teahouse and then went to the baths to sweat out the sickness. The next morning, he could hardly get up; he dragged himself to the forge but all he did was spend the day at the teahouse, sitting there in a daze.

'You've not looked at all well these last few days,' Fatma said that evening.

'I think I'm getting sick.'

Fatma felt his forehead.

'I'll make you some broth, you've got a bit of a fever, and tonight we'll wrap you up nice and warm and you'll just sweat it out.'

Timur didn't mention that he'd been to the baths, but that night he sweated again. Fatma gave him fresh pyjamas, and when he was changing by the light of the petroleum lamp, she saw reddish blotches on his chest and back.

'Timur,' she said, 'you should tell the doctor about this, it doesn't look like a cold.'

Timur looked down and he saw the blotches too, if not as clearly as Fatma did. He was completely dazed; everything appeared to him as if through a haze which wouldn't clear, no matter how much he shook his head or rubbed his eyes.

But he said: 'Nonsense, what's the good in seeing the doctor? You'll see, in two days I'll be well again.'

Two days later his fever was even higher. He no longer had the strength to stand, and in his rare lucid moments he listened for his heart. It seemed to be beating very slowly. With each day, his fever worsened, and the rattle on his lungs was enough to frighten Fatma. Through a farmer who had business in the town, she got a message to her mother-in-law about her son's condition. And she made no secret of the fact that she had begun feeling ill herself and feared she would soon be unable to tend to Timur and the children.

The very next day, Zeliha had the whole family brought from the village on a lorry. Timur was so weak that the driver had to help him up into the cab. His fever had raged uninterrupted for over a week, and now he had diarrhoea too. His skin was yellowy and seemed stretched over his cheekbones, his shoulders fell forward wearily, he could no longer stand upright, and there was a glint in his eyes, a crazy, if exhausted glint.

Melike and Gül had only ever seen him lying down to sleep, and now they were both silent at the sight of the weakened man they knew had once been able to carry them both with no effort at all.

The whole way to the town, no one said a word. The only sounds were the hum of the lorry, matches being struck and the driver taking a deep drag. Fatma felt dizzy and unwell, and a few times she tried to ask if they could stop for a moment, but then her stomach seemed to settle again and the queasiness was bearable.

'Typhoid,' the doctor said. 'I assume it's typhoid.'

'Are you feeling ill too?' he asked Fatma, who gave only a slow nod as an answer.

'It's an infectious disease. You've come from a village?'

'Yes.'

'Do you have a toilet? Or do you go in the bushes? Typhoid is transmitted by gut bacteria.'

'We do have a toilet, yes. The only one in the village... Is it dangerous?'

'It's not *not* dangerous,' the doctor said. 'Take your children to relatives; it doesn't look like they've caught it. It's almost the last stage of the illness, your husband will probably be over the worst in a few days. He has a robust constitution, don't worry.'

Zeliha sat at the head end of the bed and dabbed her son's brow, shiny with fever. Once the doctor had packed his bag and left, she said to Fatma: 'Take the children to Hülya's, they'll be well looked after there.'

Hülya had married a prison guard last spring, but she still wasn't pregnant. In the coach with her daughters, Fatma had to ask the coachman to pull over. She got out and vomited by the side of the road. The coachman gave her a sip of water after she'd wiped her face with her handkerchief. Melike and Gül sat in the coach, watching in silence. Their little sister lay between them, asleep.

'Are you ill too? Does it hurt?' Gül asked her mother.

She wanted Fatma to say that there was no need to be scared, that everything would be fine. She didn't understand what was happening, and she wanted her mother to make the world smaller with her words, to tear it into pieces that didn't seem so threatening, pieces she could grasp.

'No, my darling, it doesn't hurt. I think I'm getting ill but it's nothing bad.'

'Are we going to Auntie Hülya's?'

'Yes, I'm taking you to Auntie Hülya and Uncle Yücel. You'll just stay there for a few days. And be good, alright? Look after your sisters, Gül. We'll come and pick you up soon, and then we'll all go back to the village together. Your father is sick, but there are doctors here in town. We'll get better and then we'll go back to the village.'

Hülya welcomed them very warmly. She kissed her sister-in-law and the girls, made tea and offered pastries, but Fatma wouldn't stay.

'I must get back,' she said. 'I have to be with Timur. Please take good care of the girls. Keep both your eyes on them so I don't have to keep looking around.'

'Don't you worry.'

Fatma kissed Gül and Melike, and just as she was about to kiss Sibel, the baby started screaming, and Fatma said: 'I want to feed her one last time.'

Hülya looked her sister-in-law in the eye, and she would have liked to reassure her; she would have liked to say, *You'll have plenty more chances to feed her*, and she'd have liked to laugh as she said it. Fatma was still as beautiful as a piece of the moon, even though her cheeks had caved in, but her eyes seemed to be looking inwards, into a darkness longer than the evening sun's shadows. Then her gaze turned outwards again, and she smiled, put Sibel to her breast and let her suckle. Gül was still scared. Her mother had made the world smaller, but it hadn't helped.

The next day, Fatma couldn't get up either. The fever had seized her, and the mist had folded in around her, but she did see that her mother-in-law took much better care of her son than of her. There was nothing she could she do about it, left to lie in her sweat-soaked clothes, not getting clean sheets every few hours, no more than half a cup of broth being spooned into her mouth because she swallowed so slowly. There was nothing she could do, and little changed over the next few days. She lay next to her husband, who got better and better from day to day. He could already get up and take a few steps, while she lay there in fever dreams and was incapable of almost anything.

In a moment of clarity, she said: 'Timur, get them to take me to hospital. Your mother's not caring for me like she is of you, and I don't have anyone else. Get them to take me to hospital, please, I'm very sick. You can get better faster, your mother can take better care of you, and then you can come and pick me up from the hospital and nurse me back to health. Timur, I beg of you, for the love of God, get them to take me to hospital. I'm very sick... I'm scared.'

Timur kissed her brow and nodded.

Sibel cried all through that first night in the strange house. Yücel, who had work in the morning, walked back and forth through the house with her in his arms; he rocked her, placed a hand on her back and hummed songs to soothe her. Melike wet the bed three times that night, and Hülya, who couldn't sleep either, changed the bedclothes three times, while Gül lay there and pretended to be asleep. She liked her aunt and her uncle, who was a quiet man and often seemed quite serious.

Early in the mornings, Hülya would take Sibel to her mother, so that Fatma could nurse her at least once a day, and each time Hülya would say: 'See, there'll be many more times like this.' But Fatma's milk had all but dried up.

The sisters had been at their aunt's for a few days when Yücel went to the mosque for Friday prayers.

'Come here,' Hülya said to Gül. 'You know how we wash ourselves before prayers, don't you?'

Gül nodded, her mother had taught her how, so they did their ritual ablutions together and then they prayed. While they were praying, Melike came into the room and, though she knew she wasn't to disturb them, said: 'Look, I can do a backward roll now too.'

Gül tried to keep going, unfazed like Auntie Hülya, but she was distracted by Melike's fidgeting, and hissed: 'Go away!' But that only made Melike keener to perform her latest trick. And when they had finished praying, Auntie Hülya didn't scold Melike; she acted as if she hadn't noticed. She changed her clothes, took Sibel in her arms and told Gül not to let go of Melike's hand.

'We're going to Nene's.'

Fatma was being taken to hospital that day, and Uncle Yücel was already at Zeliha's, as were a few neighbours and friends of the family. There were so many people there that Gül was completely bewildered and forgot to keep an eye on Melike, who ran around trying to find someone to play with. Gül knew which room her mother was in, but she didn't dare go in.

Eventually, Zeliha brought Fatma out of the room. The carriage was waiting outside, and when she saw her mother, all Gül could say was: 'Mum.'

Fatma smiled and said: 'Gül, my rose.'

Then she kissed her children one more time, and her voice cracked as she spoke to everyone around her: 'Friends, forgive me if I have sinned against you.'

Gül didn't understand what this meant, but she knew that it couldn't be good. There was so much she didn't understand. At first, her mother had been the one who made the world smaller with her words, but it didn't help, and now the words she spoke made the world big again, so big she didn't know what to do with herself. The world grew so huge that Gül just stood there.

She just stood there again when they went to visit her mother in hospital seven days later. For seven days Hülya went with Sibel to the hospital, for seven days Melike wet the bed every night, for seven days Sibel cried half the night in her aunt's arms without her losing her patience, for seven days Uncle Yücel rocked Sibel back and forth on his feet, as was the custom. He sat down with his legs outstretched, placed a cushion on his feet and Sibel on the cushion and rocked the little one back and forth gently to soothe her. Seven days in which the blacksmith felt a little better each morning. He could soon feed himself again, he was able to walk a few steps and slowly he found his strength. He had been able to visit his wife three times, and soon they'd be out of the woods. Soon they'd return to the village and be together at home as a family, soon he'd be back at the forge and hold[ing] the heavy hammers in his hands, soon he'd be able to ride his horse again – soon, so soon.

Seven days passed and it was Friday again. Auntie Hülya and Gül did their ritual ablutions together and Melike joined in this time, copying the motions of prayer and giggling, failing to get anyone's attention.

Then Uncle Yücel, Auntie Hülya, Sibel, Melike and Gül went to the hospital together, where Zeliha and Timur were already waiting. Gül was frightened when she saw her mother. Fatma had violet rings around her eyes; the colour was almost garish, like the methylated spirits they kept in brandy bottles at home. Like lilac mixed with dark green, then illuminated.

'Don't get too close,' Zeliha hissed at Melike and Gül. 'It's catching.'

But Melike didn't listen. She climbed up onto the edge of the bed and then simply sat there.

Gül felt that her mother's eyes were almost disappearing into the rings around them and they looked sad, sad and like they were trying to hold onto something. Gül wanted to be a good girl, so she stood there, she stood on the same spot the whole time they were in the hospital room, unmoving, and nobody seemed to notice. Since Timur was nearly better, Gül and Melike went back to their grandmother's. Sibel would spend a few more days with her aunt. Gül couldn't sleep that night and wanted to get into her sister's bed, but Melike woke up as Gül crept under the covers, and just said: 'Go away.'

Gül went to her father.

'What's wrong, my girl?' he asked.

'I can't sleep.'

'Go to your Nene, I toss and turn all over the place.'

So Gül went to her grandmother's room, and her grandmother groaned but took her into her bed. The same image lingered in Gül's mind's eye; how she had stood in the corner of the hospital room and how wretched her mother had looked. It took a long time before she finally fell asleep, and she woke in the middle of the night to her grandmother snoring. She turned away from Zeliha's body and closed her eyes and waited until the images faded away at last, until the darkness came and took her.

It was usually only in winter that they had soup for breakfast, a warming soup that gave them energy for the day, a thick lentil, yoghurt or tripe soup. But Timur had to regain his strength, so they had beef broth the next morning. Melike, Zeliha, Timur and Gül were sitting on the floor, where the cloth lay spread with the steaming pot, bread, bowls, cheese and olives. Zeliha ladled out the soup until they all had a bowlful, but Timur didn't have a spoon.

'Run and fetch a spoon for your father,' Zeliha told Gül, and Gül leapt up.

On her way to the kitchen, she passed the front door and recognised her aunt's voice outside. Hülya seemed to be talking to the woman next door. They'd soon be finished, and she'd hear the heavy door knocker. Gül stopped to listen.

'I don't know if it's better to have them bring her home first, or if they'll take her straight from the hospital…'

'May the Lord give you all strength,' the neighbour said. 'May the Lord give you strength. What will become of the poor children, now that their mother is dead?'

Gül walked briskly into the kitchen, took a spoon and then ran back to the other room, hearing her aunt cry as she passed by. She gave her father the spoon, and at that moment she heard the door knocker.

'Mummy's dead,' Gül said.

For an instant, Timur remained motionless, then he slung the spoon in his hand against the wall, with all his might. A trickle of plaster fell to the floor.

II

Gül sees her father throw the spoon, she hears it hit the wall, but she doesn't see the plaster crumbling to the floor. Only at that moment is it clear to her that something has happened. Only when she sees her father's reaction does she get an inkling of what she's just said means. The neighbour's words didn't change her world, but the blacksmith and the spoon do. Gül runs into the room where Melike has been sleeping and locks the door behind her.

The tears must have been flowing before, but only now does she cry out loud. Perhaps she knows it from stories and imitates it, perhaps it simply comes out of her – she wails and weeps out words: 'Mummy, you're not dead, are you? You're just playing, aren't you? You will come back, won't you Mummy? Don't leave me alone, Mummy, we'll bake bread together again, Mummy, I love baking bread with you. You're just playing, aren't you, Mummy? Please don't go away, Mummy!

'Please stay, Mummy.

'Mummy!'

The door handle jiggles and Zeliha says: 'Gül, sweetie, open the door, will you?'

But Gül won't even think of it. She has lain down on the unmade bed, drawn up her legs and is hugging the pillow. The smell and the damp sheets don't register with her. And she only takes vague notice, through her tears, of everyone taking turns to knock on the door and try to calm her down. Gül lies there and cries. She's not going to open the door, she's going to stay in this room until her mother comes back.

She doesn't know how long she's been in the room when someone starts fiddling with the window frame. A little later, a boy wriggles in through the small window. To begin with, she thinks it's Recep and stops crying.

But it's one of the neighbours' boys from the summer house; one who laughed at her because she had a village accent. Gül turns her back on him and goes on crying as he unlocks the door. She's still crying when her grandmother picks her up and carries her out of the room.

She doesn't stop until she sees her father.

He's crying.

Gül has never seen her father cry.

The blacksmith is still sitting right where he took the spoon from her earlier, staring at the floor and crying so quietly it can barely be heard. He's sitting cross-legged, staring at the floor, and the sound of the tears dripping off his chin onto the cloth is louder than he is.

People are bustling around the house, but Gül doesn't know where Melike and Sibel are. She sees Auntie Hülya and Uncle Yücel, she sees neighbours and people she's never seen before. She has stopped crying and she thinks: *I have to be a big girl, I have to look after Melike and Sibel.*

'Where are my sisters?' she asks Auntie Hülya.

'They're at the neighbours. We'll go back to our house in a minute, alright?'

'Is Daddy coming too?'

'No, he's staying here.'

Auntie Hülya speaks calmly, but her eyes are red and swollen.

'I want Daddy to come too.'

'He'll come later,' Hülya says. 'We're taking a coach to our house now, and I'll make bread and butter with sugar for you and Melike, shall I?'

Lots of people come into the house, stay for a short while and then leave again – they have unfamiliar faces, but they all give Gül sad, pitying looks, and Gül keeps hearing the same phrases from their lips: *Poor children, may the Lord give them strength, half-orphaned*. And she hears the whispered words: *Istanbul, uncle, Sibel, Gül.*

Auntie Hülya takes the children to her house; there's bread with butter and sugar. Gül eats hers, but Melike holds her slice at an angle, trying to make the sugar spill onto the floor. Soon ants appear, which Melike squishes with her foot. Finally, when no one is looking, she slaps her slice on the wall, where it sticks.

When it gets dark, her father is still not there, and whenever Gül asks for him, she's told that Timur will be there by the time she wakes up in the morning.

Gül can't get to sleep. Just as she feels herself drifting off, she hears the sound of the spoon on the wall. She sees her father's face before her and she understands a little and she understands nothing.

Her mum is never coming back.

Unless she wishes really, really hard. As hard as she can. Her mum will be able to feel it; she'll feel Gül longing for her so keenly, feel her unshakeable will, and then Fatma will return. Gül will go to sleep now, and when she wakes up in the morning her mother will be back. She wouldn't do this to her, she wouldn't just disappear. Now, she'll pull the covers over her head and count to a hundred without making any mistakes, and in the morning, her mother will be there again.

Only once she's counted all the way to the end does Gül hear the front door open and, moments later, she hears Uncle Yücel's voice, a whisper. Perhaps her father has come back after all. Softly, she opens the door and creeps towards the room where the petroleum lamp is burning. The door stands open a crack, and Gül sees that Auntie Hülya is crying and Uncle Yücel is readying his shisha pipe, as he says: 'He's stubborn, but I think it would've been best for the children. He's got it into his head that he's going to keep them. We could talk our tongues dry and he still wouldn't change his mind. We should have waited before we suggested it, we should have waited a day or two.'

Yücel sighs and lights his shisha pipe, it bubbles. He takes a few short drags then inhales deeply to let his lungs savour that this difficult day is over. As he exhales and leans back, he spots Gül.

'What are you doing there? Can't you sleep, little one?' he asks, not getting up, and Hülya, who has been sitting with her back to Gül, jumps up and looks at her. At least, Gül thinks Hülya is looking at her, but her aunt's squint is so severe that she can never be quite sure.

'Come on, I'll take you back to bed. Did you have a bad dream? Come along, I'll sing you another lullaby.'

Gül lets herself be scooped up and taken back to bed. Her aunt's soft voice sings her to sleep.

Two days later, she sees her father again, at last. Two days later, Fatma is buried. They don't lay the body out at home; the blacksmith's wife is taken straight from the hospital to the graveyard. Like someone without a home to go to.

But many people come to mourn with them; she was well-liked, and nobody who knew her and who has heard of her death has stayed away. It is one of the longest funeral processions the little town has ever seen. The men are at the graveyard while the women have gathered at Zeliha's. Hülya has brought Gül and Melike, leaving Sibel with her husband because the baby has a fever and is crying. Everyone thinks she has caught typhoid too and will die soon. Gül listens to what Auntie Hülya and her grandmother are discussing while she plays on the floor with Melike.

'He won't give up the children,' Zeliha says. 'What else can I do? I pleaded with him so sweetly, for hours on end. He won't listen to me. You'll keep these children over my dead body, I said, but he's so stubborn, worse than his father. So I had another idea. Do you know Arzu, the coachman Faruk's daughter?'

'The young woman with three brothers, the ones who live over by the yellow mosque?'

'Yes, her. I'm sure her father would give her to us.'

'Why? Why should he? Why should he marry his daughter to a widower? Just because Timur has a bit of money? Why would Faruk give his daughter to someone with three little children to raise?'

Zeliha shakes her head slowly.

'Don't you know the story?'

Hülya knits her brow quizzically.

'She's already been married, surely you know that.'

'No,' Hülya says.

'They married her off when she was 14 and then' – Zeliha glances down at the children, who don't seem to be listening – 'then it turned out he couldn't get it up. Faruk took her back and told them: *If you can find a way of curing your son, then I'll be happy to give her back, but until then she stays with me.*'

'So, she's still…?'

Zeliha nods.

'I'll go straight over to the coachman tomorrow evening.'

'It'd be good for the children, at least they'd have a mother.'

A little later, the men come back from the burial. Timur takes his daughters in his arms, and Gül notices that he smells quite different than usual. She has smelt her father's sweat often enough, when he's been working in the glow of the furnace all day. She knows how he smells when he's been in the stable or when he's spread manure from the outhouse on the garden, and Gül has never found the smell unpleasant before, but now her father smells sour. Like soured tears.

Gül hasn't quite understood all she's just heard, but it's enough for her to tell her father: 'Daddy, they've found a mummy for us.'

For a brief moment, the blacksmith's eyes blaze. But the blaze turns to tears, which flow softly down his cheeks. He puts Gül down and, without saying anything, turns away and goes out towards the yard. Gül follows him without a word. She sees her father open the door to the outhouse and when he's inside, she crouches in front of the door and says it again: 'Daddy, Nene and Auntie Hülya have found a mummy for us.'

'What are you doing out here?' Timur asks, as if he hadn't noticed she'd followed him. 'Why aren't you inside?'

Gül says nothing, just crouches there, as she often will in the coming days. She will almost always be in the same room as her father. When he goes to the toilet, she will follow him and wait outside the door until he's finished.

When he has a wash, she'll sit outside the door to the little bathroom, which you still have to carry water into, to heat it in the boiler. She will be shocked that he manages to wash away the smell of his tears.

Gül will follow her father wherever he goes; she will see him stop chewing suddenly during breakfast in the mornings and see the tears caress his unshaven cheeks, see how he comes back from the toilet with wet tear tracks still shining on his face, she'll hear the tears dripping onto the prayer mat as he prays. Later, it will seem to her that during this time she never saw his eyes dry and that he barely spoke a word.

Sibel is very ill, and when Zeliha goes to sit with the coachman, Faruk, to convince him to give his daughter's hand in marriage, she tries not to mention her youngest granddaughter at all. It would be one less new child for Arzu to worry about, one more reason for Faruk to marry off his daughter for the second time.

Yet she says: 'Three girls: six, four and two months. The youngest is very sick, we don't think she'll make it. Two children, let's say then – just two children.'

'I'll think about it,' says Faruk.

If he and his daughter are to agree, he asks that they not breathe a word of it, on grounds of piety, which doesn't much interest Zeliha at that moment. She has to take care of her son, and who will raise his children? Is she supposed to do it? At her age? She's had enough of that.

For four days, four long days, Sibel fights for her life; she is a small, peaky child, her baby fat now all but disappeared. Hülya is with her day and night. She doesn't think it's typhoid, even the doctor said it could just be a normal fever. For four long days, Sibel has feverish spasms while Hülya is sweating blood with worry. As for Timur, he seems dead. He doesn't go to work; he spends all day sitting cross-legged on a cushion, drinking tea with lots and lots of sugar, and smoking – smoking till you can barely see him. Gül is always at his side.

Melike still hasn't grasped what's happened. She plays in the street with the children and brags that her mother's soul is now at peace. She doesn't ask for Fatma, but she still wets the bed every night.

When four days have passed, Sibel's fever comes down. When Timur learns that she seems to have survived, he gets up in the morning and wants to go to work. Gül cries and clings to his leg like a toddler.

'Don't be scared,' Timur says, 'I'll be back this evening. Promise.'

'Promise?'

'Promise.'

And now he sits outside the forge, and every little while someone comes to offer their condolences and take his mind off things. He orders tea for each of them and is glad there's no need for him to start work just yet. He hardly feels ready to pick up a hammer.

In the evenings, he calls Gül and Melike over to him and says: 'We'll go back to the village in a couple of days. We're all better now, Gül has school to go to, Auntie Hülya will come with us and look after you. And soon… soon… you'll have a mother.'

He doesn't say mummy or a new mother or stepmother, he says: 'Soon you'll have a mother.'

It's much like when Timur slung the spoon at the wall. Only when she hears it from her father does Gül really believe it:

they're getting a mother. She's very excited and curious too. She looks at Melike, who doesn't seem to quite know what to do with the information. Timur smiles, gets up. Gül follows him to the toilet door.

On her first day back at school, Gül notices the other children sneaking furtive glances at her, but at break time no one comes to ask curious questions. The only one who comes is Recep.

'May the Lord give the survivors strength,' he says, the way he's learned from the grownups.

'Amen,' says Gül.

'Your father was away too long,' Recep says. 'Tufan has riled the whole village up against him.'

Gül isn't worried. She senses everyone will be nice to her father to begin with. She herself is glad to be back in the village, talking to Recep and not having to see her grandmother so often – such a strict, cold woman. In the village, no one laughs at her accent, and Auntie Hülya plays with her and Melike every evening. Her aunt cooks, cleans, does the laundry and the dishes, but Gül would like to give Sibel her bottle herself, she'd like to undress Melike and wash her and make her breakfast.

And Hülya lets her, a sad smile on her face but encouraging words on her lips: 'You're such a hard-working girl. Bravo, sweetie, you're such a treasure.'

Not a day goes by without Hülya telling the girls they'll soon get a new mother, telling them it's something to look forward to. She sews them special dresses for the occasion; blue fabric with white flowers.

Fifty-two days have passed since Fatma's death, when Timur rides into town, marries, but returns alone. Arzu will be coming on a lorry with her dowry the next day.

That day is a Sunday, and Auntie Hülya has put the girls in their new dresses. They're sitting at home, waiting impatiently, when Recep comes running in: 'They're down on the road, you can see them already.'

If they can see the lorry on the curving road to the village, it won't be much longer. Gül picks up Sibel and runs after Melike to the ladder leaning against the stable. Melike is already at the top, because Gül can't run as fast with Sibel in her arms. She leaves the baby on the ground at the foot of the ladder and climbs up until she's standing on the top rung next to Melike. They have the best view from there, and she wants to be sure to be the first to see their mother. Or at least not have Melike see her first.

'You go down and get Sibel,' she says.

'No, you go.'

'I'm older, you have to do what I say.'

'I'm not going, she can stay down there.'

'She's our sister.'

'I don't care. I'm not going. You go!'

They go on squabbling for a while, not looking at each other. Their eyes are stubbornly fixed on the road.

'You get her!'

'No, you! If you carry her up, I'll carry her down.'

Then Melike might see their mother first.

'We'll both go.'

Gül grips Melike by the arm and tries to pull her down with her, but she resists. Sibel is sitting perfectly still on the ground, looking up at her sisters. Now Gül puts her arms around Melike and tries to climb down a rung of the ladder like that, but Melike wriggles so wildly that they lose their balance. Gül lets go but it's too late, and they both fall on the ground, right next to Sibel. Melike grabs Gül by the hair and pulls, Gül grips Melike's wrist to halt the pulling and at the same time tries to push Sibel out of harm's way with her other hand. Melike goes to bite the hand pushing Sibel away. Sibel starts crying, and Gül stops for a moment, finds her hair pulled all the harder and yells while Melike screams to drown her out.

That's when they hear a cautious voice: 'Children, be nice. Children, don't fight.'

A young woman with plump cheeks that make her look friendly is standing right in front of them. Gül and Melike look up. Gül has a scratch from Melike's fingernail on her forehead, Melike has cut her knee open, and later they'll notice they both have grazed elbows.

That's how Arzu first meets the children. She sees three girls on the ground, two of whom have just been wrestling, the third with snot running down her face.

'Lord, give me strength,' she murmurs.

The woman doesn't look anything like their mother, but still Gül carefully asks: 'Mother?'

'Yes.'

Gül stands up but doesn't step towards the woman or say another word. Melike gets up too, walks over to the woman and snuggles up to her leg. *Serves Gül right*, she's obviously thinking.

Though Timur has regained his strength, he's been feeling a constant pressure on his eyes. He doesn't want to go to the doctor about it; he doesn't trust doctors. They let his wife die, and probably the pain is only from all the crying anyway. He has never cried as much in his life as over the past few weeks.

He notices the villagers are reluctant to sell him their wares. Some of them would rather deal with Tufan, even though he pays them a lower price. Timur is convinced it won't be that way for long; people follow the money in the long term. He simply let the trading slide for too long because he had other worries.

They wanted to send the children to relatives in Istanbul – Gül and Sibel at least. Their great-uncle didn't want Melike, though, because he knew she was difficult. *No*, Timur said, *they're my daughters, and I'll be there for them as long as I can.* And now he's married this woman. She's not as beautiful as a piece of the moon, but everyone says she's a hard worker and she has a pure heart.

The last time his mother picked a wife for him, she made a good choice. Who could decide better for him than his mother, who nursed him at her breast and raised him? And what else could he have done, how would he have kept his daughters without a wife?

Arzu isn't as beautiful as a piece of the moon, but she's not ugly either. She really is a hard worker, she takes care of the children, she can cook; what does it matter that she can't or won't weave, that they won't have any carpets to sell? Timur gets a good price for the loom.

Her new mother has only been with them two weeks when Gül gets sick. She lies sweating in bed with a fever, and when she opens her eyes she feels as if the ceiling beams are bearing down on her, about to crush her. When she closes her eyes, the sensation only grows stronger.

But sometimes the feeling disappears too, and then Gül hears her sisters or her new mother cooking. She can always tell exactly where Melike and Sibel are in the room, she can see the odd motions of her mother's hands and even her facial expression – but as soon as Gül opens her eyes, it all disappears. She's only imagined the sounds.

She quickly closes her eyes. She wants at least to hear the sounds, but again she feels as if the ceiling beams are looming down on her, trying to crush her and squash her. She cries. She doesn't want to be alone, she doesn't want to disappear beneath the beams. Her sudden, frightened cries ring out, time and again.

Arzu sits on the bed and strokes Gül's brow. And cries. She isn't crying for the sick child. She's crying for herself. What did she do to deserve this? How was she to know her first husband wasn't a real man? And is it her fault she didn't want another one after all that? What is she doing here? She's only nineteen and has three children to look after. Three girls, complete strangers to her, and a husband still nursing the pain of his wife's death.

63

Arzu's tears spill onto Gül's forehead, and Timur smiles because he doesn't know the reason for her tears.

Soothingly, he says: 'It's not typhoid. I might not know everything these doctors learn at university, but it's not typhoid. The child just has a fever.'

And they rub Gül's body with alcohol to bring the fever down. They call a hodja to the house; he prays, assesses her fever and recommends leeches. They are to place three over the sacrum, to suck out the bad blood.

Four days after applying the leeches, which her mother brings home with her in a glass bottle, Gül is well again. But she still has fever dreams, for three days. She's almost grown used to the dreams where the beams are bearing down on her. What's worse is that she now feels lost and dreams of giant leeches; the entire weight of them on her back as they bite the nape of her neck, ready to devour her, skin and hair and all. For three days she whimpers over and over, 'Mother, Mother,' and often sees Arzu's face as she cries out.

Once Gül is better, the family's life in the village continues, to all appearances, quite normally. Gül goes to school, Melike plays in the street, gets into fights, while Sibel is at home with her mother who does housework or natters with the neighbourhood women. The blacksmith rides into town and tries to boost his business, but it just doesn't seem to work out. Tufan has spread the wildest rumours. People are mistrustful, they think that Timur might scam them. Some even believe he has a car in town.

Yes, he's rich, but not that rich. There's only one car in town, at this point. And what would be the sense of sweating away every day in the forge if he had so much money he could afford a car?

He'd like to clarify these things, man to man, but Tufan is a snake hiding in the long grass. 'He should come to me if he's got a problem,' Timur tells people. 'He should tell me to my face if he thinks I'd rip you off. God knows I'm nothing but honest in my dealings. That son of a whore should come to me himself if he's got something to say!'

But Tufan doesn't demand satisfaction, even when Timur has publicly insulted him, so craven is the man.

None of this stops the blacksmith from taking the money he got for the loom and going to Istanbul for a week in the first days of summer. As ever, he's happy as soon as he's sitting on the train. Thinking about nothing, drinking, smoking, watching the dancers and cheering on the footballers, sitting on stools at low tables outside little restaurants on street corners and eating kebabs – two or three portions, taking his time. He enjoys a chinwag now and then with the city types, and not having to think about sickness, death, birth and marriage.

Still, the pressure behind his eyes doesn't let up, reminding him that these are hard times. It's especially bad in the mornings, and sometimes in the evenings too, but in Istanbul he's usually drunk enough in the evenings to no longer feel the pain in his eyes. Drunk enough to forget.

While Timur is in Istanbul, someone in the village throws a stone at one of their windows in the dark. Arzu thinks she's seen Tufan running away. She knows the ways and habits of villagers; unlike Fatima, she's not as innocent when it comes to village life. She's not like Fatma at all, and by now she's resentful of the young girls who come to her and ask if she can tell them fairytales too. She knows her way around the customs. It's not about the broken windowpane, the message is: *I've got my eye on your wife. You ought not to leave her alone, or you'll soon find yourself a cuckold.*

First no one wanted her, and now there's one suitor too many. Arzu hasn't done anything, she hasn't looked another man in the eye or encouraged anyone in any other way. Sometimes in the evening, when the children finally go to sleep and her husband is far away in the big city, Arzu sits there, turns the flame of the petroleum lamp down low and weeps quietly to herself as she begs the Lord to give her the strength for another day.

She has no one in the village to talk to, so she tries to tell Gül. Gül doesn't understand it all, but she understands enough to feel frightened, enough to know that it's not a matter between Tufan and her father – it's between the family and the villagers. She's scared that someone too cowardly to face up to her father might ambush him somewhere. She stays close to the house when she goes out to play now, and after school she walks home quite quickly instead of hanging around with Recep.

Soon, they'll all move into the summer house. Arzu is looking forward to it too, she'll be able to see her parents regularly again. But when Timur returns and they do move, that happiness quickly vanishes, at least for Gül.

She had forgotten how the children in town make fun of her accent. And she hadn't realised she'd no longer have anyone at home to play with.

There are no tickles and no little scraps, and there are no more pet names, here or in the village. That's what Gül misses most of all, her mother's tender words: *My little girl, my treasure, my lamb, my little dove, sweetheart, light of mine eyes, my heart's joy.*

When Arzu goes to her parents' or the neighbours', she leaves the older children on their own, often for hours. One day, when the blacksmith comes home much earlier than expected, Arzu is with Sibel at a neighbour's house, and Melike is playing outside while Gül is bored at home alone.

Timur's moustache looks dark and sticky, and he spends a good while cursing loudly to himself before telling his eldest what has happened.

'I had to go to the village,' he says, 'I had some business to do, I bought vegetables from a couple of farmers and told them I still needed to go to the mill. I rode over to the mill, and it was slow-going because I'd loaded so much onto the donkey. Tufan was hiding behind the door to the mill with a shovel in his hand. He went to hit me in the face with the shovel, but the Lord protected me and the shovel flew off, so he only caught me with the handle. Right on the nose. I had tears in my eyes. If he'd had the shovel made by a decent blacksmith, that wouldn't have happened. I was too shocked to give him a thrashing in return. Imagine: one minute you open a door and the next, you've got a big chunk of wood coming at your nose! He dropped the handle and ran away, he ran for his life – that dirty little coward. And my nose was bleeding from both nostrils.'

In the years to come, Timur will often tell this story, but in two weeks' time he'll take to finishing the tale by saying: 'I'll have to find the man and give him my thanks. After he gave me that awful nosebleed, my eyes stopped hurting and the pressure disappeared. Honestly, I'm grateful to the man.'

On this day, however, he's furious and out for revenge.

'I'll beat the bones from his body,' he says to his wife that evening, but she waits until he's calmed down a little and then carefully, very carefully, says: 'We don't have to move back to the village, do we? We're both from town, after all…'

'Are you mad, woman? It'd look like I was afraid of him. No, it's out of the question.'

Later, lying in bed feeling the pleasant drowsiness that takes hold of him when he's been with his wife, he thinks it might not be such a bad idea. After all, he only moved to the village because his mother was jealous of Fatma. She won't be jealous of this wife. He could sell the house in the village and his vineyard and find a new house in town, close to his mother. If it came to it, they'd pawn the gold bracelets Arzu brought to the marriage. The journey to the forge would be shorter, and he could still do some trading on the side. Ride proudly into the village and show Tufan he wasn't afraid.

Over the following days, Arzu twice mentions moving to town, away from the simple-minded villagers who still squat in the bushes, have lice and flees and bedbugs, and can't speak properly. And though both times Timur says no, she still hopes he really means yes. If she's got to bring up three children, she'd at least like to live in town and not in one of these villages where they all wear the same clothes and only wash once a month. And since she's discovered by now how stubborn Timur can be, she stops bringing it up and goes to her mother-in-law instead.

'Mother,' she says, 'wouldn't it be better for you if Timur moved back into town? If something happened to you one of these days, God forbid, we'd be far away. I know you've got Hülya here and you're blessed with good neighbours. But Timur rides back and forth every day, his business in the village isn't going as well as you think, and no one can be master of two kingdoms. Don't you think the forge would be better run if he was always here? If he didn't have to stay in the village in winter because the roads were snowed over? Oh, I don't know,' she says, 'I'm just thinking out loud.'

Gül stays at home a lot again that summer. She doesn't skip and she doesn't play hopscotch or mummies and daddies. She does like inviting her friends to her imaginary house, making them tea, offering them pastries, hugging her little children and her husband when he comes home from work, bringing him his beans in a tin cup, with freshly baked bread and a wooden spoon.

But here in the summer house, she stays inside or goes out to the back garden, plays on her own or talks to Sibel like Fatma did with her when she was that age. She can spend hours with her little sister, kissing her cheeks and changing her nappies when needed.

Arzu is with the neighbourhood women a lot, chatting or inviting them over for coffee. Hardly anyone can afford coffee, but Arzu's husband earns enough and she's proud of it. When Arzu is at home, she tells Gül to stay within calling distance, because it often occurs to her that she needs water pumped from the well, the rooms swept, the pillows and covers beaten. Gül doesn't mind doing these chores; all that bothers her is that Arzu doesn't praise her like her mother so often would.

Sometimes Melike gets given a job too. But she shirks her chores, goes to the toilet after breakfast and then climbs over the low wall, disappearing until almost dark. Or she claims to have a tummy ache. She knows what it feels like when you've eaten too much unripe fruit and she's good at pretending.

The summer passes, the apples ripen. Melike keeps pretending to have a tummy ache, Sibel says her first words, and Arzu gets pregnant and doesn't know how to tell Timur.

Without a word, Timur has sold the house in the village along with the vineyard. His mother is probably right; the forge will do better business if he lives in town. He buys a house in his mother's neighbourhood, half an hour's walk from his summer house. All his money goes on a town house, not freestanding like the house in the village but squeezed in between two others. Like the village house, it has two rooms and a kitchen, but the rooms are larger and the floor is made of stone, not hard-packed earth. There's also a small larder down a few steps inside the house, and there's a yard and a shed built against the stable.

Gül won't see Recep and her friends for a long time. She'll be in a class with children who laugh the moment she opens her mouth. The house where her father hid the guns in the hollow wall will be far away.

She no longer has to fear Tufan lying in wait somewhere. Or her father coming home hurt, or not at all. She still sits outside the toilet sometimes when he's in there.

On the second day after they've moved into the town house, her father takes her and Melike to school; it's Melike's first time. He walks up to a woman teacher, pats Gül on the cheek and says: 'Here's my daughter.' And then he leaves with Melike. To his younger daughter's teacher, a man, he will say what parents often say in those days: 'The flesh is thine, the bones are mine.' Meaning: Go ahead and beat her if she deserves it.

Gül stands in the corridor with this stern-looking woman and can hardly open her mouth when she asks her name. She had a man as a teacher before, and now she's facing a woman who takes her by the hand and leads her along the hall. The school looks enormous to Gül; she'll get lost. At her old school they simply played outside at breaktime. Here there's a schoolyard where all the children are already lined up to sing the national anthem. There are so many children that Gül wonders how they'll all fit inside the classroom.

'Stand here,' the teacher says, pushing her towards a group of children.

Gül joins in with the anthem. At least it's the same song. Afterwards, the teacher leads the group she was standing with into a classroom. Now Gül begins to understand why the school is so big and confusing. The children are divided into different classrooms. It takes her another day to work out that hers is class three, that not the entire school sits in one room together.

The girl next to Gül is called Özlem. At breaktime, unprompted, she tells Gül that her father is a general. Gül quietly says her own name and her father's profession. She thinks if she speaks quietly, people won't hear that she's from the village. But she soon finds that hardly anyone laughs at her accent here. She has a much bigger problem instead. Up to now, she could always pretend to read well, because the teacher worked strictly from the book. When it was her turn to read aloud, she would look at the book and recite from it by heart. She had heard all the passages so often, it was easy. But the new teacher doesn't stick to the book, and while all the others can read and write fluently, Gül has major difficulties following the lessons. She can barely read. The teacher tries to help Gül, but there are 40 other children in the class, and Gül quickly loses interest because she can't keep up. Her teacher isn't as strict as she looks, but when she canes someone, which isn't often, it makes no difference if it's a boy or a girl; the ruler swishes down on the palm or the cheek.

In the first few weeks, Gül is very glad she can go home for lunch, which lasts for an hour and a half here. It doesn't bother her that there's always something to do around the house. Sometimes she has to look after Sibel, sometimes pick stones out of the rice or lentils, or sweep outside the front door. Not until later in the evening, once it's dark outside and calm has descended, once the only sounds are the hiss of the pneumatic lamp and the snaps of insects flying into it, does she get to do her homework.

After a while, Melike rarely goes home at lunchtime; she goes to her friends' houses or plays on the street. When she's hungry, she runs home, makes a sandwich in the kitchen and disappears again before her mother can give her a chore to do. She's made friends quickly and has rapidly picked up the town dialect, although no one has made fun of her accent. She's not one of those girls people laugh at – she's the best at skipping, she wins at chase, never makes mistakes at hopscotch, and if she doesn't like something she's not afraid to start a row.

By the time it gets colder, Gül has got more used to school, and lunch breaks no longer seem like salvation, but she's still having difficulty following lessons. She has made friends though and gets on especially well with Özlem. The two of them run into each other a few times at the house of Gül's grandmother, who is proud to be friends with the general's wife.

'Özlem is a good girl,' Zeliha says to Gül, 'and her mother's very nice too.'

Gül doesn't like Özlem's mother much, because she always strokes her head without even looking at her, and because she laughs so loudly when she tells stories. And Gül doesn't like meeting them both at her grandmother's because then she gets jealous. Özlem gets sweets and words of praise every time, while Gül only gets a piece of chocolate once a year, at Eid.

When harvest season comes, Timur rides proudly to the village; they're not to think he's scared. He offers the farmers a good price for their fruit and grain, and several of them sell to him.

'Warn that son of a whore Tufan that I'll squash him like an ant, I'll squash him under the sole of my shoe! I won't even deign to look at his tears,' he says at every opportunity.

On the edge of the village lives a childless widow, Filiz, who was a very good friend of Fatma's and often sells Timur tarhana; dried spiced crumbs of grain and yoghurt for making into soup.

'The man may be a coward,' she tells Timur, 'but he can talk. He talks the men so dizzy they hardly know their own names. If tomorrow he tells them you suddenly support Galatasaray, they'd believe it.'

'He wouldn't dare. I'm a Beşiktaş fan, from the cradle to the grave – everyone knows that. If he went that far, I really would break all his bones.'

'If you want to get at him, you'll have to talk to people too. Just making threats and riding off again isn't enough.'

'What should I do? You want me to waste my time on women's gossip?'

'If you want to do business, you'll have to talk to the farmers.'

'I offer them good prices. If they can't see that I can't help them.'

Filiz sighs.

'Yes, I know,' she says.

Every year, once the grapes have been harvested, a portion of the juice is cooked up with starch, dried and cut into strips. These firm little treats, köfter, are eaten over the winter, ideally with walnuts as a source of energy for the cold days.

The blacksmith stores his wheat, rice and the winter bread that the community bakes every autumn, in a small cellar inside his house, but the walnuts and köfter are kept at the very top of the shelves in the kitchen.

One evening, while Gül is despairing over her homework in the lamplight, her mother is crocheting near the stove, and her grandmother, who has dropped by as she often does, is sitting even closer to the stove and drinking tea, while Timur drinks rakı and smokes. It's the sort of evening that promises another hard winter ahead.

Zeliha goes into the kitchen and when she comes back, she says to Timur: 'I was right. There's much less köfter than there was. Gül keeps taking it and giving it to the other children at school.'

Gül has heard what her grandmother said, but she can't believe it.

'Is this true, Gül?'

Gül shakes her head.

'Özlem saw you giving it out at school,' Zeliha says.

Gül hasn't given anyone any köfter, but now she doesn't know what to say. She feels hot and she knows people think you can tell someone's lying if they blush. But she's just hot.

'I didn't take anything.'

Arzu looks up and fixes her eye on Gül.

'Özlem saw you do it,' Zeliha says, 'and why are you turning red if you're telling the truth?'

Timur stubs out his cigarette and says, sharply: 'Gül, I don't want to hear of such a thing ever again.'

Now Gül is completely silent and nods. What else can she do? Her grandmother mutters something that no one understands, shaking her head. Soon after, when Timur goes out to the toilet, Gül follows him and crouches outside the toilet door in the darkness of the yard. It's been a long time since she's done this. *It wasn't me, it wasn't me, I'll tell him right away,* she thinks, but the words won't come.

When her mother puts her to bed later that night, she says: 'Gül, you mustn't lie and you mustn't steal. Only bad people do that. We don't do that sort of thing... Do you understand me, Gül?'

Gül nods. What else can she do? She can't sleep and she stews until morning. At school, she goes straight over to Özlem.

'Did you say I brought köfter with me to school?'

'Yes,' Özlem says.

'But… but why? I didn't do it.'

'Yes you did, I saw you.'

This is the first day Gül doesn't go home at lunchtime, instead she sits in a lonely spot by the stream. She feels as if someone's opened a door and an icy wind is blowing in, chilling her to the bone. And she knows she must cross the threshold. She has no choice.

They all lied. She knows the truth, but she can't tell anyone. She's alone. For the first time in her life she is completely alone. There's no one she can go to, no one who'd believe her. Alone.

Once it's come to this, it will never stop, but she doesn't know that yet. Over the next few days, she sits by the stream at lunchtime, unable to think about anything but the köfter. How can Özlem say she saw Gül handing it out at school when she didn't do it? How can she get anyone to believe her?

On the third evening after her grandmother lied, she takes her father's hand and leads him into the kitchen. Surely *he's* got to believe her. Gül points up at the shelf where the köfter is kept.

'How would I get up there?' she asks Timur.

They don't have a table; all they have is the old, heavy wooden chair in the other room, which Gül can hardly move.

Timur looks up at the shelf, down at his daughter, then up again, furrows his brow for a few moments, then relaxes it again and nods.

'I understand,' he says.

He shakes his head gently, then picks Gül up in his arms, carries her into the warm room, tickles her with his moustache and whispers in her ear: 'I know you didn't do it, I know. The others won't believe us. But the two of us, we know my little girl doesn't

74

steal. Don't we? And that's the most important thing, that we both know it.'

Not only can he not prove that Gül didn't do it, but he also can't accuse his mother of lying.

The next day, Gül is back at the stream, but this time she stands with both her feet in the cold water, scouring the stony riverbed with her hands. Timur came home in a bad mood; his trousers were wet and he smelt of alcohol.

'Bloody hell,' he said, 'I've lost my watch. I didn't attach it to the chain and when I went to cross the stream it fell out the pocket of my waistcoat. Damn it, my watch is gone – the water's taken it, the water's stolen my watch.'

There aren't many people with watches, and all the other parents on the street rely on Timur's daughters when they want to send their children to school on time. If Gül and Melike are on their way, it's time to go. It's not just Timur who's proud of his silver watch.

'Where did you lose it?' Gül asked. 'Show me the place.'

'It's gone,' her father replied. 'I've already looked.'

'Show me the place,' Gül repeated, and they went to the stream together.

Now Gül is standing in the water, the cold creeping up her legs, and she's slowly losing the feeling in her fingers. Timur is crouching on the bank, staring at the riverbed, muttering to himself: 'Her own granddaughter... She probably sold it... Buy, sell, buy, sell... Just a bit of köfter...'

'Are you sure it was here?'

'Yes. Or maybe a bit further down, but not much.' The words come droning out of his mouth.

Gül feels the watch – it's slipped under a stone. Before she pulls it out, she turns to her father and says: 'Look!'

Timur looks up and Gül pulls her hand out the water, holding the watch aloft. The smile on the blacksmith's face is that of a child; he's overjoyed, like he's found a lost toy.

'Bravo, my little one. Bravo, my treasure.'

Timur gets up, takes a step towards the stream, breathes in briefly and then drops lengthways into the water. He soon picks himself up, Gül looking on in disbelief with the watch in her hand.

'I didn't fall,' Timur says, still smiling. 'I let myself drop.'

He picks Gül up. For a moment, she feels the wetness from his clothes seeping through into hers, but it feels good. It feels good to have found the watch and to be carried by her father, staggering a little, all the way home.

When it gets even colder, Gül often doesn't go home for lunch. Her father's forge is closer; it's warm and there's food there too. Sometimes Timur's assistant cooks, but more often he sends him out for something from the nearby restaurant, and then the three of them sit on the floor on a thick blanket, unpacking the Adana kebabs from their newspaper, the lemons and tomatoes, a big bunch of parsley – and often Melike comes dashing in at just that moment, as if she'd been watching from a hiding place and waiting until the food was ready.

As soon as she's eaten, Melike disappears again, and Gül works the bellows; sometimes her father gives her a few kuruş for it. After the first snow has fallen, Melike spends her whole lunch breaks at the forge too, even straining away at the bellows to earn a few kuruş as well, which she spends instantly on sweets or snacks at the grocer's.

Gül keeps her money in a hiding place instead of buying things, so Melike often comes begging: 'Buy me some roasted chickpeas, please.'

She always says no to start with. But Melike knows she'll says yes if she keeps pestering her for long enough.

Lunch breaks are often the only time of the day when Gül feels warm. The school is chilly, only sparingly heated, because no one knows how hard and long the winter will be.

Timur is still regarded as wealthy, but what with buying the house in town, this year's apple crop being poor, having blown part of his money in Istanbul, and trade with the farmers not going as well as it used to, he also has to save now. Tufan now has almost everyone from the village on his side; they think the blacksmith bought several fields and another two vineyards with the money he cheated them out of; they believe his rival's words and not Timur's good prices.

Because they have to save money, they only heat the big living room where Arzu, Timur and Sibel sleep at night. The door to the small room is only opened shortly before they go to bed, so that the warm air can flow in, and Melike and Gül crawl under their thick quilts soon after.

Before it got so cold, Gül would know whether Melike had wet the bed by the smell when she woke up. Now she can no longer tell. And often enough, she can't simply drink a glass of water when she wakes up at night. There's a small bowl in the room from which they can pour themselves water, but there are many nights when it gets so cold that Gül has to crack a layer of ice with her thumb before she can drink.

'It's cold,' she said to her father. 'We're so cold at night.'

'You could sleep in the stable,' Timur answered, 'it's warmer in there.'

'No,' Gül said.

She'd rather freeze than sleep in the stable with the mice.

The first winter in town passes; Arzu's belly begins to bulge, and she doesn't say anything to Timur until he sees it for himself. Only his eyes on her midriff tell her he's noticed. She conceals her pregnancy, just as she conceals her joy that she'll soon have a child of her own, of her flesh and blood.

Although they don't have much money, there's hot soup every morning, and they often eat köfter with walnuts, and sit together in the light of the pneumatic lamp in the evening, Gül sometimes falling asleep over her homework. Zeliha comes by many evenings; it's much rarer for them all to go to her house together.

Gül always makes sure not to sit too close to her grandmother. And she only goes to her when she's sent. She doesn't want to meet Özlem there; she doesn't sit next to her any more.

Even when it gets warmer, Gül still regularly goes to the forge at lunch, but not too often or her mother tells her off. Arzu needs someone to help her around the house. *Lord, give me strength,* she murmurs to herself as she does the housework with her fat belly; *give me strength and patience.*

When there's not much to do at the forge, Timur sometimes gets Gül to scratch his back and gives her a few kuruş in return now and then.

One day, Gül has just scratched her father's back and his coin is at the ready, when she says: 'I'm going to have to repeat the year.'

She's known it for a few weeks, but she hasn't dared to tell him. And now, with her father sighing in such ease, it has slipped out.

The blacksmith lowers his hand and looks at the coin for a moment. Then he smiles, takes out another coin, gives them both to her and says: 'That's not so bad. But try harder next year, promise me that.'

'I promise,' Gül says, and it feels wrong to take the money but she does it anyway. She won't save it; she'll buy her sisters the chocolate in the brightly coloured foil that Melike likes so much. They like that chocolate best, because the colours on the foil are so bright and the smell lingers on the paper for a long time. Weeks later, Melike holds the crumpled wrapper under her nose and breathes in: 'Chocolate…'

That summer, Gül quickly forgets about having to repeat the year. Her accent has disappeared over the year, and she has no inhibitions about playing with the other children: hopscotch, chase, hide-and-seek, and mummies and daddies.

It's warm; she can drink water at night without boring a hole in the ice, she doesn't have to get up early to go to school. The only disadvantage is that the smell of Melike's pee spreads better in the heat, sometimes penetrating Gül's nostrils with the sun's first rays.

At the summer house, her parents sleep together in one bedroom, Sibel sleeps with her sisters in the other, and Zeliha in the living room. Gül's grandmother spends the summer with them, but she's not in the house all that often. Right after breakfast she goes outside to sit with the other grandmothers, drinking tea, smoking, and usually not returning until late in the evening.

Arzu milks the cow every morning, mucks out the stable, and picks cucumbers and tomatoes for breakfast. After breakfast, Gül has to wash the dishes, sweep the hall where the summer dust from the unpaved road gathers, and make the beds – her own and her sisters'. They have large, flat cushions for mattresses, which are put together in the evening; two each for Melike and Gül and one for Sibel. If Melike has wet one of the cushions, it is put out to dry on the grass in the morning. Gül piles the others in a corner of the room and then puts the folded summer covers on top, followed by the sheets and pillows. Over the top she drapes a cloth to protect the bed things from dust, and to make them look nicer. Meanwhile, her mother takes care of the vegetable patch, clears up and makes a start on lunch.

Thursday is market day, and everyone gets up earlier. Arzu goes into town right after breakfast, and Gül runs outside as soon as she's out of sight. The other children also enjoy being able to run out and play in the streets so early. Gül's favourite is hide-and-seek; she can forget everything while she's playing. It's so wonderful to run to an isolated place and then sit perfectly still there; it fills her with joy, and often enough no one finds her.

For a few hours on Thursdays, she forgets everything, but when she realises it's noon she dashes home. She has to hurry – she has to make all the beds today, wash the dishes, tidy up, and she has to sweep all the rooms. She has to sprinkle the road outside the house with water just before her mother comes, so that dust doesn't rise when the carriage stops and the shopping is carried inside. It doesn't bother her that she has so much to do and always has to rush to get finished on time. It bothers her that her mother comes home, sees that everything is done, yet never has a word of praise to spare.

A neighbour, Uncle Abdurahman as they all call him, a retired village teacher with a full, grey beard who lives alone, has heard that Gül has to repeat the year and has suggested he help her study. The man likes children and Gül likes this man with his deep, dark voice, so every Tuesday that summer she goes to Uncle Abdurahman, and he spends an hour or two helping her study, gives her homework and has her show what she's done next time.

'You did wonderfully,' he'll say, 'but have a look at this, look closely now. I know you can do it, you just need to concentrate a little. Yes, you see, you were only out by two, that happens, but now it's correct and you did it all by yourself.'

'Excellent,' he'll murmur into his beard, grinning at her.

Sometimes Gül can't wait till Tuesday and goes to Uncle Abdurahman on Monday to study with him. Sometimes Gül goes by three times a week. She knows she won't be kept back another year this time.

Meanwhile, Timur's bedstead has grown famous throughout town, rarely spending more than a month in his own bedroom, even now. Inspired by its success, two rich men order identical beds from Timur. One is a businessman; the only man in town to own a car, and the other is a general; Özlem's father. Both believe they've got themselves a bargain, but Timur is proud to be able to forge such beautiful bedsteads. And though they've haggled him down, it's still a tidy sum. He'll sweat for his money. He'll sweat for the money in the sweltering summer heat and he'll use it to buy a radio.

It's the only radio on the street, and the neighbours gather at the blacksmith's to listen to the voices coming out of the machine. When her father explains it to her, Gül realises there are no little people sitting inside it, acting it all out. She understands, but she can't quite grasp why the programmes keep going when the machine is switched off. Why can't you pick up from where you left off the day before? Where do the voices disappear to if they can't get out of the box?

Once the blacksmith has spent a fortnight playing host to the whole street, he's had enough. He buys a loudspeaker and fixes it to the roof of his summer house. In the evenings, he turns on the radio, and the neighbours sit outside their front doors or on benches – some on cushions, others on the bare stone. Some drink tea and others nibble sunflower seeds as they spend their summer evenings listening to radio plays and news reports and the old singers playing the saz and singing of longing, their voices cracking. Singing that beauty isn't worth a dime, this world barely lasts a week, and nothing matters more than friends who let us live on beyond the grave. Singing that they don't know why they came here, they can't put their troubles into words, let alone into song. They listen to songstresses who hope always to smile at the future and accept their fates, for what else can we do, though it may seem like sorrow will never leave us. Look ahead and see the light – it must be shining there, not just your heart's reflection.

Timur likes this music and Gül does too. Though she doesn't understand the lyrics, she can tell that this melancholy, this Anatolian blues, has something to do with death, with suffering, futility and the understanding that we still have to try, despite it all; that we can love, protect and grow.

And Timur enjoys the football commentary; at last he can follow the game without relying on getting the news from others who can read and write Latin script. When he went to school, the language was still taught in Arabic script. Gone are the days of stopping in at the teahouse to find out from someone who's only heard second-hand which player got in a crucial header.

Arzu's belly grows bigger and bigger, and one day she tells Gül she must now do the washing for her. In the forge, they keep old square cans once used for storing sheep's cheese or olive oil. All households have these; five or ten or fifteen-litre cans with a wooden handle nailed on to make them easy to carry once the lid has been cut off. Gül pumps water out of the well into several small tin canisters and pours them into the big copper pot. Then she brings another canister of water to the boil, adds it in and squats on the low wooden stool while her mother piles up the washing nearby. When Gül sees this mountain of laundry, she feels she won't be able to do it all by herself; tears prick her eyes, but she doesn't say a word, nor does she cry.

On the next washing day, she knows she needn't be scared. She quietly sings the songs from the radio to herself, getting the words wrong. It will pass, like everything in this life, and in the end the washing will be clean, and once again Gül won't have the strength to tip the water out of the copper pot, so her father will have to empty it in the evening.

Even once her sister Nalan is born at the end of May, Arzu often still has Gül do the washing for her. She helps her daughter to empty the basin and hang the washing out, just as she did when she was heavily pregnant. Gül can't reach the washing line and she still can't lift the old wooden chair.

When school starts again, they're still living in the summer house. Early in the morning, the neighbourhood children meet up and walk into town together. This takes over half an hour because they dawdle on the way, scrumping apples, playing, getting up to mischief. But Gül is never one of those who arrives late. She likes going to school now, she likes her new classmates, she likes the plump new teacher, an unmarried woman, who everyone likes and who hardly every smacks anyone but tries to solve problems with words, showing impressive patience.

Gül likes going to school, but she always leaves home heavy-hearted in the mornings. Sibel isn't yet five and she cries every morning as the children set off, her summer playmates now leaving her alone as they go to school. Sibel doesn't know what a school is or what the others do there, but she doesn't want to be left out. She's a pale, thin child who's often sick. But when she starts crying in the mornings, stamping and screaming and turning red with rage, new strengths seem to awaken inside her.

It's Abdurahman who goes to Timur one Sunday and asks: 'Don't you want to send Sibel to school this year?'

'She's still too little, we can't put her into school until next year.'

'She's cried every morning for the last six weeks. Six weeks! How can you stand by and watch? Doesn't it break your heart?'

'Of course it breaks my heart, but what am I supposed to do? She's too small and she won't be up to it. What should I do?'

'Send her to school, the worst that can happen is that she has to repeat a year. It's no great loss.'

'Uncle Abdurahman, she's too young. They won't take her.'

Abdurahman nods and smiles.

'You'd let her go otherwise?'

'Yes,' says Timur.

'I know someone at the admin office. We can just change her age. Let me handle it. I'll talk to the teacher too, just send Sibel to me early tomorrow morning.'

And so, on Monday, Abdurahman and Sibel take a carriage to school, where he hands her over to the teacher. On Tuesday, the sisters walk the whole way together, Sibel holding onto Gül's hand while Melike dilly-dallies and keeps hanging back. Sibel is included now and she's happy the whole way there, but

83

she feels uncertain as soon as she sits down in class. It's all so unfamiliar to her, she hardly dares open her mouth, but despite her nerves she's very attentive. By the end of the school year, she'll not only be moving up, she'll be one of the best in the class, even though she missed the first six weeks.

Timur and a neighbour have shaken the walnuts from both his trees. Zeliha and Gül are to gather them up and divide them into three piles, two about the same size and one slightly smaller.

'One share for us, one share for your Nene and a small share for our neighbour because he helped us,' Timur explains to his daughter before leaving her and her grandmother to it.

Once they've finished, they wrap each of the larger piles in a cloth, the ends knotted together. There are a lot of nuts, and Gül has trouble dragging one of the cloths behind her.

'And now,' her grandmother says, 'we're going to bury this small pile in the ground. Then it'll be a surprise for the neighbour. He'll be really pleased. But you mustn't tell anyone, otherwise it won't be a surprise any more, will it? Promise? Don't breathe a word.'

Gül gives a hint of a nod. Then the old woman digs a hole with a spade, drops in the walnuts and shovels earth over them, pats it down and scatters leaves over the spot so no one can see it.

Gül is well aware their neighbour won't see the nuts either, so it's not hard for her to break her word. That evening, when she tells her mother what happened, Arzu says: 'That may be. It may be that others tell lies, even grownups. But we don't do that kind of thing, you understand? She's an old woman who likes to do deals, sell things here and there. But we don't do that kind of thing. Your father has never done it either.'

'We don't do that kind of thing,' Gül murmurs.

'Right, and now go and fetch me a can of water from the well so I can do the dishes.'

Melike has pinched a couple of walnuts; she's got to try out something she heard about from a boy in her class. She collects sap from conifers in four halves of walnut shells, then she calls Gül, not telling her what she's planning.

'I've got a piece of bread – let's go and find the neighbour's cat and feed it!'

Gül is surprised by Melike's idea but she likes cats; they eat the mice she hates so much. They find the black cat, and Gül holds out the bread, wondering what Melike is digging out of her pocket. In one swift motion, Melike grabs the cat and after a brief struggle, she has pressed three of its paws into the walnut shells. The poor creature manages to escape while Melike still has one shell left and her lower arms are scratched to pieces. With walnut shells stuck on three paws, one at the front, two at the back, the cat's gait is asymmetrical, but the worst thing seems to be the unfamiliar sound and the lack of traction when it tries to run away. It slithers but makes a quick getaway.

Melike laughs: 'It sounds like our horse.'

The cat tries to jump up onto a wall, slides off, runs in a circle and eventually disappears around a corner, Melike still laughing.

'You're cruel,' says Gül, and she hopes her sister doesn't notice she's having trouble stifling her own laughter. It did look pretty funny and Gül watched in fascination, but at the same time it repelled her.

'What do you mean *cruel*?' Melike asks. 'It's the cat's fault for getting caught.'

Gül is becoming her father's favourite. He likes having her around, calls her *my daughter who found my watch*, or sometimes *the blacksmith Timur's daughter*, calls her *my treasure* and *my rose* and *light of mine eyes*, as her mother would. He often takes her along on errands and he's glad when she comes to the forge. No matter what he asks her to do, she never says she doesn't want to, unlike Melike. And so, that autumn, she makes three or four

85

trips with him to the big orchard a little way from the summer houses to rake leaves. After the first time, Gül already feels scared before they even set out. But it's not the hard work she's afraid of.

The first time they went to the orchard, her father said: 'Try to rake the leaves together here in the corner. I just have to pop over to see Farmer Aras.'

He pointed at a tiny patch, and Gül raked up the dead leaves, covering more ground than she was supposed to, but in the end she stopped. All was quiet. Every crackle of leaves made her jump. Her father had been gone a long time, very long. If her mind wasn't playing tricks on her, it'd soon be dusk. Then it'd be dark, and she wouldn't dare go home alone. She knew her father would come, but still she felt more alone than ever before. Even when she played on her own in the garden or found a remote nook for hide-and-seek, she always knew that someone was nearby. She had never felt abandoned before.

What should she do if a bad man came along? Where in the orchard could she hide?

The gardens were only divided by low stone and clay walls; Gül shrunk against the wall, trying to make herself as small as she could. And sure enough, the sun had set, and Gül's fear grew with the onset of darkness.

When she saw her father at last, in a light that seemed to her like semi-darkness but in reality was still red from the refracted rays of sun, she ran towards him and threw her arms around his hips.

Timur lifted his daughter as if she weighed nothing at all.

'I was scared,' Gül said.

'What on earth of? There's no need to be scared. You knew I was coming back, didn't you?'

Gül nodded; yes, she knew but it was no use.

'I was scared,' she repeated in a low voice.

'There's nothing to be scared of here. And look how well you've raked the leaves, light of my eyes.'

He tried to change the subject, but Gül was close to tears, he could tell.

'What were you scared of?' Timur asked again.

It was a nameless fear; she had no words for it, but she had to say something.

'I was scared I had nothing to eat. I was scared you'd come even later and I'd starve.'

'I get caught up in conversation, I didn't mean to be so late.'

When he asks her the next afternoon if she'll come with him, Gül still says yes. Timur packs bread and cheese so that his daughter has nothing to fear. He might pop off somewhere again. Which doesn't happen that day, but it does a few days later. Leaving his daughter in the orchard with bread and cheese and olives, he quickly rides over to the mill.

This time, Gül will have to hide her fear when her father returns. She can't explain where her fear comes from. She crouches against the wall again, and soon after she thinks she hears footsteps and voices, too. Is it really voices? Is it bad people? Gül barely dares to breathe. The footsteps and voices grow louder; they're women's voices but that doesn't reassure Gül.

'Let's have a quick smoke before we get started,' one says.

They're obviously in the neighbouring garden, not far from Gül's hiding place; she can hear every word clearly and also the sounds as they sit down, even the stroke of a match. Gül breathes very quietly.

'Did you hear about Nuray's son?'

'Which Nuray, from which family?'

'Nuray from the Ismails.'

'Limping Ismail?'

'Yes, Nuray's his niece.'

'And who's the father?'

'I don't know, I don't know her personally. She's limping Ismail's niece.'

'And what about her?'

'Her son died, he was only six months old. It was a safety pin, you wouldn't believe it, would you? The pin must have been in the sheet, in the bed they put him in. It came unfastened somehow and dug into his back, a big safety pin. And they didn't know why the baby was screaming and crying, they picked him up and dandled him on their knees to calm him down, they threw him up in the air and tickled him, and he went on yelling at the top of his voice. He didn't stop until he fell asleep hours later. That's what they thought, anyway, but he was unconscious – and the next morning he was dead. The safety pin bored its way into his backbone while they were trying to calm him down.'

'Oh, my God, is that true?'

'Yes, Aylin told me, and she knows Nuray's sister.'

'May the Almighty protect us from such ills.'

'Amen.'

Now Gül is more afraid than ever. The women finish smoking and start raking leaves. Gül sees her father coming towards her but she doesn't feel relieved, only anxious. If the women hear him talking to her, they'll know Gül was there all along, and then they'll know she was scared. So she gets up quietly and walks a few steps towards her father, slowly at first but then breaking into a run, trying to look happy. Timur crouches down, spreads out his arms and waits for her.

'You didn't eat anything,' he says a little later.

'I was... I wanted to wait for you.'

On the day the first snow falls, Gül notices her mother's belly has started to swell again. She knows enough to understand that she'll be getting another little brother or sister. Sometimes in the evening her mother will sit cross-legged on the floor, a cushion behind her back, quietly stroking her belly, smiling. A similar smile plays across her lips from time to time when she holds Nalan in her arms. It's a smile Gül scarcely sees on her face otherwise.

Gül's getting on well at school this year. She's far from top of the class but thanks to her lessons with Uncle Abdurahman, at least she no longer struggles with reading and writing. Sometimes she has trouble learning things by heart, but perhaps she simply doesn't find the time to do it properly.

One day, the teacher reads out a story in which a man goes into the woods alone to gather branches. He has a donkey with him, which he loads up until the creature can hardly walk. On the way back, it begins to rain and the man takes cover in a small cave, and darkness falls soon after. At this point in the story, a lion appears outside the cave as if from nowhere, a lion that hasn't eaten for days and whose roar freezes the very marrow inside the man's bones.

'Alright, now take out your exercise books and write an end to the story,' the teacher says. 'Then I'll collect your books at the end.'

Gül dithers; it's some time before she finally begins to write.

The man is scared of the lion. He steps back and then he stands with his back to the wall. It is dark. The lion can't see the man. He can only smell him. But the lion doesn't want to go into the cave. The lion is scared of mice. The only thing it is scared of is mice. It can't help it. The lion is scared there will be mice in the cave. It also smells the donkey and wonders who it will eat first. If they come out. The man stands with his back to the wall and is totally silent. If he's silent, maybe the lion will forget about the man. He can see the lion's eyes glittering with hunger. But in the night, the lion gets tired and shuts its eyes. The man waits until the lion is fast asleep. Then he quietly runs past the lion until he is safe in his village. His donkey stays behind and gets eaten. His wife and his children are happy when he gets home, and they have a big party.

At breaktime, everyone is talking about what they wrote. Gül seems to be the only one who let the man live. In most of the others' stories, he gets eaten or at least loses a leg, then dies because he can't get home on one leg. One child had the man gather wood and make a fire; lions are afraid of fire after all. The lion ate the man once the fire had burned down.

The next day, the teacher returns the children's exercise books and says to Gül: 'Can you stay behind after the lesson, please?'

She says it in a friendly way, warmly, but Gül still feels uneasy. Was it wrong to have let the man live?

'Gül,' the teacher says when they're alone, 'did you know that everyone else in the class let the man die?'

Gül nods and looks at the floor.

'Why didn't you want him to die?'

'I felt sorry for him.'

'Why did you feel sorry for him?'

Gül thinks for a moment.

'I felt sorry for his wife and his children. The children would have lost their father.'

'You've got a father though, haven't you?'

'Yes.'

'And a mother?'

Gül looks up into her teacher's face.

'Yes… a stepmother.'

Gül keeps looking at her teacher.

'And she looks after you properly, doesn't she?'

'Yes,' Gül says.

'Are you the eldest?'

'Yes.'

'They say a girl becomes a mother the day her mother dies. Did you know that?'

'Yes.'

People usually think Gül isn't listening when the ancestors' maxims are uttered in her presence. *He who is motherless is also fatherless. Stepmothers serve watered-down ayran and burned crusts of bread.* She knows these proverbs and they all mean the same thing to her: she must take care of her sisters.

'You can always come to me,' the teacher says. 'Don't be shy. I'd be happy to help you'

'Thank you,' Gül says politely.

She knows she'll never go to her teacher. She said it herself: Gül is practically a mother now.

Sometimes, Sibel wakes in the night needing the toilet. Then she wakes Gül up because she's scared to go out in the dark. Gül is scared of the dark too, and when she wakes in the night with pressure on her bladder, she turns over and tries to go back to sleep. They do have a torch, but the little light it gives out doesn't help banish Gül's fear. When Sibel wakes her up, though, Gül takes her sister's left hand, holds the torch in her right and waits at the open door. They put on their cardigans, but once it gets colder, they often don't make it the 20 steps to the outhouse and Sibel simply pees in the yard, right by the stable wall.

On one occasion, Gül wakes Sibel in the middle of the night and asks her if she needs the toilet too. They go out together and take turns using the toilet.

And every time Sibel wakes in the night, Gül gently shakes Melike awake: 'Melike, do you need the toilet?'

'No,' Melike always replies, turning over and going back to sleep. Yet, often enough, Gül will still have to change the sheets in the morning. Now there's a tarpaulin under Melike's sheet.

That winter, Auntie Hülya comes to visit several evenings in a row. Without Uncle Yücel. Almost every time, she drags Timur into the kitchen, and Gül hears their muffled voices but can't understand what they're saying. Nor can she read Auntie Hülya's expression when she looks at her. But she understands what it means when Auntie Hülya says to Arzu: 'Timur was a father and a brother to me.'

She understands it is possible to fill that space, that her father was big enough to take on that role. And she feels small herself.

Small but strong. She's not afraid of hard work, she's afraid of pain, the kind of pain she felt when Özlem said: 'Of course you handed out the köfter, I saw you.' A pain like the one she feels that winter in the kitchen.

Arzu is sitting on the floor rolling pastry as Gül comes into the kitchen and stands to one side behind her. Arzu looks up at her and then smacks at Gül's legs with the wooden rod she's using on the pastry. She hits her just below the kneecaps and Gül's breath stops.

Gül hears her say: 'Where's the yoghurt? I told you not to eat the yoghurt, it was for our visitors this evening. Go and get some more, right now!'

Gül hears her voice as if from far away. She didn't eat the yoghurt, didn't even dip a finger in it, and now she feels both the pain in her knees, which has spread all over her body, and also the pain of being punished for something she didn't do. And that's much worse than the other kind.

She's afraid of pain like that, pain she can't give a name to.

Only once has her father wanted to beat her. It was towards the end of the summer just past; one of the girls in the neighbourhood had pinched henna from her mother and shared it out among her friends. To paint her hands and nails in peace, Gül had found a sheltered spot among broken boulders above the orchards. She didn't realise how long she'd been sitting there, trying to gather enough spit to make the powder into a paste, until she saw her father. Leaping up, she was pleased to see him, though it soon dawned on her that she'd been there far too long. She'd been gathering spit in her mouth and imagining what it would be like when she dyed her hands with henna on the night before her wedding. She had imagined a big celebration and a husband without a face, her sisters in shimmering dresses, herself in radiant white; she had got caught up in daydreams and missed lunch. They'd been worried at home, and now her father had come looking for her.

Melike could skip lunch as often as she liked; their parents were used to it, and sometimes Gül envied her for it. She thought it unfair that her father now had a line of rage between his eyebrows. When he bent down to pick up a stick, Gül understood what was coming to her and she bolted. She heard her father break into a run behind her, and she squeezed between two narrowly placed boulders, knowing her father wouldn't fit through. That gave her a head start he could barely make up.

Sometimes Melike gets beaten by their father; she gets her ears boxed or a slap on the back of her thighs with a stick. But when he doesn't get his hands on her in his anger, he usually forgets all about it. That was what Gül hoped as she went home, that his anger would burn off when he was back on his horse, at the forge or somewhere else. And when they sat together that evening, the blacksmith and his daughter, it really was as if nothing had happened.

'Then that's how it has to be,' Gül hears her father saying to Hülya one of those evenings. 'Then that's how it has to be.'

Gül hears no more than that, and nor does anyone tell her any more. Three days later, Hülya moves back to her mother's place, as Gül happens to pick up on the street. The neighbours whisper about her aunt, their conversations seeming to be about nothing else, and Gül decides to ask Arzu about it, not understanding what's happened. When Gül thinks of Uncle Yücel, she sees him in her mind's eye rocking Sibel on his feet with a contented look on his face, his chubby cheeks lending him a cosy friendliness. Uncle Yücel and Auntie Hülya have separated, that much Gül understands, but she didn't know you could do such a thing. It seems unheard of.

So Gül asks: 'Mother, what's happened to Auntie Hülya and Uncle Yücel?'

'Don't you go poking your nose in grownups' business. You wouldn't understand, you're too little,' Arzu says and sends her away.

Gül goes outside, but she doesn't go out to play like her mother suggested; it's far too cold anyway. Gül goes to her grandmother's house, even though her nene's deep, droning voice still scares her. Auntie Hülya opens the door and squints at Gül. Or at a child she sees out on the street. She strokes her niece's head.

'Come in.'

Gül stays at the door for a moment, watching her aunt's stiff-legged, ungainly walk. She won't have the guts to ask.

Zeliha is sitting on a cushion, her back against the wall, drinking tea.

'Who is it?' she asks as Gül enters the room.

'It's me, Grandmother,' Gül says, and Hülya adds: 'It's Gül.'

Gül doesn't know what to do; she hasn't been here alone since the incident with the köfter. But before she has time to think, Auntie Hülya says: 'I'm busy stuffing peppers in the kitchen, will you give me a hand, my treasure?'

In the kitchen, Hülya whispers: 'Her eyesight's got very bad lately. God forbid, but I fear she'll go blind if it goes on like this. The other day she didn't recognise Timur. And he's the only person who blocks out the whole door frame.'

Gül helps her aunt stuff peppers, listening to Hülya talk about this neighbour and that neighbour, how the winter will probably be a mild one this year, how she's looking forward to visiting the summer house in spring. She doesn't mention a word about Yücel. The only thing Gül asks, half an hour later, is: 'Can I go out to play again?'

'Yes, but wash your hands first.'

Gül goes to the only tap in the house, turns it on and picks up the olive soap. There is no tap in Timur's house; even in the town, not everyone has running water. But there's at least one public tap in every neighbourhood. Gül sometimes gets sent to fetch a can of water, and she's always happy to do so because she sees other children there. It's not like at the summer house, where everyone has a well and they have to pump the heavy handle. While their can is filling up underneath the thin stream of water, the children play tag, hopscotch, skipping games or even hide-and-seek, and Gül often forgets the time.

Once, Gül put her two cans in the queue and the next time she checked, they'd disappeared. She looked everywhere for them, but they were nowhere to be found. In the end she went home. How was she to explain to her father? Timur met her with the words: 'We were waiting hours here for water, do you know that? And Madame's off playing tag with the other children. Did I send you out to play? Tell me, did I send you out to play? I went and fetched the water myself!'

He shook his head.

'You're not a little child any more. I don't want this to happen again, is that clear? I said, is that clear?'

Gül nodded.

While Timur smokes a cigarette after supper, Arzu says to the children: 'Don't tell anyone anything about Auntie Hülya. If they ask you, just say you don't know anything.'

But I really don't know anything, Gül feels like saying, but she holds her tongue.

'We don't want to be the laughing stock of the town,' Arzu says.

Gül has often heard that phrase. Melike hears it even more often. She has made a friend at school, Sezen, a doctor's daughter, and she often goes to visit. Doctors are rich and respected in the small town, whereas word gets around that the blacksmith is no longer doing so well since the villagers have started trading with Tufan instead of him; they say Tufan now invests his profits in gold coins.

Timur's money has melted away. He'll soon have another child to feed, but thanks be to God they want for nothing; there's still soup every morning and no lack of eggs, sausage or dried meat. He just can't splash his money around like he used to. Arzu doesn't seem to be as good with money as his beloved Fatma, and Timur himself never was. Just as he couldn't convince the villagers to sell to him even though he paid better prices. Tufan had spread rumours that he was only promising the money but wouldn't be able to pay in the end, because he spent their money on trips to Istanbul to watch Beşiktaş play. It was no use Timur offering to pay the farmers cash. Empty words were worth more than his banknotes, because he didn't know how to tackle the rumours.

So whenever Melike goes to play at Sezen's house, her mother says: 'And don't eat there. They'll think you don't get anything at home. We don't want to be the laughing stock of the town.'

Gül knows Melike does eat there, she knows because Melike keeps the brightly coloured foil from the chocolate she gets at the doctor's house.

Arzu has her reasons for not wanting people to talk about them. She's glad they've started forgetting what happened with her first husband. Glad they might even one day forget she was married once before. Once gossip gets around, there's no escaping it. Arzu doesn't want to stand out, except for having a big strong husband with plenty of money. Except for having a headscarf made of pure silk from Bursa. People *should* be talking about her, but with admiration and slight envy.

Certainly not for her children wearing gaol socks. For years, Gül thinks gaol socks are a certain kind of socks, thin grey cotton ones that get holes quickly, usually in the toes. Her mother taught her how to cut a bit off the front of socks, which don't have heels anyway, and then sew them up again. It's Gül's job; the socks are too thin to darn, they just get shortened every two or three weeks. Soon enough, they don't even cover their ankles and Timur buys a new load of gaol socks.

For as long as she can remember, Gül has heard those two words together, and she thinks it's like with spoons. Just like dessert spoons, tablespoons and teaspoons, there are knee socks for winter, of which each of the sisters has only one pair to wear to school, there are stockings and there are gaol socks. Not until years later will Gül realise that they're socks made by the inmates of the local prison, to keep busy and earn money. Less than she earns when she blows the bellows.

But before she works it out, she sits in the light of the lamp at night, like many others in the town, and sews up the tips of the threadbare socks, trying to make the seam as fine as possible so that they're more comfortable to wear.

In the spring they don't need them, in the spring the children wear the only pair of shoes they possess, only to school and nowhere else. As soon as it's warm enough, they run around barefoot, like almost all the others. Or in cheap plastic sandals that turn slippery as soon as it gets warmer and their feet start to sweat.

Money may be tight, but there would still be enough to buy the girls a second pair of shoes, except two pairs of shoes are an unnecessary luxury. Everyone agrees on that in the town, rich or poor.

The radio is an accepted luxury though; lots of people benefit from it. Visitors come over now and then just to listen to the radio, but in winter the voices from the box don't have the same lure as in summer. As time goes on, the radio stays off in the evenings unless there's a Beşiktaş match on. It's not just that the radio has lost the allure of the new. Timur hasn't put a speaker on the roof in town, and it's as if the pleasure lessens if it's not shared.

This year, Gül is at school when the first snow begins to fall. Fat flakes descend, scattered at first, but the flurries soon pick up, and when Gül goes to see her father at breaktime, the snow crunches underneath her soles, and Melike and Sezen are building a snowman.

Inside the forge, it's lovely and warm as ever. Timur is sitting on a stool with a pained expression. His face brightens a little when he sees Gül.

'Come on in, little one. Fancy earning a few kuruş?'

He never normally greets her this way. Gül puts down her bag and goes straight over to the bellows, but her father says: 'No, no, come here.'

He pulls his trousers right up to the knee, revealing his calves, dotted only here and there with hairs. There are curls of hair at her father's shirt collar, and he doesn't shave every day, so Gül can often feel his rough stubble, but she's never had the opportunity to study her father's calves. If anything, she imagined they'd be as hairy as his arms.

Not only are there few hairs growing, but the skin is scaly and inflamed. There's every shade of red imaginable, from deep pink to dark lilac, and Timur says to his daughter: 'It's dreadfully itchy, could you give my legs a scratch?'

At first, Gül is disgusted by the blaze of colours and doesn't know quite how she's supposed to go about scratching. Timur's sighs soon make clear what brings him relief and pleasure. Gül feels the dry, chapped skin. She sees the flakes flutter down to the floor and is surprised that her father's legs are almost rougher than his hands. But it brings her satisfaction to hear her father purring so contentedly at her hands, and she's soon used to the colours, too.

The day when the first snow falls is the first day that Timur has his daughter scratch his calves, and it soon becomes a ritual. The blacksmith is reluctant to go to the doctor a second time.

He has no faith in doctors: despite her treatment, his sister still cannot walk properly, she squints so badly that he sometimes thinks she's staring at strange men's trousers, and his first wife was in the care of doctors when she died.

The first time he showed his eczema to a doctor, once his wife and sister had talked him into it, he was given a foul-smelling salve. He was to rub it into his calves in the mornings and at night, and it burned as if all the sparks he'd seen that day had gathered on his legs. He did this for two whole weeks and when he got no relief, he chucked the salve away and grumbled that he wouldn't have used such a thing on his own cows.

So he has his daughters scratch his calves; first Gül, and later Melike and Sibel too. When she wants a little money, Melike asks her father at the most awkward moments if she can use her fingernails to bring him a little relief. Timur often sends her away, because Melike will lose interest after five minutes or soon begin to draw blood. He sends her away and waits for Gül or Sibel, who does it the best. Sibel is fully immersed as she glides her fingers over her father's calves, just like when she does her homework. She focuses completely, and sometimes her lips move and she murmurs soundlessly to herself. Timur can't help but smile when he sees his daughter's far-away look, her lips moving softly.

Timur prefers cows and donkeys to horses and almost looks down on the latter, since they're so happy to do man's bidding. A horse will obey almost anyone who can ride it. His stubborn donkey is quite the opposite, and his cow is even more headstrong. In the mornings it won't leave the stable, and in the evenings it won't come in from the pasture, galloping home, then taking a wrong turn. Though it knows the way well enough, if Timur is to be believed. One day, it proves too much for the blacksmith. As he's driving the cow home from the pasture, it once again takes the wrong turning at every fork, and he bellows: 'That's it, I've had it! Tomorrow I'm selling you. I could find a better cow than you anywhere.'

And the rest of the way home, the cow trots obediently at the blacksmith's side, crying. Or so Timur says when he tells Gül the story. It's true, at least, that the cow is never as stubborn again.

Since that day, the cow and Timur have had a game they play. Timur lowers his head to his favourite cow, and the cow knocks

Timur's hat off with its nose. Timur grabs it up and laughs and pats his *little girl*, as he calls the cow.

One day they play this game and the cow injures him. One of its short horns leaves a deep scratch on Timur's cheek, but Timur laughs it off. That evening, when his wife finds out what happened, she says: 'What on earth are you playing with cows for? You're too good to them, you spoil them and this is how they thank you. How can a man be so besotted with a cow?'

'You know nothing about it,' Timur says, in a voice which makes it clear that the matter is closed.

And Arzu says nothing more. Her husband can be more stubborn than a cow. And more hurtful.

Arzu doesn't approve of him regularly visiting his dead wife's grave. She rarely accompanies him to the graveyard, because it always takes too long. Timur crouches down, shuts his eyes and stays in this position, unmoving, for minutes on end.

'What are you doing, why's it taking so long?' she asks one day.

'I'm talking to Fatma.'

'What are you saying to her?'

'I'm saying: Fatma, you've been lying there such a long time now, couldn't you come and swap places with Arzu for a few weeks?'

On the way back to school on the day Gül first scratches her father's itchy calves, she sees the man who the sieve maker took her to, back when they lived in the village. He doesn't recognise her, of course, but Gül instantly remembers that day when she got lost, and she hears the man's voice in her mind: *Don't be silly, that's not my daughter. I've already got four girls, what I want is a son. The merciful Lord hasn't granted me one son. You get out of here with yet another girl.*

Gül knows her father would like a son too, though he never talks about it. And at the moment when the other blacksmith's words occur to her, she knows her father's wish will soon come true. It's a picture. A picture of a little brother, a little screaming brother with blue-green eyes and fair hair. It's a picture as strong as the one she had with the fever, when the ceiling beams bore down towards her and she screamed in fear. The picture of the brother has the same strength, but this time Gül is healthy. She is sure of it. Emin. His name will be Emin.

And that evening, Gül knows with the same certainty that her father will stop smoking. He's sitting there with a glass of rakı, smoking; the radio is off and Timur seems annoyed, the contented sighs of that lunchtime when Gül scratched his calves now long past. Perhaps he got riled up about something or his assistant had two left hands today, perhaps he played backgammon at the teahouse after work and lost, or perhaps he was bothered by the way Arzu holds her fork at mealtimes and the way she never stops talking – in any case something he wouldn't admit to right now. When Beşiktaş lose he always moans long and loud about his team. Now, he murmurs to himself: 'Four daughters, thanks be to God.'

He strokes Gül's head absent-mindedly, leaving his hand on the back of her neck.

'But if the Almighty were to send me a son…'

He looks at Arzu's belly; it's the first time he's spoken that wish out loud in front of his eldest daughter.

'If the merciful Lord sends me a son, I swear I'll stop smoking.'

Gül doesn't mind whether her father smokes or not, but she knows before he does that he will give it up. Her mother seems to have no idea. Later, when Gül is married herself and has started smoking, she will often think back to this day when she knew her father would have the strength to give up his vice.

The school holidays have come and they're back at the summer house, when Arzu's contractions set in early one evening. The sisters are sent to the other room, where Melike and Sibel soon start squabbling.

'You hid inside the house yesterday when we played hide-and-seek,' Sibel says.

'No, I didn't,' Melike lies; she's a sore loser.

She almost always wins when they play tag, skipping, ball games. She's nimble and quick. At middle school, she will play on the volleyball team. When she hides, though, she might find tiny nooks where she'd never be spotted, but she's too impatient to stay put for long enough.

'Yes you did. Nalan saw you hide inside the house.'

'And you believe a little kid?'

'She saw you.'

'No, she didn't.'

Melike stamps her foot.

'Stop it, you two,' Gül says.

'You keep out of it,' Melike bites back.

'Inside the house,' says Sibel.

'Did not!' Melike counters, hitting her sister on the shoulder.

Sibel ducks and dodges away, but she insists: 'Inside the house.'

'Leave her alone,' Gül tells Melike, who has taken a step closer to Sibel. As Melike turns to look at Gül, Sibel takes the opportunity to kick Melike in the shin and run straight to the divan. Melike leaps after her sister, grabbing her. Gül tries to smooth things over. There are arms, legs, kicks, elbows, slaps, pulled hair, scratch marks and spit, a tangle of three sisters from which Gül extracts herself.

Is that Melike's shoulder on her tummy? Where are her own arms? Why aren't they stretched out? From the divan onto the floor, she falls head-first down Melike's back, her feet pointing up in the air. And down there, where she lands on the bridge of her nose, is the upside-down copper bowl from which they pour water at night. The bowl is upside down, Gül thinks, before the pain is there all at once.

She doesn't even scream. She's perfectly quiet. Her sisters fall silent too, as if sensing something bad has happened.

Come here, the pain is behind this door, someone must have said, and then opened a door and shoved Gül into a room, a big room, dark, without walls, without floor or ceiling, nothing but all-devouring pain.

Over the next few minutes, she registers nothing; the world has stopped. A moment ago, she was a tangle of arms, hands, legs, feet, and now she can't feel her limbs. There is only the pain, making her head throb and stealing away her breath.

When she takes her hands off her nose five minutes later and looks in the mirror, the skin below her eyes is already shimmering pink, her face looking strange and swollen around her nose. And she must have been crying without realising.

She knows her mother has other things to worry about now, she knows Emin is being born and she can't go to her mother. Gül feels guilty because she didn't manage to stop her sisters squabbling, because she joined in the scrum. She's scared of leaving the room and telling someone what's happened. And her own face scares her too. She simply lies down on the floor and abandons herself to the pain.

In the space of a quarter of an hour, she gets rings beneath her eyes like Fatma just before she died. Her face swells up so much that her nose barely sticks out.

She doesn't know how much time has passed when her father comes into the room, she doesn't know if her brother's been born yet or not, she doesn't know whether Sibel might have called their father; all she knows is that she's in pain, pain and fear, fear of looking like No-Nose Abdul.

'Show me,' her father says, leaning over Gül's face. Gül sees the shock in his eyes.

'How did it happen?'

'Playing,' Gül says.

Her voice sounds like a stranger's.

'No need to cry if you fall while playing,' her father says.

It's something he often says, but this time he doesn't seem to mean it the same way.

'Does it hurt?'

Instead of an answer, tears run out of the corners of Gül's eyes; first slowly, one on the left and then one on the right, but after that too many to count, running soundlessly down her temples. Timur places a careful finger on the bridge of her nose.

The midwife has gone, he has a son he will call Emin, he will stop smoking, but first he has to take care of his daughter.

'Arzu, Gül's fallen over and hurt herself. I'll bet it's Melike's fault again. I'm going to fetch the doctor,' he says as he comes to get his hat from the room where his wife is cradling the new-born boy. He never leaves the house without a hat; his summer hat to protect him from the sun in summer, and his winter hat to keep him warm in winter.

'What's the matter with her?' Arzu asks.

'Her face is swollen up, it looks frightful.'

'What?'

'She might have broken something.'

'Don't fetch the doctor.'

'Why not?'

'No one will believe it happened while she was playing, people will say you beat her. The neighbours will gossip about you, they'll say you weren't capable of looking after your daughters while I was giving birth. We'll be the laughing stock of the town.'

Uncertain, the blacksmith stands in the doorway. What she says is not unlikely.

'But what shall we do?'

'It's bound to heal. She won't go out for a few days, then no one will notice anything. She's a child, it'll heal quickly.'

Timur twists his hat in his hands. His son doesn't make a peep. The blacksmith doesn't know which way to turn. After his father died, he was the man in the house from a young age, but he often let his mother tell him what to do, and later Fatma. It has become a habit to think women know better about certain things. Didn't his mother marry him to Fatma? Didn't he have a good life when Fatma was still weaving carpets and taking care of his money? Mightn't everyone really gossip about him if he fetches a doctor?

'That unscrupulous man tried out his strength on his daughter, they'll say. You'll bring shame upon this house if you fetch the doctor. Hasn't everyone already seen you beating Melike? They'll all think you thrashed Gül so badly the doctor had to come. If you love your God, you won't do that to us.'

Timur puts his hat down. He feels like smoking right now, but the Lord has sent him a son and he won't smoke any more, never again. He goes out to the garden and takes the pack out of his pocket. He stopped rolling his own a while ago. The pack is still half-full; one cigarette after another crumbles between his fingers. A son. Today ought to be a day of joy. And anyway, doctors are all quacks who've studied for a few years and learned nothing. He's heard of that vet from Istanbul who'd never seen a living cow, only pictures in books. They're all the same, doctors, they haven't got a clue.

Gül lies on her back on the divan; Sibel has brought her something to drink. Even Gül's lips feel swollen by now, swollen and numb like the rest of her face. When she touches her face with her fingers it seems to have no feeling in it, but the pain is still there underneath the skin, throbbing and pulsing, alive. Gül has her eyes closed, and she keeps seeing No-Nose Abdul and an image that etched itself into her mind at their last Eid sacrifice.

Her father had slaughtered a lamb. She was sorry for it but she felt neither fear nor disgust, and she knew very well they'd be eating the meat later on. Timur let the lamb bleed dry and then butchered it, but as a piece of one leg lay in the big bowl, the muscle began to tremble, tensing and untensing in quick succession. That was the moment that scared Gül. Because there was life where there should be none. She stared at that leg, not daring to touch it, even though that's what she wished she could do. The life existed independently of the lamb. And it's exactly the same now with the pain, it's there all the time. It exists independently of her – it is bigger than Gül, it enshrouds her.

She must have fallen asleep after all; she doesn't notice her father coming into the room. She hadn't heard the birds singing; the sun will soon be up.

'Gül,' her father whispers. 'Gül, wake up, I've fetched the doctor. Get dressed and come out.'

Gül leaves the room for the first time since her fall. She doesn't need to get dressed, seeing as she didn't get undressed yesterday. Standing up, the pain feels different, but she can stand it without moaning.

In the small hallway where the doctor is waiting, bag in hand, she takes a quick look in the mirror. The dark green and violet rings below her eyes go all the way down to her cheekbones, only there fading slightly, yellowing. Her nasal bone is no longer visible at all.

She'll soon look just like No-Nose Abdul. That's why the doctor has come, to take her nose away. She'll be No-Nose Gül, and the children will interrupt their games and run away when she walks along the street, she won't dare to leave the house. She feels the tears, but they won't come out, they gather up somewhere inside her.

'Sit down, little one,' the doctor says. 'Don't be scared.'

He lays a careful two fingers between her eyebrows; the skin is taut and hot.

'Does that hurt?'

'No,' Gül says. She'd rather shake her head, but she senses that *would* hurt.

The doctor moves his fingers gently down the bridge of her nose, stopping at one place and increasing the pressure, and that pressure sends tears shooting into Gül's eyes, but she doesn't say a word.

'It's broken,' the doctor says and then he nods at Timur, who has been standing next to her all along, his hat clutched in the hand that would usually be holding a cigarette.

Timur stands behind Gül and holds her head while the doctor feels her nose again. Gül thinks she's safe because she feels her father's hands as he murmurs calming words.

With one swift motion, the doctor jerks her nose bone back into place. Now all the gathered-up tears shoot through Gül's eyes at once and she screams, screams in the voice that sounds like a stranger's.

'It's all over, my girl, it's all over,' the doctor consoles her.

He hands some tablets to Timur and says: 'These are for the pain. Only give her half a pill a day. She's a child, it'll heal quickly. There'll be nothing to see in three days.'

Gül knows the doctor is saying that to calm her down. She knows no one would say: 'You're going to look like No-Nose Abdul.' Even if it were true.

'You can just stay at home for a couple of days,' says Timur, winking at the doctor. 'It's sure to be better if you don't go out.'

'Yes,' the doctor says, 'you should stay inside for a few days.'

Gül sees everything through a veil of tears and she seems to hear that way too, as though there were something between the world and her ears. But she's fine not having to leave the house.

Melike will be starting her fourth year at school in autumn, but she still wets the bed now and then when she doesn't wake up at night. That morning, she doesn't disappear like usual; she changes the sheets herself. Gül went to bed after the doctor left and now she lies there, lulled by the painkiller and exhausted from the night spent awake. She is grateful for the glass of fresh milk Melike brings her, and she drifts off.

Zeliha and Hülya come to see the new baby, and Timur tells them Gül has broken her nose. Hülya goes to see her; Gül wakes as the door closes behind her. When Hülya catches sight of her, her auntie's eyes reveal what she must look like. Hülya swiftly dons a smile and removes her headscarf, which has slipped. Perched on the mattress, Hülya says: 'My sweetheart.'

The rings below Gül's eyes are exactly the same colour as her sister-in-law's before she died.

'It'll pass, my sweetheart,' she says. 'It'll pass.'

Gül has only ever seen her auntie without her headscarf at the steam baths. Hülya looks beautiful and at the same time unfamiliar.

'Does it hurt very much, you poor thing?'

Hülya gives Gül a cautious kiss on the forehead, which is still numb.

Gül saw her auntie's face an instant before, she saw the moment when her auntie was more naked than without a headscarf, more naked than in the steam bath. She saw the horror in her squinting face. For the blink of an eye, all the masks were lowered, all the words fell away, every laugh and every tear. For the blink of any eye, she saw the truth. For the blink of an eye, the world was the sound of a spoon hurled against a wall.

Her grandmother doesn't make that face; when she looks at Gül, she says, unconcerned: 'It's almost healed though. It's not that bad.'

She puts a cigarette between her lips; it takes her a long time to fumble a match out of the box.

When Gül next wakes up, there's chocolate lying near her pillow. Wrapped in silver paper, like the chocolate Melike sometimes brings home when she's been at Sezen's, and which she never shares. Gül unwraps the chocolate, carefully so the paper doesn't rip, and takes her time eating it. She hears voices from outside, people coming to see her newborn brother, who she hasn't set eyes on yet. She recognises the voice of Uncle Fuat, Arzu's brother. He's only a few years older than Gül, and Gül knows he's apprenticed to a barber and always steps on the backs of his shoes so they soon look like slippers. Quite a few men do this, but most of them are much older than Fuat.

Just before Gül goes back to sleep, she thinks she hears Uncle Yücel's voice. She hasn't seen him since Hülya has been living back at her grandmother's. Again, she remembers how he rocked Sibel on his feet. She would like to get up and run over to him. But she manages, just about, to turn over and doze off.

When she wakes up, in pain, everyone seems to be asleep. Gül feels weak and ill, and her head is throbbing dully. She needs her tablets; she needs her tablets to be well. They're probably in the kitchen, in the cupboard. To get to the kitchen, she has to go through the room where her parents sleep. She doesn't take the torch with her; there's a full moon, it's bright enough.

As she quietly opens the door, her mother wakes up. Gül sees her little brother next to her and hears her whisper: 'What is it?'

'My medicine,' Gül replies just as softly.

Arzu gestures to the kitchen with her chin, and Gül goes across and takes the tablets out of the cupboard. Her mother is a very tidy person, she never has to look hard for anything. So Gül knows the tablets must be in the green cupboard with the wire mesh, probably at the bottom on the left. That's where that sort of thing would be.

It's important to put everything back in its place, Arzu is always saying. And Gül thinks she's right. The tablets look bigger than before, as if they've grown since she last took one. She pours herself a glass of water from the carafe and manages to swallow one down with some effort. Then she goes back to bed. She soon wakes up again. It still hurts, and Gül creeps into the kitchen and swallows another of the big tablets.

At some point, she opens her heavy eyelids because someone is slapping her face. Her eyelids seem stuck together. Her cheeks are wet and someone is dabbing her brow. Gül would prefer to be left in peace, she wants to sleep, everything feels so heavy, she wants to turn over and sleep.

Gül closes her eyes and hears voices which seem familiar, maybe they're asking questions, but she can't seem to move her tongue to answer, even if she had understood the question.

She mumbles in reply, not hearing what her mother says: 'See? If you hadn't called for the doctor, this wouldn't have happened. Calling the doctor before dawn so the neighbours don't see, honestly! And what if these tablets kill her, what will you do then?'

It's light when Gül next wakes up. It seems like mid-morning, and she hears Uncle Abdurahman's voice in the other room: 'I just wanted to see where my little one's got to.'

Tuesday, today must be Tuesday – the day when she studies with Uncle Abdurahman. It was Sunday when she broke her nose, wasn't it? Where has the time gone? Gül is hungry, really hungry, and she's not keen to study. Not now and not at any other time either. When summer's over, she will be going into year five, and then she'll get her primary school certificate. She can read, count, write, and she doesn't mind that she always gets her Ottoman sultans muddled. Besides, she doesn't like the girl who is staying at Uncle Abdurahman's this year.

Every year, like many other single men or young couples with little children, Uncle Abdurahman goes to a village before summer begins, to find a poor family whose daughter sees to the chores in his summer house in return for bed and board over the summer.

'Gül's not well,' Arzu says, but Gül calls out: 'I'm here.'

Her voice is a hoarse croak.

Uncle Abdurahman comes in, and his eyes reveal nothing when he sees Gül.

'Oh, you're not very well, my girl,' he says. 'Will the young lady be visiting me again next week?'

'Yes,' Gül says.

Her skin is still a little taut.

'Well, until then I'm bringing you a book, so you don't get bored lying in bed like that.'

When Uncle Abdurahman is gone, Arzu says to Gül: 'I don't want people seeing you like this, we'll be the talk of the town. You're not to leave this room until I tell you. And you're not to call anyone in either, is that clear?'

'Yes,' Gül says.

'If you want another tablet, you'll have to ask me, alright? You took too many of them. It was dangerous.'

And just as Gül goes to ask for something to eat, Arzu says: 'You slept for nearly two days, I bet you're hungry, aren't you? Shall I warm something up for you? We've got aubergines, rice, beans, yoghurt, bread. Would you like a bit of everything?'

Gül nods mutely, so that her voice doesn't scratch at her throat, and smiles.

It's a big book for adults that Uncle Abdurahman has brought her. But she doesn't have much else to do; Arzu gives her gaol socks she's to sew new toes on, but other than that, nothing is expected of her. So she begins to read the book. She imagines the big houses it describes, the people in fashionable dress, the foreign country. She quickly mixes up the foreign names, but the characters grow more alive with every page; they grow closer to her, though the world of the book is almost nothing like her own. Eventually, she's rooting for the young woman who's supposed to be tainted. Nobody believes her when she tells them the truth, no one believes she is pure. Gül can tell there is something going on that she doesn't quite understand, something big, something secret, but she can also tell she's not supposed to ask anyone about it. But she knows what it's like when no one believes you're telling the truth. The woman feels the same as she does.

Over the next four days, Melike keeps bringing home chocolate for Gül.

Ten days later, there isn't much left to see on her face and Gül is allowed out on the street again, where she's to say she's had a summer cold. She can play, she can take the book she's finished reading back to Uncle Abdurahman. It will be a few years before she reads another book.

This summer, the girls play a game usually reserved for the boys – they play marbles. Gül has a glass marble which she takes along but never uses. Inside the marble, there's a streak of fire, orangey-red, with blue stars.

Meltem, who's two years older than Gül, argues and argues until Gül agrees to use her marble. And loses it to Meltem.

'Again,' Gül says, adding: 'You have to play my marble in the next round.'

'No,' says Meltem, 'I'm playing a different one.'

'But I wagered my marble.'

'No one forced you to.'

'I did it as a favour to you. And now you can play it as a favour to me.'

'No,' Meltem says, and Gül knows there's no use saying anything more. She has lost and she feels the tears come.

Melike looks at Gül, stands up, snatches the marble with the fire-streak from Meltem and runs away. Meltem can't catch up with her.

That evening, Melike gives her elder sister the marble.

'You shouldn't have used it,' she says. 'You always do what other people want and then you're sad. It really belongs to Meltem now, it's your own fault.'

'I'll never take it outside with me again,' Gül vows.

The whole house is cleaned every Saturday: the dust wiped away, the stone floors scrubbed, the ground in the cellar swept, the windows cleaned. This is the day when Timur mucks out the stable.

'Go and pump some water, children,' Arzu says to Gül and Melike.

The long lever on the pumping well behind the house has to be moved up and down to draw out the water. Once they've filled the basin in front of the pump, Gül and Melike must scoop the water out with five-litre canisters and take it to their mother. Gül starts pumping, and when the basin is a third full, she calls to Melike, who's sitting on a rock a little way off: 'I'm tired, my arm's going funny – can you do it for a bit?'

'In a minute,' Melike says, and throws a stalk of grass into the air. Two minutes later, Gül asks again.

'In a minute,' Melike says.

'The basin will be full in a minute.'

Gül pumps a bit longer, until she can't any more.

'Come on,' she says, 'just while I'm resting.'

'In a minute.'

'Just five pumps, come on.'

Gül still wants to rest a while but she starts to pump again, angrily. She has to use both hands, but once she's pumped another two times, she takes her left hand off the handle, picks up a stone off the ground and throws it at Melike, who's busy not looking at her sister. It seems a clumsy throw to Gül, who's right-handed, and she's horrified when Melike yelps. She hadn't thought she would hit her.

Melike holds a hand up to her eye but doesn't make any noise. For a moment, Gül can't move, then she runs over to Melike and puts her arm around her shoulders.

'Sister dear, did I hit you? Are you hurt?'

'Go away!' Melike says, and tries to shake off her sister's arm while Gül attempts to pull Melike's hand away from her eye. Only when Melike gives in does Gül see that her sister's palm is completely red.

'It's nothing,' Gül says, but she has that strange voice again.

Now Melike looks at her hand and starts to cry when she catches sight of the blood.

'Don't cry, it's nothing. It's not that bad,' Gül says.

The stone, the stone she threw with her left hand, the stone not much bigger than her favourite marble, seems to have hit Melike on her right eyebrow.

Gül has seen this sort of thing before. Before she started school, they were at the market with her father when they saw a big crowd of people shouting. Her mother had quickly pulled her away, but her father picked her up and pushed past the people until they were standing at the front.

Two men were standing opposite each other at a market stall, in front of which lay a smashed watermelon. One of the men had no shirt on, and his naked torso looked like a spider had woven a nest over it in blood, covering half his face and his neck too. The man was screaming, and with every sound more and more blood seemed to run from the wound on his brow. The other man was walking backwards slowly. He didn't seem to be injured. Gül didn't understand what they were saying, but she was overwhelmed by the scene. Her father shook his head, smiling, and they walked on.

'What's happened?' Gül asked.

'They're arguing over watermelons. The seller had sworn they were ripe and the man complained.' He shook his head again. 'Over watermelons.'

'Will that man die now?'

Timur stopped.

'No, no, my rose. It's not serious, his eyebrow has just split. It looks terrible, but it won't kill him.'

But Melike is bleeding and crying, and Gül feels her eyes welling up too. She never hits anyone when they play dodgeball. And now she's hit her sister, left-handed.

'Come here,' she says. 'Come on, don't cry, it won't hurt for long.'

She washes Melike's face and goes inside with her, presses a piece of fabric to the wound and hopes it will stop bleeding. Melike lets herself be tended to, but she's in a sulk now and says nothing. At least she's no longer crying. It stops bleeding soon after.

'Stay here. And don't say anything to Mum, alright?'

'I'm going to tell on you.'

'Please don't. I'll be your sacrificial lamb, just don't tell,' says Gül, as she's learnt from the adults.

'I will. And then Daddy will smack you this evening.'

'No, he won't.'

'No, he never smacks you. But you have to do everything Mum says and stay home all day. She's not my mother; I won't put up with it.'

'If you love me, you won't tell on me.'

'If you love me, you won't force me to pump water.'

'But...'

'Go on, you need to get the water.'

Gül fills the basin and carries the water back to her mother.

All day long, she's scared Melike will tell their father what happened, but Timur only sees the scab on Melike's eyebrow that evening.

'Who have you been squabbling with today?'

'I... I jumped on the back of a horse and cart,' Melike says. 'I wanted to ride along for a bit.'

Farmers often drive carts down their street, transporting fruit and vegetables.

'And the nasty man threw a stone at me because I'd jumped on his cart,' Melike continues.

'Serves you right,' Arzu says.

Melike will always have a small scar over her right eyebrow. Years later, she will have a son named Oktay, who will have a scar in exactly the same spot, from a fight. For a while, Melike's scar will remind Gül that she hurt her sister, but a time will also come when she sees the scar and remembers that things with Melike were hard. She'll have the smell of pee in her nostrils and feel the damp sheets beneath her fingers. The scar will remind Gül of the years when she did almost anything to make Melike happy. Anything she could do at that age – which she needn't have done, because Melike would always rather fight than endure anything.

Sibel is still pale, thin and sickly, but she gets very good grades even though she spent a week ill in bed three times over the winter. In art she's the top of her class, and even when she's sick she's rarely seen without a pencil and paper. She draws cows, sheep, hens, trees. She draws her hand or the wardrobe. She uses up her stumps of pencil until they're as small as cigarette butts.

'What, another new pencil?' Arzu once asked. 'You got one just a month ago.'

Timur picked up on it and brought her three pencils the next day. Sibel's eyes lit up; she worked out she'd be able to draw for almost three months now – if she was thrifty enough. Three pencils were a luxury she'd never imagined; not even Sezen had three pencils. Now she could spend hours sitting and drawing somewhere, forgetting herself, as long as she found enough paper.

That summer, Sibel draws walnuts and köfter when she's sick again. She doesn't know why she draws them or why she suddenly feels like eating them, but she calls Gül and says: 'Abla, big sister, I'd really like some köfter.'

'We only have it in the winter,' Gül says.

'But I feel like it.'

'We'll see,' Gül says, fobbing her off, but the next day Sibel brings it up again: 'Abla, I really wish I could have some köfter.'

'We'll see,' Gül replies again.

But once she's finished the housework, she doesn't go out to play. Though their mother told them not to, she sets off for town on her own, to her father's forge.

'Hello, my girl,' Timur says. 'What have you come for, to scratch my legs? Melike's just left.'

Gül says nothing, simply stands in the doorway, and her father is soon immersed in his work again; he seems to have forgotten her. The air is heavy with the smell of the coals and his sweat, which falls from his chin in big drips, leaving wet spots on the floor. When he takes a break, Gül says: 'Can you eat köfter in summer as well?'

'Yes – if you can find some, you can eat it in summer too.'

Why köfter, Gül wonders, *why that of all things?*

'Can we find some?' asks Gül. 'Sibel really wants some.'

'My skinny little Sibel, nothing but skin and bones,' the blacksmith chuckles.

Then he gets back to work. A while later, Gül leaves without saying goodbye.

That evening, her father hasn't brought any köfter home with him. While the neighbours and their mother are sitting outside their front doors listening to the radio, Timur is in the stable taking care of the cows. Gül stops a few steps away from the stable door and calls inside: 'Did you find any köfter?'

'Yes,' he says, 'one of the villagers still has some. It'll help our Sibel get a bit of meat on her bones… Come here, come on in. Don't be scared.'

Gül takes cautious steps closer, then once she's over the threshold she runs to her father and leans her head against his belly. He strokes her hair.

'Your wishes are enough, you understand? You only have to tell me what you want, that's enough. Then I'll do everything my hands and mouth allow, my rose.'

She wishes she didn't have to help so much around the house, but then her sisters would have to do more. She wishes Melike were better behaved, she wishes Arzu would sometimes call her *my rose or darling* or *treasure*, she wishes she could sleep in a warm room in the winter, she wishes her parents didn't argue. She doesn't know what they argue about; she just notices they've been arguing when her father doesn't speak a word to Arzu for days. Like in the two weeks after Gül broke her nose.

The next morning, Timur asks Gül at breakfast: 'I've got business to do in the village. Do you want to come along? You can play with your old friends for a bit, and I'll go and pick something up.'

He winks.

'And then we'll ride home together.'

'She's got to do the–' her mother begins, but Timur interrupts: 'There's nothing she's got to do today.'

And so not much later, Gül is on the back of the donkey. Her father rides the horse and they arrive at the village long before the midday heat. Gül is excited; she hasn't been there for such a long time, but nothing seems to have changed. She jumps down and runs along to the road where they used to live, and her father calls after her: 'I'll pick you up from the village square in the afternoon, awright?'

When her friends recognise Gül, there's much joy and laughter, but soon one of the girls says: 'You talk like a biscuit brat!'

Gül immediately falls silent. Biscuit brats are the children of the rich people from town; they're brats who don't eat dry bread, spoilt brats who crumble like a biscuit dunked in milk.

For 10 minutes, not a word passes Gül's lips; she doesn't have to open her mouth to skip rope.

The next time she says something, she speaks more or less like all the others. At first, the words sound strange out of her own mouth, but she's soon used to it. And if another biscuit-brat word does slip out, no one seems to notice.

'Is Recep still here?' she asks Kezban, one of the girls she used to like the most. A chubby girl two or three years older than her. Kezban titters.

'Do you want to play with the boys?' she asks.

We always used to, Gül would like to answer, but Kezban's tone makes her shake her head.

'He's staying with his aunt,' Kezban says. 'He probably won't be back until after summer. His aunt needs someone to herd the cows.'

Gül nods and wonders whether Recep makes friends with the cows, like her father.

At lunchtime, Kezban takes Gül home with her to eat, and they play in the fields in the afternoon.

Only when the day grows cool does Gül notice she's forgotten the time. Like the day when she sat on the rock and dyed her hands, like the day when her father took the water home. Like she always does when she's happy. She hopes her father isn't waiting for her. But when a slightly breathless Gül and Kezban reach the village square a little later, there's no sign of the blacksmith.

Dusk is falling by the time Timur comes. He's walking, holding his horse by the bridle. The donkey's reins are tied to the horse's saddle. The kilim-fabric double bag thrown over the back of the donkey is full to bursting. Gül says goodbye, and her father lifts her onto the donkey.

Not until they get to the edge of the village does he say: 'Have you heard? Tufan is dead. I managed to do a few deals. His heart just stopped beating, a week ago. He was eaten up inside, I tell you, eaten up by greed.'

In the years that follow, when the blacksmith wants to curse someone, he won't ever wish the plague upon them, nor cancer, death, affliction or poverty; he'll say: 'May the Lord give you greed.'

Timur looks at the sky and says: 'We won't make it home before nightfall now. It's too dangerous to ride in the dark, it's better if we stay here.'

Perhaps he's remembering how he and his wife used to sleep in graveyards.

'Remember Auntie Filiz, the one we used to buy tarhana from?'

Gül shakes her head, which her father can't see because he's ahead of her. But he seems not to expect an answer.

They soon get to Auntie Filiz's house on the edge of the village. Filiz is a jolly, fat woman who presses Gül to her bosom warmly. Gül likes her heavy scent of sweat and earth and something else she's not familiar with.

For dinner, which they eat by the light of the lamp without speaking much, she makes white beans, bulgur and village bread. Gül is amazed to see the same pneumatic lamp here as they have at home, one that no one else has; it shines brighter than the usual petroleum lamps.

'I'll put a mattress on the roof for you,' Filiz says to Timur, 'and the little one can come in my bed.'

Timur nods – of course he can't sleep under the same flat roof as a widow.

Shortly after Gül has gone to bed, Filiz comes too, puts an arm around her and wishes her good night. Gül feels her warm breath on the back of her neck, the softness of her breasts against her shoulder blades. She's tired and exhausted and happy. It has been a lovely day: she rode on the donkey alongside her father; it only took her 10 minutes to get rid of her biscuit-brat accent; she played with Kezban in the fields, those endless fields; she ate beans and hard village bread; she can breathe in Auntie Filiz's scent. And moments later she falls asleep. When she wakes up in the night, Auntie Filiz is gone. She turns over and goes back to sleep.

On their way back home next day, Timur says with a sigh of contentment: 'We'll do good business in town.'

Gül is glad to see her father so happy.

Someone else will soon take Tufan's place. Times have changed. More money has come to the village – the farmers expect more and don't want to wait a long time for a middleman, so they'll soon sell to Tufan's nephew instead of the blacksmith.

It always seems like a holiday to the children when they all go to the baths together: Gül, Melike, Sibel, Nalan, their mother, their grandmother, Auntie Hülya and one or other of the neighbours and their children. That winter, they take little Emin along too. In the morning, they pack a big basket with bread, cheese, olives, bÖrek, soap, flannels, hairbrushes and fresh underwear.

'Why can't you women just use the hamam to wash, like everyone else?' Timur asks.

'If we're going, we're going to do it properly,' Arzu replies. 'Why should we be done in a couple of hours?'

They go early in the morning and stay until late afternoon. From time to time the women sit in the antechamber, which isn't as hot, or relax in the entrance hall, have something to eat, chat, laugh, gossip, huddle together in twos or threes and whisper. They often fall silent when Gül or someone else approaches.

It's always a joy; the children run around in the nude and spray each other with cold water, lather up the soap or skip it across the floor, screeching, laughing and listening to their laughter echo off the arched ceiling. Sometimes, Gül looks at the other women's breasts or her auntie's hefty bottom and the improbably bushy triangle of hair between her grandmother's legs.

At first, she was fascinated to see her brother naked, too. She's since got used to it because she often has to change him. She also often has to wash his nappies, but it doesn't bother her. She likes picking him up, trying to soothe him when he cries. She rocks him to sleep on her feet and thinks of Uncle Yücel, who no one ever talks about.

She likes Emin, but sometimes she gets jealous when she sees her father cooing over him. Her father, who stopped smoking just because the Lord granted him a son.

Everyone knows Zeliha's eyes are getting worse by the day. It occurs to Gül that her mother sometimes guides her Zeliha along, that her grandmother can't find the soap when it's right in front of her, and she knows she sometimes won't know who her granddaughter is until she opens her mouth.

They're by their grandmother playing when Sibel, who ate a lot of köfter in the summer but hasn't gained any weight, says: 'She can't tell us apart at all any more.'

Just at that moment, Melike tips a dish of cold water over her head. Sibel screams but only briefly, then she stops and acts as if nothing has happened. She does this a lot these days, so that Melike stops trying to annoy her. Gül hits upon an idea, which she will later say the devil gave her; she can't explain it any other way. She can still hear her grandmother's deep voice, the voice that claimed Gül had stolen the köfter.

Gül fills one of the dishes with cold water and creeps up behind her grandmother, who is sitting on the edge of the circular marble slab in the middle of the baths. Gül climbs up onto the marble above the water boiler and tips the dish of water over her grandmother's head. She hears her cry out as she runs away.

Noticing the noise, the women are soon standing around Zeliha. By now, Gül is sitting quite innocently beside one of the marble basins, dabbling a hand in the water. But her heart is pounding, and she's sure everyone can see that it was her. How had she dared to do it?

'Who did that?' Zeliha wants to know. 'Which of you little brats tipped cold water over me? Call those wretched children over.'

All the children have to gather around and present themselves before the old woman. Gül can't bring herself to look up, but no one seems to notice. They stand there in a line, Gül at the far left, then Sibel, Melike, little Nalan on the right and the neighbour's two daughters next to her.

'Who poured water over her?' Arzu asks. No one answers.

'Melike,' Arzu says after a pause, and it doesn't sound like a question.

'It wasn't me.'

'Come here,' her mother orders, and Melike steps forward.

'It was you, wasn't it?' her grandmother says.

'No,' says Melike, 'it wasn't me.'

'Don't lie,' her mother says. 'God punishes liars.'

'If you lie, you'll be struck by lightning,' Zeliha says.

Melike is now standing half a foot from her grandmother, who is still sitting on the marble slab. Her towel has slipped and her heavy, hanging breasts are exposed. Melike stands there with a clear conscience, but before she can react, her grandmother strikes her face. She's lucky Zeliha's eyes are so bad, or she would have got a proper smack that echoed off the walls. Melike steps back. It makes no sense to run away, where would she even go?

'It was me,' Gül says. 'I did it.'

Melike visibly relaxes. She relaxes and doesn't see her mother raise her hand. This time, it echoes off the walls.

'You see?' her mother says. 'Follow your sister's example. She's ready to sacrifice herself for you.'

'It really was me,' Gül says, and her voice somersaults.

The second smack finds its mark. Melike turns and runs into the antechamber. Their mother goes to follow her, but Gül grips her arm and says: 'It was me, it really was. I swear to God!'

'Don't swear false oaths, it's a sin,' her grandmother says, and her mother shakes her off and runs after Melike. Melike is in the entrance hall, right by the door.

'Come any closer and I'll run right out!' she calls out.

Arzu slows her pace.

'It's cold outside, there's snow. You'll catch your death.'

'I'll run outside,' Melike says. 'If you come any closer, I'll run outside!'

Arzu stops.

'I'll be telling your father what you did this evening.'

'It wasn't me,' Melike says, and she can't help but laugh.

'You're lying,' says her mother. 'You're lying.'

'No,' Melike laughs.

She knows no one will believe her if she laughs like this, but the laughter is stronger than her. She doesn't know where it's come from, she can't hold it in.

Her mother takes another step closer, Melike opens the door. The air is so icy, she gets goosebumps, her neck muscles tense and she clamps her teeth together. If her mother takes one more step, she's going to run outside.

'You'll get what's coming to you tonight,' her mother says, and turns around. As soon as Arzu turns her back, tears flow down Melike's face.

When they're back home, Gül prays to God: *Forgive me for pouring cold water over Nene. The devil put the idea in my head.*

When Melike is petulant or plotting something, or when she's really silly, Timur always says: 'The devil's really farted up your nose.'

And that's exactly how it seems to Gül now, like the devil farted up her nose and she enjoyed the smell.

'Where's Melike?' Timur asks at dinner. 'Has she been up to mischief again?'

Arzu tells him what happened. Gül watches her father listening. She won't say she did it. It will only make him be even nicer to her and angrier with Melike. But maybe he's not angry at all. A smile flits briefly across his face when Arzu says: 'And then she tipped cold water over your poor old mother.'

For a second, just a second, Timur looks like a little boy who's pulled off a good prank. Then he runs his thumb and forefinger along his moustache, a gesture which seems strange to Gül.

'... she got herself dressed and left. We hadn't even got round to giving her a proper wash. Thanks to her, we'll have to go to the hamam again next week. She's not clean.'

The blacksmith strokes his moustache again, covering his mouth with his hand.

'Wait till she gets home, I'll show her what for.'

Melike comes through the stable into the garden, and Gül smuggles her inside before anyone sees her.

'Were you at Sezen's?' Gül asks, nodding towards the silver paper in Melike's hand.

'Yes.'

'I'm sorry.'

'I always get the blame,' Melike says, and her eyes brim with angry tears.

Gül nods, yes, it's unfair. She put her arms around her sister. 'Daddy won't smack you.'

'I don't care.'

'I know,' Gül says, tears rolling gently down her face too now. Soon they're lying in each other's arms, crying, until Gül pulls herself together.

A few days later, Arzu asks Gül to look after Emin while she pops out.

'It won't take long,' she says, but Gül knows she usually stays out longer than she plans.

Shortly after Arzu has left, Emin starts crying. He's lying on the divan, full of milk and with a clean nappy; he ought to be asleep, but he's screaming at the top of his voice.

Gül picks him up and walks him around the house patting his back, but Emin yells so hard his veins show underneath his skin. When he screams his face turns first pink, then red and then violet. Only when he needs to take a breath does he get a yellowish tinge, but the first sound out of his mouth turns him pink again.

'It's alright, baby,' Gül murmurs. 'It's alright, my treasure, no need to cry.'

She kisses the fluff on top of his head, but there's no calming Emin down. After over a quarter of an hour, Gül no longer knows what else she can do. He spits out his dummy, cries even more when she rocks him on her feet, and he doesn't want to eat or drink anything.

For a while he goes quiet, and Gül breathes a sigh of relief, but the quiet only lasts two minutes; her brother seems to have been gathering his strength. Now his face goes even darker.

Gül starts to get scared. What should she do? Take the baby over to her mother's friend's place? Won't her mother say she can't even look after a little baby? Gül starts to get scared.

Fear, an old familiar acquaintance paying a visit. Feelings are like invisible people. They come, they go – they can be very close or you can see them as if from a distance, blurred and unclear. Some are beautiful, so beautiful it hurts when they stand right in front of you; others give you a shock like No-Nose Abdul, but they all have a life of their own. You can never get them to do what you want. And no one knows when they're there, apart from you. You recognise them like you recognise people. Some soft and warm, and some cold and lumpy like fear. Cold and lumpy and jagged like a bolt of lightning, and bigger and darker than her father's shadow in the evening sun.

Time and again, fear comes into Gül's life and whispers something she can't quite understand. *I'll take it*, the fear seems to say, *I'll take it away*. It usually leaves empty-handed. But Gül knows that one day fear might act on its threat.

Gül flushes with heat; sweat coats her brow as she begins to undress Emin. She has to undress him, get him bare naked; she has to see if a pin has pierced his skin, perhaps one of the safety pins fastening his nappy.

Quickly, quickly, perhaps she can still save her brother.

She has to rush, but at the same time she has to be careful so the pin doesn't bore deeper into his flesh. She pulls his jersey over his head, then she carefully removes his vest, inspects his little chest, his belly and back, but there's nothing there. Emin cries, cries and screams and kicks his legs so hard Gül has trouble taking his trousers off.

His nappy is a folded cloth fastened with a safety pin. Over the top, he wears rubber pants with tight cuffs so that nothing leaks out and runs down his legs.

Now Gül sees that the elastic around his right leg has slipped out of place. Her mother must have been in a rush earlier. The elastic that ought to be around the top of his leg runs from his crotch up to his hip. Gül takes off the rubber pants, undoes the safety pin and unfolds the cloth nappy. She sees her brother's little penis and scrotum, their circulation cut off by the elastic. They're darker than his screaming face. Darker than the circles under her mother's eyes before she died. For a brief moment, Emin stops crying.

Gül stares at his violet genitalia, not knowing what to do next. Emin starts crying again, kicking and screaming, but it doesn't sound as strained now. What should she do? She can't turn her eyes away. It looks dangerous. Can you die of it? Or will he end up a girl now too?

'It's alright, it's all over,' she whispers, and watches as his penis and scrotum gradually lose their dark tint. Or is she just imagining it? No. No, no, they're slowly returning to his normal skin colour. It's a slow process, but holding her breath and staring seems to help. When she breathes out at last, tears run down her face.

For many years, she won't tell anyone this story. Her mother would have shouted at her and denied doing anything wrong when she changed his nappy. Why should she have told her father and her sisters? Only much later, once she has children of her own, will she tell anyone what happened that day, and she'll add: 'That's what makes a person lonely; when you can't share things.'

The winter's snow has melted when Gül's father sends her to the grocer's one day to buy cigarettes for the visitors they're expecting that evening. During that winter, Gül has started to dawdle. She doesn't dilly-dally on her way to school, or over breakfast in the morning, nor when she's washing dishes, doing the laundry, changing nappies. She dawdles when she gets sent somewhere. She looks around at her surroundings, watches other children playing, wishing it was summer and she could sit in the summer house garden, all alone, in the shade of a tree. She enjoys the time she takes for herself.

If Arzu catches her at it, she says: 'You're daydreaming. You daydream and then you have to rush later on and you forget half your chores. Look at Sibel – she always does everything straight away, and then she sits down and draws her pictures. My God, nothing but pictures, that girl has nothing else in her head!'

At school, too, Gül often daydreams, looks outside or examines the peeling paint on the window frame. Dawdling on the way to the grocer's, she spots something brightly coloured next to a semi-circular stone. She goes closer and sees that it's a bank-note. Two and a half lira – 250 kuruş! When she scratches her father's legs, she gets 10 kuruş, which she spends on sweets or a small bag of sunflower seeds.

Gül picks up the note, puts it in her pocket, buys a pack of cigarettes at the grocer's for 40 kuruş and goes home. She gives her father the cigarettes and the 60 kuruş change, and then she takes out the two and a half lira, holds it out to him and says: 'I found this.'

Her father gives her a searching look.

'Where did you get it?'

As though she hadn't just told him.

'I found it in the road.'

'Two and a half lira in the road?'

Gül is a little confused and nods, worried now.

'Was the grocer in the shop when you got there?'

'Yes,' Gül says, and now she understands what her father is trying to ask. 'I found it. Really, I swear to God.'

'Where?'

'In the road. Out the front of the carpenter's house, next to a stone.'

'Are you sure you found it?'

'I can show you the stone.'

For some reason, that seems to convince the blacksmith. He knows she can't make up a stone next to the carpenter's house. That would be more Melike's style. He pockets the two and a half lira, gives her 25 kuruş in return and says: 'Profit and loss are brothers. They always meet again. There's no point running after one of them. So if you lose something tomorrow, you needn't be sad.'

Sometimes, Timur has nothing to do at the forge for days on end, just drinking tea and playing cards with his assistant. He hasn't done any business with the villagers since Tufan's nephew took over the trade. Word has got around by now that the blacksmith is not as wealthy as he used to be. Neither the radio nor the pneumatic lamp can cover that up. Timur doesn't much mind having less money; the only thing he really misses are his trips to the big city. But he's hopeful for the next autumn, the next apple harvest. Perhaps there'll be enough left over to go away for a few days.

In the old days, when he saw men of around 40 in the night-clubs, he used to think: *What are those old codgers doing in here? These places are for us.* He'd thought it especially about rich men, men with sagging shoulders, men with thinning hair and gravi-ty-embracing bellies. He had often enough wondered what they were even still doing in the world. Hadn't they lived long enough already?

That was back when he was 20, and 40, 40 meant they had lived twice as long as him. Surely that ought to be enough. And now the blacksmith is pushing 40 himself and can well imagine reaching 60. Another 20 years? Why not.

So it hardly bothers him that he has less money. It bothers his wife. And it bothers his near-blind mother, who always says: 'You still have to learn not to waste your money – you mustn't throw it out the window, you have to learn to clench your fists; hold onto your money.'

He doesn't like the sound of that though. He'd rather tell the funny story of how a woman came to his workshop in the winter, patted the snow off her long coat and didn't say a word in greeting. Women don't usually come to his workshop; it's a place for men. The blacksmith often starts a conversation about football with people he doesn't know, checking the men out. Beşiktaş fans get their orders faster than Galatasaray and Fenerbahçe supporters.

He asked this woman: 'Can I help you?'

'My husband and I just got back from Ankara,' the woman said.

'Yes?'

'We stayed in a hotel. They didn't have a stove. There was this iron thing on the wall that heated up the whole room.'

'Yes?'

'Could you not make us one of those things, so we don't have to lug coal every winter?'

'A radiator,' he said with a laugh. 'Sister, that was a radiator. It's hollow inside with warm water flowing through it. The warm water comes from a stove. A stove that has to be heated.'

'Oh.'

How was she to know that? For the first time ever, she saw an iron thing on the wall that heated up the room. She turned on her heel and left without a word.

'How I'd love to have made a radiator,' the blacksmith rounds off his story, every time.

This year, they've already moved into the summer house by the end of April. The days are warm and sunny, and at lunchtime many of the children play in the street, only a few of them going home for a break or something to eat. Melike sometimes goes home with Sezen, while Sibel sits in a corner of the forge and draws her father working, once she's finished her jobs. She knows she won't be able to concentrate in the evening. After dinner in the evenings, Melike and Gül will sit in front of their exercise books – the pneumatic lamp doesn't cast enough light; they can hardly read their own writing. Nalan will sing along to songs on the radio, Emin will grizzle, their mother will have Sibel do the dishes. Sometimes at lunchtime, Sibel will paint pictures for other girls who can't draw well but need something to show in art class. The teacher spotted the scam the first couple of times, but now Sibel paints the pictures so the teacher can't tell whose work they are.

It's Gül's final year, then she'll be done with primary school, but not even on some far-flung shore of her mind does she entertain the question: And then what?

What she does know is that she needs official photos for her leaving certificate. So she goes to her father at the forge one afternoon. She'd be happy to scratch his calves for him, but she knows that photographs cost a lot more, plus her father has lots to do today. She stands quietly in the doorway. Her father turns to her, briefly: 'What do you want?'

He knows she's not there to watch him.

'We'll be getting our leaving certificates soon,' Gül says, 'so we need photos. Can I have some money to get photos?'

'Yes,' her father says, 'just a tick.'

A minute later, her father is absorbed in his work again.

Gül doesn't budge. She waits. Five minutes, six, seven, ten, a quarter of an hour.

He doesn't want to give me the money, she thinks. Quietly, she turns around and goes, not knowing where she's off to. Soon she's on the small town's main street. Where will she get the money now? Maybe she could ask Melike to borrow it from Sezen. But how would she pay it back? She can't ask Auntie Hülya or her grandmother. Now she won't get a leaving certificate because she doesn't have the photos. She has cheap plastic shoes on her feet, plastic shoes and gaol socks. She doesn't have a cardigan like a lot of the other girls, and she can't even get the money for photos. Gül is gulping back her tears when she hears swift footsteps behind her.

'Stop.'

Gül turns around. Her father is standing in front of her, breathing hard.

'You're an ass,' he scolds. 'You need a proper hiding once in a while, then perhaps you'd learn some sense. Good God, Melike would've had the money ten times over in the time you were waiting. You've got to learn to open your mouth.'

'But I did,' Gül mumbles.

Her father is incensed, his breathing not slowing. People turn to see where the loud voice is coming from, then look away discreetly.

'Of course you can have the money, you nit. You've just got to open your mouth, understand? Otherwise you'll always miss out and then you'll kick yourself.'

He fishes a five lira note out of his pocket and holds it out to Gül. She shakes her head.

'Take the money.'

'I don't need any photos.'

'Take it,' her father says, and goes to slip her the note. Gül steps back and shakes her head again. The tears which had been sitting behind her eyes, and which she gulped down, have disappeared.

'Enough of this nonsense, my girl.'

Gül stares at the ground. Her father takes a step towards her and says: 'If you don't take this money now, you'll get such a whack with the back of my hand, you'll go deaf and blind for a week.'

Now she looks up, looks at him. She thinks she can see in his eyes that he's not going to hit her. She takes the money. He rests a hand on her hair, but Gül shrugs him off, and he turns around. Gül would like to just run away now, but she doesn't dare. She watches her father walk back to his workshop. She can't cry, she can't groan, she can't walk away, she just stands there. There's just so much – defiance, self-pity, anger, fear, love – she can't feel it all at once.

Gül would like it best if she could have her photograph taken with a bow in her hair, like all the other girls. It will be her first photo of just her and no one else, and she'd like it to be perfect, with a snow-white ribbon sitting just so in her hair. So Gül washes the ribbon, but her mother won't give her any starch; that's only for holidays and weddings, not for official photos for leaving certificates. So Gül uses sugar water, as her mother suggests, and while her bow is stiff once it's dried, it's brown around the edges from where the sugar has caramelised under the hot iron. Gül washes the bow again, and even though she's much more careful this time and the iron isn't as hot, she can still make out the brown edges.

'Don't make a fuss,' Arzu says. 'You won't be able to see it in the photo.'

She's right, too, but Gül doesn't believe her, and once the bow has been washed, starched and ironed another five times, it falls apart almost by itself. Gül spends the whole evening howling with rage, then the next day at school, she asks the girl who sits next to her, who wears a starched bow in her hair nearly every day, if she can borrow the bow at lunchtime to have her picture taken with it. It takes some effort, but she can't think of any other option. And so Gül wears Nebahat's bow in her hair for her leaving certificate. Decades later, whenever she sees the photo, she'll remember how the bow in her hair wasn't hers; it will always seem like a foreign body of sorts. As if everyone could tell at once that the bow was borrowed.

The photos will never appear on the certificate or the school's records. Gül will fail her final exams and her final year.

Her parents don't make a fuss of her failing. She's a girl, she can read and write – there are plenty who can't. The blacksmith can only read the old Arabic script and has no certificate himself; Arzu is illiterate.

Gül is annoyed that she's failed, but she simply couldn't study enough because she didn't have enough time. She knows she'll never be as good in class as Melike or Sibel, but if she'd studied more, the photos would have been stuck onto her leaving certificate. The photos disappear into her mother's trunk. The only person who really seems bothered is Uncle Abdurahman.

Abdurahman has another young village girl staying with him this year, Yasemin. She's about Gül's age, a dark, strong girl with bushy eyebrows and colourful clothes like Gypsies wear. She's a bit cheeky, interrupting adults in her rough dialect, and sometimes letting slip cursewords only ever heard from the mouths of men. Abdurahman wants to wean her off her bad manners. 'She'll be a young lady when she goes back to her village,' he says.

And he wants to make Gül understand that it's important to have a leaving certificate.

'My father doesn't have the money to send us all to middle school,' Gül says.

'If you can't go to middle school now, you can always go later,' Abdurahman says, 'when you've got money. You're a smart girl; you can do it. Would you like to start coming by once a week to study again?'

'Maybe,' Gül says, because she daren't say no.

She likes Uncle Abdurahman; he's always friendly to her, calls her *my little one*, makes time for her and sometimes runs his fingers through her hair. It strikes Gül that she wishes she were one of the girls from the village who spend the summer at his house. She would take care of the housework and cooking and the washing-up – it can't be that much work taking care of a bachelor.

Yasemin comes into the room where Abdurahman and Gül have been speaking. She glances at Gül for a moment. Yasemin has big dark eyes and never seems to blink. She asks Uncle Abdurahman: 'Is this the blacksmith's daughter?'

Just like that, as if Gül can't hear her.

'Yes,' says Abdurahman, 'this is Gül. Gül, this is Yasemin.'

Gül likes the dialect she speaks and is fascinated by the way Yasemin stands there with such confidence, how little shyness she seems to feel.

'Can you play beştaş?' Yasemin asks Gül and, without waiting for an answer, she says: 'Let's play a round.' 'You'll have to find your own stones to play,' she adds when Uncle Abdurahman is out of earshot, 'you can't touch mine.'

Gül goes and finds five good stones. The rules of the game say that the loser must hold out their hands at the end and receive a certain number of slaps. Yasemin slaps the backs of Gül's hands with unconcealed gusto.

'That's how you play it in town,' she says, laughing.

Gül tries not to let her see how much it hurts. Sometimes she loses to Sibel on purpose, to make her happy, but Sibel doesn't hit anywhere near as hard. She never wins against Melike – no one ever beats Melike in any game except hide-and-seek. Over the summer, Melike and Yasemin will go head to head for games of beştaş. They will both cheat and trick the other and fight, but in the end, it will almost always be Melike gleefully slapping Yasemin across the backs of her hands. Gül will be proud of her sister and she will also feel sorry for Yasemin, who will always keep a straight face.

'Why do you keep playing with her when you always lose?' asks Melike. 'It can't be any fun.'

Gül shrugs.

'I don't get it either,' Sibel says. 'I just won't play with Yasemin.'

Gül can't explain why it is. She can't explain the way everyone has something they're especially good at: Melike has sport, Sibel has painting, Nalan has singing, and they don't know what Emin's will be yet. Hers is bearing pain. And she often thinks that everyone must be able to, because she doesn't find it all that hard.

Gül and Yasemin become friends this summer. At first, Gül admires Yasemin's bravery and waywardness. When the others try to tease her because of her dialect, she simply lets fly a few cursewords, calls them biscuit brats and laughs. And she enjoys Gül's admiration.

But their relationship changes over the course of the summer. Yasemin turns quieter, more cautious, more withdrawn. Abdurahman's efforts to make a young lady of her seem to be bearing fruit. And the quieter Yasemin gets, the closer she and Gül seem to become. One day, when it's nearly time for the apple harvest, Yasemin lays her head in Gül's lap. It's the first time Yasemin forgets her pride and lets down her guard.

'I'll be happy to be back in the village soon,' Yasemin says.

'Are you homesick?'

'Yes… homesick.'

After a pause, Yasemin asks: 'Did Uncle Abdurahman teach you a lot?'

'Yes,' says Gül, 'he gave me lessons. He used to be a teacher.'

'I want to go home; I'd go today if I could,' Yasemin says.

Now that they've spent almost every day of the whole summer together, it hurts Gül that Yasemin wants to go back home to her village as soon as she can. A few days before school begins, she vanishes suddenly, without saying goodbye to Gül.

On the last evening of the holidays, Gül watches as Melike and Sibel pack their school bags. She watches her mother and then her father. No one says anything.

And the next morning, when Sibel and Melike have left the house, she simply watches the children walking into town in groups, big and small. She hears her mother making a start on the washing-up. Gül bangs the front door shut and shuffles into the kitchen.

They won't talk about the fact that Gül simply stays at home. She helps her mother, dawdles around in the garden, and is surprised by how quiet and lifeless everything is when the others are all at school. She's used to sitting alone in the garden, but all of a sudden, she no longer feels alone; she feels lonely.

A week, almost a week, passes in this way. It's Friday – the men have been to Friday prayers at the mosque at midday, and towards evening there is a knock at the blacksmith's door and Melike opens it. When Gül hears Uncle Abdurahman at the door, she quickly runs off. Without thinking, she runs straight into the room Uncle Abdurahman will soon be invited into. Where can she hide?

Gül opens the door to the cupboard; she can just about fit inside. If she pulls her knees up to her chest and rests her chin on her knees, she can, with a little effort, pull the door shut from the inside. Her mother sees her hide, but before she can ask what Gül's up to, Abdurahman is in the room, greeting Arzu.

'Is Timur home?' he asks.

'Yes,' she says, 'Melike, call your father from the stable.'

Inside the cupboard, Gül can hear Uncle Abdurahman walking around the room. She's scared he'll discover her, but then she hears her father's heavy footsteps. Timur and Abdurahman greet each other; Arzu goes to put the tea on; Melike, Sibel and Nalan come into the room. They like the man with the long beard who often gives them sweets. He doesn't seem to have any on him today.

'I hear your daughter's not going to school any more,' he says to the blacksmith, not lingering over pleasantries. He is old; he can be forgiven his directness.

Abdurahman speaks very loudly, as if he knows Gül is nearby and listening. Perhaps the blacksmith is nodding, but all Gül hears is Uncle Abdurahman pause, then continue: 'It's not too late; we can still send her to school. Little Sibel here managed it and she'd missed the first six weeks. And look at her now – she's the best in her class for most subjects. And Gül's a clever girl too, it's a shame she failed her final exams. She'll be sure to get a good mark on her leaving certificate this year. These things matter nowadays. Times are changing; soon everyone will have to go to middle school and even high school. There will be ever more young people wanting to learn and study. Times are changing, Blacksmith – the world is turning on its axis and our children will inherit it. And they ought to be well educated when they do so.'

'Blacksmith,' he says again, but it seems to Gül that he really means her.

'Yes,' Timur says, 'the world is turning; soon everyone in the town will have electricity – the world is turning, and you count up every penny and try to put something aside but in the end you have nothing worth anything.'

'Blacksmith, I'm talking about your daughter.'

'Yes, I see' he says, 'but we haven't forbidden her from going to school.'

'She doesn't need to be ashamed about repeating a year. Gül should finish school either way.'

Where is she anyway? – Why isn't he asking that question? Gül's arm hurts where she's holding the door shut. She hears the little melody of spoons on glass as the men stir sugar into their tea.

Abdurahman takes his time drinking his tea, discussing this and that with the blacksmith, but he doesn't forget to keep turning the conversation round to the idea that Gül must finish school.

Eventually, he pulls four small chocolate bars wrapped in silver paper out of his bag, gives one to each of the girls and gives the last one to Sibel, saying: 'This is for your sister.'

Gül's knees ache, her arm's gone dead, her back hurts – she listens for the sound of fading footsteps. But before she knows if she can come out or not, her father says: 'Come out of there now, Gül.'

They didn't say anything, Gül thinks, as she opens the cupboard door. Neither her father nor her mother. One word, one word would have been enough, and she would have stood before Uncle Abdurahman and promised to be back at school on Monday. So they don't want her to. They don't want her to finish school. She will stay at home.

When they finally move back to the town house at the end of September, Gül finds being at home very boring. She can no longer sit in the garden, underneath apricot trees or by the well. Now she gets up with everyone else in the morning, helps her mother make breakfast, says goodbye to her sisters, washes dishes, helps prepare lunch. Once all her chores are done, she plays with Nalan and Emin; sometimes her mother goes out to visit a friend or a neighbour and leaves Gül at home alone with her brother and sister.

It's boring but Gül isn't unhappy. It's her mother who seems to be upset, often irritated and snapping at Gül over nothing. Perhaps there are too many children under her feet all the time, or perhaps there are other reasons. Whatever the case, one evening she says to her husband: 'She shouldn't be sitting at home doing nothing and getting used to idling around. She should be making better use of her time. We could send her to the dressmaker so she learns something useful.'

A week later, Timur takes Gül along to the dressmaker in the morning. Esra is about 10 years older than Gül and has a workroom at home. Lots of women come to her for fittings of dresses, şalvars, blouses. Esra sews wedding dresses and underwear, and she also takes up or lets out men's trousers if their wives bring them in. Men's clothing isn't really her territory. How would a decent woman measure up a grown man? She'd have to touch him everywhere.

The workroom is strewn with scraps of fabric, patterns, unfinished pieces of clothing, spools of thread and bobbins, pin cushions, measuring tapes, fabric chalk, safety pins, scissors.

'Hello,' Esra says, 'you must be Gül.'

Gül gives a shy nod.

'Don't be scared. I'll be like a sister to you; we'll get on just fine.'

'I'll be getting along then,' Timur says, strangely stiff in the presence of this young woman. He puts on his hat and is gone.

Esra sits back down at the foot-powered sewing machine but makes no move to start work yet.

'So you'll be my little assistant,' she says to Gül.

She has a round face with a scattering of freckles and very full but pale lips. Her hazel eyes look almost piercing at first glance. Gül thinks Esra is beautiful.

'Come,' says Esra, getting up and holding her hand out to Gül. 'Come, let me introduce you to Candan first of all.'

The two of them go into the next room, where a girl of about two is lying on a small mattress, asleep.

'She's a bit sick,' Esra says. 'My little lamb's poorly. But now she's got you as her abla to take care of her, hasn't she?'

Gül smiles for the first time, and Esra says: 'And now I'll show you everything else.'

Within three days, the sewing room is transformed. The fabrics are neatly folded and piled, the unused measuring tapes rolled up, the spools of thread in an old tin, arranged by colour, as are the pins in the pin cushion. Gül takes pleasure in finding a place for everything and never having to look for long when Esra needs something.

It's a little bit like going to school. Gül leaves the house soon after her sisters, goes home for lunch, plays for a while and then goes back to Esra's. Sometimes she dawdles along the way, looking at stones that might have money underneath them, or watching the slightly richer women strolling to the high street to go shopping or eat gateau at the patisserie. Gateau – Melike ate it once at Sezen's house, but Gül only knows it by name. Gateau, the epitome of luxury; something eaten by women who wear furs in winter. Gül watches the ladies strolling along in their high-heeled shoes, their hair artfully pinned and draped; she watches these women who have seen Brigitte Bardot, Elizabeth Taylor and Marilyn Monroe at the cinema but can't lead their idols' swinging lives in this country. And she notices the young men with brilliantined hair watching those women too, watching while pretending to lounge on street corners and smoke cigarettes. The young men who already have moustaches – some thin and peachy like her Uncle Fuat's; some bushy, black and walrus-like. The young men whose marbled plastic combs stick out of their back pockets, whose eyes flash with furtive desire.

Esra doesn't say a word if Gül turns up a little late now and then. It's better than school, where she always had to be on time. While Esra teaches Gül to sew, she doesn't hold back on praise and she never gets impatient if something doesn't work out right. In the evenings, Gül now often sits by the light of the pneumatic lamp with her mother's huge rusty scissors and snips newspapers into shapes that look like the patterns once scattered around at Esra Abla's place and now neatly stacked in cardboard boxes. Esra Abla, Gül calls her – Big Sister Esra. She calls her that because Esra wants her to, because she feels old if people call her Auntie Esra. At last, Gül has someone to call abla, like her sisters call her.

Even though Gül doesn't often see people reading them, newspapers are everywhere she looks. The grocer wraps things up in newspaper and so does the butcher, and Timur uses it sometimes to stoke up the fire at the forge in the morning. Arzu lines the cupboards with it. When Gül fetches something out of the cupboard, a word or two occasionally catches her eye – MURDER, MANSLAUGHTER, UNREQUITED LOVE, BLOOD FEUD, INNOCENT CHILDREN – and then Gül immerses herself in the newspaper articles, moves the glasses carefully back and forth, lifts up the plates, almost crawling into the cupboard if the print is upside-down, and having to hold her head to one side, so she can put the unfamiliar-looking letters together to make words.

She no longer bumps her head when her mother calls her. It happened a few times, but now she's learned to remember the place where she stopped, and simply goes on reading later.

Sibel cuts the white margins off the newspapers and uses the thin strips to draw miniature animals. Arzu tells her off; it'll ruin her eyes, she says. But there's never enough paper, and she has to use her few coloured pencils sparingly. Until Uncle Abdurahman notices how talented she is. From then on, he buys her pencils and paper, so she doesn't draw on both sides of each sheet any more.

That also means Gül has the newspapers to herself again, and now she sits there in the evenings, scissors in hand, and sometimes half an hour passes before she makes the first cut. Her schoolbooks were never this thrilling.

'Cut if you're going to cut,' her mother often says. 'Why are you reading the newspaper like a grown man?'

Gül barely sees anyone but Uncle Abdurahman reading the newspaper in public, and she's never seen a woman doing it.

When her mother tells her off like that, she starts cutting, the sound of the scissors enough to make her mother look elsewhere; and Gül tries to go on reading as she cuts along the edges of the stories. She reads articles about brothers killing brothers, family honour, about babies with two heads and the spoilt children of the rich – the editorials and pieces about business, politics and football, she cuts up unread.

The first time Gül sits down at the sewing machine and tries to glide two pieces of fabric under the needle at the same time, she can barely reach the pedal, which she has to push evenly up and down to make the machine run smoothly. It's even harder for her to coordinate the movements of her hands and feet. She takes a long time to learn it, longer than someone else would probably take. It will take months before she coaxes the same calm purr out of the machine as Esra does. Yet she will often think back to that first day. She will remember it years later, sitting at an electric sewing machine in Germany and sewing bras, paid by the piece; 400 to 450 a day, while her workmates rarely manage more than 350.

It will take a while to master Esra's machine but sewing will bring her joy. And she will still feel a gentle echo of that joy even when she's sitting in a room with 70 other women, with toilet paper stuffed in her ears to block out the terrible din.

'I'm not afraid of hard work,' she'll always say later. 'I've learned that I can load any pile of work onto my shoulders without collapsing underneath it.' But she won't say how offended she can get when no one values that hard work.

At the moment, she's not only helping her mother with the housework, learning to sew and looking after Nalan and Emin, but also taking care of Esra's daughter Candan.

Candan is besotted with Gül, and Gül sometimes buys her sesame rings or sweets with the money she gets from her father for scratching his calves. She hopes Nalan and Emin never find out. She loves her brother and sisters, of course, but she loves

Candan differently. The way you can only love people who aren't as close to you.

Even now, the few kuruş her father gives her for the calf-scratching is the only money she gets. She doesn't get paid for working with the dressmaker. Learning the trade is payment enough.

The same goes for her Uncle Fuat, who works for a hairdresser and wants to open his own barbershop one day. Gül can't even dream about that kind of thing, but perhaps she'll marry a man who'll buy her a sewing machine.

One Saturday, once she's dusted both rooms, washed nappies and done the dishes, Gül says to her mother: 'I'm going to Esra Abla's.'

'But it's Saturday.'

'I miss Candan so much, I'll just play with her for a bit and then come straight back.'

'Good God,' her mother says. 'As if there weren't enough other children to play with around here.'

But she lets Gül go, that Saturday and the one after too. Every time they see each other, Candan runs into Gül's open arms, and sometimes Gül imagines she's her own daughter. But where would the matching husband be?

She doesn't want a husband, really; all she wants is a daughter. Gül is always in a great mood when she's played with Candan. She feels good and thinks it must be to do with Esra Abla's daughter. And nothing to do with not being at home, no one giving her chores, not having to do heavy lifting or break up arguments.

One day, Melike and Nalan gang up on Sibel. They copy everything she does, follow her around, imitate her every move – and when Sibel sits down in a corner to draw, always her way of escaping, Nalan and Melike don't know what to do for a moment, until Melike starts chanting: 'Picasso, Picasso, Mona Lisa!' Nalan joins in, and they repeat the words over and over until Sibel bursts into tears.

'Leave her alone, please. If you love your God, leave her in peace,' Gül says.

She says it the way her mother and the neighbourhood women always say it: *If you love your God, you won't do that to me. If you do that, you'll end up sitting vigil over my dead body. Eat a bite or two, for the love of me, for the love of God, for fear of my death.* The grownups' language is full of exaggerations which the children like to adopt.

But Gül can't stop her sisters from teasing Sibel, who eventually exclaims in a thin, tear-choked voice: 'You two are *always* against Gül and me, just because you have a different mother.'

Nalan doesn't understand what Sibel means, and Melike just laughs at her. Gül puts her arms around Sibel to console her. Once the tears are flowing more slowly, she tries to explain to her eight-year-old sister how they are related to each other.

'You've got that wrong, my treasure. Melike, you and me – we have a different mother to the others. You were very little when she died, you were still a baby.'

Sibel stops crying. The tears have left pale streaks down her face.

'After our mother died, father married again and we got a new mother, and then came Nalan and Emin.'

'She's not our real mother?'

'No, she's our stepmother.'

'And how can you tell the difference?'

Gül needs a moment before she answers: 'You can't.'

'So how do you know she's not our real mother?'

'I… I was bigger when our mother died.'

'What did our mother look like?'

'A bit like Melike. Her skin wasn't as pale as yours or mine; she was dark like Melike, and she had beautiful eyes.'

The moment she says it, she can't help thinking of the circles beneath her eyes; the deep violet circles underneath her eyes when she was in hospital.

'And her hair, what did her hair look like?'

Over the next few days, Sibel and Gül huddle together a lot. Gül tells her sister what she still remembers. Dresses all the images in her head in words for the first time. And Melike soon joins them and listens, not interrupting. Gül remembers the village, their father's rifles, the fight in the village square, how her mother said, *Now you've tickled me to death*, the hospital, Auntie Hülya and Uncle Yücel.

The pictures are as clear and sharp in her head as if it had all happened only yesterday. She sees her father throwing the spoon, and she feels what she felt then. She doesn't see the images as she saw them; she sees everything as if from above; she sees herself standing there, but she feels what she felt then.

She cries as she tells her stories. Even in 50 years' time, she will still see those images in sharp focus, but she will live through those feelings again and again; unlike the images, she won't be able to examine the feelings with any detachment.

It soon becomes a ritual for Sibel, Melike and Gül to huddle together as Gül tells stories of Fatma and the old days. It becomes a ritual they practise often over the next few years. Yet Gül will always keep the story to herself about when Timur very nearly threw Melike off the roof of the stable.

So Gül plays with Candan on Saturdays and thinks her good mood is all down to Esra's daughter. Sometimes on the way home, when she sees some girls of her age skipping or playing hopscotch outside in the cold on a patch they've cleared of snow, Gül asks if she can join in. Though she's usually shy, on Saturdays she finds it easy to ask, and she quickly loses track of time as she's playing, loses track of the weather, her sisters, her father, her mother, and she forgets Candan too, ruining her shoes playing hopscotch.

When she's late home again after forgetting lunch one Saturday, her mother says: 'Why do you spend all week long with strangers? You must be a burden on them.'

And even her father says: 'You shouldn't go there so often. I'll come and pick you up so you're not so late next time.'

And so the blacksmith picks his daughter up from Esra's house the next Saturday. He's wearing his good shoes and he's shaved, even though he doesn't usually bother at weekends. The week after that, he blows on his hands as he stands in the doorway. It's a gesture Gül has never seen her father make before.

'It's cold outside,' the blacksmith says.

Esra agrees: 'It certainly is, the Lord has sent us a hard winter.'

'Do you want to run ahead?' Timur asks his daughter. 'Your mother's making bÖrek today; I'm sure she could use your help.'

'Oh, I'm sure she doesn't want to,' Esra butts in before Gül has a chance to answer. 'She was so looking forward to walking home with her father today.'

Her father only picks her up this one time, and Gül plays hopscotch plenty more times that winter with the girls on the street. She soon finds out why they play outside; it's no warmer inside their houses than it is out in the cold. When Arzu finds out about it at the end of the winter, she won't let Gül go to Esra's at all on Saturdays.

'What will people say if they see you playing with poor children?'

The first piece of clothing Gül makes at the sewing machine is a pair of knickers made from a leftover piece of brown fabric with orange flowers. Gül sews a pair of knickers for Melike, but she doesn't take them home straight away because she wants to sew a pair for each of her sisters.

Come spring, she's managed it. She has four pairs of knickers and is pleased with her gifts for her sisters. When her mother sees the pants; one brown pair with flowers, one purple, one lemon-yellow and one frog-green with blue drops, she says: 'Who's going to want to wear them? Those are Gypsy colours.'

Gül, Sibel, Nalan and Melike are standing there – Sibel and Nalan are holding their knickers, Melike's are on the floor. But before the tears can prick Gül's eyes, before anything happens, Melike says: 'But you wear them underneath your clothes. No one's going to see them. I'm wearing mine anyway, no one's going to stop me.'

And so in springtime, the sisters wear their knickers, which blaze with colours no one can see. One day, Melike and Sibel come to Gül, giggling, and say: 'Nene can't see any more.'

'Her eyes aren't too good these days,' Gül says.

'No,' Melike says, 'she can't see at all.'

'How do you know?'

'I sat down, really rudely; I had my legs open and Sibel did too, and you could see our bright knickers under our skirts. And Nene didn't see them; she couldn't even tell how rudely we were sitting.'

Zeliha can identify the money she has in her hand; she can tell notes and coins apart by their size. She can tell who's who by the sound of their footsteps, but she can hardly see any more. If her daughter didn't live with her, she'd have trouble going about her day. Hülya does everything that requires a good pair of eyes, and Zeliha spends her time sitting cross-legged, her back supported by a big, hard cushion. She orders people around, with a glass of tea in one hand and a cigarette in the other: *Open the window, shut the window, put the kettle on, bring me a glass of water, give me a light, buy some cigarettes from the grocer's.* There's always something Gül has to do when she's there, but the situation is no different for her sisters and her mother. Zeliha seems to take pleasure in giving orders to as many different people as possible.

Her grandchildren find her even scarier now that she's blind and moves so little. Since her sight has gone, her voice has got deeper too; she smokes more now that she has less to do. Gül doesn't like her heavy odour, her smell of smoke and old sweat, of tar and a little of well-fingered money, which she carries in a wad in her sock.

Zeliha gets money from Timur and has Hülya do a little business here and there, selling a few walnuts, half a kilo of köfter, homemade jam, a few old copper pots. The woman never went to school, but she can count well; she remembers prices and profit margins; she lends money to earn a little interest, and Hülya is amazed her mother always knows exactly who owes her what.

Sometimes, Zeliha will take out her wad of money and count it slowly, deliberately, a cigarette in the corner of her mouth, her eyes fixed ahead and a faint smile on her wrinkled lips. The years have dug great furrows in her face, deep furrows – a dark, vertical line just above her eyebrows, two lines which run down from her nostrils to the corners of her mouth, and her cheeks are scored with countless wrinkles.

Gül's other grandmother, Berrin, is much younger and has an almost smooth, round face. But their mother usually only takes Emin and Nalan to see Berrin Nene. Gül never feels quite at ease there, though Berrin Nene is friendly and laughs a lot. There are too many people there for her – her grandfather Faruk, who often reeks of spirits; her Uncle Fuat; Fuat's older brothers Levent and Orhan, who are already married. Her grandparents have a big house, and Gül feels strange among so many people who know each other so well. And who rarely pay her much attention.

Melike has a leaving certificate. In her official photo, she's wearing Sezen's bow in her hair; a big looping bow, so stiff with starch it almost cracks when you look at it. Melike isn't an especially good student, but she's never had to repeat a year and she's good at learning by rote. A few days before her exams, she annoys everyone with her revision. She takes her book and reads it while walking around. She has to walk all around the house; she can't sit still and do it. With the book open in her hands, she walks through the rooms murmuring to herself. Or at least she seems to, from the way she moves her lips and nods her head at odd moments. Her approach will change with time, but Melike will succeed at school not because she understands, but because she learns by heart.

She learns the material by heart until she knows which word comes at the end of each page. Then, each time, she motions slightly with her head, moving it from right to left, turning the page in her mind.

Just as they don't talk about the fact that Gül has stopped going to school, it's now clear that Melike will go to middle school after the holidays.

Gül doesn't go to Esra's while they're at the summer house, and so the long summer spreads out ahead of her; a carefree summer stealing cherries, playing beştaş, hide-and-seek, tag and – towards evening when it's cooler – dodgeball. Dodgeball is a game for older children that takes up the whole breadth of the dirt street, but by now Gül is allowed to join in. And Melike is allowed to play too, but only because she's so good, and everyone scrambles to have the scrappy little girl on their team.

When Melike's side loses, she sulks and blames her teammates. She's a sore loser and quick to pick a fight; all her energy has to go somewhere, her anger and her disappointment, her ambition unsatisfied.

At dusk, people usually sit on their front steps and listen to the radio, the sound from the loudspeakers on the blacksmith's roof. They listen and chat, the women knit or crochet, and sometimes the men sit in the garden, the sad songs on the radio just an echo, a hum in the air they fill with lungfuls of old smoke and the aniseed scent of their breath. They sit there with their legs crossed, talking about the old days, when people were wiser, they say, less greedy. When they talk of their elders, their ways and their quirks, of strength and pride, of brave highwaymen in the mountains, of rebellion and heroism, they feel the magic which makes the past into a land of legend. The men sit side by side and they know the words to the songs of the old gods.

It's a summer of grazed knees, of thirst turning the spit to wool in their mouths; a summer where Gül is caught scrumping pears, but the owner of the garden lets her run away when he recognises her: 'Gül, it's you! Run, run along after the others, and here, have a pear. And say hello to your father from me.'

Emin can walk now. He can run, turn somersaults, and he's already trying to climb trees. Only talking seems to elude him. By the end of the summer, he is one and a half, but he only makes a sound when he cries. Nalan, on the other hand, talks all day long, and when she's not talking, she sings. She sings the songs she knows from the radio, and her voice is so beautiful that some of the neighbours, the older girls, often gather round and promise her a sweet or some chewing gum if she'll sing for them.

Since Gül, Melike and Sibel have started huddling together now and then, Gül has stopped feeling sad whenever they talk about the past. Instead, it's Timur who feels his eyes shine when he sees his daughters sitting together: *Thanks be to God, thanks be to God for letting me see this, thanks be to Him though he granted Fatma her eternal rest so early. Fatma, who was as beautiful as a piece of the moon.*

Though he often thinks of Fatma, he has to admit that he thinks of her less often in recent years. But if an angel of the Almighty came down and asked him: *Timur, Timur the Blacksmith, would you give up Arzu to get Fatma back?* He would say yes. And if the angel of the Almighty asked: *Timur, are you happy? Do you praise God? Are you thankful for this life with its joys and sorrows and hardships?* He would answer yes with the same sincerity.

Praise be to the God of the Heavens, he has five healthy children, he has a wife, he'll have strength in his arms and his back for a good while yet. He is still a man who few are happy to cross, because he knows how to use his fists – yet this fair-skinned man with the blue eyes still gets scammed because he's trusting and doesn't know how to keep money from slipping through his strong fingers. He no longer lends to everyone who wants to borrow from him – just to anyone who softens his heart. And that heart's not much harder than freshly baked bread.

The sunny days pass like this: Gül washes the laundry, sweeps the house, looks after Nalan and Emin; they go to the hamam, in summer too; and Uncle Abdurahman still sometimes says that Gül could have finished school. Gül thinks often of Candan, but the two of them see each other just four times in the 18 weeks the blacksmith's family spend at the summer house. When they bump into each other at the hamam, Gül notices that her mother greets Esra only briefly, then ignores her completely. Gül would like to soap Esra Abla's back, but she senses her mother wouldn't like it, though she can't explain quite why. She just plays with Candan, lets her spray her with cold water till she squeals and is glad when the little one laughs.

It's an easy summer for Gül, a carefree summer, even if she doesn't know it yet. She's got used to its struggles and can enjoy its pleasures. It's a long, hot summer, and by the end of August the branches on the apple trees threaten to break under the weight of the fruit. Timur supports the heaviest branches with forked sticks, driving the tips into the ground. He may have been to slow to hire harvest workers, but the trees bear such a remarkable number of apples that, come harvest time, day labourers need no encouragement to knock at the blacksmith's door.

When it's time at last, everyone pitches in: Arzu, Gül, Melike, Sibel, Auntie Hülya and four hired labourers. It takes five days to harvest all the apples. And since they're the first to sell their apples, they get a good price. Once Timur has paid the workers, there's still plenty of money left over, much more than in previous years. In the evenings, Timur sits there, exhausted, a cushion at his back, his legs stretched out in front of him, and he'd like to smoke a cigarette to chase the tiredness from his limbs. He wonders how many days he should rest before going to Istanbul.

Gül wants to scratch his calves, but he's so worn out, his legs don't itch. Gül stays with him a little longer, she's tired too.

'Daddy?'

'Yes, my treasure.'

'Can you pay me too?'

'What?'

'Like the workers.'

'Like the workers? You're my daughter, you're not a worker. You're the light of my eyes, you're not a day labourer.'

There's so much Gül could say in reply, but she just goes to the room where she sleeps with her sisters, disappointed; she wants to go to bed earlier tonight. Once she has lain down, her mother comes into the room and sits by the head of her mattress.

'Tired?' she asks.

'Yes,' Gül says.

'You'll sleep so well, you'll feel reborn in the morning… Gül, I want to ask you a favour.'

Arzu never uses her first name, except when she calls her.

'Your father listens to you. He can't deny you anything. I would so love a fur coat for the winter. Like the general's wife. It's bound to be a hard winter after a summer like this. Could you ask him?'

'Yes.'

'A beautiful coat, just like the one Neslihan has. Shall I bring you some more milk? I've just milked the cow.'

Gül shakes her head, though she'd like to drink milk that's still warm from the cow's udders.

I raised her, Arzu might think, *I clothed her and fed her, I've looked after her and her sisters seven days a week. I did everything I could to please their father, but I've never been able to replace his first wife. I even gave him a son, and she didn't. I treated the children like my own daughters, as well as I could, I'm only 13 years older than Gül, I did my best. I've never refused the man, but have I ever once got what I wanted?*

It takes Gül a long time to fall asleep. She'd like to buy the fabric she saw in town, dark blue fabric that shimmers like velvet. She'd like to sew a dress from it. A proper, fancy dress, just for her. Like the one Özlem has. Or the daughters of the women who go to the patisserie. She'd love a midnight blue dress and a bow in her hair, a bow stiffened with starch. She'd like shoes to go with it, with small silver buckles, but she won't be able to buy them. She could sew the dress herself, though. If she had the money for the fabric. She worked just like all the others.

I won't ask him, she thinks, *I won't ask him for a fur coat for Mum. I'll just tell her I did. Even if she asked him herself, he probably wouldn't buy her it. Why should she get a fur coat when I don't even get the money for fabric?*

But if she doesn't ask her father, she'll have to lie. Like Özlem did that time, like Özlem and her grandmother. And she can't lie. She gets all hot and she always thinks everyone can see her sweating.

But it wouldn't be a proper lie. It would only be fair. It would be fair if both of them got nothing.

Let others do as they will, we don't do that sort of thing. Those were her mother's words. *We don't lie and we don't cheat. We are honest, even if it comes at a cost. We'll always have our integrity.* But this time, Gül would rather have a dress.

Five weeks later they're back in the town house; Arzu has a black fur coat that goes down past her knees, and the blacksmith hasn't been to Istanbul.

'What on earth does she need a fur coat for?' Timur said, and Gül answered: 'But she wants one so badly. I bet she'd be really happy.'

Arzu was happy, and she has promised to take Gül to the patisserie for gateau. As soon as it gets cold. Gül has never tried gateau and she'd really like to. If only she had something to wear to the patisserie.

Every day now, she eyes the leftover fabric at Esra's and wonders how to sew a dress out of the scraps. Esra, who notices her searching look, asks: 'What would you like to sew for yourself, then?'

'Nothing,' Gül says, 'I'm just seeing what's left over.'

'Maybe a dress?' Esra guesses.

For a moment, Gül feels caught out, but in the blink of an eye she answers: 'No, no, not a dress.'

More than a week later, Gül is tidying up the sewing room while Candan whines to her mother, wanting to go outside. Esra has a lot to do but she seems to give in to her daughter, and asks Gül: 'Shall we go shopping?'

'You go,' Gül says. 'I'll finish cleaning up.'

'Let's go together. Come on, sweetie, get your coat on.'

Gül doesn't know quite what to think. Esra has never taken her along on a shopping trip.

Esra walks slightly ahead as Gül carries Candan, her little head bedded on Gül's shoulder. The sun is shining, the sky is clear, but it's cold, the leaves already swept off the streets, and Gül wonders whether her father would leave Nalan alone if he took his younger daughter along to sweep leaves.

'Let Candan walk on her own,' Esra says for the second time. But although it's hard for Gül to carry the little girl for so long, she doesn't put her down.

A boy is walking towards them. Gül stops in her tracks when she recognises him. He stops too; they're three or four steps apart. Gül notices the peachfuzz on his upper lip. For an instant she's afraid, scared she might fall into his blue eyes. Her heart beats very fast, but she can't move a muscle.

'Hello,' Recep says, but Gül can't answer.

What is he doing here in town? How long has it been since she last saw him? Why can't she be glad and simply talk to him? And why is she lowering her eyes now?

'Gül!' she hears Esra calling; she's stopped and turned around.

Not looking Recep in the eye again, Gül walks past him. She doesn't run; she walks as fast as she can, carrying Candan. She notices Recep watching her pass. Perhaps he smiles.

Once they've turned the next corner, Esra asks: 'Do you know him?'

Gül doesn't answer.

'Gül,' Esra stops to say, 'you're a young woman now. It's not proper to look at men in the street. I won't tell anyone, but do you know what your father would do if he heard you exchanged glances with a young man in the middle of the high street? Do you know what people would say then?'

'Yes, I know.'

They don't say another word the rest of the way. Gül can't think. All she can do is feel like she's made a mistake. Like she's made a wrong decision, resulting in an empty space. Like an invisible person who had always been by her side were suddenly gone.

Esra slows her pace and eventually stops outside the haberdasher's, wavering. She knows the desire in the blacksmith's gaze, but she might be surprised to spot a similar longing in Gül's eyes. Perhaps Gül might get into trouble if she has a nice dress on top of that.

She says: 'I've forgotten my purse.'

'They'll give us credit, won't they?'

'Yes, they might… But… No, no, not today.'

Gül looks past Esra into the shop. The shopkeeper has got up from his chair and come to the door: 'Hello, how can I help you three ladies?'

Perhaps Gül is imagining it, but she can see the midnight blue fabric glinting on the shelf. It seems to be calling her.

'What's the matter, Esra, aren't you coming in?' the shopkeeper asks.

'No. No, thank you, Uncle Serdar, not today.'

'Hang on a tick.'

The man goes to the counter and comes back with two walnuts. One for Candan and one for Gül. They both say thank you. On the way back, Gül holds Candan by the hand and walks a little way behind Esra again. They don't run into Recep again.

For the rest of the day, Gül is conspicuously quiet; Esra sometimes smiles to herself and sometimes shakes her head in the middle of her work. Gül knows it wasn't right to stop, but she was so glad to see Recep again. She almost felt like hugging him. How he's changed! His hair is no longer shorn off, and even though there was no brilliantine in it, she'd bet he had a marbled comb in his back pocket. His scruffy jacket was a bit too small for him; he must have been cold. But he is tall too, almost as tall as her father. His eyebrows have grown thicker, his nose more pronounced, and his eyes seem to sparkle even more brightly than before.

He didn't look like someone from the village who herds cows, he wasn't wearing baggy trousers or plastic shoes; he was wearing suit trousers, and everything about him looked like he came from town. Had he been here a while, perhaps? Would she see him again? And if she did, what should she say? She couldn't just stand there speechless again, not even returning his greeting. She'd have to say something. But what?

Esra is right, though. She can't talk to young men in the street, she's too old for that now. So it's better if she doesn't meet him again. She hopes today was just a coincidence. And she also hopes they'll run into each other again. She won't speak to him and she won't stop either, she'll just lower her eyes and walk on by.

She'd so like to see him again. Just see him, just for an instant; that would be enough. It was so short today, it was just like a dream today.

Over the next few days, she keeps her eyes peeled in the mornings when she goes to Esra's, on her way home for lunch, then on her walk back to Esra's, and one last time as she walks home again at dusk.

She doesn't dawdle now, takes no unnecessary diversions. She's scared of seeing Recep again. She's scared because she doesn't know what to do if she did, and she's scared someone might see them and tell her father.

The days go by, turning to weeks, and after a while Gül's heart no longer thuds when she sees someone in the distance with a passing resemblance to Recep. It seems to get a little colder every morning, and by the time the nights are ten degrees below freezing Gül almost never thinks of Recep. Neither on the way to Esra's nor on her way home, nor in the evenings in the heated room, where Melike tells them how Sezen buys chestnuts for the two of them almost every morning to warm their hands on the way to school. They tug the sleeves of their jackets right down and clutch the chestnuts with them, so they don't burn their palms. Even though Sezen's parents have plenty of money, there are no small gloves to be had in the shops, and who wants to be the only girl with hand-knitted gloves. Gloves are something you get when you're grown up.

Recep isn't wearing gloves either when Gül meets him again one morning. He's suddenly there; he must have just turned the corner, and now he's standing right in front of her. Gül looks at him, her heart not thudding, not showing the slightest sign of excitement, stiff as a board. Recep holds his hand out to her, a little awkward. At first, all Gül sees is his pale fingers, the black lines under his nails, the cracks and creases. Only then does she notice the envelope he's holding between his index and middle fingers. She still can't move.

'Here, take it,' Recep says, and Gül hesistantly reaches out her hand. As soon as she's taken the letter, Recep turns around and runs off.

Only now can she move again, and she looks around to see if anyone was watching. As she hastily slips the letter underneath her vest, she feels the cold of the paper, though it soon warms up.

Perhaps this wasn't the first time Recep followed her? The thought makes her heart beat faster; she feels warm. Warmer than Melike could ever get from her chestnuts. Slowly, very slowly, she puts one foot in front of the other. She might fly if it was only joy she felt. But there's the fear too, there's confusion and amazement, there's excitement, and there are questions heavier than the big hammer at the forge. Is this the feeling they sometimes sing about on the radio? The feeling that makes people write lines full of sorrow. *I gathered your tears in my pocket and cried them all, one by one. Death is the Lord's command, if only needn't part. You've left but I'm still standing, not falling to my knees. Since he's been gone, even the air I breathe tastes sour.* How can she hide it, this feeling? And this letter?

Gül moves very carefully all morning long so that the crackling underneath her jumper doesn't give her away. She doesn't dare go out to the cold outside toilet with the letter; she doesn't have the guts. Esra told her not to talk to young men on the street. What would she do if she found out Gül accepted a letter from one?

It doesn't occur to Gül that she could simply feign a tummy ache and leave early, leave early and find a quiet spot. Gül waits until Esra sends her home, but waiting is not quite the right word. She endures, simply endures the hours.

The first steps after leaving Esra's house, she manages a normal pace, but then she starts running. She runs without stopping once, all the way to the stream on the edge of town, just before the first summer houses. There, she squats down breathlessly, the paper clammy with her cold sweat. Her hands trembling, she pulls out the letter. Running through the icy air has brought tears to her eyes. She opens the envelope carefully, and when she sees the sheet of paper with pencilled writing, the letters blur before her eyes. Even when she's wiped the tears away, she can't read. Her gaze flits across the lines, can't find a resting place, can't anchor itself to any word. It's as though language were not a river but a maelstrom, only single words flashing up: *you, your, saw, very, longing, beauty, then, always.*

Gül can't find the calm to connect the words, and the longer she can't find calm, the greater her fear grows of being discovered. And what if someone finds the letter? Where could she hide it? Nowhere. And she can't read it either; her hands are trembling harder and harder, her fear growing, and then a twig snaps. She hears footsteps.

She scrunches up the letter and throws it in the water. The stream carries the words away.

When she turns cautiously around, she sees two little boys clutching boats folded out of newspaper. The boats will follow the letter downstream any moment now.

The next day, Gül stays in bed with a fever, and once again the ceiling bears down towards her, and in her fever dreams she sees leeches and the newspapers with which her mother lines the cupboards. They turn into letters, the newspapers all turn into letters written to her, and she is frantic because she knows she'll be found out.

For almost a week, Gül keeps waking from her feverish imaginings with a scream. Sometimes she sees her father standing by a bend in the water, and he fishes the letter out from between two stones like she found his watch on the bed of the stream.

'Gül, is this letter for you?' he asks, and Gül shakes her head as fast as she can, but her mouth simply says: 'Yes, yes, Recep wrote it to me.'

Timur likes going to the cinema to see double bills of Turkish or foreign films; a romance and an adventure film, a drama and a western – it almost doesn't matter what they show. It's a treat, but not as much as going to Istanbul; drinking, listening to the beautiful singers and cheering on the footballers. The blacksmith likes sitting motionless in the pleasant darkness of the cinema, soaking up the film music and the actors' voices. It lets him forget his day. His cares, his work, his itchy calves, his lost wife, his assistant's mistakes, the heat of the fire in the forge, his favourite cow – all of it vanishes and he grows blissfully tired. He usually nods off, enjoying the feeling of abandoning himself to the heaviness. It's not like slipping into sleep in bed; sleeping in the cinema is far sweeter.

When he starts to snore, which happens regularly, or when his head droops onto one shoulder, he wakes with a start. Then he gets up and goes for a stroll so as not to bother the other cinemagoers with his snoring. The streets are empty at this time of night, and Timur pulls on his hat, puts his hands in his pockets and saunters through the darkness, savouring the silence and the stars. Then he goes back, but he usually nods off again not much later and gets up for another walk. Timur likes going to the cinema, but not for the films. Even the ones he sees all the way through, he usually forgets by the next day.

Not so for his daughters, who will remember some films for as long as they live. It's like the radio, only with pictures, he explained to Gül and Melike the first time he took them along. But cinema surpassed Gül's imagination. Radio with pictures, but her father never said it would get as dark as inside a stable. Nor that you watched people shouting at each other, or sitting alone in a room and crying, and that you were right there but couldn't do anything about it. Nor did her father tell her that he'd fall asleep and then go outside, leaving her alone with her sister in the big auditorium. Gül put her arm around Melike, not to protect her but to feel that someone was still there, close to her.

Later, she remembered the laughing face, the face of an elderly woman who'd come up with some plan, something Gül didn't get. The laugh was an evil laugh, a laugh meant to scare you. But not for weeks on end.

Melike seemed to be less afraid, though she'd been grateful for Gül putting her arm around her on their first trip.

Melike likes films; they're another world that she can live in. Later, she will begin to write down the films she's watched in a notepad, keeping a film diary. She might change things here and there, making a rich man even richer or inventing an act of selflessness for one of the baddies, giving a woman another daughter or taking a girl's toy away. But for three years, she will write down all the films she watches, and she'll dream of one day being in Istanbul too, in Rome or in New York. One day, she too will live in a big city; she'll be rich and have her hair done just like the women in the films. Her film book is a diary like any other, meant to record her life because she's yearning for something.

Sibel has nightmares after her first trips to the cinema, but she still goes back again with her sisters and soon she starts drawing film scenes from memory. Eager and proud, she gives her drawings to Melike to put in her book.

The sisters get used to going to the cinema regularly with their father. Even when they're at the summer house and it's a long walk, Timur is always glad to take them along. Arzu rarely joins them; she doesn't like sitting still for so long, and besides, she says she can't sleep properly after the cinema.

There's more than one film in which children find out at the age of 12 or 14 that their parents aren't their real parents. The adoptive parents are rich and the real parents are poor, but the children still want to go back to them. In one film, a maidservant finds out that the master of the house is really her father. In another, a boy finds a letter to his stepmother in his father's drawer. *My beloved, it says, my dear, don't worry about the boy. Once we've got rid of my wife, we'll send him to boarding school and then nothing will stand in the way of our happiness.*

All of this stays in Gül's mind, but nothing leaves as much of an impression on her as the scene where a young man is at his mother's deathbed and she asks him for a glass of water. When the man returns, she is dead. Gül is 14 and she knows the woman sends her son out of the room because she knows death was on the threshold, because she wanted to be alone with it. *I wouldn't send my child away,* Gül thinks.

A few days before New Year's Eve, Gül, Melike and their father are at the cinema, which is heated by glowing sawdust in a specially made stove; wood or coal would be too expensive. The three of them sit in the heated cinema and watch *Spartacus*. For the rest of her days, Gül will remember the scene where the Romans have captured the slaves and want to know which of them is Spartacus. They threaten to kill every one of them if they don't betray their leader. Kirk Douglas stands up and says: 'I am Spartacus.' Once he's revealed himself, one slave after another stands up and claims likewise: 'I am Spartacus.' The Romans are confused.

When the film is over, Timur isn't sitting with his daughters.

'He must be waiting outside,' Melike says, and the sisters go to the exit. They lose each other in the crush, and all of a sudden, Recep is next to Gül. Out of nowhere. Gül looks at him for an instant; they only have an instant's eye contact, and then she looks away hastily. Her heart thuds as she tries to push her way faster to the exit.

'The letter?' Recep asks in a whisper. She can feel his breath on her ear. And she doesn't answer. She can't. She can't speak, can't whisper, can't think; she can't even walk properly, the crowd helping her on towards the doors. Gül feels something being pressed into her hand and she lets it happen. A moment later she's outside. It's bitterly cold and she daren't turn her head, but she senses that Recep is no longer by her side. She closes her hand tightly around the folded piece of paper. She will read this letter, She will find a way, soon, very soon. This time she'll find the courage.

It's easy to make out her father in the crowd; he's taller than all the others. Melike is already with him, and as Gül reaches the two of them, she hears Recep's voice: 'Uncle Timur! Uncle Timur, good evening to you. How are you?'

'Fine, son, thanks be to God, and how are you?'

'I'm fine too, thanks for asking.'

Recep avoids looking at Gül or Melike; he smiles at the blacksmith who is only a head taller than he is. A pomaded strand of hair falls across his forehead.

'Do I know you, son?'

'Yes, Uncle Timur, I'm from the village – you often came to visit us, bought things from my mother... Leyla is her name...'

Timur looks more closely but doesn't seem to remember him.

'Recep,' Recep says now, 'Recep whose father disappeared to Istanbul.'

'Oh yes,' Timur says. 'So tell me, Recep, how's your mother?'

Gül bends down to tie her shoelaces.

'Fine,' says Recep, 'she's fine, thanks for asking.'

There is a pause in the conversation. Timur asks: 'Well, young man, what team do you support?'

'Beşiktaş, because they're the best!'

'That's what I like to hear,' the blacksmith grins.

'I won't keep you,' Recep says. 'My friends are waiting.'

He gestures towards an empty spot, says a polite goodbye and leaves. Gül doesn't spy a comb poking out of his back pocket. The little letter is now in her gaol sock.

At home, she takes the letter out on the toilet. Her hands tremble as she carefully puts the torch down on the ground and removes the piece of folded paper. It's not white, as she expected; it's printed in different colours. And when she unfolds it, she sees it's not a letter this time. It's a lottery ticket for the big New Year's draw. Recep has given her a ticket. Why did he do that? And why is she so happy about it? She stares at the ticket number as if it's concealing a secret message. 430512389. It's a quarter lottery ticket; she can hide it and keep it as a memento. Nothing bad can happen. Gül is too nervous to smile, her heart is still beating too fast, her breathing is still too short. She folds up the ticket and puts it back in her sock.

Recep, she's sure, would be one of the first to stand up and call out: 'I am Spartacus.'

On New Year's Eve, lots of people often gather at the black-smith's house. They all praise Arzu for her stuffed vine leaves, which Gül spent the whole afternoon making; for her börek, which Gül spent the morning kneading the dough for, not to mention washing the spinach in ice-cold water until she could no longer feel her hands. They praise her for her pastries, and when Gül is out of the room, she hears her mother say: 'Gül helped me. She's a young woman now and she's not just a good cook; she's thorough, shrewd and quick too.'

'Thorough, shrewd and quick, thorough, shrewd and quick,' Gül murmurs to herself as she puts on a new pot of tea to boil. The house is packed. Hülya and Zeliha are there; her Uncle Fuat; her Uncle Orhan with his wife and child; neighbours and their families; the blacksmith's assistant, who has no one else and now sits, quiet and shy, in the corner, not even piping up when he wins the game of bingo. Gül sees his numbers have been called when she serves him his tea, but he just looks blankly at the worn bingo card in front of him and squints as the smoke from his cigarette gets in his eyes.

They always play bingo at New Year's. Every adult gets a card, and this time Melike is allowed to draw the numbers out of a little bag and call them out. The children sit with their parents or their favourite aunts or uncles, and Gül pours the tea. The minute the game is over, the men and women will separate: the men will sit in the big room and the women will sit in the girls' room, where Timur has fitted a stove. He's made a stove just like the one they have at the cinema, because wood shavings cost next to nothing. He's annoyed that he didn't think of it sooner.

Only once it approaches eleven o'clock will the men and women huddle together around the radio, which broadcasts songs, sketches, good wishes for the new year and, finally, the results of the New Year's draw. They sit clutching their eighth, quarter or half tickets excitedly, holding their breath and hoping to start the new year rich.

Timur buys an eighth ticket and a quarter ticket every New Year's too, and Arzu lays them both out in front of her, muttering to herself before holding her breath when the speaker announces the numbers loud and clear, one after the other, starting with third prize: 'Four, three, zero, five, one, two, three, eight – and last but not least, ladies and gentlemen; the last number on the winning ticket is…. nine. Congratulations to the lucky winner. And now we come to second prize…'

Gül knows the numbers on her quarter ticket off by heart, but she hadn't reckoned on it winning. Just like the blacksmith's assistant, she keeps her victory under wraps. The speaker repeats the numbers and someone curses to themselves. Perhaps Gül's eyes are glazing over, or maybe it's just from the smoke in the room.

No one can see how agitated she is, her heart thumping, and when she takes a tray of empty tea glasses into the kitchen, no one hears the spoons chinking against the glass, the saucers rattling on the tray, and no one sees her walking oddly like Auntie Hülya. Everyone is hoping for second prize, or the jackpot. But before the announcement, they play another song to ramp up the tension.

Gül's legs seem all tangled up, her hands are trembling. She puts the tray down in the kitchen and goes to refill the tea glasses, when the kettle slips out of her hand and she tips boiling water onto her foot.

She cries out, her screams cutting into a singer singing of pockets of love filled with pain. Arzu comes running into the kitchen at once, followed soon after by Hülya and a neighbour. Gül stands there, still screaming. Her mother shouts: 'Off, get those socks off!'

Gül can't respond; she stops screaming but she can't move. Her mother stands behind her, grabs her under the armpits, and links her hands across Gül's chest. The neighbour woman kneels down and pulls Gül's sock off. She was lucky, there wasn't much water left in the kettle. When she starts to cry, they sit Gül down on a stool and plunge her foot into a basin of cold water.

'You must have been a bit clumsy,' Arzu says, and Gül cries even more. But she no longer knows if it's from happiness or pain. Or bewilderment. Third prize, and she has a quarter ticket; it's so much money she can hardly imagine it. What could she buy with it? Dresses for her sisters; and shoes, so they'd each have two pairs; the chocolate that Melike likes so much; pencils for Sibel – paper and coloured pencils, even watercolours; a toy for Emin, maybe a spinning top; a musical instrument for Nalan. And the midnight blue fabric – she could buy the midnight blue fabric to sew herself a dress, and she could buy a cardigan. She could give some to her father and her mother and Auntie Hülya, and still there would be some left over.

'I won,' she mumbles through her tears, but no one seems to hear her. They take Gül to bed, and Auntie Hülya smears honey on her foot.

'It will ease the pain,' she explains. 'It's not too bad, you don't have a blister, it will stop hurting soon. You were lucky.'

She brushes Gül's hair out of her eyes gently and smiles at her. Gül smiles too. She *has* been lucky.

'My big brave girl, what a way to start the new year.'

Gül hears the quiet rustling of paper in her pillow. Or is she just imagining it? She folded the ticket up small and sewed it into her pillow. And every day since, she's thought about what would happen if someone found it. But who would find it? Their mother never makes their beds. Melike might hear the rustling and guess at once that Gül has hidden something. When they're playing, Gül always knows the best hiding places, but now that it's serious, she's scared.

Much later, when everyone's asleep, Gül cries quietly into her pillow. There's no way she can show her ticket to anyone. Who would believe her if she told them she'd found it on the street or saved up for it herself? And the truth? Who would accept the truth? No one. No one would believe that Recep had given her the ticket as a gift: Why had he given it to her? What for? Where did they meet? How long had she been meeting up with him? Why was she talking to him?

What should she do now, what should she do with this cursed winning ticket? Why did Recep have to give her such a thing? Can't she just slip in into her father's trouser pocket? And what if she gets caught? She could never explain how she'd got into the situation in the first place. And even if she did, he'd just be baffled when he found it. He'd be baffled and throw it away. How would he know it had won third prize in the big New Year's draw?

Three days later, she's still limping, but only a little, and the ticket goes the same way the letter went. It floats downstream to the sea Gül's never seen; it ends in salt water.

'Gül, the neighbour needs someone to help move her wooden trunk – will you run over and help?'

When Gül arrives at the neighbour's, there's a couple there with their son. Gül hasn't seen them before. They could have helped too, she thinks, and helps the neighbour move the trunk.

Only when the same couple comes to visit them that evening with their son in tow does it dawn on Gül. She looks at the young man again. Dark eyes, short, jet-black hair and a face like butter wouldn't melt. He looks so innocent – not pure, but innocent. Gül serves the guests tea with her head bowed and then quickly disappears from the room. When the three of them have gone, Timur comes to Gül and says: 'You know why they were here?'

'Yes.'

'And?'

'I don't know.'

'Did you like him?'

'I don't know.'

'They're a very rich family. You'd have a good life with them. His father's a jeweller... they say he's a good young man, no bad habits.'

'I...'

'Take your time and think it over. By tomorrow. By the day after tomorrow. By next week, my girl.'

Maybe Gül's just imagining it, but her father's eyes seem to grow moist.

Rich, Gül thinks when she's lying in bed, *and we're not rich. I'd definitely feel small there. They're different people, they're not like us.*

The next morning, while her father is eating his soup, Gül looks at him until he stops and looks back at her. Gül shakes her head, her father nods, puts another crust of bread in his mouth and mutters something. Gül thinks she hears the words *too early anyway*. She doesn't want to leave home yet, but she knows she's the age her mother was when she married.

A few weeks later, the girls are home alone, which doesn't happen all that often, and as usual they run straight to the wooden trunk belonging to their mother. Their real mother. Almost every woman brings a trunk like this with her when she marries, using it to store her trousseau: pretty clothes and shoes, hand-made lace, her wedding dress, her headscarves.

Sibel, Melike and Gül dress up in their mother's clothes, slip on her shoes, which are too big for them, and strut around the house, admiring each other. When they've had enough, they marvel at the soft handkerchiefs, the fine lace edging inwrought with little beads, they breathe the napthalene scent of moth balls, and Gül tells them about how their mother used to crochet in the light of the gas lamp.

Later they will sometimes open their stepmother's trunk and try on her clothes too. And it's always Gül's job to fold everything away neatly at the end and arrange the trunk so no one knows they've been there.

The trunk not only holds the bridal trousseau, it contains other precious things too. The plastic ball that Timur brought back from Istanbul once; a small ball with multi-coloured stripes which Arzu only gives the children for an hour at a time.

'Alright,' she says, after they've begged for long enough. 'Take the ball, and when the muezzin calls for afternoon prayers, bring it back.'

As soon as they go out into the street with the ball, everyone wants to play with the blacksmith's daughters, because no one else has a plastic ball. The boys play football with scrunched up rags bound with cord.

When the girls take the ball out of the trunk in secret, they don't take it outside; they prefer to play with it indoors. Someone might snitch on them.

On this day they are sitting on the divan, sweaty after playing with the ball, drinking water out of a big tin beaker.

'They want you as their bride, don't they?' Melike asks.

'Yes.'

'Are you getting married now?' asks Sibel.

'No, no, I'm not getting married yet.'

'You're staying with us?'

'Yes. And even when I do get married, I'll stay nearby, my lovely; we'll still be able to see each other.'

'I don't want to stay here,' Melike says.

'What do you want, then?' Gül asks.

'I want to get away, to Istanbul or Ankara. Somewhere where I won't constantly hear: *We'll be the laughing stock of the town*. I want to go to the city and wear nice clothes and nylon tights, I want to play volleyball without someone telling me that girls can't. I want to have electricity and running water. What is there for me in a dump like this, no bigger than fat Ayşe's bum?'

'Sssh, don't talk like that,' Gül says. 'God sees and hears all.'

'I don't care, it's just a dump! I'm going to finish middle school and then I'll go to the state high school where you can train to be a teacher.'

'If you're allowed,' Gül says.

'Why wouldn't I be allowed? Then I'll be able to earn money.'

Gül looks at the ground with a hint of a nod.

'I could be a teacher too, then, couldn't I?' Sibel asks. She could teach art.

'Yes, of course,' Gül replies. 'You can be a teacher too. But let's worry about middle school first.'

'I'll manage it.'

Gül doesn't doubt for a moment that Sibel will do well at middle school. She's not so sure about Melike, she might fail the entrance exam for high school. *Maybe I should get married*, she thinks.

It's not yet properly spring, but it's warm – it's around the first days of March, and Gül is sent to the summer house.

'Tell Esra you won't be coming in for two days; take the broom and a duster and clean the summer house from top to bottom,' Arzu says. 'We're going to move in earlier this year. The first people are there already.'

There aren't very many of what she calls the first people; only two on their road, and Gül feels daunted at being so alone. Three doors down is a tiny old woman, widowed at an early age. The boys often pick on her, calling her a dwarf. And at the very far end of the road, a young woman called Handan is also doing her spring cleaning.

It's the first time Gül has been there all alone to clean, and she's afraid. She tries to make as little noise as possible; she feels safer that way. If she's noisy, she worries she might not hear something important, though she couldn't say what that would be. What would a burglar take from an empty summer house? She knows what a man might want if he found a young woman all alone. But there are people nearby, she could scream at the top of her lungs. But could she really, after not daring to breathe loudly for so long?

'Help!' She hears a loud call. 'Come quick, now, help!'

Someone is screaming their heart out, but the voice also seems to be trembling, like Gül's voice when it sounds like a stranger's. Gül drops the broom and runs.

Entering the old neighbour's house, she sees Handan kneeling on the floor, her hands raised, keening. Gül has heard of people singing in tongues when they find out about a death, but she's never seen it for herself. She's never seen a dead person either.

The old neighbour seems to have slipped on some soap and fallen. She's lying on her back with her eyes open.

Handan's voice ebbs away. After a moment's pause, she says to Gül, who is standing motionless next to her and staring at the old woman's body: 'She's dead. May the Lord bring peace to her soul.'

'Amen,' Gül says.

Then Handan begins another lament. Gül stands by her side, not knowing what to do. She can't turn her eyes away from the dead woman's vacant gaze.

Gül doesn't know how much time has passed when Handan's voice grows quieter and then falls silent. The next thing she hears is the door creaking; she turns around.

In the doorway is a very old woman who lives on the next road; a woman Gül has always found odd. She's a resolute woman who looks robust despite her bent back, one who raises her voice in the company of men and whom everyone respects; their respect coloured with fear. Muazzez, that's her name, but everyone always calls her Muazzez Hanım, using the formal title as a mark of respect. Muazzez Hanım has so many wrinkles in her sun-browned face that no one dares look at it properly any more. Her eyes are slightly dimmed; she does have a few teeth left in her mouth, but her lips seem to have disappeared, and the rest of her face looks to Gül like a muddle, a mess that she can't get the measure of. Aside from that, Muazzez Hanım often talks to herself, jiggling her chin as she speaks, her eyebrows twitching up and down, her right eyelid fluttering – and sometimes her mouth is nothing but a dark round hole.

'May the Lord bring her peace, she had it tough,' Muazzez Hanım says, and then she turns to Handan: 'Find two hankies, my beauty.'

Handan runs off and Gül is alone in the room with Muazzez Hanım, still not knowing what to do.

'Ah well, my girl,' Muazzez Hanım says, without turning to face Gül. 'That's how it goes; one moment you're alive, the next you're dead. That's life. Nothing times nothing and nothing's left over. No one knows the hour when the angel of death will come to visit. The poor woman; she didn't have it easy in life, brought up three children all on her own. And then she dies before she's finished cleaning the house, in her old clothes – and she doesn't even manage to close her eyes. Ah well, my girl, take a good look. One day you'll be dead too.'

When Handan comes back with two handkerchiefs, Gül is glad not to be alone with Muazzez Hanım any more. The old woman takes the hankies from Handan and, shaking her head, says: 'Three children, and only one lives nearby. Go and fetch her son from town. And drink a glass of water first; you're white as a sheet.'

'You too, my girl,' she says to Gül. 'Drink a glass of water. And don't be scared.'

With a groan, Muazzez Hanım kneels down next to the dead woman, folds the hankie diagonally, places the middle under the dead woman's chin and ties the ends together on the top of her head. Then she shuts the woman's eyes and lays the other hand-kerchief over her face.

'What's the matter?' she asks Gül, who still hasn't moved. 'What's the matter, don't you want a drink of water? Go on. Handan will be back from town any minute.'

Gül goes to the pump in the kitchen and drinks from her cupped hand.

'I'm outside,' she hears Muazzez Hanım saying, and now she has to walk alone through the room where the dead woman is. At first, she wants to dash across as she would if walking through a stable, but then she stops to stand by the dead woman.

Her children are grown up.

That's just a brief thought.

She doesn't look dead, more like she's asleep.

Another brief thought.

Death is invisible, like feelings.

Another one.

Did my mother get a sheet over her face? So no one could see the circles beneath her eyes?

Gül walks out slowly to where Muazzez Hanım is sitting on the steps outside the front door, smoking.

'Not easy, not easy,' Muazzez Hanım says, and breathes out smoke. 'Three children, three children. Who are you, child?'

'Timur the blacksmith's daughter.'

'Ah yes. Yes, your father's wife doesn't have it easy either. Five children and three of them not even her own. And then a mother-in-law who rips everybody off, even though she can't see any more. No, no, life's never easy, my child.'

She puts her cigarette out with her shoe and spits on the ground.

Gül doesn't know how, but the news travels fast. Soon there are nearly a dozen women outside the house, telling stories about the dead woman and wishing peace upon her soul. Just as one of the women is bemoaning that Cem, the dead woman's son, only ever visits on the weekends, the town's only taxi swirls up the dust of the street.

They all fall silent when Handan and Cem get out. She seems to have been crying, but his face is like stone. Not showing the slightest emotion, he goes into the house past Muazzez Hanım, who barely shifts aside to make room but murmurs a few incomprehensible words.

When he comes out again five minutes later, Cem's eyes are reddened, but there's no sign of tear streaks on his face.

'What shall we do?' he asks in a weak voice.

'You have to take her into town,' Handan says. 'She can't stay here.'

'No, he can't do that,' one of the women pipes up. 'You can't carry the dead past a graveyard.'

'That's true,' another woman confirms. 'She's dead, she can't pass the graveyard.'

'But where's she supposed to go? She'd have to stay here, and then the rats will get at her at night.'

'And where's she to be washed?' another voice asks.

'But it can't be, not past the graveyard, that's never been done, it just won't do.'

Cem simply stares at the ground, at Muazzez Hanım's cigarette butt; everyone starts talking at once. The taxi driver waits in his car and smokes a cigarette. Chattering women, he might be thinking, *they talk so much, not even a lentil would get wet in their mouths.*

'Then that's just what's written in her book,' Muazzez Hanım says, and they all fall silent as the old woman raises her voice. 'Then that's just her fate, that her last path leads past the grave-yard and not into the graveyard. Carry her to the car...'

'Cars, did we used to have cars?' she adds in a murmur, stand-ing up with the aid of her stick and turning to Cem: 'She brought up three children, do you know what that means? Do you know what this woman did for you three? She went without food so you wouldn't go hungry, she went without water so you wouldn't go thirsty, would have given her life for you children. And you three? You didn't even turn around and call her "Mother". You didn't even look back after she brought you on your way. The three of you are such a disgrace; you didn't honour her and didn't value her. May the merciful Lord give no mother children like you! A curse upon you all! The Lord shall give you children who won't care for you when you grow old and fragile either. What was the old woman doing here alone? Not once, not one time did you turn around and look at her like a mother. You're a disgrace, you and your brother and sister!'

Muazzez Hanım spits, hobbles down the steps, rests on her stick and walks down the road, back bent. Not the slightest reaction shows on Cem's face. It still looks like a mask someone with stiff fingers has shaped out of white candlewax.

'His mother's just died,' Handan whispers after a while, and Gül watches Muazzez Hanım as she inches away. Hard words. What does the woman know to make her talk that way?

The taxi driver and one of the young women lay the corpse on the back seat. Someone presses a glass of water into Cem's hand; he raises the glass to his mouth and swallows. Gül thinks she can make out his Adam's apple labouring to move up and down. Lacking a will of his own, Cem lets someone take the empty glass from his hand; Handan holds the passenger door open for him and he gets in. What remain are a few women, a cloud of dust that soon settles and Gül, wondering whether she too will die alone.

'May the Lord not leave me to lie for long,' her blind grand-mother always says. 'When the time comes, I want to lie in bed for two days at the most and pass away on the third. May the Lord bless me with a swift death.'

But what if swift also means lonely? What if you don't even have anyone to fetch water for you? *Dear Lord, don't let me die alone*, Gül prays. All of a sudden, she feels like crying, but not in front of all these strange women. She goes back to the summer house and cleans the windows while the tears flow; crying and working, and she doesn't know which she'll be done with first.

Her father comes to pick her up in the early evening. When he finds out what happened, he says: 'Let's go to the graveyard on the way home, you and me.'

And so Timur and Gül go to Fatma's grave in the dusk. Gül doesn't dare go there alone, and her father rarely takes her along.

'Your mother and I used to sleep in graveyards, you know, he says, when we were travelling. Highway robbers are scared to go into graveyards at night, and we'd lie side by side and look at the stars. Your mother was as beautiful as a piece of the moon. And one night she just said *Gül*. I didn't know what she meant, but she said she was pregnant and our daughter would be called Gül. The stars blurred before my eyes.'

'Ah yes, Fatma,' he adds after a while, 'what times we had in the old days.'

I should have gone to her, Gül thinks. *I should have gone to her bed in the hospital like Melike did. I shouldn't have listened to the grownups. I always listen to the grownups, but Melike does whatever she likes. She gave our mother a last kiss and I didn't.*

'You see, Gül,' her father says now. 'There's no cure for the past. What happened happened, my girl, and we can't bring the dead back to life.'

Gül thinks of what her grandmother says when she's bitten into a particularly hot pepper: 'This pepper's so hot you could wake the dead if you tickled their bums with it.'

But no, you can't bring the dead back to life; you can only tie a handkerchief around their chins.

'We do that, so the mouth doesn't gape open when the body goes stiff,' Timur explains. 'You children will do that for me too. That's the path we all take.'

Gül says nothing. The blacksmith will live another good 40 years, and when he dies, Gül won't be sitting at his bedside like his other children; she'll be in Germany, in a hospital after an eye operation, and Timur's last word will be 'Gül.'

When father and daughter get home, Arzu's father, the coach driver Faruk, is there with his son Fuat.

'What kept you?' Arzu scolds and sends Gül straight into the kitchen to make coffee for the visitors. A moment later she comes up and says: 'What happened? Is old Hatice dead? Were you there when it happened? Is it true Muazzez Hanım cursed her son? Tell me everything.'

Gül tells her mother, who paces up and down the kitchen nervously. Gül is still mid-story when the coffee is ready, but Arzu says: 'Now go through and serve the coffee.'

Gül notices Uncle Fuat's eye fixed on her, but she just looks at the floor. Yet she's still surprised when her father wants to talk to her in the yard later that evening.

'Do you think Uncle Fuat could be the man for you?'

So that was why she served the coffee, that was why her grandfather was there, that was why Fuat had stared at her like that, that was why her mother had managed to tame her curiosity for once. Now she understands.

'No,' she says. 'No, I don't think so.'

'Why?' She hears Arzu's voice; she's been standing at the threshold by the back door and must have been listening.

People say things about him, he's got bad habits. He smokes, he drinks, he gambles.

'So why not?' her mother asks again. 'He's still a good-looking young man, and he's got a job too, he'd be able to feed a family.'

Yes, Uncle Fuat is good-looking. And he probably would be able to feed a family. But people also say he was friends with Engin, who made socks in gaol.

'What have you got against him?' her mother asks.

'He walks on the backs of his shoes,' Gül says.

'What?' her father asks.

'He always walks on the backs of his shoes. I don't like men who walk on the backs of their shoes.'

'Alright,' her father says carefully, 'it's your choice.'

'But,' her mother starts up, yet Timur interrupts her: 'It's her choice.'

That night, Gül dreams she is in bed, unable to move. The quilt weighs heavier and heavier on her and suddenly Fuat is there with his Clark Gable moustache, gaol socks on his feet, with a marbled comb, a pair of barber's scissors and a razor in the pocket of his short-sleeved shirt.

'It's just what's written in her book,' Gül hears Muazzez Hanım say. 'It's her destiny.'

177

Gül wakes up in a fright, gulps some water, and tosses and turns until daybreak. She can't help but think of the dead woman's open eyes. If the covers smothered her, would she rather have her eyes open or closed? Would she stay on her back or would she turn onto her front? On her front, she decides at first, but then she wouldn't be able to see the covers pressing down on her. She can't decide, and eventually she does fall back to sleep, lying on her side, her legs pulled up to her chest.

Summer comes, and sometimes Gül can't sleep for the heat. Perhaps it's not the heat, perhaps it's the taste in her mouth; black feathers and something metallic. Perhaps it's not the taste of down or blood or old coins, perhaps it's a smell like crumbly feta that's gone off. Summer comes, and sometimes Gül wakes in the morning and thinks, *Today will be the day when everything falls apart.*

Gül loves the summer, a time when she has so much less to do, when she can roam the big garden with the others. A time when her father sometimes takes her with him when he goes to spray insect repellent on the trees with a machine strapped onto his back. Gül carries the big can of repellent, standing to the side while he sprays. A time when she doesn't have to feel cold, when the washing dries quicker, a time when, sometimes, the whole street sits out to listen to the radio. Gül likes the summer, but this year it seems to her like the end of something.

Melike and Sibel often play with Yıldız, the girl helping Uncle Abdurahman around the house this summer, but Gül doesn't get on too well with her. It might be because Yıldız is 11 or 12, while Gül is nearly 15. Nearly all the children in the street call her Gül Abla now; she's a young woman, and there's a new man asking for her hand every couple of weeks. If these men sent someone to see Gül just as Timur once sent his sister to look at Fatma, they'd learn that Gül already has budding breasts.

And, unlike her mother when she was her age, she's already had her period twice. The first time, she was at Esra's when she went to the toilet and saw the blood. Quietly, she crept into the sewing room.

'Esra Abla, I'm not well, I need to go home.'

Esra looked at Gül curiously, knit her brow and asked: 'Are you bleeding?'

Gül looked at the floor.

'You know what it is, don't you?'

Gül didn't reply.

'You'll get it more often from now on – you're a woman now, you're not ill.'

And she explained to Gül that women use cloths to catch the blood. Gül wondered why she'd never seen the cloths her mother uses.

From that day on, Gül washes her cloths in secret, just as her mother does, never saying a word about it.

Everyone knows she's hard-working, capable, and she can sew too. No one bothers about her nose, which healed crooked. Men aren't after looks, a woman need to be able to cook and run a household.

Gül doesn't speak much in company, which is put down to ladylike reserve, a kind of maturity. She doesn't know why most people can't tell the obvious: she's shy.

Over the summer, five young men visit with their parents, but Gül doesn't want to leave home yet. It's not hard for her to find excuses for not liking them. But in reality, they all have the same flaw: they're strangers.

Gül's father smiles each time she turns one away. He doesn't put pressure on her like other fathers do.

'I'll have to make you one at the forge,' he says one day. 'You've found a niggle with every one.'

But he says it with a good-natured smile and suppressed pride.

Timur has forged a door for Abdurahman's summer house, a door decorated with scrolls and ornaments that proves he knows his trade and is more than a jumped-up farrier.

'Who made the door?' the glazer asks when he comes to measure it up for the pane of glass.

'Why do you ask?' Abdurahman wants to know.

'You have to watch out with some doors,' the glazer says. 'You put the glass in, but there's still a bit of wiggle room in hidden spots here and there. Then as soon as the door slams on you, the glass smashes, and then there's trouble and the glazer always gets the blame. But really it's down to the doors. Who made this one?'

'Timur the blacksmith.'

'Then there won't be any trouble,' the glazer says, putting away his yardstick and pencil.

Almost back in town, the glazer realises he's left his note with the measurements at the house. Half an hour later, he's back outside the former teacher's door and hears screaming from inside; it stops abruptly at his knock. He knocks again and listens. Not a sound. He reaches through the hole in the door where the glass is not yet fitted and opens it from the inside.

'Sir!' he calls, and he hears a quick scream that's immediately stifled. It sounds like a girl's voice, coming from the room on his right. Not thinking long, the glazer opens the door. Abdurahman has one hand pressed over Yıldız's mouth, the other is trying to pull up his trousers.

That kind of news travels fast, and as always Arzu is one of the first to know.

'What's happened?' Gül asks, noticing the agitation but not knowing what her mother is whispering about with Auntie Hülya.

'Uncle Abdurahman was doing indecent things to Yıldız,' Auntie Hülya says.

'It's not for children's ears,' her mother says. 'Mind your own business.'

Then Arzu turns back to her sister-in-law: 'He swore on the holy book it was the first time... What are you doing still here?' she says to Gül, who goes out to the apricot tree where she often sits this summer.

Uncle Abdurahman has always been good to her. She sees his thick grey beard in her mind's eye, hears his warm voice, thinks of all the sweets he's given her.

Sometimes it's easier not to know certain things. Sometimes it's easier not to really know a person.

Yıldız will be taken back to her parents in the village. Her father will be relieved she's still a virgin for two reasons: it doesn't reduce her chances of marrying, and it doesn't force him to take action. What was he to have done – shoot a respected teacher?

Abdurahman will drink a bottle of rakı every night for the whole of the summer, barely leaving the house, and in the autumn he will disappear, people say to Istanbul. After the initial gossip, most people will stop mentioning the secret.

Sometimes it's better not to know, but Gül will also never find out whether it really was the first time. Who can a person trust?

Several times from spring to late summer, the big water comes, as they call it, but Gül has never thought to ask where exactly it comes from. It is channelled from upland streams to the orchards and gardens near the summer houses. People water their apple trees, vegetables and flowers – they let the earth drink its fill and then they channel the water along ditches to the next garden. Or they channel it across the road to the opposite gardens through a hole left in the wall on purpose. Sandbags are piled up, and soon the road is almost knee-deep in water, all the way across. The children play in it, cooling off, sinking paper boats, splashing each other.

Gül knows neither where the water comes from, nor how the first person finds out about it or what the last person does with it if there's too much left, or how they react if they go empty-handed. She does know the big water is a huge adventure for all the children.

This time, the big water comes a few days after the old woman's death. If he weren't relying on a good harvest, Timur could let the water flow past unused, but this time he and Gül are waiting in the garden, armed with sandbags, spades and rags to plug any gaps. As they sit together in the darkness, the blacksmith feels like smoking a cigarette, that yearning still hasn't left him. Gül is excited; she gets up and pulls at a few weeds.

'Save your energy for later,' her father says.

It's the first time she's helped him channel the water. He usually gets a neighbour to come over, but most of them haven't moved into their summer houses yet. Gül seems strong enough to Timur now, though it's actually Melike who ought to be doing it.

'I've got school in the morning,' she'd said, and Timur let her get away with it.

Once the water is there, Timur gives Gül instructions. Gül likes following the arc of the torch, listening to the rush of the water and her father's voice. *Bring me another cannister. Get that sandbag. Give me the small spade. Plug this gap. Shine the light over here.*

The sun is rising as they finally channel the water into the neighbour's garden. Gül didn't notice the time passing. But now that everything is done, she feels suddenly exhausted. She's not tired, she can't imagine going to bed now, but she feels drained. Her father wordlessly hands her three two-and-a-half lira notes.

They came on foot and they walk home as well. The grocers aren't open yet, not even the bakers, and there are no children playing outside the school gates. It is quiet in the town, utterly silent but for their footsteps on the dusty ground. As if the silence of the night had carried into the morning. It seems to Gül like when the sound cuts out during a film, only in the cinema a murmuring would soon start up, get louder and louder. They hear a single donkey braying in a stable.

Timur takes out his pocket watch. 'Perhaps it's not telling the right time,' he says, but he doesn't seem to believe it.

'Quick, quick!' Arzu beckons to them as they turn into their street. She's standing in the doorway, her face stricken with fear and alarm.

'Inside, get inside,' she says in a hushed voice when Gül and Timur are still 10 paces away.

Her father hasn't quickened his step, and Gül walks alongside him.

'Quick,' Arzu shouts now, 'before they see you!'

'Who?' asks Timur, taking his shoes off outside the door.

'Leave your shoes on, get inside,' Arzu says anxiously.

'What is it, woman?'

'There's a curfew, they've brought in a curfew.'

She shuts the door behind them. The shoes are outside.

'Who?'

'The soldiers. No one's allowed out.'

Melike comes running over: 'Isn't it great? School's closed today. And probably tomorrow too.'

'Get out of it!' her father barks at her.

'A coup?' he asks, and his wife nods.

The blacksmith sits by the radio, his face grim.

He will often be seen like this in the coming days, sitting by the radio, his brow furrowed, shaking his head every once in a while.

'What's happened to democracy,' he will murmur to himself. Or even: 'Whoremongering bastards.'

He's always been more interested in football than politics, but he's voted for the Democrat Party for years, and now the military has seized power, claiming democracy was under threat. Prime Minister Menderes is accused of corruption and running a dictatorship, but the blacksmith is convinced that all power ought to come from the people, from men like him. Though the coup will have no real effect on their day-to-day lives, the blacksmith will only be reassured a year later, when a new constitution is approved by a national referendum.

Gül follows her sister into the room.

'What happened?'

'I don't know. But I don't have to go to school. Mum says the soldiers are deciding things now.'

Gül nods as if she understands.

'You want to go to high school when you've finished middle school, don't you?'

'Yes, you know I do.'

'But you don't like school.'

'Not really, but it doesn't matter. I need qualifications; it's hard if you've got no qualifications. I want to get out of here.'

Gül nods again. She knows Melike is right. You don't have many options if you've got no qualifications.

A few days later, the curfew is lifted. The sisters go back to school, Melike listless, Sibel full of anticipation. Timur re-opens the forge, and Gül buys the midnight blue fabric with the money her father gave her. She sews herself a dress which she won't wear all summer, but when she's alone she'll take it out, try it on and marvel at it.

At the end of the summer, her grandmother Berrin comes by one evening and brings Uncle Fuat with her. And afterwards, Timur says to his daughter:

'I don't need to ask you again, do I?'

'I want to.'

'What?'

'Marry me to him.'

'You don't have to. Even if they come another 100 times, you can say no a 100 times more.'

'Maybe it's my destiny.'

'He's certainly not a bad man. He has a job, he'd be able to feed you, he's capable. Then again, he walks on the backs of his shoes.'

There is a pause.

'Do you really want to?' the blacksmith asks.

'Yes.'

'Really?'

'Yes.'

When Gül wakes up the next morning, she still wants to. Maybe it's preordained. That's why Fuat came twice. And what is there for her at home? She makes no money. Even if there's enough for soup every morning in winter, there's not enough money to support that many children. Melike wants to go to high school. And Gül wouldn't be far from home; Fuat isn't a stranger, he's already family. She will have to marry sooner or later. What else is she supposed to do? Sooner or later, everyone gets married. Or they wither at home and get funny looks in the street. Fate. She said yes for some reason, last night she said yes for some reason. And it felt right. Didn't it?

Once the apples have been harvested, they will have a little engagement party. Arzu no longer has to worry about what people will say if Gül is seen in public in the company of a young man with brilliantine in his hair, a smooth-shaven face and a marbled comb in his trouser pocket. Gül is now the kind of young woman she often used to glance after with quiet longing.

It's exciting walking along the main street with Fuat, but it's not thrilling. Gül is nervous, glad of the man at her side, but she doesn't know what to say. Nor does she really know what other engaged couples talk about. Fuat talks about his friends, about customers at the barbershop, and he also tells her about times he's won money playing cards. Gül listens attentively and nods.

For Gül, the best thing about the engagement is that she can now go to the cinema more often, with Fuat, who doesn't fall asleep at almost every film. You don't have to speak at the cinema and Fuat takes Gül home afterwards, and on the way they can talk about films, about Humphrey Bogart, Cary Grant, Cüneyt Arkın, Belgin Doruk, Bette Davis, Ava Gardner, Fatma Girik, Elizabeth Taylor, Ayhan Işık, Filiz Akın, Ediz Hun, Türkan Şoray, Gina Lollobrigida, Kirk Douglas, Erol Taş.

When he sees his friends in the hall during a double bill, Fuat says: 'I'll just nip over and say hello.'

Then he stands there with his friends, smoking, laughing, and if he's not standing too far away, Gül sits up and looks to see if he's been walking on the backs of his shoes. Which he sometimes does when they leave the cinema, but never when they go in; when they go in he's always neatly dressed. She doesn't know what Fuat talks about with his friends. She assumes it's the same kind of thing the men talk about at her father's workshop. Football and politics. And though as a young girl she would listen in as the blacksmith's customers and friends chatted at the workshop, she knows almost nothing about footballers or Menderes or Kennedy. It has never interested her.

When Gül and Fuat sit side by side in the dark, sometimes their shoulders touch. That's it. Sometimes Fuat smells of alcohol, and when he does, he talks louder in the breaks and laughs more. And he runs his fingers through his hair more often.

But he doesn't often smell like alcohol, not that autumn when Gül goes to see lots of films. Films about young love, about love that crosses every line, about people who deny themselves for the good of their beloved, about people whose lives began with great suffering and who can now see a light at the end of it all. Or who hope they will. About people simply trying to survive, or about people who are prepared to endure anything for love. About women rescued from a mire of drugs and prostitution or liberated from insufferable toil and burdens; about men rescued from a swamp of drugs, alcohol and pimping, or from gaol where they've been locked up, innocent. Or just because they avenged their father's murder. They're all saved. All the good ones.

The more of these strange dreams she sees, the more she longs for other worlds. She starts reading photo love-story magazines which come out every other Saturday. Doctors fall in love with nurses, young men from the upper classes abandon unscrupulous lifestyles in a flash because love has struck them like a thunder bolt, sisters fall for the same man, whose long-lost brother miraculously appears. But there are also stories which end bloodily, in which mothers hold their dying daughters in their arms and men can't escape their pasts, stories in which evil demands a sacrifice: 15 years in prison, a father in a wheelchair or a mother who's lost her sight. Stories like the old songs, where it always ends in bitterness because there's nothing in this world worth a dime, where your love is never returned and you keep going anyway, stories like the Anatolian Blues.

Usually Timur buys the magazines for his daughter, but sometimes Fuat does too. Melike is only allowed them once Gül is done with them. Later, when Gül comes to reread them, there will be greasy marks on the cheap, rough paper, the pages will be dog-eared, and sometimes a few will be missing. When Sibel begins drawing her first little stories, they're based on the plots of these love-stories or on sequences from films she's seen at the cinema, which she changes slightly and makes her own. Unlike her pictures, she won't show these stories to anyone, instead hiding them away carefully among her school things.

Towards the end of autumn, Gül and her mother are at the shop choosing fabric for her wedding dress, which she will sew herself. The fabric Gül likes best is expensive. Her mother pulls a pained smile and signals with her eyes for Gül to pick a different one. But Gül would rather have fabric she likes than a long train. When she tells the salesman how many metres she wants, he gives her a questioning look: 'Isn't that?' he begins, but Gül interrupts him: '...exactly the right length.'

The matte white fabric has a silky sheen to it. It is cut from the bale, and Arzu takes out the money as if in agony, but the only thing she says on the way home is: 'What will people say when your train's so short?'

Gül sews, she sews with great care and concentration. She keeps asking Esra: 'It's going to be fine, isn't it?'

And one day, after she's asked the question at least 10 times, she says out of the blue: 'Esra Abla, what do I have to do?' She tacks on a whisper: 'On the wedding night?'

Esra hesitates.

'Has your mother not told you anything?'

Gül blushes.

'There's no need to be scared. Try to relax, get undressed and just try to relax. Leave it to Fuat. It doesn't hurt. Maybe a tiny bit to begin with, but actually it's nice... very nice.'

Gül has gone even redder; she's sweating. So it's very nice, Esra says it's very nice. There's no need for her to be scared.

Gül sews a perfectly fitting, waisted wedding dress, which she tries on again and again. She twists and turns in front of the mirror, looking at what she's made out of the fabric with her hours of work. They are peaceful, oblivious hours that Gül spends at the quietly humming machine, her foot on the pedal, her brows drawn together, her eyes focused. Nothing can disturb her – her thoughts are directed entirely on her work, she doesn't daydream of what her wedding will be like and nor does she notice the cold creeping back into the houses, through the gaps in the doors and the shutters. The cold slowly takes possession of everything again; the only place it doesn't dare set foot is near the stoves. Otherwise, though, it is everywhere and seems to grin with pearly white teeth: *Just you wait, this year I'm going to really bother you all.*

The dress is finished long before the wedding date. It's cold outside, bitterly cold; first comes so much snow that they sink up to their knees, and then the stream freezes over. Melike, Sibel and Nalan, who's now in her second year, get a fortnight off school. This time, though, Melike can't enjoy it for long. There's lots to do; inviting their neighbours and relatives, ordering musicians – and the sisters need something nice to wear, otherwise they'll be the laughing stock of the town. Arzu decides she definitely needs new shoes, Timur's good suit has to go to the cleaner's, orders need placing with the grocer. Melike gets sent out in the cold on so many errands, she almost wishes she were back at school. She wants to get out of here, she wants to leave, but not in the same way as her big sister.

On the morning of the third of December, Gül opens her eyes and her first thought is: *This is the last time I'll be waking up here.* She looks over from her bed at Nalan, Melike and Sibel. She'll be leaving them behind; she won't be able to protect Sibel and Melike any more. Never again will she wake up to that acrid smell of urine, never again will she make Sibel eat at least half of her breakfast egg to grow bigger and stronger. Never again will she fetch her mother's ball out of the chest and play with it indoors. But they're sure to huddle together again sometimes to talk about their real mother. Gül is staying nearby and she'll come home often. There will be one less mouth to feed, and Melike will be able to go to high school.

Gül stares at the ceiling as tears run slowly down the sides of her face. No one sees it, and later, when someone might see it, she won't cry any more. Why should she? She's getting married. It's the day they always look forward to in the photo love-stories, the day when everything turns out fine. But those girls always have a real mother.

Gül won't live far away and everything will turn out fine. *Almighty God, escort me on my way*, she prays. *Your will be done, but please protect me from harm.*

There are people around her for the rest of the day. First Gül is taken to a neighbour's house, where someone does her hair. Not only her straight hair is curled with hot tongs, but also her sisters', and even her mother and Auntie Hülya have decided not to wear headscarves that evening. Zeliha is the only one who doesn't care what she looks like.

As there aren't enough curling irons, the handles of the little copper pots used for making coffee are inserted between the coals. Melike is too impatient, and the place soon smells of burnt hair, but she doesn't make a sound; all that shows are her tears of rage.

Everything is done according to tradition. When the time comes to collect the bride from home, Melike stands in front of the door to her room and blocks the way, only giving way when she gets a tip. The blacksmith ties a red sash around Gül's hips as a sign that he's giving away his daughter a virgin.

Years later, Gül will attend the official opening of a highway, and in the moment when the mayor cuts the red ribbon and announces that these 25 kilometres of asphalt are a major step into the future, she will remember her wedding.

When Gül is led into the bridegroom's house, the couple are given bread and honey so that they may want for nothing and may brighten each other's lives with sweet words.

The day passes swiftly. There are people around Gül all the time, wanting to give her advice or predict the ways in which her life will change. But she can't concentrate; she gets dizzy from all the words and sounds.

There is loud music in the hall in the evening; a drummer and a man who blows the zurna; children running around; girls of Nalan's age showing off their belly-dancing skills, still without the slightest inhibition and probably not even guessing it will soon be unseemly for them to move their hips that way in public. At one point, an astounded Gül spots her teacher, the one who read out her story about the man, the forest and the lion. She sees the sieve maker who took her to the wrong blacksmith, and Cem, the son of the dead Hatice.

Fuat makes a dapper bridegroom, his dark blue shoes so shiny he can see his face in them. When he sits down, his matching dark blue suit only wrinkles stiffly in five or six places, and when he stands up, the suit stands firm too, as if it has a life of its own and feels proud to present its wearer at this celebration. Fuat has shaved three times in a row today, and only one little black lock, now gently brushing against his eyebrow, has come loose from his slicked-back hair.

The bride and groom sit at a table decorated with flowers, receiving congratulations and listening to all the well-meaning advice and comments. Someone has put two cushions on Gül's chair; one so that she's sitting comfortably, and one so that she doesn't look so short. Her feet don't touch the ground, but there's an old tradition where the couple try to step on each other's feet while the registrar carries out the marriage ceremony in the hall. Whoever's foot is on top will wear the trousers, they say, and often enough, women simply leave their foot under the bridegroom's to make him feel superior. In a household without a capable wife, they say, no one knows which way to turn. Or, as they also say: *A man can only ever be as good as his wife.*

Fuat holds his right foot above Gül's left one, but as the words *I hereby pronounce you man and wife* are spoken, she shifts it aside a little so that their feet are no longer touching. If it was quiet, the guests might hear Fuat's leather sole tapping on the floor in search of Gül's foot.

In all the excitement, Gül notices a pale-skinned young woman with full cheeks and tears running down them. She's never seen this pretty woman before, a woman in a midnight blue dress that seems to be made of the same fabric as hers.

Gül knows why her father is crying, though. His oldest daughter is leaving home and she'll never be his little girl again, she's in the hands of this stranger now, she'll be gone. Not as far away as Fatma, but she too is being taken from him.

The bride and groom accept the gifts: Fuat, the banknotes he is handed; Gül, the bracelets; both, the household goods and towels. They are even given an electric iron. Never in her life has Gül as much as touched an electric iron; she only knows them from films and photo-love stories.

Melike dances and laughs, her scorched strand of hair apparently forgotten, Sibel sits quietly in a corner, Nalan and Emin run around with a crowd of other children, and Arzu beams brightly, looking much younger without her headscarf. Her long black hair glints in the light, but Gül is certain she hasn't used brilliantine. Her mother has beautiful hair; Gül envies her. Her own is naturally thin and dull, but she likes the way the hairdresser has done it today. Gül hopes her hairdo and dress direct attention away from her bent nose. She doesn't think she's pretty, and sometimes she also looks at Melike with a slight sense of envy because she looks like their mother, because someone might also call her as beautiful as a piece of the moon.

Timur flits from one guest to the next, almost competing with the bridegroom in his white shirt and black trousers and waistcoat. His bald head makes him look older than he really is, though. 'My good luck and my hair left me with Fatma,' he often says, and he will repeat those words as long as he lives. But as soon as Timur is alone for a few seconds that evening, he looks at his daughter and his eyes well up.

'Like they're ripping out part of my lung,' he murmurs to himself, and: 'Will my heart ever get used to this pain?'

The woman with the midnight blue dress and the full cheeks keeps looking over at Gül, and her eyes keep filling with tears. Gül sees it but she can't explain it. She watches the woman closely, and her father and her sisters and her old teacher, so she doesn't have to think about how she feels – so she doesn't notice how hard her heart is beating and how her throat feels like she can't speak. Gül feels very small at this big party.

'Hey, you little runaway!' Gül suddenly hears, and she turns her head. The sieve maker seems to have barely aged since he carried her all the way across town on his shoulders.

'Good evening,' Gül says.

'So the blacksmith's daughter is getting married,' the sieve maker says. 'There are four of you sisters as well now, but at least you've got a little brother, eh?'

He leans down to Gül and puts his mouth close to her ear, and Gül can smell the aniseed liquor on his breath.

'I wish you both the best of luck. And if you get lost, you can always come find me again.'

He laughs as he stands up straight.

'Thank you,' says Gül, rather confused.

A band begins to play, and when the bride and groom dance, Gül lays her head on Fuat's shoulder. Perhaps because she thinks that's what's expected of her, perhaps because she's a bit tired, or perhaps because it means she can hide her face. She breathes in his scent; he smells good, her future husband. No, he's no longer her husband-to-be, now he's the man by her side. They belong together now. He will be there, he will always be there for her. Until… She can't think that far ahead right now, it's too difficult. She doesn't even have to suppress the thought; it disappears of its own accord.

After the reception, they are driven to her in-laws' house, where they will live in a room on the first floor. Fuat's brother and friends are waiting outside the front door; they pat him on the back to lend him strength for his wedding night. Laughing, Fuat carries Gül over the threshold. He carries her all the way up to their room.

There, he lays her on the bed Gül's father forged, and takes off his tie, jacket and shirt. Gül lies motionless and looks at the fur on Fuat's chest out of the corner of her eye. She can barely make out any skin beneath the curly black hair. When Fuat turns off the light, Gül begins to undress slowly. She doesn't know whether she's excited. The whole day has been too much for her, it's a little like she wasn't there herself; everything flashed past her.

When she closes her eyes a moment later, she can feel Fuat's chest hair. It feels rough. Rough and like a protective shell preventing her from getting close to him. The kind of protective shell she wishes she had too.

The next morning there's a little blood on the sheet, and Gül hopes it only hurts the first time. Her hope is dashed that evening; Esra lied to her.

Forty days, for 40 days she's been living with Fuat in this room on the first floor. Forty days living with Fuat in this house, of which she'll later say: 'It brought me luck. All the prayers I said to the Lord in that house were answered.'

The room next door belongs to Gül's brother-in-law Orhan, his wife and their two young sons. Her in-laws, Faruk and Berrin, have a room downstairs, and Levent, the eldest brother, has another, which he shares with his wife and their two daughters. Only the big living room and Fuat's parents' room have stoves.

There's a lot to do in such a large household, but Gül adjusts quickly. The first few days, she does anything that is asked of her quietly but reliably, but soon she begins taking on every possible chore, lending a hand where it's needed, and her initial shyness lessens because she sees she can make herself useful.

When Fuat and his brothers come home from work in the evenings, they eat, and Fuat disappears into their room soon afterwards. Gül clears the table, washes the dishes and goes to Berrin, who she has always called grandmother until now, and asks: 'Mother, does anything else need doing?'

If the answer is no, she asks if she can go. If her mother-in-law nods, she takes the stairs up to their room. But not before sticking her hand in the pocket of Fuat's coat, hanging in the hall.

Fuat can't smoke in front of his parents, because it's disrespectful to indulge in such pleasures in the presence of your elders. You mustn't sprawl on the divan or cross your legs when sitting down either.

So Fuat hides his cigarettes in his coat, and there's often also a little bottle of rakı, which would make Fuat's trousers bulge, but Gül can hide it under her broad skirts as she makes her way upstairs. Fuat is usually on his back on the mattress; he would still be smoking if there were any cigarettes left in the room. Instead, he often has his hands folded behind his head, eyes closed. When Gül opens the door, he sits up dozily.

Gül hands him the cigarettes. If there's rakı, she pours him two glasses. One with just water, from her beautiful glass carafe, one half and half: half water, half rakı. Some men like to take a sip of water after they've drunk the aniseed-flavoured spirit. A sip which, after the rakı, tastes as sweet as coffee with lots of sugar.

'Coffee must be hot,' Fuat often says, 'as hot as a girl's stolen glances, as sweet as her first kisses and as black as her mother's mood when she finds out what's gone on.'

He's not a coffee drinker, though, and he could give up the cigarettes too, he likes to think, but the booze, that he really enjoys, that has to stay.

'Put the carafe on the windowsill,' Fuat suggests, 'it keeps the water cool.'

But the carafe from Gül's trousseau is too lovely, too precious for that. So before dinner, she places a copper dish of water on the window sill and she often has to crack the layer of ice on top to pour the water into the carafe. She never would have thought she'd one day enjoy doing such a thing.

'Have a smoke with me,' Fuat says almost every evening, but Gül always says no. Her father doesn't smoke anymore, her mother has never smoked. It's a filthy habit, they say, why would she start? Fuat drinks almost five evenings a week and always offers Gül some, and she'd like to drink to keep him company, but she's seen drunks before and she'd be scared to find herself in that state, one where you obviously lose control.

And yet she often does get drunk on these evenings. She no longer finds it as hard to talk as she did in the days when they walked along the main street together. She talks about her sisters, tells the story of the sieve maker, how the other children used to tease her because she had a village accent, she talks about the colour of the circles beneath her mother's eyes before she died. And Fuat sits on a cushion, another at his back, a soft veil of smoke across his face, and he listens. He listens and nods and says 'mmhm' and 'oh' and 'I wouldn't have liked that', or he shakes his head and says: 'It beggars belief.'

Gül is often drunk on the words, drunk on the strange hum they leave behind in her head – on the sound, on the rhythm, drunk on how far her words carry, though she never raises her voice. She's only told her sisters this much before.

The words also delay the moment when it's time to put out the light. On some evenings, Gül talks for hours, but Fuat is never too tired to turn to her in the darkness.

Once a few days have passed, Timur grows used to dropping by to see his daughter before work in the morning. It's just a little out of his way – sometimes he stays for a tea, sometimes he just asks how things are, says hello to them all and disappears. He tells her that Emin has lost a milk tooth or that Melike has been skiving school. Gül tells him she gets on well with her mother-in-law and is slowly settling in. She doesn't tell him about her drunkenness; she doesn't have the words to describe what words do to her sometimes. Father and daughter spend at least a few minutes together every morning, on some days half an hour.

On her seventh day as a married woman, Gül runs into the woman with the round face and full cheeks in the street, the woman who cried at the wedding. She looks about 10 years older than Gül.

'Hello, pet, how are you?' the woman asks Gül.

'Fine, thanks. And yourself?'

'I'm well, thanks be to God. But how are you?'

Gül doesn't know how she's supposed to answer. The woman has a very friendly face, but there's something sad about her eyes.

'How are you?' she asks again, adding: 'They say a new broom sweeps clean.'

She smiles a little, as if she's said something funny.

'Thanks be to the Almighty, I am well.'

'I'm Suzan,' the woman says. 'We're neighbours now, I live in the little house next door.'

She points towards it.

'Gül,' she says, 'if you need anything, no matter what it is, my door's always open. Don't be shy... It's hard to be married so young and have to live with new people. I know what I'm talking about. When I saw you at your wedding, it reminded me of my own. You poor little thing; they propped you up on a cushion and your feet didn't even touch the floor. But that's how it is, believe me – they pay your tears no mind, you're married off when you're still a child. I was 14. How old are you?'

'15.'

'Yes, and so it goes. I'm 25 now and have three children of my own, but don't ask me what I've been through. Oh, my poor little one,' she says and strokes Gül's face.

It's the first real smile Gül has seen on Suzan's face. A warm, vigorous smile, one which looks back on the obstacles it has overcome, one which is grateful for the stones in its path, stones it has almost forgotten, a smile Gül will see a lot from now on.

'You can always come to me,' Suzan says again, and Gül murmurs: 'Thank you.'

Does Gül really have no clue of what marriage will have in store for her? She wonders who Suzan's husband is. He must be a happy man with a woman like that at his side. She's a beauty, her clothes are clean, her windows are washed, and Gül's certain she sewed that midnight blue dress herself.

In time, Gül gets to know Suzan's children too, a boy of around 10 and two girls aged seven and eight, but she never sees her husband. She doesn't want to ask her mother-in-law.

Gül and Suzan always have a chat in the street, a little gossip, a little about the weather, about Levent and Fuat; and two weeks later, Gül feels able to ask: 'Where's your children's dad, Suzan Abla?'

'He's doing time,' she says, looking Gül in the eye.

Gül feels too shy to probe further. Suzan says nothing on the matter.

When they've been married four weeks and haven't even been to the cinema once, Fuat starts going out with his friends now and then. He likes company when he drinks; they sing songs when the booze has made them gutsy and loud, and Fuat can talk with his friends, whereas he mostly just listens when he's with his wife. He can talk to them about football, about the mopeds some of them have, about cars, which they'd all love to have, about the brothel which is supposed to be somewhere halfway towards Ankara. When he comes home around one or two, he shakes Gül's shoulder and whispers her name with his boozy breath while he fumbles with her nightie.

Forty days: the young couple spend 40 days together, 40 nights of sleeping in the bed forged by Timur, 40 days in which it becomes a morning ritual for the blacksmith to visit his daughter, 40 days in which Gül gradually makes friends with Suzan, 40 evenings she often spends in their room with Fuat, talking more than she used to in a whole week. Forty days in which she cooks, washes dishes, does the laundry, tidies, dusts, shops. She's the youngest in the house and has the least rights and the most duties. She's the first to get up in the morning, making breakfast, fetching wood from the cellar and taking care of her new nieces and nephews.

After 40 days, almost 20 people gather at the station to say goodbye to Fuat, who has to report for national service in a province in the east.

'May the Lord reunite you,' Suzan says when Gül gets back from the station.

'Thank you,' Gül says.

'You see,' Suzan says, 'both our husbands are far away. Yours is in the military, mine's behind bars. There isn't a war on; yours will come back in 24 months' time, but only the Lord knows when mine will come, if ever.'

'Why... why is he in prison, Suzan Abla?'

'Highway robbery. Alleged highway robbery.'

'What happened?'

'Oh, don't ask, honey. Murat comes from a village near Erzincan. His father was killed by the village mayor in an argument. Murat wanted to avenge his father, but the mayor had his dogs everywhere, his helpers and brownnosers. When people heard he wanted to avenge his father, Murat had to escape to the mountains. And he was a highwayman out there – no, you can't say he was a highwayman, he was a child *playing* at highway robbery, he was 15 years old. After a year, he turned his back on that life and moved here. He bought and sold horses, he knows about horses. He earned his money by the sweat of his brow; he bred sheep, bought land, and my father married me to him because he was such a hard worker, because he never complained and always trusted in the strength of his arm. And especially because my father comes from Erzincan too. And then five months ago, some village idiot, another village mayor or whatever he is, went and shopped Murat. The man felt hard done-by in some deal and he knew about Murat's past. They didn't even have evidence, but the mayor must have had his people in the right places. May he be cursed, may he end up blind, deaf and homeless for taking my husband away from me.'

Gül stares at Suzan; Suzan's eyes are firm and tough.

'Anything can happen at any time, in this world,' she says, shaking her head. 'Now he's gone, and only the Lord knows when he'll be back. If it wasn't for my old father, we'd have to go out begging. Children need a father, don't they? You can't raise children without a father. Unless you live like your family. God forbid, but if one of your brother-in-laws died or had to move away, there'd still be enough men in the house, and if something happened to one of your sister-in-laws, her husband wouldn't even need to remarry to make sure his children were looked after, because everyone takes care of each other. But us, we're not from around here, and my brothers and sisters have all moved to Istanbul to find work, we haven't got anyone... Oh, look at me going on, goodness me, you don't have it easy either, do you? We none of us have it easy.'

'I'm fine,' Gül says, and she believes it herself. Just as Suzan was saying children need a father, she thought of Recep. Recep, who she will never see again.

These days, Gül sometimes sits with her sisters-in-law or their mother in the evenings, but often enough she's in her room, reading books by the light of the petroleum lamp. Books she's borrowed from the library, or books that were on sale cheap. She reads anything she can get her hands on. It reminds her a little of the summer when Uncle Abdurahman gave her that book she had trouble understanding but enjoyed reading in the end. Every time Gül thinks of Uncle Abdurahman, she doesn't know whether she ought to be disgusted, afraid or feel pity.

Unlike the photo love-stories from the autumn of her engagement, the plots in the books Gül reads often span many years. The people change, get tied up in something just because they once made a tiny mistake and tried to hide it. The books say how young women feel; they say things about shame and scandal and suffering, about gossip and chatter, sincerity and courage.

But nowhere does it say what it's like to live like a servant in your in-laws' house, because your husband is on military service. That's how Gül begins to feel as spring sets in. Like a maidservant. She's constantly being told: Gül, do this, Gül, do that –

Gül, the nappies need washing; Erkan needs the toilet; Gül, the baby's crying, go and have a quick look; Gül, fetch wood from the cellar; Gül, pop out and buy potatoes. Gül, Gül, Gül!

She doesn't grumble. How could she? She's expected to show respect. But no one here praises her when she does everything quickly and well either. It's like at home, except she has even more to do in this larger household. And the more she manages, the more they pile onto her plate.

Is it all work and effort and separation? No, there are the letters she and Fuat write to each other. Gül writes about playing with the children, about ending up in fits of laughter some nights with her sisters-in-law, about going to the cinema together, about Fuat's mother never watching the second film in a double bill, always going home first. She writes that her father looks in on her every morning, she writes that she visits her mother and sisters, and she even writes that she's sometimes sad when she sees life there going on without her. Sibel keeps things up and running, even though Melike's the oldest now. But Melike speaks up more now, says what's bothering her when she thinks Sibel is being worked too hard, says: 'No, she can't do the washing on Saturday, she has to do schoolwork. She wants to go to boarding school just like I do.'

That's what Melike has set her mind on. She wants to take the entrance exams for boarding school. The schools are state institutions set up so that children whose parents don't have enough money can attend secondary school, where they're trained as teachers.

Gül writes too that she's made friends with Suzan, and she even drops occasional hints that the work around the house is getting too much for her. And in the final lines, she always writes that she's longing to see him, because she thinks that's what she ought to write.

Fuat writes about his new friends; all great guys from all four corners of the country, some of them good card players, some good drinking buddies. He writes about the daily routine, the stresses and strains, the marches and the unbearable boots that even give you blisters on the tops of your feet. Sometimes he writes passages full of images and similes, full of rose petals and mountain lakes; letters in which shirts are aflame with the heart's burning embers. He obviously copies these parts from somewhere, or someone else writes them for him. But does it make any difference if he has to use someone else's words to express his own feelings? Does it make any difference that Gül sometimes writes two or three letters before she receives one from Fuat?

And does it make any difference that they have their first argument by post?

In the living room one evening, Gül looks at a photo of Fuat and his friends. Some of them she's met before, but she can't remember the name of one of them. She goes to Faruk the coachman and says: 'Father, look – this is Yılmaz, this one's Rıfat, that's Can, but what's this one's name again?'

'That's Selami – but that other one, the one you called Yılmaz, that's Savaş.'

'That's Yılmaz,' Gül says, stubborn.

'That's Savaş, the cobbler's son, he's been in and out of this house since he was five.'

'It's Yılmaz, I know it is.'

Gül is sure of herself, and unlike at home she tends to react defiantly with her in-laws. She doesn't have to consider her sisters here; she doesn't need to keep the peace in this house. She still feels she doesn't belong, but she also feels freer.

When Faruk and Gül fail to agree, Gül promptly puts the photo in the envelope with her next letter and adds: 'The third from the left, is it Yılmaz or Savaş?' She wants to prove herself right to her father-in-law and she thinks no further than that.

Fuat tears up the letter, tears up the photo too. He feels like going straight home and showing his wife what for. Yes, his name is Yılmaz, yes, he's a good-looking guy, and no, he's not married, but what business is that of Gül's? Why is she so interested in this man that she's sending him his photo? Just wait until he gets home; he'll give her what's coming to her!

It takes four letters by express mail, two in one direction and two in the other, for Fuat to calm down a little. Gül understands it was inconsiderate, but she feels as flattered as she is offended. She would never look at other men. Other women might do that, but she wouldn't. She knows right from wrong. What does Fuat think of her? She's a respectable woman. But one who won't refrain from telling her father-in-law she was right and that it *was* Yılmaz in the photo.

'They're using you,' Suzan says. 'They're using you like a maid. No one can force you to take their children to the toilet. You have to stand up to them, Gül, my love. These people don't see your tears, you have to carve out a place for yourself, it's not enough to get in a huff and then do what they want anyway. It's hard and you're still so young, I know what it's like. Murat's mother and sister lived with us for the first three years, it wasn't easy for me. Then my mother-in-law died and the sister married. She was twenty. That's just how it is; that's the way the world works. If you've got no one to look out for you, you have to look out for yourself. Gül, you have to do something.'

It's a cool evening with a hint of spring when Suzan says this to Gül. An evening that gives an inkling of how soft the air will soon be, an evening that brings with it the scent of earth and greenery; the kind of evening Gül would usually rejoice in. Winter is finally over; their muscles and faces can relax at last, as soon as the last vestiges of cold have left their bones.

But the next morning, Gül is sitting in the yard, in front of the huge copper basin, washing nappies and crying into the sudsy water when her father comes by. Gül wipes her tears, holds her head up high and puts on a smile.

'What's happened?'

'Nothing.'

'What do you mean nothing? Why... at this time in the morning?'

'I had a fight with Mother.'

'But that's normal; mothers- and daughters-in-law are *supposed* to fight. What was it about?'

'I wanted to wait until this evening to do the washing, and she said I had to do it now. But I wanted... I would have done it, just a bit later, but she shouted at me and cursed me. *I hope you never see your husband again*, she said.'

'She didn't really mean it. It's normal, see? Mothers- and daughters-in-law rarely get on. You know how I had to pull your mother into our room and start punching the cushions, so your Nene would think I was hitting her.'

'I know,' Gül says, holding her head high again. 'I know, but...'

'Don't take it to heart, my girl.'

He crouches down and Gül returns to her washing. They stay like that in silence for a while until the blacksmith gets up and says, 'I'll see you tomorrow.' He pats her on the shoulder and then heads for the stable: 'I'll just have a quick chat with the coachman's cows.'

Finding Gül in the yard like she is this morning, he would usually talk to her and then go up to the house to say hello.

'Father,' Gül says, and the blacksmith stops and turns to look at her. Gül sees the tears in his eyes and doesn't say anything. She doesn't cry until her father is out of sight.

Gül works less as the trees come into bud. She no longer does everything that's asked of her; sometimes she drags her feet, or pretends she's misheard or forgotten. Suzan is right – why should it always be her taking her nieces and nephews to the toilet? She dawdles in her work so she can say: 'Yes, yes, when I'm done with this, I'll get right to it.' She works less, but just as diligently as before; when she does something, she does it properly. It irks her to do a sloppy job.

The only thing she's always happy to do is ironing. Once she's plugged her iron into one of the two sockets in the house, the iron seems to glide over the fabric of its own accord. There's no longer any need to heat the iron on the stove, waiting until it reaches the right temperature, pressing harder as it slowly goes cold, and there's no need to worry about leaving rusty marks on the clothes, as almost always used to happen.

On the ground floor, a naked bulb hangs from the ceiling of each room, but there's no electricity on the first floor, so they still use the old petroleum lamps. The blacksmith has electricity in his house in town now, but it will be another 15 years before the summer houses get it.

What am I doing? Gül wonders. Even in summer there's so much to be ironed, but she knows she can get the job done; she's managed it all so far.

Though Gül sometimes has a laugh with her sisters-in-law, though she's made friends with Suzan, though her books keep her company in the evenings, though she writes letters, though she's rarely alone, she still feels lonely. She's a stranger here.

'It can't go on like this,' Suzan says.

'What do you mean?' Gül asks. 'I'm doing less work.'

'Yes, but your heart's not at peace, you look troubled. Are you happy?'

Gül doesn't answer.

'What are you doing here, anyway?'

When Gül fails to reply again, Suzan repeats the question.

'What do you mean, Suzan Abla?'

'There's lots to do, but *you* don't have to do it, do you?'

'Who else?'

'Look, sweetheart, why are you here? Because of your husband. And where's your husband? On military service. He's not here. So what are you doing here? Your mother's a daughter of this house, isn't she? Why doesn't your mother come to this house and you go home for a while? Then the two of you can give your own fathers a bit of a hand.'

Gül thinks it over for two nights. On the second morning, she asks her father what he thinks. Timur looks at the ground, thinking.

'We'll see,' he says.

He doesn't bring it up for a week, and Gül doesn't ask. When a week has passed, Melike comes by at lunchtime, which is odd for her. She wants to talk to Gül in her room.

'You've got it good here,' Melike says.

Gül shrugs. She doesn't know what her sister wants.

'Why do you want to leave? I wish I had a room all to myself.'

'I get lumped with all the work, like a donkey.'

'Why should it bother you? You've always worked hard.'

'Well, it does bother me.'

'Father wants to send Mother home, and you could come and replace her.'

'Maybe.'

'But she doesn't want to. She and Dad are arguing nearly every evening. You're tearing the family apart.'

'What?'

'You're tearing the family apart. You want to take our mother away from us.'

'Are you mad?' The words slip from Gül's lips.

Silence.

'Think about it. Mother doesn't want to come here.'

'Because she knows how much work there is to do here, and she's lazy.'

'You don't know what it's like at home.'

Melike says something else, but Gül isn't listening anymore; she can't listen, the thoughts in her head are too noisy now: *What mother am I taking away? Do you really prefer her to me? Has she ever treated you like a mother? Didn't I always do everything for you? Didn't I try to be a mother to you as best as I could? I was only a child myself. Have you ever heard a single word of praise from the woman you call Mother? She doesn't even praise her own children, I know… But still. What am I tearing apart? What's got into you? Are you mad?*

But what can she do? She's her sister. She swallows them down; she swallows down the thoughts and the words, like a drowning man swallowing water. But she's not drowning; she just feels tight around the chest, and she wishes it were night-time already, so she can be alone.

Gül used to keep the peace at home, and now I have to do it, that's what Melike probably thought and it's why she went to Gül. What else was Melike to do? It doesn't bother her that much, but Sibel's taking the nightly rows hard; she just sits in the corner and stares into space as the raised voices come through the thick walls. She's not even drawing any more.

For two more nights, Gül lies awake and moves the words around in her head. She shifts them, rearranges them, rejects them, but they always come back. *Melike's wrong,* a voice whispers inside her; it whispers though it would like to scream.

The morning after these two nights, her father says to her: 'We're moving into the summer house next week, everything's arranged – your mother will spend the summer here and you'll come to us. I've already spoken to your in-laws.'

'Thank you,' Gül says, 'you won't regret it.'

'Of course I won't regret it. Come by the forge again at lunch-time, I'll let them know that I need you there.'

When Gül arrives at the workshop at midday, it's so hot that the sweat beads on her brow at once.

'Will you scratch my calves?' Timur asks, and later he murmurs: 'How I've missed this.'

'God be with you,' a farmer greets as he enters the shop, Gül stops scratching her father's calves and the blacksmith gets up: 'God be with you, what can I do for you?'

'I need a spade,' the farmer says, 'and I'm a Beşiktaş fan too, just so we're clear. What's the trouble with your legs, if you don't mind me asking?'

'A rash,' Timur says. 'This itchy rash, it never goes away.'

'Can I take a look?'

Timur pulls up his trouser legs and the man crouches down to look.

'I used to get this too,' he says, stands up, smiles, takes his hat off and scratches his head.

'Used to?'

'Yes, used to.'

'How did you get rid of it?'

'I showed it to one of the old girls near our place in the village – she had a special remedy.'

'What kind of remedy?'

'When can you have that spade ready for me?'

'Come back in an hour. And woe betide you if I find out you're not really a Beşiktaş fan.'

'Cow piss,' says the farmer. 'You rub your calves with cow piss seven nights in a row, that'll make it go away.'

'You're having me on.'

'I swear by the Almighty! It worked for me.'

'If this is your idea of a joke, if you're taking the piss, or if I find out you support Galatasaray or something, then I'll come after you, and may God have mercy.'

'I'll be back in an hour,' the farmer says.

'Are you mad?' Arzu asks him that evening, but Timur just mutters: 'Be quiet, you know nothing about it.'

'And you're planning to come to bed like that?'

'I'm going to bed like this seven nights in a row, woman, whether you like it or not.'

On the second day, the itching stops, and in two weeks the redness and flakiness have all but disappeared. All that remains are scars and a man who sighs contentedly and says:

'I could have figured out myself that cow piss is better than any salve.'

It will be the last summer the sisters spend together for a very long time. The three of them will sit on their mother's wooden trunk very often over these three weeks. Often, they will let Nalan join them. The few times they don't let her, they will enjoy the fact that Nalan has no one to run to to tell on them. Emin will be spending the summer with his mother because he's still so little, and sometimes Nalan will also stay the night in her oldest sister's room at her grandparents' house.

Yet for the first three days, Melike refuses to speak a single word to Gül. Twice Gül tries to say something, but Melike turns on her heel and walks out.

On the fourth day, Gül is just about to go in the kitchen when she hears Sibel and Melike talking in there. She stops outsides the door and eavesdrops.

'We're sisters. You can't treat her like that. We have to stick together. We have to stick together because we haven't got a mother any more. Who else have we got but each other?'

'She shouldn't have done it,' Melike says, though she no longer sounds that convinced.

'She didn't do anything. Dad did it.'

'She's married now, she's not one of us any more. She's left us.'

'Be nice to her, Melike Abla, please, just be nice to her, alright? Do it for me. You do still love me, don't you?'

'Yes, of course.'

'Then do it for me. Do it for the love of God.'

'I wanted us to live in peace here. Was it good for you when they were fighting every night, was it? Mother will come back and take her anger out on us. And Gül will be sitting tight at the coachman's house. She's sitting pretty and I'm always the one on the wrong end of trouble, no matter what happens. You know how often Mother hits me. And just because I open my mouth and don't sulk all day long like you and Gül.'

'We might never be together like this again. She's our sister, we belong together. And that little bit of trouble…'

'We'll see,' Melike says.

On tiptoe, Gül goes out in the garden, lies down in the tall grass and cries.

Later that day, Melike pushes a book into Gül's hands: 'Test me! Page 49.'

And she starts reciting the text of her biology book by heart. In the middle of a sentence, she tips her head to the left at the exact point where Gül has to turn the page.

'Good,' Gül praises her, and Melike gives a quick smile, against her will.

After a few days, it's as if they'd never lived any differently. Now they don't need to wait until their mother leaves the house if they want to open the chest and try on the dresses. They often take out the ball and play with it. Usually inside the house, but sometimes they take it outdoors with them. Never for more than an hour though. For years, they were never allowed to take the ball outside for longer than an hour, and now they're perhaps scared the ball might burst or come apart in some way if it's outside for too long on the dusty, stony street in the bright sunlight.

Their mother comes over every few days to check on them, but Gül tidies and cooks, Sibel washes the dishes, and even Melike lifts a finger sometimes, helping to hang up the washing. Almost every time Gül tips the water out of the copper basin, she can't help thinking how she was doing the washing even before she had the strength to empty the tub.

The days pass – it's the summer holidays and there isn't much to do. Gül enjoys being able to plan her own time; she likes not having anyone around to boss her about; she does everything by choice and she's happy to do it. It seems to her that she's working less than before her wedding; less than when her mother was still doling out the chores. And she knows she probably won't have that same freedom again for a very long time.

Melike revises for her exams, which are coming up soon. As a distraction and a reward, she plays volleyball. Sibel wanders through the gardens, perhaps pinching cherries or playing with clay; in the evening, she usually draws by the light of the pneumatic lamp, and Gül watches her purse her lips and frown in concentration. Gül visits Esra a couple of times, but only to play with Candan. She's tempted to ask Esra about her lie. But she doesn't dare. Esra might've only lied so as not to frighten her, but she still can't forgive her.

'Nothing,' she says, 'it's nothing,' whenever Esra asks what the matter is.

Sometimes Gül slips out for a glass of tea at Suzan's, always making sure her in-laws and her mother don't see her. Now and then, she goes to visit her parents-in-law as well. Then she's really a kind of guest, no one asking her for anything. But she knows that will change as soon as she moves back in.

When Arzu comes home for a day, she calls the sisters together, enraged.

'You've been playing with the ball from the trunk!'

'No, we haven't,' Melike cuts in. 'Why would we be playing with the ball?'

Gül is grateful for her lying, and hopes they'll get away with it.

'Hush,' Arzu snaps at Melike. 'See those marks on the wall? Where do they come from, eh? Did you borrow a ball from someone else? There's a mark on the wall from a ball.'

She's yelling now: 'Ungrateful, that's what you are. I've hardly turned my back on you three and you go rummaging around in my trunk. Who gave you permission? That was the last time, I promise you that. You spoilt brats; may you get cancer, all three of you!'

She sometimes says the thing about cancer when she's gone red in the face, and none of the three sisters know what it means.

Once she finds out, Gül will think a proper mother would probably curse differently. *Oh, if only I hadn't had you!* she might say, but she'd never wish her children dead.

That evening, Sibel, Melike and Gül hear their parents fighting. Their loud voices find their way through the thick walls, but they can't understand what they're shouting about. Gül goes very quiet. And she hopes Melike stays quiet too.

After breakfast, the blacksmith asks his eldest to come into the garden with him. His wife has spent the night.

'She didn't want to go back,' he says. 'She says you can't behave yourselves. I'm going to make a lock for the chest. But you have to promise me nothing of the sort will happen again. Is that clear? Otherwise, she'll come here and you'll have to go back.'

'Yes, but…'

'But?'

'I promise it won't happen again,' Gül says, though she knows she can't speak for Melike.

That same day, a lock is fitted to Arzu's chest; the other remains unlocked. And Gül thinks there'd be more gold jewellery in there now, if that chest had also had a lock on it after her mother's death. They only took a ball and put it back afterwards, but their grandmother pocketed the gold bracelets which had been in there. Gül didn't see her do it, but she's sure it was her. Where else could the bracelets have gone?

They don't play with it any more that summer, but next year Melike will have found a way to get her hands on the precious plastic ball. Perhaps just to prove to herself that she can't be refused anything.

'What's it like being married?' Melike asks a week later, admiring herself in her mother's dress in front of the mirror.

'It's nice,' Gül says, a little offhandedly.

'Sibel, give me the shoes,' Melike says, and then she asks: 'What's Uncle Fuat like?'

She and Sibel still call him Uncle Fuat, and that will never change.

'How should he be?'

'Does he hit you?'

Melike puts the shoes on. For a long time, they were too big for her, but now they almost fit. Smiling contentedly, she twirls around again in front of the mirror, the one with the dark spots.

'No, why would he hit me?'

'Are you in love?'

'I think so.'

'Why hasn't he come to visit you?'

'Because it's not easy getting leave in your first year in the army, and it's such a long journey. He'll come in the autumn.'

'I won't be here in the autumn.'

'God willing.'

'In autumn, I'll be at boarding school. And I'll only come home at the weekend.'

Sibel has put a dress on too. Gül crouches next to the chest and runs her hand over the crocheted doilies.

'I want to go to boarding school too,' Sibel says.

'You can come next year. You'll manage it, you're doing well at school,' Melike says.

'So are you,' Sibel says.

Gül puts a dress on too. There are precisely three dresses in the chest, two pairs of shoes and two cardigans, two lamb's wool blankets, and the wedding dress. It used to be the first thing they'd try on, taking it in turns, but this summer the wedding dress holds little interest any more.

The three of them jostle in front of the mirror, all three of them in dresses that are too big for them; only Gül is nearly big enough to fill one. 'I would love to have a photo of that,' Gül will say later, when she thinks back to this day. 'The three of us in our mother's dresses in front of the big mirror in the hallway of the summer house. The three of us; we must have been happy.'

Melike passes the entrance exams for the state high school and moves away to a boarding school in a town nearly two hours away by train. When she comes home, she's always very irritable and fights with their mother almost daily. But she tells Sibel excitedly about her new friends, about the dormitory, about the food – the only thing she doesn't like – and about the teachers. Sibel listens intently. If Melike weren't already at boarding school, Sibel might not have wanted to take the exams, out of fear of never finding her feet in a strange, new place.

During her first year at boarding school, Melike starts smoking.

'You try it,' she says to Sibel and gives her a drag.

It makes Sibel cough. She feels dizzy and she squats down in the narrow alleyway where they're standing.

'Father would kill you,' she says, when the coughing fit has passed.

'Don't you say a word. If you do, I'll tell him you smoked too.'

'I only took a drag.'

'Then you can tell Dad that.'

In the future, the sisters will smoke together like this more often, but soon Melike will stop coming home every weekend. Because the train is so expensive, she says – and the little money her father gives her only just covers chocolate and cigarettes. Not that she says that.

Sometimes Melike comes home completely exhausted because she doesn't get much sleep in the dormitory. It has nothing to do with wanting to keep talking and smoking in secret after the lights go out. There are four or five girls who meet at the back of the dormitory at night, smoke, whisper and clamp their lips tightly shut to hold back the giggles so they don't get caught, but Melike isn't one of them.

She can't study during the day; it's too noisy, she can't concentrate, and she's quickly distracted. No lights are allowed in the dormitory after 10 o'clock, so the night before a test Melike gets up, takes her blanket and her book, and sits in the toilets. She sits by the sinks and learns her texts off by heart – from her chemistry book, her history book, her physics book, her Turkish book. She memorises the texts just as she has for a long time now, and later, when she's an adult, fragments of these texts will occur to her in public toilets, and she'll always remember at which point in a sentence she'd have to turn the page.

It's cold in the toilets, and Melike always hurries because she wants to go back to the warm dormitory. But sometimes she sits there until her fingers are so stiff she can hardly turn the page.

On more than one occasion, Melike comes home and pulls an old blouse or a crumpled jumper of hers out of her bag – the jumper might have a hole in the elbow, the blouse might be missing a couple of buttons. She holds the piece of clothing aloft and says to Sibel: 'Would you like this?'

'Yes,' Sibel always says, 'yes please.'

And she takes it, sews on the buttons, patches it, darns it or threads through some new elastic, and on Sunday, when Melike is packing her bag, she sees her old clothes looking good as new and says: 'This is in better nick than I thought. I'm taking it with me, you can have it next time.'

'But you... you gave it to me.'

'Yes, yes, it's yours, I just want to take it with me this time.'

And often enough, Sibel won't see the clothes again until there's nothing left to salvage. And yet she always repairs her sister's clothes; she just can't refuse the gifts. But sometimes Sibel will just hide them once she's fixed them, and she won't put them on until Melike's gone.

When it comes to order and diligence, Sibel takes a little after Gül. She makes the breakfast, plays with Nalan and Emin, does the washing at the weekends, and no one ever hears her complain. She can do whatever Gül can. And since she's had less time recently, she cherishes all the more the hours when she can paint undisturbed.

One day, Timur brings her some watercolours, and when Arzu sees them, she says: 'What's the girl supposed to do with them? She's no painter. Since when can we afford this sort of thing?'

But except for Sibel, there are only three other children in her class who have watercolours, and when a neighbour asks Arzu if it's true Sibel has started taking watercolours to school, she proudly replies: 'Yes, her father bought them for her. She paints beautifully, it was about time we got her something special.'

Once Gül is back at her in-laws' house, it doesn't take a week before she gets in a row with her mother-in-law. She's accused of losing a sock while doing the washing, a good wool sock, not one made in prison. Gül is certain the sock was missing before and she says so too, but her mother-in-law yells at her that everything went better when she wasn't around.

That can't be true – there was a thick layer of dust on her in-laws' radio, a device many people own these days; the glasses in the cupboard were stained; the cabinet was in a mess; the hall rug obviously hadn't been beaten all summer; and Gül found a pair of pants in the cellar that definitely didn't belong there.

But despite the row, things are better for Gül with her husband's family now. One of her sisters-in-law helps her with the washing and the dishes, the other borrows the iron regularly, and they seem to be putting less work on her plate in general. Berrin has even stopped calling Gül's name impatiently across the road when Gül is deep in conversation with Suzan.

'You see,' Suzan says, 'it was good that your mother came to stay. It made them see how good they have it with you. I've always got on well with her. You may hate her sometimes, but she can't help it that you're not her real children. She's an honest woman, sometimes she pays a bit too much attention to appearances, but I've never seen a bad side to her.'

She looks Gül in the eye and Gül says nothing; but she decides to talk to Suzan less over the next few days.

Fuat doesn't arrive until the night frosts set in. They wouldn't grant him leave before then. 'You've only just got here,' they told him, 'are you homesick already?' And he answered that he was newly wed and his wife was waiting for him at home. They all laughed at that.

In the 10 months he's been away, he's put on a bit of a belly, and his cheeks look even fuller with his unfamiliar cropped hair. He has three weeks of leave, and four days of that are spent on buses and trains.

Gül has been looking forward to seeing him, to the days he'll be at home. She will feel less like she doesn't belong once everyone can see why she's living in the house. But at the same time, even though the thing with Yılmaz was a few months ago, she's scared their argument won't stay confined to the page.

Fuat arrives in the evening, and the whole family eats together, talking into the night. Until the moment they're alone, Fuat doesn't pay much attention to Gül. And then, once they're in their room, Gül is glad he's not cross with her any more – but she does find herself wishing for that protective shell again.

Fuat leaves the house right after breakfast the next morning. He wants to meet his friends, most of them older than him and finished with their national service. Some of them are unemployed now and spend their days killing time. He wants to tell them about the jeeps they drive in the military, about there being no brothels out there in the east. He wants to sit with his friends in the tea-house again, play cards or backgammon, smoke and forge plans for the future.

'Soon there won't be any carriages left in Istanbul,' Fuat predicts, 'but my father will still have work 10 years from now. We're so far away from all the modern stuff here, but I'm telling you, one day I'll have enough money to buy myself a Cadillac.'

'Me too,' Rıfat says, 'I'm going to get myself the longest car there is.'

'With chrome headlamps and leather seats,' Yılmaz adds. 'We don't want to spend our lives on the back of a donkey.'

'Right, exactly,' Fuat says, 'and then you dangle your arm out of the window, a cigarette between your lips, and you enjoy every minute of it. That's the life...'

'No,' Can says, 'you need an asphalt road as smooth as cream, and then you put your foot down and drive so fast you think you've got wings. That's how to drive a car...'

In the end, the three of them squeeze onto the back of Can's moped and head for the stream to drink a glass or two and pass the time talking about football; sharing their dirty jokes, dreams for the future, and smutty songs.

In the evenings, Fuat and Gül go to their room, and once again Gül savours the words that come out of her mouth. It's enough for her to just sit there and talk and hear Fuat's identical comments: 'You wouldn't believe it' and 'I understand' and 'That's the way it is'. But after five days, he starts going out after dinner as well.

One morning, steam rising from their mouths, Suzan says to Gül: 'You look tired. Not getting much sleep at night?'

Gül stares mutely at the ground; Suzan laughs.

'That's what I'll have ahead of me, if they release Murat one day.'

'Oh, if only they'd let him go soon,' Gül says.

'They've transferred him to Istanbul. God alone knows why, and I've stopped getting letters as well.'

Fuat doesn't get home until one or two in the morning. Gül usually wakes up because he can't coordinate his movements, swaying from wall to wall and into the wardrobe. Gül pretends to be asleep, but often he shakes her awake, only rarely falling into bed beside her and starting to snore straight away.

After 17 days, they take him to the station. His mother can't hold back her tears and Gül cries too – partly because she'll be alone again now with no one to listen to her like Fuat did at least those first few evenings, and partly because it's expected of her. Arzu won't be outdone by the two of them, loudly bewailing that her brother has to leave home again.

Even Gül's grandmother Zeliha is there. Not knowing whether anyone is listening to her, she says: 'Why all the tears, I thought the boy had put on weight? He's having a grand time out there, kebab and baklava every day, so there's no need for cry for him.'

Suzan shakes her head and gives the old woman a disapproving look. On the way home, she puts her arm around Gül.

'It won't be much longer. You've managed half of it already.'

'354 days,' Gül says, imagining her life will change when her husband moves back home.

'Oh, what are 350 days?' Suzan says, rounding down. 'Have I told you the story of Murat's army mate, Mesut? You could write a book about the man. Mesut was in love with this woman from his village, the poor guy – as infatuated as Mecnun was with Leyla, as Romeo with Juliet. He'd fallen in love like he'd been struck down by a rock, and her father promised to give her to him once he'd finished his national service. Mesut went to the military with a heavy heart. But once he got there, he heard she was just about to marry someone else. So he went AWOL and made his way to the village, only to find out it was all just a rumour, not a word of truth. When he got back, they gave him two extra months as punishment for leaving without permission. He stuck it out for almost six months, but the longing chewed him up and spat him out; every morning his yearning spat him out again and every day he got smaller, and every night the yearning got bigger. He couldn't resist a day longer, he had to see her. So he spent three days traveling to his village, saw her in the barn for a couple of hours and then left again. This time they gave him another four months extra. And once again, he heard she wanted to marry another. He needed certainty, and the letter got lost in the post or something – anyway he went AWOL again... You get the point. By the time Murat met him, he'd been in the military for three and a half years. And he still had 120 days to go.'

When Suzan stops talking, Gül asks: 'And?'

'What shall I say? It's not a fairytale, who can wait four years? She might have done, who knows? But her father gave her to another man, one with more sense in his head than Mesut, as he put it. Oh yes, that's how the world works, my dear. No one takes any notice of your tears.'

On the cold mornings when he goes to visit his daughter before work, on Sunday evenings, in the breaks between a double bill at the cinema, when Sibel comes to the forge during lunch, and on many occasions that winter, the blacksmith rummages in the pocket of his waistcoat and brings out a stained envelope. He will keep up this habit all the years that Melike is at secondary school and later, too, when she's at teaching college.

'Read it to me, would you,' he says, and he sits down, props his elbows on his knees, lowers his head and listens attentively. Sometimes he mouths the words as they're read, because he knows the letter almost by heart. Sometimes he has tears in his eyes when he looks up at the end.

'Oh, Gül, go on, read your sister's letter to me again, please.'

Or: 'Oh, Sibel, I've already forgotten what Melike wrote, can you read it to me again?'

On these winter mornings, when, for the 15th time, her father pulls out the same letter and, for the 15th time, listens with the very same devotion, Gül wishes she had at least finished her basic schooling; she wishes she had a leaving certificate.

She knew little of life then. Now that she reads books and she's the one her father comes to most to read his letters, now that Melike is far away and will probably be a teacher soon, now she would like it if the same doors were not closed to her. She'd like a certificate.

A few weeks after leaving Fuat at the station, it's Bayram, the end of the Ramadan fast. From morning until night, relations and friends pay little visits to Gül's in-laws. On days like these, it's good to have something special to offer your guests, and Faruk, the coachman, hands out chocolate and a small glass of liqueur. Every time guests arrive, Gül pours the liqueur and heads for the living room, a tray full of glasses in one hand and a crystal bowl of chocolates wrapped in silver paper in the other. Men before women, elders before children, and anyone who says no will be invited again to help themselves. And again. And again, by Gül's mother-in-law. Most people take the chocolate. If they don't eat it, they slip it into a pocket. But many turn down the liqueur.

For most, it's a long day with lots of visits to make. Only older people like Gül's in-laws are allowed to stay at home on the first day of Bayram and wait for others to come and pay their elders a visit. Berrin has bought plenty of chocolate and three bottles of sour-cherry liqueur. She daren't think what people might say if the guests arriving in the morning were served something different to the guests arriving in the afternoon. There are only six liqueur glasses, and Gül doesn't want to leave the glasses of rejected liqueur sitting out until the next guests arrive. Ants could crawl all over them, dust could fall inside. Until midday, she carefully pours the contents of the glasses back into the bottle, but eventually it gets too laborious and there are still two full bottles left. So she simply finishes off the glasses herself and then washes them up. This way, she doesn't have to keep wiping away the sticky drips which run down the outside of the bottle, where a little spills every time she pours it back in.

The liqueur is sweet, but not as sweet as the chocolate, so Gül soon begins eating a piece of chocolate after each glassful. Berrin is sitting in the living room talking to the guests; she doesn't know what Gül is doing in the kitchen. As long as her daughter-in-law appears with the tray and the crystal bowl whenever new guests arrive, it's alright by her.

Gül has never drunk alcohol before in her life. She's seen what alcohol can do to a person, in Fuat and in others, and it scares her. Wine and beer and rakı, that's alcohol – what she's drinking now is something you can offer to guests even on a religious holiday, a sweet drink with an enticing scent, blood red like Snow White's lips. Gül's only really drinking it out of convenience, because she doesn't want to have to pour the tiny glasses back into the bottle. And the chocolate tastes better with every glass, so now and then she scoffs two pieces in one go.

In the afternoon, fewer guests turn down the liqueur, but by that time Gül's drunk eight or nine glasses, or maybe 11, she's hardly keeping count. At first she feels a little dizzy, and at the same time [she feels] light-headed. She has no trouble offering round more chocolate and liqueur; her movements are still coordinated when she starts to feel unwell. For the first minute, she tries to push the feeling down, but she has a sour taste in her mouth. She tries to swallow it down, but seconds later saliva pools in her mouth again, saliva she thinks must smell like rancid butter. She tries to wash the taste away with a glass of the sweet liqueur. When the drink reaches her stomach, she feels its contents coming right back up.

She runs but doesn't make it to the toilet. She throws up on a wall in the yard. Her stomach tightens painfully, the warm torrent shoots out her throat. It feels as if she's going to throw up her innards, ribs and all. There are tears in her eyes, and she tries in vain to suppress the rhythmic retching, which doesn't stop even once her stomach's empty. A thick, brown pool steams in the cold air. Gül watches her tears drip into it.

'What's happened?'

Gül only notices her mother-in-law now.

'Poor thing, you look a fright!'

'I felt a bit sick.'

'Are you alright now?'

Gül nods.

'Come inside, give your face a wash. I'll make you a mint tea. You should have a lie down.'

After two glasses of mint tea, Gül is feeling a little better. Her stomach feels queasy and her limbs are limp. When she tries to stand up, her head spins and her legs won't behave. So she lies back down and dozes off.

She hears the knocks at the door, she hears the guests coming and going, but the noises reach her ears as if from some vague distance, and sometimes the sounds seem to symbolise something important, but Gül can't quite grasp what they mean.

It's early evening when she comes round. The first word that appears in her mind is: chocolate. As soon as she's thought it, she starts feeling sick again. She banishes the word and the image, the whole thought of it. She will drink alcohol a few more times in her life, but she'll never eat chocolate again.

Her mother-in-law comes into the room as Gül is folding the blanket Berrin had placed over her.

'I think I ate too much chocolate,' Gül says.

'It doesn't matter,' Berrin says. 'Don't worry about it. Why have you got your cardi on, where are you going?'

'Out to the yard.'

'Your sister's already cleaned it up.'

Gül reddens: 'Oh... May the Lord reward her.'

The next morning, she makes it to the toilet. And the morning after that. She feels fine during the day – no dizziness, no nausea. Except she sometimes gets tired from one second to the next and all she wants to do is lie down and sleep. Then she sits down for a few moments and closes her eyes. Often, she wakes with a start from her head tipping down as the tension leaves her body. She gets up quickly, eats a walnut with köfter and goes on with her work.

'It won't go away,' she tells Suzan. 'I'm scared. It's almost a week ago now and I still feel sick, every morning the Lord sends us.'

Suzan smiles.

'What? You're not taking me seriously.'

Still smiling, Suzan shakes her head.

'Suzan Abla, maybe I'm ill, maybe I've got cancer or something.'

'No, honey, you're not ill. You're probably pregnant, that's what it'll be. When was your last period?'

Gül draws her brows together and then quietly mouths: 'I'm pregnant.'

'Come here, let me give you a hug.'

'May the Lord bless me with a healthy child.'

Gül waits another two weeks, during which she no longer feels sick every morning, and then she's sure of it. She's going to be a mother. She's going to feel what her own mother felt. Two weeks, and then she tells everyone; her mother-in-law gives a knowing smile and embraces her. Sibel doesn't know quite how to react to the news, and nor do Nalan or Emin. Timur's eyes glaze over and he looks away, while Arzu says: 'Aha, so now you'll be a real woman too.'

Back when Timur noticed *her* first pregnancy, he wasn't the slightest bit emotional.

Most of the day, Zeliha sits on a cushion, another one squeezed behind her back. She's still lending money and she still never gets her debtors muddled up. She talks to the neighbours who come to visit her, to friends and relatives. People who don't know what to do come to see her. Women whose husbands drink away the money for food, women who know their sons are stealing, women who often argue with their husbands. Suzan comes to her to find out whether Zeliha knows someone who knows someone who might be able to help her husband. People come who trust in her age and experience, especially her age. And with all these visitors, the blind woman always picks up the latest gossip without even having to stand up. She's very well informed of the events in her small town, and it instils trust in people that she always knows who's doing what with whom, and why. Why little Bülent doesn't look like his father, why Derviş is a secret drinker, where Derya hides her jewellery, why Begüm is angry with her sister, and who kicked Bora's dog.

She barely moves from the warm stove and she can tell almost anyone by the sound of their footsteps now. But this winter she wants to go to the hamam with all the family again, at least that's what Arzu says.

Perhaps it's just Gül's imagination – no one else complains about it – but this winter seems to be even colder than the last. So she's looking forward to warming the marrow of her bones again in the hamam.

'We're all going to the steam bath tomorrow – my mother, my grandmother, Sibel and Nalan. Would you like to come with us?' Gül asks her mother-in-law.

'Where are you going?'

'To the steam bath. My Nene wanted us all to go.'

Berrin seems to think it over. Gül is busy picking over lentils, but if she were to look up, she'd see the shadow on her mother-in-law's face. Her expression growing hard, firm and thoughtful, the slight movement of her chin, her head leaning to one side as if she were resigning herself to something.

'Your grandmother?'

'Yes, my grandmother wanted us all to go together.'

'I… I won't be coming with you.'

Berrin leaves the kitchen and murmurs, inaudible to Gül: 'Taking a pregnant woman to the steam bath… What a wicked woman.'

Gül spends the next day in the hamam. It's almost like the old days, except it's calmer without Melike, almost dull. Emin starts school next year; he's too old to go along with the women now.

Sibel casts a curious glance at Gül's belly once they're naked.

'You can't see it yet,' Gül says.

'What would you like to have,' Sibel asks, 'a girl or a boy?'

'A girl. No. No, actually, a boy. I've written to Fuat to tell him I'm pregnant. The baby might be here next time he comes.'

'And what will you call him?'

'If it's a boy… we'll call him Timur. He's bound to grow as big and strong as Dad.'

'Yes, just look at Emin. And if it's a girl?'

'Ceyda. If it's a girl, we'll call her Ceyda.'

'Ceyda?'

'I read a book about a woman called something like that. People start talking about her because they all think she's… she's sullied, you know? Even her mother thinks so. But Ceyda knows she's pure, so she doesn't let it worry her.'

'Ceyda. I'll be an auntie.'

'Yes.'

'Did you hear Nene just now?'

'What?'

'She wants to leave already, she said it's too hot for her, and she asked why we dragged her all this way. And Mum said: "But you wanted to come, don't you remember?" And she answered: "I might be blind, but I've still got my wits."'

Not until years later does Gül make sense of it.

They've been at the baths for a long time and they want to take their time sitting in the anteroom before heading out into the cold. The door is wrenched open, and Aunt Hülya, who didn't come with them, storms in and runs over to her mother, who recognises her from the sound of her footsteps.

'Hülya?'

'Yes, Mother. Mother, Yücel is dead!'

The family hardly mentions Yücel any more since he and Hülya separated. Uncle Yücel, who lived alone in a little house on the edge of town, seemed to have no contact with Hülya, nor with the rest of the family. There'd been rumours he wanted to move in with his married sister, there'd been rumours he'd got mixed up with men doing illegal deals, it was said he was drinking, he was soon to marry; a beauty from Fertek, a nearby village. And now he's dead.

Zeliha sits there, entirely unmoved.

'Where are you getting this?'

'The whole town's talking about it,' Hülya says. 'He was getting a shave, and the barber thought he'd fallen asleep.' Hülya starts to cry. As far as Gül knows, she hasn't spoken to him for years.

'Calm down, child, it's just the way of the world, some come, others go.'

'Just like that,' Hülya sobs, and when she drops to her mother's feet, Gül notices there's a hole in the sole of her shoe. 'He fell asleep at the barber's, just like that.'

'Calm down,' Zeliha says. 'He wasn't worth all this.'

'But he was my husband.'

Gül folds her hands in her lap and drops her gaze, looks at her fingers. The first teardrop falls on the nail of her right thumb.

She doesn't know what the rumours said, she doesn't know why Auntie Hülya and Uncle Yücel split up, she doesn't know what flaws he might have had, but she sees him before her, Sibel on his feet – she sees him before her, playing with Melike, tending tirelessly to his nieces, and Gül can't remember ever seeing him impatient or even annoyed. She sees that friendly face before her – she still remembers the feel of his moustache, and she still remembers his smell. Like eau de cologne and something that might have been shaving foam. No, she doesn't know what flaws he might have had, but when he stands before his maker, she's sure the Almighty will consider how he cared for the three sisters.

Lord, let him rest in peace, Gül prays, and she'll repeat this prayer a few more times in bed, in the darkness of her room. She will grieve for a man she hardly knew, she will spend days thinking of him, and by the time he slowly vanishes from her thoughts, her belly will have grown a little.

Gül gets up in the morning, makes the breakfast, sometimes she washes up, sometimes someone else does, she does the housework, knits, and goes to the cinema. She writes letters to Fuat and she reads books of scripture, she puts more wood on the fire, tidies her room and crochets doilies. She eats and sleeps, and now and then she argues with her mother-in-law. Sometimes when she lies in bed at night, she's surprised by how short the day has been, and sometimes the day never seems to end. She plays with her nephews and nieces, but it's not the same as playing with her siblings or with Candan. She sits with Suzan, who hasn't had word from her husband for months. Gül laughs and cries and yawns and wakes in the night when she's hungry or her baby kicks.

Winter passes, spring comes; Gül feels lighter, more lively, the light seems to seep into her bones and render them weightless. The green delights her eyes; with every new bud her belly seems to grow rounder, everything is blooming and flourishing. Springtime feels like a fertility ritual, an ancient feast held to honour the gods, in a dance hall with huge columns, where worries have no place and everyone forgets whatever they've been yearning for.

When summer returns, so does Melike, and on the second evening after she gets back, the blacksmith has her read aloud all the letters she wrote in her own voice. Melike often goes to visit Gül; now they've been apart for so long, they get along well. Melike likes to put her ear to Gül's belly and listen.

Melike plays with the precious ball from their mother's chest again. She can't unlock the padlock, so she simply unscrews the hinges on the other side of the trunk and takes the ball out, screwing the hinges back in when she's put the ball back.

She plays with Sibel or meets up with Sezen, who goes to a secondary school in town. Her parents have money, so she doesn't have to go to a state boarding school. Full of pride, she tells Melike she's now on her school volleyball team, and her team are going to take part in the championships and win.

Melike acts very self-assured; she knows what she wants and she always has the courage to ask for it, and loudly. Sibel thinks her sister has become more grown-up in the year she's been away, more grown-up than Gül. And she knows she'll never be as brave as her, brave enough to follow her dreams. She's scared of going to the same boarding school as Melike. Even though she wouldn't be on her own there, Sibel wouldn't like to be so far from home; she wants to stay near her parents and near Gül, here in town. But she listens, fascinated, when Melike tells them about a school trip to the sea. The blue of the sea blended with the blue of the sky, the water was salty, but not as salty as the water in the salt lake, and it was warmer than the water that flows through the gardens in spring. It seemed calmer, too, though there were waves.

Sibel would also like to see the sea. To paint it. But she can also paint it from her imagination, now that Melike has described it. She shows her sister the watercolour painting the very next evening.

'No,' Melike says, 'the water is darker than that, and the waves are much higher, and they're not crinkled like that. They're the same distance apart, and the water on the shore is white, but not like soap bubbles, the bubbles are lighter.'

'Water,' the blacksmith always says, 'we're used to water from a cup, not the sea – we're Anatolians.'

'Water,' Gül says too, drenched in sweat and mid-contraction. 'Please give me some water!'

It's a boiling hot day and she's on the bed in her room – her mother and mother-in-law and a midwife are there, Gül's pillow is soaked through, she doesn't want to scream and she doesn't want to sweat. No one told her it would hurt so much. She wishes she were somewhere far, far away; she wants someone to come and deliver her from this torment. She feels her mother-in-law squeezing her hand, but she only senses the calming words, she can't hear them; there's no room in her head for any more sounds.

Two days. The baby could have waited two more days. In two days, Fuat will arrive. Gül screams, her face a grimace; sweat drips from a strand of hair directly into her ear and she shudders. She still remembers it exactly, years later, that drip, which she thinks runs down her ear canal right into her brain. Ceyda must have come shortly after that. Or perhaps a long time after that. Time no longer exists; it stretches and spreads and then concentrates in one spot and disappears somehow. But the baby comes at some point. The Lord has answered her prayers; it's a healthy baby. Her hands and feet in the right places, a scream as beautiful as birdsong in spring and her sleep as soft as lambs' wool.

Gül's in-laws have an orchard too, and Fuat has to help with the harvest. He's on leave but he spends all day picking apples, and in the evenings after cuddling his daughter, he falls into bed exhausted. Gül suspects he'd rather have had a son but she's not sure, and the only time she sees her husband in the eight days of his stay is at night. His belly has got fatter again; everyone jokes about how good he's got it in the military and how they all just laze around smoking cigarettes, eating baklava and going to brothels when they're allowed out. The latter only comes from his friends, pulling his leg.

In the first few days of the apple harvest, Fuat's muscles ache like bruises. They do laze around in the military, eating, playing cards and telling each other the same old stories from back home.

'Back home, right, back home in our village, there's this old lady, right, and she can talk to the souls of the dead.' Or: 'In the next village, this really happened, believe me, I'm not having you on, I know it's not right but that's the way people are – anyway the people from the next village, they have these unbelievable ideas! May the Lord not curse them… One of the young men there fucked a dog. I know, I know you've heard all about that kind of thing, but the bitch got a cramp and he couldn't pull his dick back out, he couldn't, it was stuck. He didn't know what to do – he beat the poor dog and he tried to feed her, but she'd cramped right up and he couldn't get his thing out again. Yes, it's a sin, I know. In the end he beat the dog to death with a stone, and she cramped up even more as she was dying, but he finally managed to pull his dick out. Ever since then, they've fucked their chickens up the arse instead, in the next village! Really, it's true, the Almighty is my witness.'

Those were the stories they passed their time with, but now he has to work like everyone else. They're busy all day long, pausing briefly at noon to eat bread and cheese under the shade of the trees – and in the evenings, their eyes are red with fatigue, their arms weak, and they can still feel the smooth skin of the apples on their fingertips.

Gül stays at home, feeding Ceyda, taking care of the household, cooking so her husband and in-laws have something to eat after work.

When they all come home from the orchard one evening, Gül sets aside the book she's been reading and goes to put the pan on the dinner table. Her brother-in-law Levent says: 'You should be helping out with the harvest, not swanning around back here! We're working our fingers to the bone all day long and you're reaping the reward. Are you just a guest in this house or what?'

Perhaps he's annoyed about something else, perhaps he's so exhausted he doesn't know what he's saying, but Gül holds her breath. She stops breathing and knows she won't be able to say a word back to him.

'Enough, hush!' her father-in-law scolds, when Levent opens his mouth to add something. 'Don't you think you're something special just because you've worked so hard today. Gül does her bit, you know that full well.'

Gül is glad he says something. But she's not satisfied. *Lord, may I not be stuck for an answer.*

Everyone in this house gives their mite, and Levent can go out to the cinema with his wife any time he likes without having to ask who'll look after their children. There's always someone there, everyone helps each other, and now her brother-in-law is snapping at her for no reason.

Melike goes back to boarding school, but without Sibel, who isn't desperate to see the sea. After a few attempts, she manages to paint it without having seen it. She doesn't need to know what the big shops look like, and what's the point of having three cinemas next to each other if you can only go into one? She does still want to go to secondary school, to boarding school, so there'll be one less belly to fill at home. Yet she hardly eats anything. It's clear, not just in her class where she's the youngest, but also among her peers, how small and weedy Sibel is.

She'd like to be a teacher: teachers are always needed, and after three years at secondary school, you can be a trained primary school teacher and earn your own money. And teach art.

Perhaps Sibel also wants to go to boarding school because she knows it's exactly what her mother expects of her, because she has the feeling her mother will be happy to have more space at home. She takes the entrance exams for the boarding segment of the state secondary school and passes with ease. From the autumn, she spends the weekdays at a nearby boarding school and at the weekends she walks the 20 minutes home. Melike writes letters, Sibel spends the weekends at home, but now it's Gül who knows most about what goes on at home, because she sees her father nearly every day. Of the three sisters, she is the closest to her family, though she thought her marriage would take her the furthest away.

Gül sleeps with Ceyda on a mattress in the living room, where it's warmest; the bedstead has been with a newly-wed couple for some time now. But it will only see another four wedding nights before it finally collapses, prompting all kinds of obscene whispers about the newlyweds from behind closed doors. And so the story of the bed comes to an end. It begins with love and craftsmanship, sweat and rigour, skill and flair and strength, but ultimately cheap jokes are all that remains.

It would easily have lasted another two or three decades if it hadn't been tied to a horse and cart every couple of months, bashed against door frames, if it hadn't fallen off a pickup truck, if it had been carried instead of shoved. And so the story of the bed comes to an end, except it doesn't end, because the bed is still lauded in the words of those who remember it today.

In the mornings, it's Gül's job to stoke the fire in the wood stove, which goes out in the night. One Sunday, her father-in-law and Fuat's brother spend the weekend in a neighbouring town. It's a mild morning at the end of December, and only at breakfast time does Berrin happen to notice that the fire's not burning: 'What's this? Are you having a lazy day today? Do you want us all to freeze?'

'It's not that cold. I'll do it right after breakfast,' Gül says. She takes a defiant sip of her tea. It's not as if the whole house will freeze if she takes another 10 minutes before lighting the stove. And they've all slept in rooms where it's been really freezing. Even her mother-in-law.

'Come on, hurry up,' Berrin says. 'Don't come the big tea lover with me, stop lazing around.'

Perhaps she got up on the wrong side of the bed this morning.

'In a minute,' Gül says, setting down her glass. It's the first time this winter that they've had breakfast before the stove has been lit. This happened more often last year, but back then it was her mother-in-law's job to light the stove.

'Are you listening to me?'

Gül gets up and goes into the room where the wood is kept. There's wood and stuff no one needs any more: old coach wheels, a rusty spade, a barrel that's probably leaky, and an enormous, battered copper salver. They call it the cellar, but it's only really three steps down, with no windows, next to the stable. In summer, the air inside is cool but heavy, damp and earthy, and in winter it seems colder in the cellar than outside.

Gül leaves the door open to give herself enough light. She sees a couple of mice scurry away. Maybe they were rats. She feels uneasy; she's disgusted as ever, but she no longer has that same fear, because she's learnt that the animals will simply flee from her. But she's not about to spend the night in a stable, not by a long chalk. She could be sleeping quite innocently and then there'd be mice crawling all over her face, biting her nose or ear.

Gül crouches down next to the wall, right in front of the wood pile. She starts gathering up a little brushwood to help get the fire going.

She hears it first. A muffled cracking and then a sound like something crumbling. She stops briefly and looks up, not understanding where the noises are coming from. Her eyes fall on an iron ring sticking out of the wall, maybe once used to tie up the animals. Then she feels the ground beneath her give way. For a fraction of a second, she thinks she might just be imagining it.

The next thing she knows, her legs are dangling in empty space. If she hadn't acted on reflex and grabbed for the ring, she would have fallen into the hole which has opened up in the floor beneath her. Her right hand is clinging to the ring, her body grating against the wall, and that's it. The floor where she was just crouching is now a hole as big as a cart wheel. In her initial panic, Gül kicks her feet and loses one of her clogs. As soon as she notices, she stays quite still and listens, listens for the slipper thudding against the ground. She hears nothing.

'Help! Mother, help!'

Gül listens again; she thinks she hears the clack-clack of her mother-in-law's wooden clogs and the sound of the besom broom on the ground.

She shouts for help again, and in the silence afterwards, she's sure the only sound is the broom sweeping. To her right, on the edge of the pit, there's a patch of ground that's still solid – or at least hasn't disappeared yet. She'd have to swap hands, hold the ring with her left, try to grab on with her right, and then pull herself up slowly.

But she doesn't dare. The ring isn't all that big, and she's only holding on with four fingers. Her forearm is already aching.

'Help!'

The clogs keep clacking, the broom keeps sweeping.

'Mother, help me!'

The clogs keep clacking, the broom keeps sweeping.

Ceyda, Gül thinks, *Ceyda*.

She can't remember the rest. Later, she struggles to explain to her in-laws, her father and everyone else how she managed to climb out of the hole.

'The Lord protected me,' is all she can say. 'I pray for his protection every night and he heard me.'

All she remembers is running to her mother-in-law, who was just putting the broom away, and wanting to say something, and her mother-in-law's face changing, and how her knees then gave way. And the next thing, she was being brought round with the smell of cologne and the first thing she said was: 'Praise be to God.'

She can see her daughter from where she's lying, sleeping peacefully on a cushion.

'You were lucky,' Berrin says. 'The Almighty clearly means well for you. You could have fallen in.'

She gives Gül a kiss on the forehead.

'I did fall in.'

'Lord in Heaven.'

'The hole opened up right under me, and I fell in.'

She'd like to cry now, but she holds back the tears.

'How could this have happened?' Berrin asks.

'I don't know.'

'I'll have someone get your father.'

Gül nods.

Her mother-in-law is speaking fast, gesturing erratically – she doesn't know what to do.

Gül doesn't ask what sense there is in having Timur come over now. And she won't ask later either. She doesn't ask whether her mother-in-law simply didn't hear her. That evening, they hear on the radio that JFK's been shot.

Some of the older people recall once-forgotten rumours. There's said to be treasure buried beneath the house, treasure from the time when Timur's father was a child, from when Faruk's grandfather bought the house. Gold coins, heaps of silver, beautiful jewellery from the days of the Ottoman Empire, jade, emeralds... Everyone with a tongue in their head feels the need to voice a suspicion. And now that everybody knows the house harbours a secret, they all know about the treasure chest too, a trunk that would feed the family until the end of their days.

Many years later, long after Gül's in-laws have died and the house has been sold, the new owners, digging a basement, will come across a box of silver jewellery, for which the jeweller will give them just enough money to cover a month-long trip to America for the two of them.

At the moment, though, the main topic of conversation is the fabled well which Gül very nearly fell into. A handful of smart-alecks claim to have always known the well had been covered up with a sheet of iron back in the day – and of course, those smarty-pants not only knew about the well, but also guessed that the sheet metal would rust under the moist tamped-down earth and give way to a death at the bottom of a dried-up hole that no one had wanted to fill in because it was so deep.

Levent and Orhan tie a coin to a length of thread, which doesn't touch the bottom until a third of the spool has unwound. It takes them two days to fill in the well with sand.

Fuat will soon be back from national service, Ceyda is healthy, Timur comes to visit his daughter almost every morning, and Gül knows now that the angel of death will one day return, to take her away for real next time. *Don't let it be before my sisters are married,* she prays. *Please, dear Lord,* she begs, *please not before my sisters have homes of their own, and please not before my daughter is big enough to walk her path alone. Lord, give me enough time to be there for these people.*

'I've had just about enough of this!' Berrin says to Gül, eight weeks later.

'Pardon?' Gül asks, all innocence.

'Alright, you fell down the well and I didn't hear you calling. But ever since then, you've done almost nothing I tell you to do. You're misunderstanding things on purpose, aren't you? If I say peel the apples, you go ahead and make apple sauce out of them; if I say put a bit of pepper on the food, you make it so spicy no one wants to eat it; if I get you to do the washing, you scrub right through the trousers on the washboard. I daren't send you to fetch wood any more; you'd go to the forest instead of the cellar. Do you think I haven't noticed? I've been going easy on you, Gül, but it can't go on like this.'

Gül feels herself blushing. She doesn't think it's right, what she's been doing, but she's made the most of her mother-in-law's obvious guilty conscience, and she's enjoyed it.

Fuat has saved a little money and is on the lookout for a vacant shop where he can set himself up as a barber. He hangs out with his old friends a lot, entertaining them with anecdotes from the past two years. Almost all of them have mopeds now, apart from Fuat, but none of them has a car, still. Their assets haven't grown but their dreams have; they talk about the houses they'll one day own and imagine what it would be like to afford a week in Istanbul, to go to the football stadium and the classy restaurants, and if their eyes kindle their desire, to the houses of ill repute as well.

Everything seems easier for Gül when she knows her husband will be home in the early evening. When they're in their room together and the baby's asleep, she talks to him in whispers, tells him her versions of the stories he's already heard, lets him know how she felt about them, and she reports on the latest neighbourhood gossip. Fuat listens in the same deliberate way to every subject, nods or shakes his head or expresses his amazement, saying *it beggars belief.* He often repeats himself; it's become a habit and it will stay that way for decades. It beggars belief how much they want for the shop, the mould creeping up the walls in there beggars belief, it beggars belief that my mother didn't hear you, it beggars belief that the winter's nearly over, it beggars belief that she's our child, and for Gül it beggars belief that he now drinks even more than he used to. He drinks almost every evening now, getting drunk once or twice a week. Then Fuat gets noisy even though the baby's asleep, or he starts singing. He couldn't drink very often in the military but he didn't need to there – he didn't have to take care of things all the time, he didn't have to worry about how to make money, he didn't have to haggle with shop landlords asking ridiculous rents. He could still dream there, and the cars still seemed within reach; he could still believe everything would just fall into place once he got back home.

The first few weeks are wonderful nonetheless. *The cold's back is broken*, people say; Gül is looking forward to the first spring she'll spend with her husband and daughter. She, too, thinks everything will fall into place now.

Fuat opens his barber's shop at the beginning of March, and with that opening comes a spring that Gül imagined differently.

Don't believe in this spring, a woman sings on the radio, often, this year; it's a popular song. *Don't believe in this spring, it's untrue, a winter will come; don't believe in the sun, it won't rise, it will leave only darkness to swallow us up one and all.*

This year, the sun's rays don't seem able to brighten Gül's mood, perhaps because she barely has time to notice them.

There's so much to do: Ceyda demands her attention, part of the running of the household is on her shoulders, and now Fuat brings towels home from the shop every other day for washing. Fluffy towels, threadbare ones; white, brown, blue, yellow, stained towels; big towels and small ones, which Fuat pours hot water over and drapes on his customers' faces to soften up their stubble.

A man of about 30, with a stature rather like Timur's but a good head shorter than him, comes into the shop for a shave every morning, wearing a three-piece suit. His stubble is so hard it wears holes in his shirt collars, he tells Fuat. And because he can't be bothered to shave every day, and it's cheaper to pay for a shave before work every morning than to keep buying new shirts, he comes to the barber's shop. He's the first customer every day and he leaves a generous tip before he goes to work for the town council. He seems to hold a high-ranking position; Fuat casts many an envious glance at his gold watch.

Fuat's days now begin with this man, Bülent Bey, and they continue with regular customers, chance customers, and empty hours in which he sits in the barber's chair and reads the newspaper and smokes, or tells the grocer next door he'll be in the teahouse if anyone turns up. Business is passable, and after Fuat has locked up for the night he still sometimes hangs out with his friends, but usually he goes home, where the whole family eats dinner together. After dinner, he drinks a glass or two or three, in their room at first and, as the evenings grow warmer, he drinks with his friends by the stream, where they play cards for money.

He's not interested in going to the cinema, neither with Gül, who asks him to, nor with his friends. Films don't make him forget his worries; they show him everything he hasn't got. They show him that other people order whisky on the rocks, while he's never even tasted it. They show him that a man can achieve many things. But certainly not if he spends his days in a shabby barber's shop.

Gül feels like she sees more of the shaving-cream-stained towels than she does of her husband, who she still doesn't know properly. She doesn't know what he's interested in; she knows he talks to his friends about football and probably about politics as well; she knows he'd like more money, but it will be a long time yet before she finds out about his love of cars. Sometimes Gül simply picks up Ceyda and goes over to Suzan's. Soon, soon it will be the summer holidays; Melike will come home, Sibel will be off school, and Gül will sit with them in the summer house, and her sisters will cuddle Ceyda and kiss her and wish for children of their own. That's how Gül pushes the bright days a little way into the future in her mind, a future from which she draws strength.

The evening before Gül's parents are to move into the summer house, Gül and Fuat are sitting in their room. Fuat is drinking rakı and telling her his future plans, or dreams perhaps – who can say for sure? He wants to own a shop; not rent one, own one. He wants to run his own business; stop spending every day holding strangers' noses just to check he's not missed a hair hidden up a nostril. He no longer wants to clip the villagers' greasy hair every market day when they combine their day's shopping with a haircut, their smell making it quite clear they've been sat on a flea-bitten donkey since daybreak. He wants something bigger and better, and he's prepared to work for it. His own shop and his own house, made of concrete, not just stones and clay – a proper, modern house where the toilet's not in the yard; a house with electricity and running water, like a couple of the neighbours have now. Not one with a washbasin which flows out into the backyard, but a house properly connected to the sewer system; a house where he can live with Gül and Ceyda in peace and quiet. Maybe even a house with heating, like they have in the big cities. One of his friends from the military was from Istanbul, and he told them how they simply switch the heating on and the house warms up; no need to lug wood or coal around. No soot, no smell, no keeping an eye out to stop the children burning themselves on the stove. He never mentions cars; after all, what do women know of such things?

'A proper solution,' he says, 'that's what we need.'

'Yes, God willing.'

'I'm sick of slaving away for nothing, for a little bread and a bit of butter! Some people live in the light and they have a great time of it. Why not us, Gül, why not us too? Are we any worse than them? No, we've just been born into different circumstances. If I could, of course I'd earn a lot of money, but how?'

He takes another swig.

'I'm sick of the sight of those holey hand towels in the shop, that mirror with the dark spots, the chairs the customers stick to in summer. I could make it better, with money. I'd need money. I want to have the best shop in town, one that sparkles from top to bottom; I want people to see their reflections in the very edge of the mirror. And I'll work, so help me God, until things are better for us. You know what, tomorrow I'm giving up gambling – no more games, no more playing cards. We'll start saving.

'Top me up with water, would you?' he says, when he's filled his glass from the bottle of rakı.

Ceyda has been grizzly for two or three days and starts to cry as soon as Gül puts her down on the bed. Gül gets up and goes to get the carafe, which she can't reach sitting down. She holds Ceyda in her right arm, reaching for the carafe with her left. She can't quite get hold of it at first and has to set it down again. She's clumsily pouring Fuat his water when Ceyda makes a noise. For a moment, Gül is distracted, and the glass spills over. She notices almost at once, but in her haste, she spills even more, some of it dripping onto Fuat's feet, onto his gaol socks.

'Can't you pay attention for once?' Fuat fumes. 'You and your precious carafe. And you won't leave that child's side for a second!'

Gül knows these sudden mood swings aren't rare when Fuat's been drinking.

'Give me the carafe,' he says, and Gül doesn't know what to do. She hesitates.

'Give me that fancy bloody carafe, come on, give it to me!'

He's standing in front of her now, red-eyed, his shoulders slightly back, his chest puffed out.

'Give me the fucking carafe, for God's sake! It beggars belief how attached you are to it.'

Slowly, wordlessly, Gül hands him the carafe. Ceyda cries.

'I'll throw it at the wall, shall I? This carafe means more to your than your own husband, doesn't it? Shall I throw it out the window?'

He swings the carafe at shoulder height.

Do it then! Gül would like to say, then he'd let the carafe slip. It wouldn't be that bad. But it would be disrespectful; he'd get even more wound up. *Are you trying to provoke me?* he'd say. *Are you the man of this house? I do what I like, understand? What I like.*

So Gül looks at the floor and waits. Luckily, Ceyda has stopped crying. Luckily, no one comes into the room when Fuat gets loud. That's marriage for you, the others might think; sometimes couples don't get on all that well at first. It comes with time. You can't interfere in a newly married couple's business.

'Learn to live with it,' Suzan told Gül. 'You have to accept him as he is. What other choice do you have? Some men stop drinking when they get a little older.'

Like my father, Gül thinks. There are legendary tales about Timur, rattling the window bars at night after everyone fled because he was so drunk he could hardly stand but still needed a showdown with someone. On a few occasions, those less drunk than him would dare to take him on. They would rely on their reflexes, their focus, their sense of balance. But the blacksmith would simply grab hold of them, knock them to the ground and thrash them. There were said to have been times where the grazes on his knuckles wouldn't heal from one week to the next. Soon enough, no one dared to fight him and, at some point – it must have been a year or two after the wedding – he had practically given up drinking altogether. Gül has never seen her father drunk, the closest she's seen him is with a glass in his hand.

Perhaps Fuat will be the same one day. But on this particular evening, he stands there, holding the carafe aloft and says: 'Look at me when I'm talking to you!'

Gül looks him in the eye, looks straight into his glassy, red, bloodshot eyes.

'I could chuck this fucking jug out the window any time, you hear? Any time.'

Gül nods and Fuats sits, sets the carafe down and knocks back his rakı. A couple of drops run down his chin.

The next morning, Fuat doesn't say a word, but he avoids looking at Gül. And he doesn't speak to her when he comes home in the evening either. Gül is even more offended, but she guesses the reason behind it. Melike also finds it hard to admit she's done something wrong. *But she's my sister and I love her*, Gül thinks. *And he's my husband; I don't want to be cross with him either.*

Perhaps his guilty conscience is to blame, but Fuat really does rarely gamble any more. Gül often sees him putting bank notes into a little box he hides at the very back of the wardrobe.

Gül knows how often her husband changes his underpants; she knows which friends he goes out with at night; she knows how much he drinks; she knows there've been a few times he didn't wake her when he came home late, whipped up from the alcohol, and brought himself relief instead. She knows when he's argued with his father, she knows what he looks like when he has to swallow down his anger, she knows so much – but she hasn't the slightest idea of how much money is in the cardboard box. She doesn't look and doesn't ask. He's the man.

The sisters sit on their mother's trunk only on two, maybe three days this summer. And their conversations are different this time too.

'I can talk to a boy in the street without anyone gossiping about it,' Melike says. 'Nobody knows you, nobody gives you evil looks. We've got a girl from the Black Sea in our class and it sounds like it's even worse there than here. You know what she told us? They have a small field, really small somewhere by the sea, a strip of fertile land between the rocks and cliffs, but you can't get there, not over the rocks. So her father would let her mother down on a rope. He'd sit at the top smoking, and once her mother had done the work, he'd pull her back up again.'

'He *could've* done the work,' Sibel says, 'only she wouldn't have been strong enough to pull him up.'

'I don't care, I want to move to the city.'

Sibel tells them about a girl in her dorm; no one knows why she's at boarding school, because she has rich parents.

'It's tough for her, no one pays her any attention. She's always trying to be friendly and generous; she invites us to tea, and a lot of girls drink the tea but still don't talk to her. She's actually quite nice, but she's rich. I don't think I'd want to be that rich.'

'But if you were that rich, you'd go to a different school,' Melike says.

'And you're not going to make friends with her?' Gül asks.

Sibel shakes her head: 'I would, but then the other girls look at you funny. And I've got a friend already, Nilüfer.'

Gül can see how hard it must have been for Sibel to find a friend at school. She can picture Sibel creeping along the side of the corridors and lying in bed by a draughty window in the dormitory.

'One girl wets the bed sometimes,' Sibel says quietly, looking at the floor. So she doesn't catch Melike's eye, Gül thinks.

'İzel's her name, İzel's bed is right next to mine, and Sevgi told everyone the smell came from me. She told all the girls I still wet the bed. Just because I wouldn't draw her art assignment for her like I did for Nilüfer. I only do that for friends, though. And Sevgi is a stupid swot, top of the class in every subject, just not in art, I'm the best at that, she just learns everything off by... She swots up all day long. And then the geography teacher came and asked me if I sometimes had problems waking up at night. I didn't know what he meant. But once I got it, I went hot all over – I was ashamed even though it wasn't even me. And he didn't believe me because I went so red, and he told me Sevgi had told him about it. I went and asked her why she was spreading lies about me. *I never did,* she said, *what am I supposed to have said? Don't believe the others, they just want to get me in trouble because they don't like me, because I'm so good in class,* she said. And I said it was the geography teacher who told me she'd said I wet the bed. That got her; she went quiet then. And I talked and talked to her until she went to the teacher in the end and said she'd been wrong. I talked to her for hours. *I'll go to İzel and make her admit it,* I told her, *and then you'll look even more stupid.'*

Gül smiles to herself. Sibel never lets go when she feels she's in the right.

'No one ever told her she was right,' Gül will say years later, talking about her sister. 'Whenever she had a row with Nalan, our mother said Nalan was right and not her. It's no wonder she's always so insistent.'

At the moment, though, Gül wishes she could protect Sibel; she feels like grabbing this Sevgi and asking her what on earth she was thinking. She feels like giving her a clip round the ear. She feels like doing what she herself wasn't capable of when Özlem said she'd handed out köfter at school.

Gül doesn't talk much during these two or three days chatting on the trunk. She mentions that Fuat has stopped gambling, she tells her sisters about the baby's teething, the baby's diarrhoea, she tells them about falling into the well. But she keeps to herself how hard she finds life with Fuat, even though she wants to love him. How noisy he can get when he's been drinking, and how he fell asleep just as she was telling him about her row with his mother, how she can't shake the feeling he doesn't listen to her the rest of the time either. She keeps her worries to herself; her sisters have their own, and they're surely enough to deal with. So far away from home, every night in a dorm with 30 other girls, the bunk beds and the smells of every one of them. And they can't see their father every day. No, the two of them are having a tough enough time, and it even pains Gül when they complain about the canteen food.

Another thing Gül doesn't tell them is that she's planning to complete her basic education this winter, by correspondence course. She will receive the document in September, and Fuat will pay the small fee. She keeps it to herself because she's ashamed in front of her sisters, both of them at high school now.

This summer, too, they sit on the steps outside the summer house in the evenings, barbecueing corncobs in the garden in August, children playing out on the street, the sky so cloudless that the holidays seem endless. Boys catch big flying beetles and tie threads around their legs because it won't be windy enough for kites until the autumn; the heat beads on their skin and runs down their faces as they annoy wasps out of cocky boredom, poking sticks in their nests or throwing stones at them. Girls play mummies and daddies and listen to Melike talking about taking a dip in the sea, or they sit in the shade and tell each other stories they've picked up – of sweat-soaked sheets after a birth and blood on a wedding night. Or boys and girls play volleyball in the cool of the evening, after Melike puts up a string as a net. She shows off a little in front of the others, who will never make it onto the school team, never mind become captain like her. But everyone wants Melike on their team, nothing's changed there.

Arzu tells her off, says it's not right, not ladylike to play ball in the street. There are always young men around the edge of the field, applauding whenever Melike thumps another ball across the string. But Melike doesn't listen to her mother and doesn't grant her admirers a single glance either.

Almost everyone thinks it'll be her last school year coming up. The first boys ask for her hand this summer, wanting to get engaged so they can marry next year. Hardly anyone knows of her plans; she's only told her sisters about them, plus her father because she needs his permission. All he did was give her a sceptical look, but he didn't say no and that's almost a yes. Melike wants to apply for a grant to study French in Istanbul. 'I don't want to be a primary teacher,' she says, 'I want to teach at a high school.'

Only for appearances' sake does the blacksmith ask her whether she'd like one of the young men who apply for her hand. He knows going to university in Istanbul is more important to her. Remembering his own escapades in the city, he smiles to himself.

It was great indulging himself; he enjoyed it and never regretted all the money he spent, but he hasn't been to Istanbul for years now. *I'm not as young any more*, he thinks, *now I'm happy to be here, children around me, the cows, my work and the songs on the radio, not on the lips of beautiful women in breathtaking dresses. The radio gave me the songs and took away the women.* It took away the stadium he used to go to once or twice a year, and it brought him the weekly broadcasts of the matches.

He'll remember this summer as the summer when the first men asked for Melike's hand and she joked about one skinny young lad: 'What would I want with him? He'd fly across the room if I gave him a clip round the ear.'

And Timur laughs and knows right away that he'll sit around the forge's fire with his assistant and one or two others and talk about his daughter taking the mickey out of skinny-malinky lads. There'll be pride in his voice and also concern for his child, who won't have it easy in life.

His words will be passed on without the pride, without the concern, but with people's enduring love for gossip, and the skinny young man will get wind of it and feel terribly small and lonely all winter long. He'll start doing press-ups, in secret. He'll be embarrassed about caring so much about his thin body, but he'll be just as proud, secretly, when he adds a little to his chest measurements over the winter. Perhaps barely visible to others, it will feel like a start to him. Later on, he'll marry a voluptuous woman from a nearby village, and on his wedding night and the nights that follow he'll have the feeling he's conquering her. They'll have children and move to Germany, his wife will put on more weight, and one day, 15 years after he asked for Melike's hand, he'll be in Istanbul with his wife, in Taksim, and he'll see Melike on the street, only she won't recognise him. He'll feel small, small next to Melike's husband who's almost six foot five, and even smaller next to his own wife, whose swaying gait sometimes reminds him of a pregnant cow. And another 10 years later, Ceyda will meet his son at a party, and he'll tell her in drunken exuberance that he prefers thin women. *Thin*, he'll say, *really thin, so I can hear her bones grinding against each other underneath me.*

That autumn, words from books find their way into Gül's head, but they're no longer the words from the novels she reads, now they're words from the school books for her distance-learning course. The apples have been harvested, and the people from Adana have moved back to the city, leaving their summer houses. Ceyda is crawling here, there and everywhere, but seems to have no inclination to learn to walk. Instead, she can already say a few words, which probably has something to do with the fact that Gül talks to her all day long. Her admittedly rather one-sided evening chats with Fuat are rarer now. Either she talked a lot and he listened, or he'd drink too much and then he would speak. Now Gül often sits in front of her books in the evenings, studying, for the first time, by the glow of the electric lightbulb. Fuat goes out, sits with his brothers, or settles back and drinks his rakı by the radio when his father's not at home. It's hardly noticeable that he doesn't follow the radio plays at all, instead indulging in thoughts of his own.

The apricot, apple and mulberry trees lose their leaves. The wind whistles through the cracks in the house, but it doesn't bring a cold draught with it just yet, and the boys who practised with their beetles are flying kites now. Emin is repeating Year 2, Arzu is happy that there are no longer so many kids under her feet and she has her peace and quiet, Suzan is preparing herself quietly for another winter without her husband, and Fuat makes exceptions to his new rule, placing one-off bets. They are one-offs, really; the money in the cardboard box keeps growing, as far as Gül can tell. And when Fuat does win, his fellow players shake their heads and say: 'There goes our money, disappearing into Fuat's pocket, and we'll never see it again. Fuat, you can't play once a month, take the cash and then come back in four weeks' time. Money has to flow.'

'Yes,' he says then, 'straight into my pockets. You're in for a big surprise.'

'What, what's this?' Yılmaz asks him. 'Are you planning on buying yourself a Cadillac with our money?'

'You're in for a big surprise,' Fuat repeats.

He often says this to his friends that autumn. *You're in for a big surprise.*

No one is surprised by the new mirror he buys for his shop; no one is surprised by the assistant, an 11-year-old boy who sweeps and cleans the shop, polishes the mirrors, doles out the hand towels and the soap. A boy who, come spring, will be able to shave the customers perfectly, long before the first hint of fuzz sprouts on his own chin. A boy who takes no money home but has the chance to learn a trade.

Hülya has spent a lot of time alone since Yücel died. She used to visit Timur, walk round the neighbourhood, sit on a stool out in the street, talk to passers-by. Everyone knew her awkward gait, and everyone had long grown accustomed to her squint. But since Yücel died, she's withdrawn into herself, even though they'd been divorced for years and hardly ever saw each other, as far as Gül knows. He must have been a good husband, she thinks sometimes, he was patient and he married Auntie Hülya, a woman with a squint, whose hips stick out every step she takes, and who can't even cook very well. He must have been a good husband, but her grandmother never talks about him and pulls a face at the mention of his name.

This autumn, Gül visits her grandmother more often, but only so she can sit in the kitchen with her aunt. There are days when Hülya talks without worrying whether Gül is listening or not, she simply starts somewhere, perhaps with the fact that she can hardly remember her father, to whom she owes so much, and then she continues with a memory of how Timur once carried her across the stream on his back because she was scared of the water – she must have been quite little then, as little as the neighbour's young daughter, but much older than Ceyda – and later she lost a coin in that same stream, those days are gone now, she can't remember how much it was and how much money her mother earned by selling things, jewellery, köfter, walnuts, what a savvy businesswoman she is, and yet her brother's never learnt to hang onto his money.

Hülya talks almost without stopping, jumping from one topic to the next, because she hardly sees anyone. She's still got her wits, and she has a great need to talk, but she always changes the subject when Gül tries to turn the conversation to Uncle Yücel.

'Oh, those days are gone now,' Hülya says then. 'How should I know? May he rest in peace.'

And that's it. But it's not curiosity that keeps Gül going to see her aunt, and so she continues to visit regularly. Gül will never find out what happened between Uncle Yücel and Auntie Hülya, she'll never know why they split up. It will bother her for a long time. Gül will find that complete strangers come to her and trust her with their life stories. Only Auntie Hülya will refuse to share her secret, at least with her.

When she's sewing bras in piecework at the factory in Germany, she'll sit next to a very young Turkish woman who cries every day. After a week, this young woman – still a girl, really – will come to Gül, who will already be in her late twenties, and she will say: 'What a heartless person you are. I sit next to you every day, crying, and you haven't even once asked what's wrong!'

Guiltily, Gül will say nothing, but the young woman will say: 'I want to tell you everything.'

And she will start with her childhood, she'll tell her how she and her friend tended the cows, she'll talk about the soldiers, the other men, her first husband, who was three times her age, her second husband, his father, about what the neighbours said, about her new town and her new husband and her new country, and Gül will try to hide her astonishment but she won't be able to hold back her tears, until *she's* crying instead of the young woman. And she'll become used to people confiding in her without ever understanding why they do.

When in pain, perhaps people are always looking for someone who knows that same pain.

Once she's spent almost a whole winter reading and studying, once she feels ready for her exams, the first warm rays of sunlight leave Gül desperate to be outside again. She's seen the poster – they're showing *The Barefoot Contessa*, a film with Ava Gardner, one of her favourite actresses. Humphrey Bogart is in it too; she's not bothered about him, but perhaps he'll help draw Fuat to the cinema.

'Don't you fancy seeing that film?'

'No,' Fuat replies.

'We haven't been to the cinema in so long…'

'And who's going to look after Ceyda?'

'Your mother. She'd be happy to do it.'

'And what if Ceyda cries? She's not used to you being away for such a long time.'

'Oh, she's big enough now. How about it? I'd like to see that film with Ava Gardner. And Humphrey Bogart's in it, too.'

'Bogart. What does he look like? A man should look like Sinatra or Dean Martin, maybe Clark Gable or Errol Flynn, now those are good-looking men. Bogart, pfft,' he says and sticks a cigarette between his lips, strikes a match and lights up. As he exhales the smoke, he looks into Gül's pleading face and says: 'Fine, what do I care? As long as Mum looks after Ceyda.'

Bogart will be drinking whisky, he knows that, and he's taken to slipping into bad moods whenever he sees someone drinking whisky: What crime did he commit that's stopping him getting so much as a whiff of it?

'Saturday night?' she asks.

'I wanted to go down the river with Yılmaz and Can on Saturday.'

Going down the river means coming home drunk.

'Please, just this one time.'

Fuat sighs. Bogart might not be drinking any whisky in this film, perhaps he'll only be driving a goddamn car.

'Alright,' he grunts.

He can always go down the river next week, Gül thinks, *and the week after that, and the week after that.*

On Saturday night, Gül gets dressed up. First she wanted to wear her midnight blue dress, but it seemed over the top, so she's put on her favourite skirt and a stylish blouse. She's curled her hair and she can hardly wait to go out. She's ironed Fuat's suit with the electric iron; his shirt is white and starched. His clothes are as important to him now as they were before they married, but he still walks on the backs of his shoes. The belly he had from his military service vanished in a flash, but he's slowly losing his hair; his hairline's receded further than any other man of his age. He still carries his comb with him, but he no longer uses brilliantine because it makes his hair look even thinner.

On the way to the cinema, Gül slips her arm through his. She's proud of her husband and looking forward to the film. It's a double bill and *The Barefoot Contessa* is up second. Dean Martin plays the lead in the first film, but Fuat just shifts restlessly in his seat, smoking one cigarette after another, looking vacantly at the big screen and exhaling loudly from time to time. He's watching some bloke up there drinking whisky while he's left high and dry. Towards the end of the film he's calmer, and when the lights go up, he looks at Gül expectantly.

'It's the second film,' she says. 'Ava Gardner wasn't even in this one, we're here for the next film.'

'Okay,' Fuat says and shakes a cigarette out the packet. 'No problem, we'll just watch another one. Why not? Are you sure Ceyda's alright? Maybe she's cried the whole time, you know she's not used to going so long without you. I could also take you home, and then drop by Yılmaz and the lads.'

Very often in her life, Gül will get the feeling that she's not a good mother, and she'll fret over it endlessly. But tonight she's feeling relaxed; it's springtime and she wants to see Ava Gardner. Her mother-in-law may be many things, but she's not bad with children. Gül would be reluctant to leave Ceyda with her stepmother, but she'd always trust her mother-in-law.

When the film begins, Fuat grows restless again, smoking, fidgeting in his seat, getting up, going to the toilet, coming back, crossing and uncrossing his legs and then re-crossing them the other way, cracking his knuckles and yawning. Meanwhile, the film has been playing for 15 minutes, and Gül hasn't been able to forget what's going on around her for a single second, she hasn't spent a single second lost in Ava Gardner's eyes the way she sometimes loses herself in the voices from the radio, not for a single moment does she forget that her husband doesn't want to be there.

'Are you sure Ceyda will be good?' he whispers.

'Yes,' says Gül, 'I'm sure, but come on, let's go and check.'

'But…'

'We'll go and check,' Gül says decisively, standing up. They walk side by side through the night, saying nothing. *Was it too much to ask*, Gül wonders, *was it too much to ask of him to go out with me for one evening? When he's been out with his friends, he doesn't come home till one or two. Was it too much to ask that he see a film with me? But maybe he really was worried about Ceyda? Why doesn't he trust his own mother?*

Fuat's thinking too. Except Gül doesn't know what he's thinking about. She knows nothing about whisky and how it feels to go dry. It's a clear night; in other circumstances it would be possible to gaze at the stars. We don't come here just to live and die, we come here to gaze at the stars and lose ourselves in the vastness of it all.

'You're back early,' Berrin says as she greets them; she's been sifting through rice in the kitchen.

'Yes,' Gül says, 'we were worried about Ceyda. So we couldn't watch the film to the end. But she's slept perfectly, hasn't she?'

'Yes, I gave her her milk and I haven't heard so much as a peep from her since.'

'You see?' Gül says to Fuat.

'But she could have…' he responds.

'But I would have seen to her,' says his mother. 'I raised four children, I think I can cope with that sweet little angel.'

'See?' Gül repeats, this time with a note of triumph in her voice. 'Our daughter's a big girl now; she's fast asleep.'

Fuat has sat down. Gül goes to the cupboard to get herself some köfter.

'She was good as gold. We could have watched the whole film in peace. But you had to upset the apple cart!'

She usually keeps her feelings under control, but she's on a roll now. And she has this pressing urge to eat something sweet, though she doesn't think it'll make what she's saying any friendlier. As she chews, she stands with her back to the cupboard. She's furious that Fuat isn't saying anything.

'Once in 40 years I ask if we can go to the cinema together and you use the child as an excuse to come home early.'

The köfter grinds between her teeth. Berrin continues picking over the rice, as though she's heard nothing.

'You knew full well I wanted to see the second film, the one with Ava Gardner.'

Fuat has stood up and walks over to her. Neither his face nor his body language betray anything. Perhaps Gül is too preoccupied with her own anger to notice. She turns back to the cupboard, opens the door and takes another piece of köfter, left over from winter. Quick energy.

'Enough!' Fuat explodes.

Gül turns around, the cupboard door still open, Berrin has stopped picking over the rice and is looking up at the two of them facing each other.

'What?' Gül snaps back.

Fuat's hand strikes the cupboard door, which only fails to hit Gül in the face because she's still holding it with one hand.

The sound of an open palm on the wire mesh of the door and then: silence. Not one of them moves, no one dares take the first breath. Finally, after four long seconds, Fuat snorts scornfully, leaves the kitchen, slips on his shoes – stepping on the backs – slams the door shut and stomps off. Gül waits, as if there's something to wait for. As if her mother-in-law is bound to say something or do something. Later, Gül will rebuke herself. *I shouldn't have spoken to him like that in front of his mother*, she'll say, *of course that hurt him. I should have just waited. It was between me and him.*

But that's later, much later. For now, she stands there and waits. As if a magician might appear and say the magic words, and she'd stop feeling as though she's been turned to stone, like in a fairytale.

Time seems to expand; Fuat's footsteps have long since faded and the more the seconds stretch on, the more the thoughts crowd in, chasing after each other, leaving Gül no time to escape them. So he can do it then, he's up to it. When will be the next time? Her father has never hit her. He's hit Melike. And Emin too. And sometimes Nalan. And she herself once threw a stone at Melike. But she was little then. Her father never hit his wives. But Fuat can.

'These things happen.' Those are the words which bring the relief of sound to the silent room.

It's not these particular words that Gül needed, only the sound, a sign she could move again. *These things happen* was just as good, or bad, as: *I'll have a word with him.* Or: *You provoked him.*

'Yes,' is all Gül says, and she shuts the cupboard door, whispers goodnight and goes to bed. Creeping under the covers, she pulls her knees up to her chin and hopes that Fuat stays out a long time tonight. A long time.

After the slap, Gül doesn't speak to Fuat for a fortnight. He seems to regret it, at least it seems that way to Gül, but all he manages is a tiny apology. And that only in passing, one morning as he's about to leave the house. One foot out the door, he turns back to her: 'I didn't mean it.'

A cool breeze blows between Fuat and Gül. When Fuat comes home one night, three weeks later, and shakes her awake for the first time since the slap, she turns her back on him demonstratively, and he waits until he thinks she's fallen asleep and then takes the matter into his own hands.

Yet the summer and Gül's muted joy about her school diploma warm that breeze. People get used to anything, and the next time they argue, it takes Gül only two weeks to stop turning away at night.

The next fight starts with Fuat saying: 'Savaş took the same train as Melike.'

'Yes, Melike came home by train.'

'She was sharing a compartment with men.'

'So?'

'Do you think it's right for your sister to share a compartment with strange men?'

'They probably weren't strangers, they were probably school-mates.'

'But what will people say?'

'What people? Does your chatterbox of a friend have to tell everyone?'

'She's your sister, you ought to forbid her from sharing a compartment with men.'

'What? What's going to happen if they share a compartment?'

Gül knows people gossip about this kind of thing, but what can have happened, really?

'You're standing by your sister, aren't you? You're standing by her because she's your sister. You're selfish, you don't care if people talk.'

'She's old enough. She'll soon be a student; she must know what's good for her and what's not.'

'I'm just saying. I wanted to help, but you only ever stand by your sisters, never mind if it's Melike or Sibel. They'll say Melike is easy, a loose woman, not that I care!'

'What are they supposed to have got up to in the compartment? In front of all the other strangers on the train. Do you know what they did? They smoked cigarettes. That was the worst thing they did. My sister smokes. And if you want to get her in trouble, go ahead and tell my father!'

'She'll be the talk of the town, you'll see.'

Melike doesn't become the talk of the town. Over the summer, she hides at the back of the garden to smoke. She usually sits down, because smoking can still make her dizzy. Occasionally, she takes Gül along and makes her smoke too. It amuses Gül, because it's normally the older children who seduce the younger ones into smoking. The cigarettes leave a dark, dry taste in her mouth, and Gül gets dizzy too and can't suppress the urge to cough.

'The devil's handiwork,' she will say later, once she's started smoking herself. 'The devil's handiwork – it gets you so hooked it'd make you knock on your worst enemy's door. Every time I try to give up, I only smoke more and I think: *Just one more to kick the habit.* But it's never the last one.'

She will smoke for more than 40 years of her life, cutting down to one or two a day for the last five years before she can go without them. A cigarette will always feel like comfort to her, something to hold onto. Something she's doing all for herself.

But this summer, she smokes her hush-money cigarettes a little reluctantly, just like Sibel, who soon stops inhaling; otherwise her coughing fits never seem to end.

'Shhhh,' Melike says whenever anyone coughs. 'Shhhh, Dad will hear us.'

Since he gave up, the blacksmith has run out of sympathy for smokers. And no one has any sympathy for young people enjoying things in the presence of their elders. It almost doesn't matter what it is.

And so the sisters sit at the back of the garden and share cigarettes, huddled and hidden, just like when they were telling stories of their mother.

By the end of the summer, Gül is pregnant again. When Fuat finds out, he doesn't say: *That's good.* Not: *May the Lord give us a boy.* Neither: *Glad to hear it.* Nor: *It's going to be tricky.* And not: *The Lord has blessed us.* He says: 'We're going to have to come up with something.'

Gül immediately thinks of the types of contraceptives she's heard about. She's heard of condoms, but if they are on sale anywhere, then only in Istanbul. The man can pull out, but that doesn't seem to cross Fuat's mind.

'What do you mean?' she asks. 'What will we have to come up with?'

'I'm still touching strangers' faces day in, day out, I'm working my fingers to the bone, I'm saving money, I'm not gambling, and what have I got? Nothing, nothing times nothing, and all that's left is nothing.'

'We're filling our bellies.'

'Yes, thank the Lord for that. But every last idiot will soon have running water and electricity. People have cars and I don't even have a moped yet; people have toilets, they have radios and televisions, people build houses, and us? We're filling our bellies, yes, but that can't be the end of it, can it? Don't you want nice dresses, nylon stockings, don't you want a washing machine? How can you sit here and be satisfied? You, you've seen how much better life is when you've got money. Your father used to be rich too. And us, we've never had anything. My father's a coachman. I used to go to bed hungry as a child, you get it? And your children, do you want to send them to bed hungry and pack them off to a state boarding school, for want of enough money? Money, Gül, money makes the world go round, money opens doors for you.'

Gül has never imagined having a lot of money, but right now she thinks Fuat is talking sense. Yes, her children should have it better one day, they shouldn't go to a state boarding school, they should get money whenever they need it. For a photo or midnight blue fabric or two metres more for a long train on their wedding dress. Yes, they should have it, but money doesn't solve problems. That's what Gül learned from her photo love-stories, at least, where misfortune clings to the children of the rich like a shadow.

'What do you want to do?' she asks Fuat.

Fuat purses his lips and then says: 'I'll find something.'

Fuat is taciturn that autumn. Not that he talked much before, but that autumn he's really taciturn. He goes out less with his friends, and drinks less. Often, he'll just sit there, the cigarette butts piling up in front of him. *Light up another one*, he may be telling himself, *light up another one, nothing times nothing, and all that's left is nothing, light up another one in this life in which we work our fingers to the bone while the rich order food, get driven around in fancy limousines and don't need to worry about people's hair growing back fast enough or falling out entirely. People who don't get an itch from a hair finding its way into their shirts – no matter how careful you are, a goddamn hair always ends up in your shirt. People who don't have to spend all day looking at the greasy yellow wax in other people's ears. Wax so thick it crumbles out at the slightest touch.*

Fuat doesn't enjoy his work, that much is clear, but he does it because it's what he can do. What else is he to do? Gül watches Fuat's state of mind with concern. *At least we're fighting less*, she thinks.

Her belly seems to grow faster this time than with Ceyda, and her appetite is far bigger too. Sometimes she's amazed how long it can take her to feel full. The morning sickness hardly makes a showing this time either. Perhaps it gets easier every time, she thinks. There are women who go out in the fields in the morning, heavily pregnant, and come home with a baby in the evening. But perhaps that's only because the village smallholders can't afford farm hands.

The money in the cardboard box mounts up, but one day in that grey, muddy autumn, Gül sees Fuat putting a note in an empty box instead. She gives him a questioning look.

'It's gone,' Fuat says, off-handedly.

Gül raises her hands, leans in and raises her eyebrows: 'Where's it gone?'

'Life's a game. If you don't take a gamble, you can't win,' Fuat pronounces.

It seems not to bother him.

'If you bought me a sewing machine, I could earn a bit of money too,' Gül says.

'How much would that be?'

'Ten kuruş is ten kuruş, it'd be better than nothing. I could sew clothes, take in alterations. Plenty of women would come to me, I know they would.'

It's spring when Fuat brings the sewing machine home. Gül's belly draws glances from every direction, some people say she'll have twins, but her cheeks have grown fuller too, and sometimes she eats in secret, embarrassed by how much she can put away. Her mother-in-law remarks that Gül could probably eat an entire tray of baklava by herself without much trouble. She's joking, but Gül reckons she really could. She'll eat anything, except for chocolate.

Her belly gets in the way while she's sewing, but that spring Gül often sits at the machine, chewing, and feeling good. The whirring pacifies her; sometimes all thoughts disappear out of her head, sometimes she drifts away with the memories that wash over her. Memories of Candan and Esra, of the hours she spent learning dressmaking. When she's sewn something, she still feels the same satisfaction as she did then.

A lot has changed, she thinks, *I have a child of my own now, a husband, a sewing machine, another life.* It doesn't quite feel like it's hers, but it has changed. Now, once she's asked Fuat, she can buy brilliant white cotton to sew a blouse for Suzan. It will be a surprise, and Gül is gladder to have something to give Suzan than she was about the sewing machine itself.

Two days after she's given Suzan the blouse, word arrives that Murat is to be released from prison. Suzan receives the letter just before midday, and come evening, her husband is standing outside the door with a small, almost empty canvas bag. He's lost so much weight, his cheekbones are visible, his shoulders poke out beneath his shirt and even his fleshy nose seems to have shrunk.

'I'm hungry,' are the first words he says.

For days, he doesn't leave the house. He lies in bed, sleeps, eats and smokes cigarettes, staring at the smoke rings, his eyes empty, lightless.

'They tortured him,' Suzan says to Gül, and Gül doesn't ask, but Suzan goes on: 'He won't talk about it. The nails are missing on his right thumb and forefinger. He sleeps all day; at night he sits in the dark, smoking. What am I supposed to do?' she asks, tears in her eyes. 'What am I supposed to do? I've got my husband back.'

Gül feels ashamed not to have an answer for her. She'd like to help Suzan, just as Suzan has always helped her, but all she can do is take her friend in her arms: 'May the Lord bring an end to his sorrow. Maybe he just needs some time.'

'Oh, you poor little thing,' Suzan says. 'You're pregnant, your belly's almost up to your nose and I've nothing to tell you except my own troubles.'

She laughs as the tears roll.

'It'll be alright,' she says, 'it will be, he's a fighter. My Murat doesn't give up. Children need a father, Gül, children need a father.'

'Yes,' Gül says, 'they do.'

She only sees Murat out in the street once in the first three weeks after he gets back. But soon enough he's out and about more often, usually grim-faced, nodding silently when someone recognises him. He chats with a few men at the teahouse, smokes shisha and displays such ambition and fury during games of backgammon that soon no one wants to play with him any more. There's no money coming in at home, but he shows no sign of going back to work.

'Where's this going to end?' Suzan asks him one evening.

'It's wrong,' Murat says. 'Everything's wrong here. What a godforsaken country! Not one honest soul in the place; they're all liars, cheats, conmen and bootlickers. Everything's wrong here, this country is full of idiots with arseholes where their brains should be. I don't know where it's supposed to end.'

'Shh, you'll teach the children new words.'

'We'll have to disappear.'

'Where to?'

Murat just nods and shrugs.

'Where will you go?' Suzan asks.

'I'll be back in a couple of days. I'm sick to the back teeth of this place.'

'Where are you going? Murat? You're not going to leave me here on my own, are you?'

'No, I won't leave you on your own. You're my wife.'

But Suzan senses he's going away. And she doesn't know if she'll have the strength to endure it.

Gül's second baby is a girl, too; she names her Ceren. Fuat can't hide his disappointment, not from Gül, nor from his parents.

'She's healthy, she's got two hands and two feet, all in the right places. We should thank the Almighty,' Gül says. 'The whole time I was pregnant, I prayed that my child would come into the world healthy.'

And at the same time, she asks herself whether Fuat would be able to give up smoking, like her father, if God granted him a son. Probably not, she thinks. But Fuat will give up smoking at the drop of a hat, long before she does, and to Gül it will look like it's easy for him. He won't be able to get a handle on the drinking, though, not until his belly finally forces him to cut down in his sixties.

Gül is preoccupied with her daughters this summer. Melike brags to anyone who will listen, about what it's like living in the big city and what famous person she saw while out walking along the Bosphorus. But she doesn't tell anyone who she's been walking with; no one hears about the huge, good-looking, gallant sports student from Izmir who has captured her heart with his reserve. Words often fail Mert when they're together, and when he hasn't drunk anything. But he's got a fiery temper like hers; he's a man who can lose control from one minute to the next. One day, when they're walking through Beyoğlu, they find themselves in the way of a man who wants to park his Cadillac on the pavement and is trying to beep the couple off it. *Beep. Beep beep. Beeeeep. Beeeeep.* Mert walks over to the car, wrenches the door open and gives the man a resounding clip round the ear which is almost louder than the car horn.

'This is the pavement, you ox, pedestrians have right of way, you jumped-up little limo driver!' he yells.

Melike is embarrassed, but at the same time she's proud of Mert because he's so much like her. He won't let anything slide.

Melike has spent the winter picturing the three of them sitting on their mother's trunk, and how she will tell Gül and Sibel about Mert, about his curly hair, his shyness and his quick temper. He's even taller than her father, a fact she'd like to save till last. But they don't sit together, not that summer, because, between the sewing and tending to her two daughters, Gül can't find the time to go to the summer house, let alone sit quietly with her sisters.

Sibel has a problem, which the blacksmith is taking care of. She's finished school, but because she doesn't turn 18 for a few more months, she can't work as a student teacher in the coming school year.

'The poor child started school early, but now she's too young again,' Arzu says. 'She'll lose a year.'

People believe her. But can you lose years or mislay them, forget them or squander them?

'We'll just get her made older,' Timur says.

But it's not like the old days now, the laws aren't as lax any more; they have to go to court, they have to produce witnesses. The formalities aren't dealt with until the end of the summer, when the judge asks one of the blacksmith's neighbours: 'And you're sure she was born in March?'

'Yes, definitely; the snow had thawed and the leaves were budding on the trees but not even the cherries were blossoming yet, so it must have been spring, it was still cool. Whether it was the beginning of March or the middle, your honour, I couldn't swear to it, it's a long time ago.'

The neighbour owes Timur a small amount of money and he has the gift of the gab.

'And why did you originally state your daughter had been born in October?' the judge asks Timur.

'I didn't want to have to pay a fine. We lived in the village back then; I didn't make it into town, and then I didn't want to pay a fine for registering the birth too late.'

'Sibel,' the judge says, turning to her before he pauses and has the others sent out of the courtroom: Timur, the neighbour and the second witness.

'Sibel,' the judge begins again, looking closely at the thin, pale, shy young woman who's obviously nervous. 'There's no need to be afraid of me, my girl, I don't want to do you any harm. Is your father trying to do some kind of fiddle, is he using you for something?'

Sibel shakes her head.

'You're doing this of your own free will, are you? Nobody's forced you? Look, this is your chance to say if anyone has forced you. If they have, I'll just reject the application and question the witnesses' credibility. The cherries weren't yet blossoming, all this is 18 years ago, how can anyone remember that? What do you say?'

'This is what I want.'

'Are you sure?'

'Yes.'

'Alright.'

By the time Sibel leaves the court she is of legal age, on paper.

In the autumn she'll begin a year as a student teacher at a village school.

Murat disappears for a few days a second time, not saying where he's going. When he gets back, he shows off his contract. He's leaving in three weeks, for Germany, a town called Duisburg where he'll work as a miner for a year.

'Germany or prison, what difference does it make for me?' Suzan asks. She sees the hope in Murat's eyes, but she doesn't want to be alone. She'd prefer a husband who doesn't say a word all day long to a man who's never around. Loving someone who's not around is harder for her than no longer being loved by someone she sees every day.

'I'll never make anything of myself in this bloody country,' Murat says. 'I'll send you money from over there. And I'll look for a place for us to live and then you can join me with the kids. Everyone in Germany has a flat with heating and electricity, everyone has a car, they have hot running water – we'll live like pashas and no one will piss me off, none of those dishonourable good-for-nothings.'

'What would I do in a strange country?' Suzan asks, crying.

'And what would I do here? I'll never get a foot on the ground in this country. I've had it up to here! I'm leaving and you'll come after me. You can do that, I asked about it.'

In the autumn, letters arrive from Murat. He writes about the clean streets, the streetlamps, the cinemas and the brightly coloured lights at night; he writes about big department stores, about escalators and lifts. He doesn't mention a word about the hostel they're jammed into, six to a room, where he feels like he's still in prison. He doesn't write that he'll probably never learn the language and that he's not working as a miner but sweating at a smelting furnace. He doesn't write about how they look at him on the streets, and how it's almost impossible to find garlic and there's no köfter to be had, how the walnuts don't taste as good as at home. Nor does he write that he never sees anyone lazing around there, that he can't see any sign of cheaters and liars, that nothing is taken from anyone, that everything is right and proper and there are probably no innocent men in prison.

Murat sends letters and he sends money, but he doesn't tell Suzan to come and join him, not yet. She's not eager to go either; Germany doesn't appeal to her, what would she want with big department stores and coloured lights?

'But what shall I do?' she asks. 'If he says come over, I'll just have to go. I can't get used to him not being here. I miss him, you know, Gül, I burn up with longing for him every night.'

'Fuat's never around either,' Gül says. 'He comes home late at night, and in the morning he gets up and goes to work.'

That's men for you, she feels like saying. The days when she told Fuat all sorts of things seem to be over. It's only from books and films that she knows it can be different. But Gül doesn't dare say anything that might sound worldly when she talks to Suzan, who has so much more experience than her.

Gül has never been as slim as Sibel, but even six months on from Ceren's birth, she's still far off her previous weight. Her appetite hasn't left her, and though she might no longer constantly feel like she could eat an entire tray of baklava, she still treats herself to a little something between meals: a bit of bread and butter, yoghurt with sugar, a little grape molasses, a few hazelnuts, an apple or a simit. Her belly bulges, her hips are full, her bosom wobbles when she walks.

'Maşallah,' Arzu and her mother-in-law say; 'The Lord has blessed you – you've become a proper woman!' It will be another 10 years, or thereabouts, before *proper* becomes *fat*, and in 40 years' time she will think long and hard before sitting on a sofa, because she'll know she'll find it hard to get up again. But for now, she's a well-fed woman like the old-fashioned belly dancers before the skinny ideal put paid to that art.

A plump young mother, her breasts heavy with milk; a wife who sits at the sewing machine nearly every day, happily putting her foot to the pedal, running the fabric under the needle, listening to the whir of the well-oiled parts and making a little money on the side, which she gives to her husband, who sometimes simply pockets it and sometimes sticks in in the cardboard box, which will never be full again.

As the man of the family, Fuat manages the money, investing it in games of chance or alcohol. But he makes sure there's always enough to eat, enough for clothes and shoes, soap and razors for the shop.

Gambling is to him now what playing the lottery will be in middle age, and what the stocks will be when he's old and has managed to put some money aside. He'll never abandon his dream of getting rich one day without having to work for it. Gül will be very late to argue for a say in how they spend the money. She'll spend years filching the little she needs for cigarettes from the housekeeping money and smoking without Fuat knowing. She'll study special offers and hunt down bargains, she'll go without a cardigan or a winter coat to fulfil one or other of her daughters' wishes. But since this won't even nearly cover all those wishes, she'll grow furious with her husband, who is happy to display his generosity to his friends and even strangers and invite them over much more often than politeness and decency demand. But he won't even buy his daughters a second Barbie doll.

Gül is still sitting at her sewing machine at her in-laws' house; word has long since got round that she does good work. When Esra has too much to do, she sends her customers to Gül. And Gül enjoys a natter with the women, makes them tea and puts it on the slate if one of them can't pay straight away.

The days pass quickly – Gül is constantly busy, and Ceren often wakes up in the night crying; she's much more restless than Ceyda was as a baby. Many nights this winter, Gül falls asleep the moment her head touches the pillow and is awakened by a cry or by Fuat shaking her shoulder.

Her father still comes round nearly every day before work, and there's time enough to swap news: Nalan's doing really well at school this year after passing her exams at last; Timur came across her teacher in the street and had a word with him. This past autumn, Timur also lent out his insect-repellent sprayer, the one he uses on the trees, and he still hasn't got it back. If he has to buy another one, he won't lend it out again; he'll charge people to have him spray their gardens, that's right. Ceyda called him 'Dede' yesterday just as he was leaving, and *wasn't it cold last night, we were freezing*, and this morning Gül's eyes were watering the minute she stepped out the house, the wind was so harsh, and *I ran out of thread yesterday* and *I'm completely worn out in the evenings*, and *read me that letter of your sister's again would you, and this one from your other sister*, and *do you remember when I lost my watch*, and *do you remember when you went to smack me*, and *can you bring me a couple of walnuts and dried apricots, from the tree at the back of the garden, by the wall, they're the best-tasting*, and *I'll soon have no hair left on my head, when Fatma left so did my hair, but now it's really gone*, and *did you hear*, and all the words they use to try to bind two lives together that bit tighter.

Gül is so absorbed by the children, her work, the housework, that she misses the beginning of spring. One day, her thread breaks, the machine falls silent and for the first time that year she hears the birds chirruping. She looks at the acacia, which is already flourishing, and suddenly she is filled with joy; a joy that usually builds slowly. It heralds the return of summer – the birds are promising once again that the air will shimmer and the crickets will chirp, the big water will flow through the gardens, people will sit on their front steps outside the summer houses and call across the street, Sibel and Melike will come home, she'll have that carefree taste on her tongue again, and the light will find its way once more all the way to the marrow of her bones.

Gül never sings aloud, at most she hums to herself quietly, but today she feels she could sing out loud. Give forth sounds of joy.

This spring takes Suzan away from her. One day she's suddenly standing there holding a letter, while Gül is absorbed in her sewing.

'May your work come easy to you,' Suzan says, and Gül jumps, her foot stops moving, and the sewing machine goes quiet.

'Your mother let me in,' Suzan explains.

'What's wrong? You look so... so lost.'

'Murat wants us to join him. He's already rented a flat. He's not coming back this summer. He promised he would.'

'Aren't you pleased?'

'What are we supposed to do with ourselves over there?'

'But everyone's going there. I'm sure it'll be good, you'll see.'

'Oh, maybe you're right. Maybe I'm worrying too much,' Suzan says, but she doesn't seem to believe her own words.

'Six weeks, we're leaving in six weeks.'

'I'll sew you a lovely dress you can wear over there. You will write to me, won't you?'

'Of course I will.'

Gül doesn't cry until she's said goodbye to Suzan. Her tears fall onto the dress she begins working on that day; they fall on her parting gift.

Spring takes Suzan from her, and at first, Gül thinks time will seem slow without her friend, but the summer's over before she knows it. During the apple harvest, Gül's brother-in-law, Levent, is sitting on a rock and smoking and smoking, and maybe he's getting a glimpse up the young girls' skirts as they climb the trees, but he's certainly enjoying the shade of the canopy of leaves and the gentle rustling – he's enjoying it with the expression of a man about town, when his father appears behind him, saying: 'Get to work, Levent, my son, you should be working! Do you want to be a scrounger in your own house?'

Levent goes red and drops the cigarette he's been concealing in his cupped palm.

'You won't fill your belly by scrounging, son, up, up!'

Once her father-in-law has gone, Gül, who has been eavesdropping, can't hide her satisfaction: 'Harsh words, eh?'

She never forgets injustices and pains suffered. Not the big ones, like when her mother hit her because she thought Gül had eaten the yoghurt, nor little ones, like Levent calling her lazy. And she likes to think that things have been put right. She prefers to suffer in silence rather than open her own mouth. Why take a stand for anything in a world that hasn't got anyone's interests at heart? She bears it, while Melike fights, and Sibel prefers to escape into a world of her own.

Gül smiles slyly to herself when Levent is rebuked. Even the cold autumn wind can't shake her smile, but that evening Fuat pipes up: 'I'm going to go to Germany. There's good money to be made there.'

'Excuse me?'

'I'm going to Germany, for a year. I'll save what I make there and when I come back, I'll open my own business here.'

'What kind of business?'

'I don't know yet. But you've got to have capital; you've got to spend money to make money. And we've got none.'

'And I'll stay here on my own?'

'No one's ever alone in this house. And it's just for a year, it'll go by quicker than my military service.'

I didn't have two children then, Gül thinks, but she looks at the floor.

'And when I'm back, we won't have to think twice about whether the coal and the wood will last the winter, or whether we'll have to borrow some.'

'Everyone's going to Germany now,' Gül says.

'It's a good country, it's clean and you can make money there. They don't ride donkeys over there, they're civilised people. And they're old friends of our country.'

Once Fuat has made his decision, the formalities are dealt with quickly, and eight weeks later they take him to the train station. The first early flakes of snow melt in their hair as Gül cries, while Ceyda clings to her leg, confused by her mother's tears and the big crowd of people.

It's a lonely winter for Gül. If it weren't for her daughters, she would spend even more hours staring at the wall in her room. Now Suzan and Fuat are gone. Gül visits her father at the forge more often. She's usually carrying Ceren, but she doesn't think of holding the little one away from the fire to keep her from getting too hot and getting a shock when she goes back out in the cold. And so Ceren sweats by the forge fire and starts crying as soon as they get outside. Gül smiles at the thought that the baby likes being around her grandfather, but Ceren will keep catching colds over the winter. *Lord, let my daughter grow up healthy, with a father and a mother, protect her from hardship, oh Lord, thy will be done. Give me the strength to fulfil my destiny*, Gül prays almost every day.

In the evenings, she sits in the dark listening to Ceyda's quiet breathing, while Ceren's lungs often rattle. Sometimes Gül is barely capable of moving. *I need the toilet*, she thinks, and then her mind drifts off again, to last night's dream, to her mother, Melike or Sibel or Fuat, to a memory of the sieve maker or of Suzan crying at her wedding – and the next time her thoughts return to her body, the pressure on her bladder, entirely forgotten in the meantime, has grown stronger.

Fuat writes less than during his time in the military, explaining it by saying he has to work so much. He's in a place called Delmenhorst, and because they both start with a D, Gül always imagines it to be close to Duisburg, where Suzan is now living. Gül receives regular letters from her.

Suzan and Murat live in a building full of Italian families, whose kitchens smell of cooking all day long, of olive oil and garlic too, and Suzan has started learning Italian. *The Germans talk so little, it's not worth learning their language*, she writes. She doesn't like Germany; it's cold, colder than at home, the people are distant, she never gets smiled at anywhere, she never feels welcome anywhere, but Murat wants to stay, forever if possible. He never wants to come back to Turkey, to *that country of cut-throats*, as he puts it. The children go to a German school and Suzan hopes they'll soon be able to interpret for her. Only two years later, though, the family will be living in Naples, and both Murat and Suzan will be happy with their lives.

Gül doesn't quite know what to write to Suzan. She sits in front of the unlined paper with its yellow tint, pencil in hand, and thinks. She's been cooking, washing clothes, washing dishes, she's talked to her mother-in-law and changed Ceren's nappies, Ceyda woke up three times yesterday, even though she usually sleeps through the night, Ceren is sick yet again, but none of it seems interesting enough to write down. And so she sits there, pencil in hand, and thinks of the film she saw last week, and of how empty her life seems to her. A life in which nothing happens, a life in one room in the cold and loneliness of winter, a life in which the children's screams seem like the petals of a flower.

'You've put on weight again, Gül, haven't you?' Zeliha asks as Gül enters the room. Gül looks at her grandmother blankly, as if the old woman could see her expression.

'Your footsteps are heavier.'

'Yes,' Gül says, a little intimidated. 'I've put on weight.' She goes to her grandmother, kisses her hand and touches it to her forehead.

'You've left your daughters at home?'

'Yes.'

'That's good. I can't stand noisy kids these days.'

'Grandmother, I've come to say goodbye.'

'May the roads be open for you,' the old woman says, but it doesn't sound like she means it. 'So you're going to the land of the unbelievers, are you? Everyone's going to the land of the unbelievers these days, as if there was anything there. Are they better than us, eh? What do all these people want in a foreign country? But you go, my child, you go, may the Lord bless you.'

It's the day before Gül leaves. A spring, a summer, an autumn and a second winter have passed since Fuat went to Germany. He has sent money regularly, and in summer he came back for almost four weeks. But those weeks passed so quickly they seemed to Gül like a dream, afterwards. A dream in which Fuat came home drunk every night and woke her. He was amazed at the words Ceyda could say, he was amazed that Ceren could walk already, but it was just that: amazement. It didn't fill him with pain, if Gül saw rightly, and it will fill her with just as little pain when she leaves her daughters behind now, Gül hopes.

It's only to be for a year, one more year for the two of them to earn money. They haven't saved enough yet, Fuat said when he was home for the summer. They won't have saved enough for a very long time, not for years – and when he does have his own house built in the end, one with European toilets, a bathtub and central heating, in the middle of the town where he grew up, they will almost have forgotten they wanted to move back to Turkey. They will have taken their daughters over to Germany years earlier, only for them to grow up there, go to school there, get married and have children. They will have postponed their return to an undetermined future date so often that they themselves no longer believe in it, until they finally admit they will probably always stay in Germany, close to their children and grandchildren.

But no one can predict any of that when Gül goes to say goodbye to her grandmother. *This might be the last time I see her*, Gül thinks, and that thought will come to her often in the years to come, with different people, and it will become a habit for her to cry when she says goodbye, because that thought never leaves her.

Gül can't say goodbye to Melike, who told her in summer about Mert, the man she's seeing. In the summer that's ahead of them, the summer Gül will spend in Germany, Melike wants to bring Mert home with her and introduce him to their parents, who don't yet know their daughter is going out with a man in Istanbul. Gül was the first to find out about him, but she will be the last to meet him. Melike will marry him, and they will have two children. She will teach French at the same school where her husband is a PE teacher, and she will be happy with the life she has chosen for herself.

Nor can Gül say goodbye to Sibel, because she's working in a village in the southeast. The hygiene there is disgusting, Sibel writes; she keeps getting cold sores. In the summer when Melike brings her young man home, another man will ask for Sibel's hand, the fifth or sixth by that point, and she will say yes and afterwards she'll explain that he looked like her destiny. A man who plays the guitar and sings, but who is unhappy with his work at the cement factory. Their marriage will remain childless, and they won't have many friends, but they will live in peace and harmony in a little house on the edge of town.

Nalan will get pregnant in Istanbul, while visiting Melike, and the baby's father, a bar owner, will leave her after eight years. She will never marry again and will watch with great pride as her daughter becomes an actor.

Emin will take eight years to get through primary school instead of the usual five, and no one will guess that he'll be the only one in the family to get rich. He will invest his money on the stock exchange, and in import-export deals hard for outsiders to understand, and he'll have made his fortune by his mid-forties. But his greed will have him chasing after money time and time again.

Gül makes her farewell visits; she goes to see the neighbours, Auntie Hülya, her parents, Esra and Candan.

Ceyda and Ceren are to spend the year with their grandparents, with Faruk and Berrin, and Gül knows they'll be well looked after there. It's the only home they've known since they were born; the lucky house. But it breaks her heart to leave them behind. She would rather stay with her daughters, but she has to go out to work so that the family can be reunited sooner. It's like Suzan always said: 'Children need a father.'

'You don't need to take anything with you,' they all say, her mother, her mother-in-law, the neighbours. 'They'll have everything there, you can buy everything you need, and it'll be much better than anything here. Why lug a load of rubbish all that way?'

And so Gül is standing at the train station with a small cardboard suitcase, and almost everyone, all those she went to say her goodbyes to one by one, has come. When her father came to see her that morning, they sat side by side without saying a word. Gül didn't look Timur in the face, but they sat so close she could smell that his breath was sour.

Then he'd held his head up and said: 'Next year, in the summer, we'll all be together again. You'll be here, your sisters will be here…' He's shunted his happiness into the future. But that is how it will be, year after year; the siblings will come to the summer house for many years, and Timur will delight in his children and grandchildren. This ritual, these carefree, glittering summers will only end after he dies.

There's not a single cloud in the sky, and standing in the sun long enough without moving, they can soon feel the sweat creeping out of their skin, though it's only just spring. A friend of her father's, an old farmer called Yavuz, will accompany Gül to Istanbul; she's not on her own, her nerves are still in check. When the train finally leaves, the tears come.

Yavuz fumbles a hankie out of his trousers and hands it to Gül: 'All things will pass, my girl, don't cry. May the Lord reunite you and yours. Leaving home is hard. Did you know, my family came here from Greece. It's a hard lot but you mustn't cry. We're alive, thanks be to God, we're alive, we're standing on our own two feet. Smile, my girl, smile,' says the old man. 'One day either one of us might not be here to smile. We will all leave this place, so smile. The whole world is a foreign land we will leave some day.'

Then he distracts Gül with anecdotes from his own life and about her father. He makes the time go quickly for her, smokes cigarettes all the while, and eagerly accepts the bread and cheese and tomatoes Gül offers him during the journey.

Gül has never been to a big city; she's seen New York at the cinema and Istanbul too, but the noise, the chaos, the trains' screeching, the crowds of people... She'd imagined it might be like the hustle and bustle on market day, but market days in her hometown are quiet compared to this train station in Istanbul.

With Yavuz' help, she finds her train. The old man speaks to a gaunt-looking woman on the platform. From her clothes, Gül can tell she comes from a village; she might be around 40, with an angular face and sunken cheeks, her hands chapped, and she's wearing şalvar.

'Sister,' says Yavuz, 'are you taking this train to Germany too?'

'Yes, Uncle.'

'Can you look out for our little girl here? She doesn't know her way around.'

The woman looks Gül in the eye and then nods briefly. She's not friendly, but something about her inspires confidence. Like she's got a handle on things.

'Come along, sweetheart, say your goodbyes. It's going to be a long journey. I've been before.'

Her name is Emine and, once Yavuz has gone on his way, she tugs on Gül's sleeve.

'Come along, the train's about to leave. Come on, what are you looking at? Is that someone you know?'

Gül nods. At first, her eye snags on a young man with broad shoulders. Not just his suit, but his whole appearance seems strange; he must be a foreigner. Curiously, looking at him makes Gül think of brilliantine, though his hair stands up busily on his head. He looks like the man Fuat and his friends were trying to imitate when they still carried their marbled combs in their pockets. When the man moves off, Gül marvels at the spring in his step and thinks he must be an actor.

Only then does she see Uncle Abdurahman; the young man is edging his way towards him purposefully. For a moment, she's unsure; the next, she'd like to call out to him. But she's too shy to raise her voice.

'Come on, we need to get on. We can't miss the train, my girl.'

Emine places an arm on her shoulder and pushes Gül towards the door of the train. Gül is so happy to have seen Uncle Abdurahman; she would have liked to run over to him.

'Come on, sweetheart, there's no need to be scared.'

The conductor blows his whistle, and Gül turns her head to get a last look at Uncle Abdurahman. He and the young man shake hands and kiss each other's cheeks. Before Gül can comprehend that this is probably the last time she'll see Uncle Abdurahman, she's sitting with Emine and four other women in a compartment, on her way to another life.

III

'I'm not afraid of death,' she says, 'believe me, I'm not afraid any more of the time when the angel of death comes to fetch me. It was different a few years ago. I didn't want to die then, right when I was happy. *Please, Lord, let me savour this happiness,* I prayed. But I don't do that any more either, I've got used to the thought that death can come at any moment. I'm not afraid any more, I'm really not. My mission on this earth is almost over; I've raised two children, I've tried to be a good mother to them, and they've both found their place in life. There's no one around who needs me now, so I can go in peace.

'I've lied but I've never cheated, and I've never sold myself in this life, I've never spied on anyone or stolen anything. Perhaps that was just because the circumstances never demanded it.

'Ending up bedridden and wasting away, that's what I'm scared of, I'm very afraid of that. Call it pride or false pride, but I don't want to be a burden on anyone and I don't want anyone to have to wait for me to die at last, and release them and me. That's all I'm afraid of now, not of death.

'Sometimes, when I'm unhappy, I wake up in the morning and think: *Damn, I've woken up again. Couldn't I have slept forever?*

'I thought one day my time had come. Such pain settled upon me, as if it would break me, settled upon my heart and soul.

'I dragged myself to bed with the last of my strength. I don't know what it was, but I felt so bad I thought I'd die. And then I remembered the lentil soup on the gas ring, and I prayed: *Lord, give me the strength to get up and switch off the cooker, Lord, grant me this request, and then come and take back your gift of life.* I was ready to die but I didn't want the whole house to burn down. I'd like to leave this world cleanly, neat and tidy. But I didn't have the strength, I couldn't get up. Then I must have passed out.

'When I came round, I didn't know how much time had passed. I managed to get out of bed, but I had to lean on the walls on my way to the kitchen. The soup was still simmering.

'I'm not afraid now. But if I had one wish, I'd like to die in the autumn. I like the spring, I like the summer, I like the light that caresses you as the waves caress the beach, but I've never liked the winter. I might as well spend the winter under the earth. In the autumn, if I had one wish I'd like to die in autumn. Or at the end of summer.'

Acknowledgements

A. H.

Seher Özdoğan, Tufan Özdoğan, Gülten Ertekin, Vedat Ertekin, Nermin Turan, Nesrin Demirhan, Svenja Wasser, Markus Martinovic, Zoran Drvenkar, Tolga Özdoğan, Lutz Freise, Tim Wasser, Filiz Doğan, Solvig Frey, Christian Goeschel, José F. A. Oliver, Angela Drescher, Marcel Vega

The Co-Translators
in Conversation

Katy Derbyshire: This book has been with me a really long time, since it came out in German in 2005. That's 15 years now – incredible! I remember it reminding me of Laura Ingalls Wilder, bizarrely, because of all the domestic detail and because of the way I really felt for the characters. I know it was one of the books that prompted my burning desire to translate literature, although back then I wasn't in a position to get any translations published. But I made a big fat dossier about the book and sent it to British publishers, who had no idea who I was and either turned me down politely or didn't respond.

How did you come to the book, Ayça, and can you remember your response to it?

Ayça Türkoğlu: I came to the book much later. Actually, Katy, it was through your blog. I spotted it again in *The Edge of Heaven*, one of my favourite Fatih Akın films, so I bought it and added it to my TBR pile, then forgot all about it for a while. I started reading it not long before you asked to co-translate it with me; it was an act of wish fulfilment, really. I remember I spent quite a lot of my first reading of the trilogy clutching my chest. I just love the sentimentality of it, I'm a real sucker for the Anatolian blues. I like the balance of foibles and virtues in every character, and how the story is peppered with these little village tales and bits of hearsay that I recognised from my own childhood (the baby and the safety pin, the man and the unfortunate dog…).

KD: I can definitely relate to the sentimentality appeal – our initial versions of the translation are dotted with comments by one or other of us saying basically: Awwwww!

AT: Did your approach to translating the book change in the 15(!) years between your finding the book and getting to translate it?

KD: I'm not sure how my approach changed over time. I like to hope I've honed my skills over the past decade and a half, so I was too scared to look at the very first translations I did from the book. But I felt a special kind of joy mixed with nostalgia for my younger self when I retranslated an early passage, about scrumping pears. I remembered agonizing over whether I could use that verb, *scrumping*, which back then I thought was very specific to English (how odd that German doesn't have a single verb for stealing fruit off a tree…). I've learned in the meantime to use the riches of the language with fewer qualms – if we're going to lose the occasional thing in translation, why not add extra flair where we can?
You mention your own childhood memories of Turkey, Ayça, and they proved invaluable for our translation. Although Selim wrote the books with German-speakers in mind, he told me he hid subtle references to Turkish sayings and such, which Turkish-speakers would spot but I certainly couldn't. Now we've re-embedded them – I hope – in a new version for Anglophone readers. Did you have Turkish-speakers in the back of your mind while you were translating, though?

AT: I think so. I could certainly hear certain people when reading some passages. I like that extra layer that's available to Turkish-speakers in the text. Sometimes I'd get an inkling of what a sentence or an expression would be in Turkish and I'd translate that instead. Sometimes I'd find I responded differently to lines once I imagined them in Turkish, particularly the song lyrics that crop up. It was interesting to see the solutions we came up with for the Turkish pleasantries that English lacks, like the phrases used before a meal, or to greet someone who's working.

Were there any sections of the book or aspects of Selim's writing that you were apprehensive about translating before we started?

KD: I don't think so! I think I was just raring to go after such a long wait... What I really wasn't sure about was the co-translation process. I'd never shared a translation before except in workshop situations, where translating ends up so drawn out that it takes days to translate a single page. That's a really valuable experience – because it makes everyone explain their word choices, advocate for certain tenses or prepositions, argue over punctuation... But it's not viable for a book-length translation with a deadline attached! How on earth would we get a translation done well by two people in a fixed amount of time?

I asked a few people who have co-translated before but there didn't seem to be a patent solution, and often it seemed rather hierarchical, with a junior and a senior translator, if you like. What I wanted was for the two of us to be on equal footing – we both bring different experiences, enthusiasms and backgrounds to the job and I hope they've flowed seamlessly into the text. And now – maybe because we divided the book up into quite short alternating chunks – I can't necessarily distinguish the passages I translated from your sections, which I edited, and vice versa. Unless they made me cry. So it was a hugely positive experience and I think the result is a genuinely outstanding translation.

AT: Yes, I did wonder how the co-translation process would work – and I worried how you'd feel sharing a book you'd loved for so long with another translator! I can't imagine I would have been as generous… I enjoyed working together so much, though. It was lovely to be able to share that instant feedback with another translator, to feel reassured that you'd made a good choice or just enjoy the other's work. I loved how, every few pages, one of us would leave a little comment on some phrase or other saying, essentially, 'Nice one.' I also enjoyed the occasional bit of bitching when a character was misbehaving.

KD: Me too! What are your hopes for the book?

AT: Besides an English-language film adaptation by Fatih Akın, based on our translation…? I hope people come to love Gül and Timur as much as we do. Gül is such a survivor, the kind of woman almost everyone knows and loves but whose story never gets told. Timur is the archetypal Turkish father, fierce and soft in equal measure.
But what are your hopes, Katy? If that's not cheating…

KD: It's not cheating! Obviously, I'm totally with you on the film adaptation and on readers coming to love the characters. One other thing would be for the book to bounce back to Germany – often an English translation lends writers more respect in their own countries, and I hope that will be the case here, too. As I see it, Germany hasn't sufficiently valued stories about the people whose labour helped build its economy in the 1960s and 70s – whether migrants or other workers – and I'd love for readers in Germany to rediscover this beautiful and important trilogy.

Berlin and London, September 2020